ALSO BY
DOUG WALSH

FICTION
Tailwinds Past Florence

NON-FICTION
The Walkthrough: Insider Tales From a Life in Strategy Guides
One Lousy Pirate

SHADOWS OF
KALALAU

DOUG WALSH

SNOKE
Valley Books

SNOKE
Valley Books

ISBN: 978-1732746787 (Paperback Edition)
ISBN: 978-1732746794 (Digital Edition)

Library of Congress Control Number: 2021914648

The characters and events portrayed in this book, other than those clearly in the public domain, are either products of the author's imagination or are used fictitiously. Any resemblance to actual persons, living or dead, is purely coincidental and not intended by the author.

Edited by Deborah Dove
Cover design by Jenny Kimura
Book design by Colleen Sheehan
Cover art: tropical leaves and background © Zamurovic Brothers/Shutterstock.com; portrait of woman © Take A Pix Media/Shutterstock.com; Kalalau mountain range © Maridev/DepositPhotos.com; Kauai mountains © fominayaphoto /DepositPhotos.com; Night sky © jocker17/DepositPhotos.com

Printed and bound in the United States of America

Published by Snoke Valley Books
P.O. Box 654
Snoqualmie, WA, USA 98065

Visit Dougwalsh.com for promotional queries, author signings, and additional info.

*For everyone who fights to protect
and preserve our public lands.*

NOTE: Though events in this book may appear to glorify illegal camping within the Kalalau Valley, the author implores all visitors to treat the land with respect, to not overstay permits, and to always pack out what is packed in.

CHAPTER 1
SELF-DEFENSE

The helicopter's approach couldn't be coincidence, not so soon after the killing.

Malia spent hours staring into the unsettled darkness, searching the ceiling of her tent for refuge, an escape from the horror she'd witnessed. Now she yanked a pillow over her head, her hair still damp with tangles, wishing she'd fled when given the chance—days ago.

Unlike the high-pitched whine of the flightseeing choppers that plagued the region like a mosquito nuisance, the incoming craft beat the air like a war drum. Its thrum advanced low over the valley, as if guided to their camp by a tether. But routine sweeps were rare, and squatters hardly warranted a predawn surprise. The police knew. But how? Kaua'i's Nāpali coast was a rugged, roadless wilderness where cell phone signals went to die. The only way to get a message out, if not by boat, was an arduous, eleven-mile hike. No time for that. *Unless . . .*

Dread tugged at Malia like an undertow. She clutched the sleeping bag to her chest, ignoring the summer mugginess, recalling the missing locator beacon. *We used to call it yuppie 911,* Tiki said. *Push button in case of emergency.* A comforting notion, but who sounds the alarm over a crime of their own doing?

The helicopter hovered overhead, bouncing their tarps like trampolines in its wash. Her instinct was to run. She reached for the zipper, to flee to Big Pool and cleanse herself of all she'd seen. But why? "I didn't do anything wrong." A plea whispered into darkness.

Craning to listen, she hoped to catch Tiki's assurance that everything would be fine. She heard nothing over the racket of dirt and twigs pelting her nylon tent, the clashing of the sword-like pandanus leaves. Despite her fright, she could practically hear Tiki correcting her. *Hala leaves,* he'd say. Just like he'd known *ihe* was the Hawaiian word for spear.

A spotlight flashed on, penetrating the jungle canopy, illuminating the camp. She bolted upright and winced as her split lip cracked anew in surprise. The beam swept the valley floor, crisscrossing the camp. She tried to yell, but only managed a hoarse cry. "Tiki, what's going on?"

As if in answer, a flurry of voices yelled amid a frenzy of flashlights. "Everyone out of your tents!"

"Kaua'i Police with DLNR. Have your identification ready."

KPD? Of course, she'd heard the stories of park rangers rounding up illegal campers on Kalalau Beach, but up-valley? And with a police escort? The searchlight slithered closer, like a snake stalking its prey. Grim certainty slid home: *they're here because of Inoke.*

Malia held her breath, thankful her tent was the furthest from the trail. It was silly to think they wouldn't see her or that, because she was a girl, the cops would leave her alone, but the thought comforted her. She didn't move—didn't even blink—hoping it merely an overblown effort to clear them from the valley.

The helicopter withdrew, taking its windstorm toward the beach, but the fury didn't cease. Amid the shouted orders rang the bells of destruction: chairs and coolers kicked over, their makeshift shelving upturned, spilling pots and pans to the ground. Closer, their pyramid of water jugs toppled in heavy thuds, the plastic exploding underfoot as boots stomped them like they were balloons at a birthday party. Elsewhere, zippers shrieked open as tent poles snapped like wishbones.

"Quit it, *braddah*. You're wrecking our camp." It was Darren. "Ouch, watch the hair."

"Grab your stuff and line up." The command was harsh, urgent.

Malia huddled in place as the others offered a drowsy but futile resistance. She hated herself for remaining hidden but didn't move. Self-preservation lodged in her throat like a mango pit. She remained kneeling as her home—the first place she ever lived without her parents—was destroyed around her.

Just as the tide of commotion began to recede, light flooded her shelter. "You in the blue tent. Come out."

She raised a hand in defense, but her splayed fingers did little to screen the blinding beam. Her two months in the valley were over. She glanced about the tent in search of something tangible to take with her. Proof it had all been worth it. The necklaces and shells, ruined sarongs, and discarded paperbacks already appeared foreign to her. Relics of a shattered dream. She patted the empty air mattress beside hers. Cool to the touch. Of course. Anger brewed within her as she took a swig of water, her throat scratchy from the tumultuous midnight swim back from Honopu.

"Now!" The officer shook the tent, sprinkling her with condensation.

"Okay, okay." Her voice cracked as she hollered, betraying her worry. She wrapped the sleeping bag around her waist and unzipped the tent door, thankful her lengthy black hair could screen the brightness. The bedding snagged as she crawled out, naked, exposed to a chorus of whistles and catcalls.

"All right, that's enough," barked one of the men. His voice carried the baritone certitude of authority.

The whistles tapered off, but not before someone taunted, "Nice birthday suit, *wahine.*"

"I said knock it off." Then, shining the light in Malia's face, the cop in charge asked, "You got any clothes?"

She shook her head, squinting at the ground, only able to see the half dozen pairs of boots fanned out around her. She'd been going topless for weeks, but never felt as vulnerable as she did right then, surrounded by police. Still, Malia refused to wilt beneath the heat of their gaze.

The cop peered inside the tent, then grunted and clicked a button, turning the spotlight into a lantern, bathing the forest floor in an unnatural white. It gave her pupils a chance to dilate. Thanks to the first pinkish rays of sunlight glinting over the cliffs, she could see Tiki and the others being marched toward the beach. The camp crawled with police, maybe a dozen. Malia expected to be told to collect her things and follow the others. But rather than order her to leave, the cop posed the one question she couldn't answer.

"Where's Jordan?"

Malia stared at Sergeant Kahale's name tag until it and the stars on his lapels swirled in a golden smear. His question struck her like a rogue wave. *They came for Jordan.* Dazed and wobbling, she felt herself drowning in turmoil as the fear of being labeled an accomplice stacked atop the shock of what she'd experienced—and the heartbreak of having her time in Kalalau end in such disaster.

"I think she's *kūpouli*, Sarge. Her brain broke."

The comment and ensuing laughter yanked her to the surface.

Sick in the head? She considered the destruction that surrounded them—the camp they'd worked so hard to build reduced to splinters—then turned to the officer in a tan shirt bearing a Department of Conservation and Resources Enforcement badge. Did he think this was funny? After what she'd been through? After what happened to Inoke? *DOCARE, my ass.* Despite her predicament, Malia's resolve hardened. She realized right then that whatever the police knew, whatever led them to Kalalau, they couldn't possibly know the full story. The drugs. The fighting. They couldn't be there for her, and she'd be damned if she was going to be left holding the bag.

Flanking Sgt. Kahale, a forty-something, broad-chested man with a doughy, honest face, stood two of Kaua'i's so-called finest, clean-cut and square jawed in navy blue uniforms. They didn't look much older than Malia, early twenties, tops. Three DOCARE officers loitered nearby, each in green cargo pants, tan shirt, and matching ball cap.

"The hippie said the suspect stayed with her," said one of the DOCARE guys. The same squeaky voice that made the birthday suit crack. No taller than she, he smirked as he eyed her from head to toe with a lecherous gaze. Malia crossed her arms beneath her breasts and scrunched her nose at him, not about to be cowed by some jerk who couldn't handle seeing a nineteen-year-old naked. He looked away, not unlike the tourists she caught peeping on her morning yoga on the beach.

"That true?" Kahale asked her. "You two shacking up?"

Malia's heart raced as she sensed Kahale connecting the dots. She had to be tough. "What's this about? You *māka'i* don't ever come out here. These DOCARE guys need a babysitter?"

Kahale allowed himself a brief chuckle then told the two cops to spread out, keep searching. He directed the conservation officers to go about their business. Facing Malia, he drew his salt-and-pepper eyebrows tight, sucked in his gut, and thrust out his jaw, successfully halving his double chin. She'd seen the look before. From her headmaster, from the owner of the bakery where she worked, and especially from her father. The stance of a man deigning to explain himself to a teenage girl. Most never failed to wilt when she stared right back, stiffening her posture, refusing to back down. Her father hated that. Yet there was something to Kahale's demeanor that felt different. Sympathy, perhaps.

"Never mind them. Where's Jordan?"

"Haven't seen him since last night." It was the truth—and part of her was glad.

"He give you those bruises?"

She sniffled the pain back. "No."

"Uh-huh." Kahale pulled a paper from his pocket and unfolded it, face up. "You're Malia Naeole, right?"

She pressed a hand over her mouth, stifling a gasp as her graduation photo stared back from a missing person's report. Age, eyes, hair, her height and weight. Each detail tugged at the knot in her stomach, drawing it tighter, causing her to nearly double over from the ache. Unwilling to read any further, Malia looked to the ground, where her toes burrowed into dirt.

"Your dad filed it last month."

She could hear Kahale's neck brushing against the polyester shirt collar as he shook his head, judging her, oblivious to all she'd been through. No way would she allow him to see her shame. "So?" she said, armoring herself with indifference.

"You're coming to Līhu'e. Detective Park wants you for questioning."

"Questioning?" Malia's eyes flashed with alarm. "Aren't you just gonna fine me? That's what they do for the *haoles*." For days, she'd been hoping for a way out of Kalalau. But not like this. Not to the police station. She spun around, tossing her hands in the air, in serious want of a door to slam, only to see the conservation officers heaving things from her tent.

"Hey, that's mine," she yelled, rushing to claim her photo keepsake. She shoved one of them, knocking him aside. Malia turned to push the other, but Kahale intervened, pinioning her arms behind her. She screamed for him to release her, but his grip was like steel. Instantly, she was face down in the dirt, her bruises aching anew, arms pretzelled behind her with a knee across her back. The forest fell quiet save for the ratcheting of plastic zip ties.

"You're hurting me," she yelled as the cuffs cinched down.

"Get me something to wrap her in."

"Get off me! You can't do this."

"For assaulting an officer? You bet I can."

Malia blew hair strands from her face and struggled to free herself, but soon realized it was no use. As she lay panting, the mossy scent of dew-dampened loam flooded her nostrils, calming her with each breath. She decided not to test him.

"Here you go, sarge."

Kahale hoisted Malia to her feet and wrapped her in a blanket, awkwardly tying it beneath her arms like a bath towel. "Okay, let's go," he said, guiding her by the elbow toward the trail leading to Kalalau Beach, a mile away.

Malia managed one final look at the camp, believing in her heart she'd never be back. She regretted it at once. As if the destruction wasn't bad enough, the other officers had already bundled the mass of bedding and tents inside a tarp, folding it like a burrito. She watched as her books, the kukui nut necklaces she sold to tourists, the photo of her mother, and the remainder of her few trail-worn possessions were tossed into trash bags. Whether to be disposed of or held as evidence, she hadn't a clue.

The other officer held her ukulele. Upon noticing he had Malia's attention, he made a raunchy show of blowing her a kiss and strummed so hard he snapped a string.

The helicopter banked in the morning light, filling the window with the diamond-cut sea below. Malia would have banged her forehead if it were not already pressed against the glass. They leveled off, framing the postcard view of the emerald Kalalau Valley, its glistening white beach, the waterfall spilling from its cathedral of fluted cliffs. Her Eden scrolled by in sparkling fantasy and Malia heaved a sigh of regret. She knew she couldn't stay forever, but hated feeling like everything she loved had been taken from her.

"I'm sorry, Mom."

They were the first words she'd uttered since the humiliation of being marched to the beach like a criminal: barefoot, blanketed, and bound. Kalalau was sacred to Malia's mother, home of her most cherished memories. Where she'd left a piece of her heart and taken home a surprise within her womb. Malia couldn't quit envisioning how she'd look to her mother now: battered and handcuffed, an insult to her mother's legacy.

She blinked away a tear as the valley fell from view. The pilot followed the coastline south, low over the water, toward Honopu Arch and the isolated cove that shared its name. From the air, the postage stamp of a beach looked so near, as if you could swim from Kalalau to Honopu on a single breath. Far too close, too exposed, to shelter a secret for long.

Malia's pulse redlined as she realized Jordan must have known this. That his only chance to avoid capture was to flee along the trail back to Keʻe Beach and the nearby town of Hanalei. But whether he disappeared out of fear or to let her take the fall, she didn't know.

Turbulence bucked the helicopter, knocking Malia off-balance. With her hands cuffed behind her back, she was helpless to avoid rocking into Tiki. She'd been so focused on her own troubles, she'd forgotten he was there beside her.

Malia was relieved to see him at the helipad, wearing his favorite turquoise board shorts and striped, gray tank. Up close, she saw his slender eyes were puffy, gaze distant, and his cocoa-brown locks of hair looked as though they'd been combed with a rake. Tiki, a New Zealander, had his own legal concerns to worry about, having overstayed his student visa by at least a year.

She knew it was selfish, but Malia craved the comfort of his warm Kiwi smile, needed to hear everything would be okay. But he only proffered a sideways glance before burying his head in his hands, his elbows bouncing atop anxious knees.

They were ordered not to speak, and the hard plastic earmuffs made it nearly impossible to hear anything anyway, but she had to try. With Kahale staring out the cockpit window, Malia nudged Tiki with her shoulder to get his attention. When he turned, she repeated the cop's earlier question: "Where's Jordan?"

Tiki sank in his seat and blinked slowly, as if to suppress a boiling frustration. He mouthed the words "You tell me" and stared back, clearly exasperated. But there was more to his look. Wounded affection, perhaps.

Malia swallowed hard and turned away, unsure how to react or feel. Instead, she replayed the events of the prior day. From the fighting to her plea for a boat ride back to town, to Inoke's suggestion of holding a contest at Honopu. Never once did Jordan hint at running—or leaving Kalalau. She gazed out the window as a wave disappeared within a cave. There, then gone. Bile rose in her throat as she considered another possibility: maybe Jordan never made it back to camp. Were there footsteps on the beach? She'd been in such a daze. So physically and emotionally drained by the quarter-mile, up-current swim that she barely reached Kalalau herself, let alone thought to look for signs of Jordan.

Deaths along the wild Nāpali Coast weren't unheard of. Hardly a year went by without someone drowning in the surf. But Jordan was a capable outdoorsman and Malia couldn't imagine her surviving the swim and not him.

He must have made it back. She was certain. Malia gasped, realizing Jordan may have left a note explaining where to meet him—or blaming her for what happened. If so, and the police found it, they'd think she was involved.

I need a plan.

The helicopter angled inland as they skirted a lengthy beach at the island's southwest corner, another state park judging by the numerous tents. Malia had no idea how fast they were flying, but it seemed only a few minutes longer before the low-rise buildings that passed for a city on Kaua'i came into view. The summer spent in Kalalau marked her first visit to the Garden Island. She didn't know where the police station was, but figured it had to be close. Time was running out.

Suspecting this might be the last chance they'd have to talk, she drew Tiki's attention one final time. When he turned, she made a show of enunciating the word "self-defense."

Tiki placed a hand atop her knee. He blinked slowly and dipped his chin. Then, without averting his gaze, his pressed lips curled into a wry smile. He lifted the ear protection from her head and leaned in, so close his breath warmed her skin, even as her predicament chilled her to the bone.

"I always keep my promises," he said. "Always."

CHAPTER 2
A NICE HAPA GIRL

Malia hugged the blanket tight against her naked form, feeling like someone who survived a house fire, swaddled in Red Cross sympathy with matted hair and a thousand-yard stare. Except it was she who struck the match; the only available pity was her own.

She thought she'd caught a break when the police removed the zip ties to fingerprint her during booking. That she might be given a seat in the lobby, told to wait. Offered a snack, perhaps. Instead she was led down the hall to the holding cell, where she'd been sitting ever since. The confidence she'd mustered in camp had long since abandoned her. And Malia knew her arrest wasn't part of some "Scared Straight" act. Inoke was dead. The cops were looking for Jordan. And somehow, they knew she was involved.

Nervous sweat burned a prickly trail down her back as she stared at the air conditioner mounted high on the wall, its knobs removed despite being out of reach. The unit's cracked ventilation grill returned a toothless smile caked in a veneer of gray dust so thick it nearly muffled its incessant wheezing. The quilted blanket smothered her in a clammy embrace, but Malia didn't dare dispense with the shelter of her wrap. Instead, she folded her knees to her chest as she sought impossible comfort atop an aluminum bench and scanned the room for the millionth time, struggling to look anywhere but at the tattooed woman cursing at the wall across from her.

The holding cell at the Kaua'i County Police Department was only slightly larger than her childhood bedroom, but Malia's room never stank of alcohol and body odor. Nor did she have to share it with someone who threatened to "snap her puny ass" for making eye contact. Malia studied the aging wooden floor. Decades of anxious pacing had left the planks so scuffed their original teak stain only showed in splotches, like wet footprints on a beach. She took to counting first the nail heads in the floor, then the divots, ultimately playing connect-the-dots as she traced the outline of a pelican, then a hibiscus and a palm. With each seaside icon came a reminder of an afternoon spent cloud spotting with Tiki—memories now overlain with the tender touch of his hand atop her knee, the scent of his breath in her ear aboard the helicopter.

I'll probably never see him again.

Malia's chest tightened as worst-case fears piled like too many textbooks atop a fragile shelf. But the realization she couldn't ignore, the one most troubling, was that if only she'd listened to Tiki about Jordan, none of this might have happened. What had Jordan's friendship gained her? Even now, detained for questioning regarding his whereabouts, it was Tiki she couldn't stop thinking about. And that, more than anything, tormented her the most.

The pressure grew so intense, she barely recognized the sound of her name when called.

"Malia Naeole, come with me." The young cop's eyes flashed briefly toward the other detainee, then settled on her. He carried a pair of metal handcuffs.

She clambered to her feet and hurried across the sticky floor, pinching the blanket tight within her armpits. "Am I going home?" Her voice oozed with youthful optimism.

The cop slammed the cell shut behind her and mock-yelled toward the lobby, "Hey, lieutenant, we let 'em go home for assaulting an officer?" He didn't wait long before pretending to hear an answer. "Ooh, negative. Worth a try, though," he said with phony sincerity. "Give me your wrists."

He led Malia down a hallway and through a locked door. The corridor's fluorescent lighting was an affront to her eyes, long accustomed to the natural light of the forest. But even that paled in comparison to the artificial sterility of the room she was taken to.

"Take a seat," he said, pointing to a wooden, straight-backed chair in a room not much larger than a department store changing room. He left without another word.

She lapped the room, alone, delaying the inevitable. Across the table from her designated seat were two drab office chairs on casters with faded burgundy cushions. No doubt the source of the mildew smell. The whitewashed walls were bare save for a video camera pointed directly at her. No posters, no clock, nowhere to fix her gaze. Beside a windowless door was a small mirror which Malia assumed hid observers on the other side.

The reality of her situation landed with a thud as she slumped into the uncomfortable chair. She imagined the mugshots of the types of people who end up in that room. Murderers, drug dealers, rapists. She knew Kaua'i didn't have the same level of crime as her hometown, Honolulu, but the thought of being anywhere near hardened criminals made her tremble. She'd never been in trouble with the police before. Never even had detention.

What if they send me to prison?

She squeezed her eyes shut, trying to escape the reality of her situation, only to picture the rocks being placed atop Inoke's corpse.

They'll blame it on me. All of it. They'll—

Malia caught herself on the verge of tears and slammed the brakes on her imagination. She focused on the pinch of the handcuffs, the inescapable flush of frigid air blowing from the ceiling, and that irksome camera leering at her like a cycloptic version of the agent outside her tent.

Her stomach growled as she fidgeted in the chair, trying to scratch an unreachable itch. Despite being accustomed to going hungry in Kalalau—a diet consisting largely of rice and fruit seldom sustained her—she couldn't help wondering if she hadn't missed only breakfast, but lunch too. How much longer? Two months spent living in paradise, experiencing a freedom few could comprehend, now reduced to a puny, white cage. She glared at the mirror, wondering who was watching. She wanted to yell. To flip them off. Or at least turn the chair around.

Instead, she focused on not making her situation worse. She knew the next one to enter would storm in full of bluster, threatening, demanding to know where Jordan was. Where Inoke went. He'd ask about last night. What would she say?

"I'm fucked," she whispered into her lap, hoping it'd be over soon. If only they'd find Jordan. Then she'd be off the hook.

Malia rehearsed her explanation as a woman in a cobalt twill suit and white blouse with butterfly lapels swept into the room, carrying a folder and bundle of clothes. She was tall with angular features and Supercuts layers that ended in a chestnut fringe below her shoulders. Malia felt a wisp of relief at having drawn a female detective. That she appeared Asian—Malia pegged her as being of Korean descent, likely no more than second generation—added further comfort. Provided she wasn't the type of woman who felt obligated to be twice as tough as her male counterparts.

"I'm Detective Park," she said, all but confirming Malia's guess regarding her ancestry. "These are from lost and found. Here." Park placed a pair of sweatpants on the table, along with a balled-up T-shirt and a pair of dirty slippers. She spoke fast with a friendly tone, but her geniality didn't continue to her eyes. Her thin, flat eyebrows didn't budge. She rolled a chair around the end of the table, closer to Malia.

Malia stood to take stock of the clothes, then lifted her bound wrists and shrugged. "A little help?"

"Still cuffed? They should have undone those before booking you into holding." Park produced a key ring from her pocket. "There. Sorry about that."

Malia thanked her, despite suspecting that Park was not, in fact, sorry. She rubbed feeling back into her wrists, then inspected the pants: navy blue and devoid of any noticeable stains, but at least five sizes too large. "I'm supposed to wear these?"

"You have any idea how bad that blanket stinks?" Park flashed Malia a salesman's smile. "Just put them on."

Tight-lipped, Malia tugged the sweatpants on beneath the blanket. Unlike her time in Kalalau, a measure of modesty seemed prudent. She turned her back to Park—and the camera—before discarding the offensive wrap. The pants were clearly menswear, and she didn't want to know how they wound up abandoned in a police station, but at least they didn't smell. She pulled the green tee over her head, noticing the detective had set a digital recorder and legal pad on the table as she did.

Malia dropped the slippers to the floor and sat, unsurprised to see that one of the thongs had pulled free of the sole.

"Be right back," Park said, and let herself out, taking the blanket with her.

Malia sighed and looked down at the shirt's University of Hawai'i logo, emblazoned in white. It stared back, a mocking reminder of what she stood to lose.

Park returned several minutes later clenching a cup of coffee and a vending machine bear claw. "Thought you could use a little breakfast. Don't want the recorder picking up your belly barks." She slid a sugar packet and creamer across the table.

After weeks of fresh fruit and fish, the cellophane-wrapped pastry appeared alien. The sweetened almond slivers called out, but Malia refused to answer, wary of being buttered up by a good cop facade. Despite the coffee's oily sheen, Malia knew the caffeine would serve her well. She mumbled her thanks and allowed herself the compromise of a hot beverage—and smiled sheepishly when her stomach growled while she added the sugar.

"Just eat. You're obviously hungry." Park glanced over her shoulder toward the camera and shifted to the right, ensuring it a clear view of Malia. "Unless you're gluten-free. I'll never understand why so many kids can't eat wheat anymore."

Malia stared across the table, searching for traces of genuine concern. She considered herself trilingual: fluent in English, Hawaiian, and sarcasm. That she couldn't translate the dialect of Park's sincerity unsettled her.

"Oh, but you're not a kid anymore, are you?" Park flipped open a manila folder containing an arrest report. Her narrow lips formed a wispy smirk as she tapped the line containing Malia's date of birth. "No, you're not."

If the dietary remark was Park's way of probing for a response to snark, then this was a smash-and-grab on the jewels of her confidence.

The reminder of her age—her legal adulthood—struck like a sledge, igniting neon warnings that she'd be tried as an adult. For years, Malia had been eager to vote, to have a voice. Now she could only wish to roll back the clock. Park opened the wrapper and pushed the pastry closer. The cinnamon scent reminded Malia of pit stops at 7-Eleven on the way home from school with friends, back when *lolos* from the neighborhood would make lewd gestures and call her jailbait. Adulthood marked her legal for the men of Kalalau, but where did that get her?

Malia sought solace in the flaky dough. A reluctant taste of comfort. She devoured the rest in quick bites as Park looked on with a satisfied grin, her pen hovering above the report like a guillotine.

"Thanks," Malia said, already craving another.

Park nodded, then tapped the page. "Mind a little housekeeping?"

Malia ran her tongue along her teeth and cautioned herself to keep her guard up.

"Malia Naeole. That's beautiful. I've always been jealous of you girls with local-sounding names. Your pop Hawaiian?"

"Japanese-Hawaiian." Malia could tell Park wanted more, so added, "Mom was Filipino-Islander mix."

"It shows."

Malia shrugged, unsure how to respond. Maybe it was different on Kaua'i, but in Honolulu, where Asian ancestry was the norm, her roots seldom came up.

"Age nineteen, graduate of the Kamehameha School. Smart girl like you, why you not at Mānoa?" She gestured at Malia's borrowed shirt.

Park wasted no time in ditching her proper English in favor of a clipped, informal pattern she probably used for dealing with delinquents. To Malia, there was nothing worse than middle-aged professionals embarrassing themselves by speaking pidgin. Malia licked a finger and suctioned up an almond slice that had come loose inside the wrapper. She answered with her finger in her mouth.

"Berkeley. I was accepted into UC Berkeley."

Park loosed an exaggerated, patronizing whistle. "Your pops must be real proud."

"You'd think," Malia said, noting Park had yet to mention her mother. She eyed the file, wondering how much Park knew.

"Of course he is. I hear that part of California's real nice."

Malia never visited the campus, or the mainland for that matter. She mailed applications to California on the sly, ignoring her father's demand to stay local. She applied to several Honolulu schools to get him off her back, but the hassle only strengthened her resolve to get away—an ocean's worth of separation felt about right.

She caught herself picking at the shirt's screen-printed logo as Park took notes. That she seemed to write more when Malia was quiet sent a chill through her. She wanted to plead her innocence, throw herself at Park's mercy, but knew she had to play it safe. Her words were the one thing under her control.

"Okay," Park said. "Why not start by telling me what a nice *hapa* girl like you was doing in Kalalau?"

Malia cradled the coffee cup in front of her. "You wouldn't understand."

"Try me. I left Oʻahu to come to Kauaʻi. I get the draw."

"I didn't run away, if that's what you think."

"Not thinking anything. I'm just the messenger." Park flashed her tight-lipped smile and swept the snack wrapper into a wastebasket. "But before we continue, I have to read you your Miranda rights, okay? It's just a formality."

Malia stiffened as Park began, just like on television. The tiny room with the table and the camera was bad enough, but now her rights were being read to her. Park didn't recite them exactly like the cops on *Law & Order*, but Malia could practically repeat the spiel right along with her, thanks to her father's love of reruns. And if his iron grip on the remote taught her anything, it was that you never wanted to be in this room.

"Does this … Am … Am I going to jail?" Malia struggled to form the question.

"No. You're not. In fact, Sergeant Kahale informed me the other officer will consider dropping the assault charges if you cooperate."

Malia exhaled and relaxed a bit. She'd been so distracted with self-pity, she'd forgotten why she'd been handcuffed.

"But I need answers for that to happen, Malia. With those rights in mind, do you wish to talk to me about the events leading to the death of Inoke Duarte?"

Malia's gaze fell to her lap, unsure what to say.

"There's no reason to be scared. I can tell you're not like the frequent fliers I normally see in here. You get it. You're smart. The Kamehameha School did you good. You know you don't need to keep silent because you're the type of girl who does the right thing."

Malia touched her bruised lip, again feeling the force of Inoke's blow, the shock of what followed. Suddenly the room felt too small to contain the whirlwind of her confusion. How did the police know to come? Where was Jordan? She wanted out. *Now.*

But how? The others were somewhere in the police station going through the same questioning—or worse. Darren and Ruby didn't matter, but she needed to believe Tiki could be trusted, that the police wouldn't flip him against her.

Would he rat out Jordan?

Probably. But did she really care what happened to Jordan? She wanted no part of jail—for herself or for Tiki. The memory of his touch left a mark more permanent than any punch could have.

"It's important you tell us what happened."

Malia had no choice. She nodded. Slowly at first, then with the eagerness of someone swimming to a life raft.

"Excellent," Park said, flipping to a clean page in her legal pad. "It's important we establish your credibility as a witness. How long were you in Kalalau?"

"Almost two months. Since the end of June."

"How'd you get there? We checked the flight records and know you didn't fly."

"By boat."

"Whose?"

"Can't remember." Malia knew she'd have a harder time keeping her story straight if she peppered it with random lies, but she had no reason to out the captain. Especially after he risked a fine for dropping her off illegally.

"Were you abducted?"

Malia rolled her eyes, refusing to answer such a stupid question.

"You scoff. But your dad didn't think it so ridiculous when he filed a missing person's report."

The breath fell from Malia's mouth in a heavy gasp. The armor she'd donned at camp, when Kahale showed her the paper, crumbled at her feet. For weeks, she'd fought to keep her father from her mind, to not grant access to the image of him sitting at home, waiting for a call that would never come. Alone.

"Did you know he did that?"

She tried to speak, but her quivering lips refused to cooperate. Her eyes refused to blink away the picture she'd drawn. When she spoke, it was barely audible.

"You have to speak up for the recorder."

"Yes."

Park leaned across the table, her eyebrows arched into double question marks. "How about dispensing with the one-word answers. Yes, what? Yes, you want me to charge you with assaulting an officer? Yes, you want me to add indecent exposure and possession of narcotics to the list? Is that what you want?"

The list of charges jolted Malia from her stupor. She'd cooperate. She had no choice. But there was a clear shift in Park's demeanor, a desperation fueling her sudden burst of intensity. A murder in Kauaʻi was big news. That it took place at one of the island's most popular tourist attractions—the Nāpali Coast—would garner national attention. The island could ill-afford to have a killer on the loose. No, the cops needed Malia's cooperation. Probably as much as Malia needed to be set free.

"Fine, I'll talk." Malia drained the last of the coffee and straightened her shoulders. She looked directly at Park and held out the cup. "But make it two sugars this time, okay?"

CHAPTER 3
THE FIRSTS
KEEP COMING

A school night.

Malia eased aside the driveway gate, doing her best to minimize the clatter as its wheels skittered along the cobblestones. It was nearly eleven o'clock and, judging by the lights on inside the house, her father hadn't gone to bed. Still, there was the chance he'd fallen asleep. She nudged the gate shut in near silence, but the latch slipped from her hand. A metal-on-metal clang echoed through the cul-de-sac calm. A silhouette flashed across the living room window. *Shit.*

Charles Naeole sat glaring from the kitchen table, drumming his fingers atop the mail as she entered. "Look who decided to come home."

Malia turned her back to him and shut the door, rolling her eyes out of sight. Hardly a week passed without her getting in trouble for something. "Sorry. Had to cover for Jenna."

"You know how I feel about you working late. You should have called to ask—"

"Well, maybe if my phone wasn't an antique. The battery died in fifth period. *Again.*"

Charles ran his hand through thinning black hair and sighed an unnerved prayer to the heavens, mumbling beneath his breath in Japanese. He slid his thick, onyx-framed glasses from his face and studied her with sagging, wrinkled eyes, looking more lost than tired. His mouth opened briefly, then closed, as if he'd forgotten the lyrics to their contentious duet. All the while, he continued his anxious drumming.

Malia slung her bookbag over a chair and fetched the carton of POG from the refrigerator.

Behind her, a lecture she'd heard countless times before gathered steam: the lurking dangers of the city at night, the importance of her senior year grades, the value of a good night's sleep. She unscrewed the cap and raised the passion-orange-guava juice to her mouth, ignoring him.

"Don't turn your back on me," he yelled, yanking the carton from her hand, splashing her shirt, pants, and the floor.

Malia recoiled from the uncharacteristic aggression. "What the hell?" Normally the quiet, seething type, she couldn't recall him ever lashing out like this.

"Lower your voice," he hissed, and moved quickly to shut the window over the sink.

"You ruined my clothes!" She backed away, holding her arms wide. Sunset-tinted juice dripped from her work shirt, puddling between them.

"You'll look at me when I'm talking. As long as you're under my roof, you'll follow my rules. And that won't change when you start college."

Malia was adrift in her frustration, wanting to scream and needing to rinse her clothes before the stain set, but the mention of college snagged her attention. She followed his gaze to the table, to an open envelope sitting atop his place mat. Only then did she notice the University of Hawai'i logo.

He released a heavy, tone-shifting sigh. "You did it, Malia," he said when she faced him, a hint of pride peeking out beneath his crust of discipline.

She'd earned a 3.9 GPA at the most prestigious prep school in the islands and been named to the Headmaster's List six times in four years. The state school? Of course she'd get in. Malia thumbed the envelope open, then made a show of crushing it with two hands. "Doesn't matter. I'm going out of state."

"Don't be ridiculous." His disbelief surfaced as a nervous laugh. "It's right in town. And you'll probably get a scholarship. Of course you're going to UH."

"No. I'm not. And why are you opening my mail?"

"It's my house. I'll open anything addressed to it." Charles ripped a spree of paper towels from the roll hanging beneath the cabinets and squatted to clean the juice.

"I'm not your prisoner." She stormed over to the garbage can and stomped the foot pedal to prop the lid. Before throwing it away, something caught her eye. Peeking out beneath a ramen wrapper and soggy tea bag was a similar envelope. This one embossed with a golden UC Berkeley logo.

She plucked the envelope from the trash and withdrew the soiled letter. Malia could scarcely believe the words before her. She'd applied to Berkeley, Stanford, and Caltech on the sly, hoping if she got in, her father would come around—and maybe even help her pay the tuition. But this wasn't merely an acceptance letter. She'd won a Regent's Scholarship, one of California's most competitive. Now she could go no matter what. She didn't need him.

And he wasn't gonna tell me?

Betrayal coiled around her like a two-ton anchor chain, sinking her back into a darkness she thought she'd escaped. She clenched and unclenched her fists, balling the letter as her pulse pounded in her ears. It was one thing for him to want her local. Another entirely to deceive her. She pivoted toward him, her nostrils flaring. "How dare you?"

Charles's lip quivered as if, for a moment, he regretted what he'd done. Then he regained his composure and reached past her to throw away the sopping wet towels.

Was he really that stupid? Did he think she wouldn't check the online admissions portal? There was probably an email already awaiting her reply. "Where I go to school is NOT UP TO YOU!"

"You can't even be home on time. And you think you're mature enough to choose a college?" He snorted.

Malia glowered, staring him down, unblinking despite the dry-eyed burn. Through clenched teeth, she hissed, "I'm. Going. To. Berkeley."

"No. You're. Not. The mainland's not safe."

"You say that about everything."

"You have no clue how dangerous the world is. The private school. This neighborhood." He waved his arm in a circle, motioning around the house. "We sheltered you. Maybe we shouldn't have, but you've never even been off O'ahu on your own. The mainland? No way."

"Stop saying *we*. Mom would have been thrilled for me. Just because you couldn't keep her safe doesn't mean you get to lock me in a tower!"

Charles recoiled as if slapped. Though he had never laid a hand on Malia, had not even given her a spanking when she was young, the vein bulging from his forehead made her wonder if now would be the first. She sensed he was reaching a boiling point—the stickiness of the POG drying on her skin indicated he'd been plenty hot already—but she couldn't give in. Ever since her mother died, he'd grown more overbearing with each passing month. The unreasonable curfews, the constant hovering, the parties she wasn't allowed to attend. She couldn't take it.

Malia stood, arms crossed and smoldering, knowing her only hope was to put an ocean between them.

Charles stomped off as though heading to bed, then stopped. He gripped the chair back, chest heaving with each breath. Through gritted teeth, he said, "I swore to raise you as my own flesh and blood. I'm sorry if my best isn't good enough."

Malia's legs trembled with trepidation, yet her anger had carried her too far to turn back. "It should have been you."

He bit his lip and nodded, slow and deliberate, then looked her square and said, "Times like this, I wish it was."

"I hate you!"

Malia sprinted to her bedroom and slammed the door behind her. She hurled herself, tear-streaked and jagged, onto the bed and pounded at the mattress. Blow after blow, she hammered away until her anger had been beaten to oblivion. All that remained was the shame of her words. She loved her dad, the only one she ever knew, but it'd gotten so hard to live with him alone.

What more does he want from me?

It would have been so easy to slack off after her mother died. The most natural thing in the world for a kid to do. But not Malia. She doubled down, got straight As, worked a job, stayed out of trouble, and still he didn't trust her. When would it end?

Malia unfurled the acceptance letter and smoothed it against her leg. She read it again, feeling the betrayal in her bones, doubting she'd ever forgive him. Sheltered. That's what he said she was. And his solution was to reinforce the walls? It made no sense. How could she ever prove herself capable of being on her own if he never gave her the chance?

Before long, Malia rolled to stare at the photo atop her nightstand, taken the year before she was born. In it, her mom, mid-twenties at the time, wore a teal bikini and a straw hat. A group of friends mugged for the camera. Her Kalalau family, she called them. A dozen of them arm in arm, they stood soaking up the sun as a wave tickled their feet. Towering, fluted cliffs filled the background. As stunning as the scenery was, it was her mother's smile that captured Malia's attention. An expanse of pearls as broad as the horizon.

When asked about the photo, her mother, Christina, would drift into a wistful smile as the air fell silent around them. Sometimes, if she were feeling reminiscent, she'd open up about her month in the valley. "With the most peaceful bunch of hippies you could ever imagine," she'd told Malia, blushing. "We were in love with life, with one another, with nature. It was pure magic. Just living off the land, working together, communing with our great Mother Earth." It wasn't until Malia was older that she realized one of the men in the photo was probably her birth father. A man Christina had only ever referred to as "that cute boy from California."

For as long as she could remember, her mother dreamed of returning to the Kalalau Valley. But Charles always pushed it off, citing Malia's age, his medical practice, or the weather. The excuses continued until it was too late. Christina died before "one of these days" ever arrived.

Her mother yielded to him time and again. Where did it get her?

Malia sat up in bed and pulled the photo close, resting it against her thighs. "I miss you, Mom," she said, tracing a finger along her mother's likeness, feeling more alone than ever.

***

The crowd sat in rapt attention as song filled the Blaisdell Center. From her perch at the head of the arena, Malia stood shoulder to shoulder within the row of Ns performing the all-girls *mele*. Two hundred voices singing in unison, a commencement tradition. Teachers and parents packed the arena floor in aluminum folding chairs; thousands of extended families filled the upper balcony. Malia worked her lungs like a bellows as she sang, but her heart wasn't in it. All she could think about was her mother's unused ticket resting atop her bedroom dresser. Malia gave all but three of her dozen allotted tickets to friends with larger families.

In lieu of a cap and gown, the graduating Warriors wore a royal blue, smock-like *kīhei* which swished against the ruffles of their white *muʻumuʻu* as they retook their seats. The girl beside Malia, last name Nagamine, said, "I can't believe we're finally graduating." Malia smiled politely, in no mood for the bubbled-up spirits surrounding her, and scratched where the blue silk lei itched her neck.

The emcee redirected the crowd's attention to the parents, asking them to rise for applause. Malia spotted her father three rows from the rear, across a sea of beaming smiles. Chin up and stoic, he reminded Malia of an old war hero standing for a long overdue medal, welcoming the acknowledgment while knowing it wouldn't erase the scars. She clapped on autopilot, looking away, unwilling to bear the sight of him. Alone. Her sole parent. Though her auntie had flown in from the Big Island, a gesture Malia genuinely appreciated, her presence couldn't dull the pain of her mother's absence.

Cheers of gratitude went out to the grandparents, then, raucously, to the few great-grandparents alive to share in the festivity. Still, Malia couldn't help picturing an empty chair, imagining it with a white lei wilting atop an unread commencement program.

Malia was admitted into Kamehameha Schools Kāpalama when she was eight, only two short years after her delayed entry into kindergarten. "The first in our family," Christina said, squatting to hold her daughter by her shoulders. Malia could still recall the wonder and pride in her mother's reaction, the scent of her hibiscus perfume as she hugged her. That she wasn't here to see this day, after a decade of struggles and expense, was an unacceptable cruelty. Malia blinked away a tear and stared at the emblem adorning her *kīhei*, where four flaming kukui nuts comprised the Royal Lamp.

Her mother's oil was snuffed out thirteen months ago, to the day, last April.

Weeks later, on that first Mother's Day without her, Malia volunteered to work a double at the bakery in effort to get out of the house. A mistake. She spent most of her shifts hiding in the bathroom in tears as one family after another came in to celebrate. Her birthday was an even bigger gut punch, as it was their tradition to celebrate together, given their birthdays were only two days apart. The June twins, her mother called them. Then there were the winter holidays. As bad as they were—movie and Thai food on Christmas with her dad, neither able to stand being in the house—Malia took comfort believing, come New Year's Day, the last of the firsts would be behind her.

But now, at graduation, she realized the firsts would never cease. And they weren't even the worst of it.

Her mother's smell still lingered in the house as the sounds of her singing echoed throughout the hall. Those daily reminders wouldn't fade, despite the grief counselor's assurances to the contrary. Nor had her father's coping abilities improved with time. He was stuck. Malia struggled to understand how he could sleep alone in that bed. How he still shared a closet with her mother's dusty clothes. Why hadn't he redecorated? How could he go on, seeing those reminders day after day?

The thought of being trapped in the house with him all summer, walking on eggshells without homework to busy herself, was unbearable. Worse still, it was harder to pull extra shifts in the summer on account of the college kids being back in town.

I can't do it. I've got to get out of that house.

An elbow nudged her side. She looked around, confused, and realized her entire row had stood. Half had proceeded down the stairs. She bunched her dress in her hands to keep from tripping and hurried after the girl in front of her, listening as one name after another echoed throughout the cavernous arena, boys and girls graduating in zipper-like fashion from two aisles. An occasional whistle or yip went up from the cheap seats. But the well-behaved crowd largely sat on their hands, as requested, containing their applause until all four hundred students had been named.

The effect was polite, but sterile, and Malia couldn't help wondering if her mother would have been so reserved. She recalled her mother's reaction to her uncovering the photo from Kalalau, the rebellious, unbridled foolishness on display. "We were so naive back then," she'd said, referring to her fellow Gen Xers. "If only we'd known what was coming. What with 9/11, the wars, the housing crisis, and ..." Her thoughts led her down a secret trail, but Malia could guess the destination: *if only she'd known about the surprise growing within her.*

Malia advanced along the line of students becoming graduates, cursing the unfairness of life.

"Malia Kaia Naeole."

She shook hands with her right while grabbing the diploma in her left. She paused, waiting, giving her dad a chance ... but nothing.

Mom wouldn't have let me graduate in silence.

She stomped her way up the steps and slumped in her seat, despising her father's obedience. Vibrating from neglect, she turned the diploma's black case in her hands and stared at the crest emblazoned in gold foil. "*Imua Kamehameha.*" The dignitary's words echoed in her mind. Her chest filled and emptied, air cycling through flared nostrils as she gripped the diploma in anger. To her right, ponytail happiness sauntered back to her chair.

"*Imua Kamehameha,*" the Nagamine girl said, waggling her diploma.

Malia narrowed her gaze while the words ricocheted in her mind. Her breathing quickened as an idea sparked from the echoed greeting. Maybe she didn't need to spend the summer at home. Didn't even need to stay in Honolulu. Not entirely. If she took every available shift, she'd have enough money for airfare to California within a month or

so. Malia rose in her chair, floating on the effervescence of a plan. She'd
escape to Kalalau. Just like her mother. And maybe, if she was lucky,
she'd find a Kalalau family of her own.

"Yes," Malia replied, returning the girl's smile. "Forward, indeed."

Malia gripped a sand-flecked sink, enduring the restroom's briny
miasma of urine, sand, and moldering paper towels as she searched
the mirror at Kaiaka Bay Beach Park for a sign she was ready. But
behind the scribbled graffiti and splotchy silver coating stared the
same uncertain girl she'd always been. The familiar round face and slim
nose. The thin, squarish lips she wished were fuller; the high cheek-
bones her mother blamed for making it impossible to tell when Malia
was lying. At only nineteen, Malia knew she wouldn't look as mature
as her mother did in that old photo keepsake atop her nightstand, but
was it too much to ask to see a little confidence reflecting back?

"I'll be fine." It was the third time she'd said it. Once or twice more
and she might even believe it.

She spent the month since graduation snagging every shift she could
at the bakery, avoiding her father, and researching Kalalau Valley—
namely, how to get there. She considered flying—inter-island airfare
was cheap—but a flight to Līhuʻe would still require at least a bus, some
hitchhiking, and a dangerous eleven-mile hike. No, a boat would be
better, she reasoned.

Malia had nearly given up after dozens of fishing charters declined
to offer passage between Oʻahu and far-flung Kauaʻi. Others told her
it was illegal to deposit passengers at Kalalau Beach and weren't about
to risk their business license. But her best friend, Jenna, knew a family
friend who owned a fishing charter in Kauaʻi. A few emails later, Malia

had her captain. Better yet, he planned to make the crossing out of Hale'iwa the same weekend Malia would be camping nearby with Jenna's family on the North Shore. She hadn't intended to leave so early in the summer. Her father would certainly make the month between her return from Kalalau and college departure unbearable, but this was her only chance. Malia had to take it.

She toggled the cold water and rinsed her hands quickly before the faucet cut off. Oh, the pleasures of public restrooms. That she wouldn't even have this small luxury at Kalalau wasn't lost on her. Nor would she have the internet, groceries, running water, or even electricity. Nevertheless, the prospect of living off the land in an unspoiled corner of Hawai'i, just as her mother had, ignited an unexpected excitement. One that nearly matched her eagerness to meet the community she hoped would become her Kalalau Family.

Malia swept her hair behind her ears and peered once more into the mirror. A spark of confidence soon erupted into a bonfire, melting her mask of apprehension. Finally, the woman she'd been searching for gazed back. Malia surprised herself with a spontaneous burst of laughter. "I'm coming, Mom." She drew her shoulders back and smiled at her visage. "I'm really doing this."

It was almost time. Malia exited the campground restroom, drying her hands on the front of her green hoodie as she went. It was nearing midnight and most of the campers were already tucked into their tents, Jenna included. Unfortunately, the fire glow and clinking beer bottles meant Jenna's brothers were still awake. These camping trips with Jenna's 'ohana had become an annual tradition, always the first weekend of July, and always to a locals' beach where the men could fish while Jenna and her cousins played in the waves. This year, same as last, they'd reserved every campsite at this small park outside Hale'iwa.

Over the years, they'd become Malia's 'ohana too, an extended family of aunties and uncles she could count on. Which was why they needed to go to sleep; she'd never get away if they knew what she was up to. Jenna promised to explain in the morning. With any luck they'd understand—and Jenna would keep Malia's whereabouts secret.

Carrying her slippers so they didn't flop against her feet, Malia skirted the campground toward the beach and sat atop a basalt boulder. The laughter of Jenna's brothers melded with the sloshing surf, the lyrics of summer sang in a round. Malia unfolded a photo from her pocket, one of two she'd bring with her, and angled it against the moonlight. She and her mother, spoons aloft, sharing a papaya-lychee shave ice with a sweet cream snowcap. Their birthday tradition. A familiar ache built below her ribs as she smoothed the well-worn print and lost herself to the memories preserved within those still frame smiles: the hopes and laughs, motherly advice, and heart-to-hearts about boys and becoming a woman. What she wouldn't give to sit across that sticky, paint-peeled picnic table one more time, sharing another bowl.

A shiver plucked Malia from her memories. The night had grown cool and clammy, and the camp had fallen quiet. Malia tucked the photo away and padded over to the tent she shared with Jenna. Once certain everyone was asleep, she ducked inside. Her duffel lay where she left it, already packed with her sleeping bag and air mattress, bathing suits, and a couple of T-shirts and shorts.

She shook Jenna's shoulder to wake her. "I'm going."

Jenna stirred behind a veil of black hair. "What time is it?"

"After midnight. I'm late," Malia whispered.

"You sure about this?" She sat up, rubbing her eyes.

Malia nodded, fighting to keep the moment's somber barbs from piercing her confidence. "It's only two weeks." Jenna looked away, chewing her lip. Malia knew how much she hated being asked to lie. And not only to Malia's father, who was sure to call, but to her own family. She squeezed Jenna's hand and said, "I owe you."

Jenna dipped her head, then pulled Malia into a hug. She squeezed so tight Malia could feel her friend's fingernails through the thick cotton sweatshirt. "Be careful, okay?"

Malia ran her arms through the duffel's twin handles and shouldered it like a backpack for the thirty-minute walk along the waterfront. Having never been to the harbor, its simplicity brought Malia relief. There were two floating docks and only one boat fitting the captain's description: a thirty-foot fishing boat with a hulking Yamaha outboard.

Using her phone as a flashlight, she double-checked the name painted on the stern, *Ka Pua 'O Annana*. Annana's Flower. A pretty name for a boat, Malia thought. She took a deep breath, hoping the captain would prove as trustworthy as his directions, and climbed aboard. She tapped gently against the dashboard near the cabin entrance and whispered, "Captain Kimo, you awake?"

She knocked again louder and nearly leapt from her skin when a groggy reply came from behind her. Kimo had been laying atop the bench at the rear of the boat, completely hidden in the shadows. "Whoa. Easy, didn't mean to frighten you." He stood, gripping the metal frame of the overhead canopy, tattoo-clad muscles bulging.

If he hadn't been a friend of Jenna's family, Malia might have turned and run back to camp then and there.

Kimo's shoulders stretched well beyond the tank top sleeves of his Iron Man shirt. An all-black tattoo of a gecko escaped from beneath the hem of his rust-speckled shorts. Around his neck, tied to a black cord, hung a carved bone *makau*, so old its coloring had shifted from white to golden. Clearly not one of the fishhook trinkets sold to tourists. Despite having never been offshore, Malia assumed this was a mark of his seamanship, or at least the number of years he'd been chasing fish.

"Was wondering if ya gonna show."

Malia fidgeted nervously, unsure this was still a good idea. She darted her eyes between Kimo and the dock.

"So, you Jenna's friend?"

Malia nodded.

"How she doin'? I ain't seen her since she was *keiki*," he said, holding out his hand waist-high.

"Jenna's good. We just graduated."

Kimo shook his head the way adults do when confronted with the reality of how fast the years have gone. The gesture eased the tension Malia had been holding in her shoulders. She took a small, committed step forward, smiling nervously as she imagined Kimo back at the campground, sitting around the fire with the others. It was the thing she loved about Hawai'i the most. It seldom took more than a mention of a mutual friend or a quick introduction to be greeted with open arms. Living in one of the world's most popular tourist destinations wasn't easy, but the locals knew how to look out for one another. Despite what her father said ...

"Anyway, you a lucky girl. I only come to O'ahu to visit my *makua* for their anniversary. I usually stick to Kaua'i, especially during mahi-mahi season." He looked at her in a way that seemed at once to understand both what she was up to and why. Then, as if agreeing with the unspoken lie, asked, "So, you meeting friends at Kalalau?"

"Yeah, someone I haven't seen in a long while."

"Uh-huh." Kimo clapped his hands, then pointed at the cabin door. "Well then, best put your stuff down below so it doesn't get wet. The crossing takes about four hours. Calm seas tonight. We'll gas up outside Poipu. Then it's another hour up the coast to Kalalau."

"Umm ... okay."

"And ... this is the part where you pay me." He smiled when he said it, but Malia could tell he wasn't doing it for charity.

She withdrew her wallet. "Oh, yeah, of course. Is there an ATM at the harbor? I didn't have time—"

"Here? What you think this is, some Waikiki yacht club? Closest one's a couple blocks away. How much you got?"

Malia's confidence drained as she began counting out twenties. "I've ... just sixty dollars."

"You gotta be kiddin' me."

"I'll get more. I can run. It won't take—"

"We're already late. No time for that," Kimo said, hands on his hips in frustration.

"Wait. Here. You can have my phone. It's a new iPhone. A graduation gift. I'll reset it and it's yours. My stuff's backed up. I just need to pop out the SIM." Malia spoke frantically, afraid to let this unlikely boat trip slip away. She turned the phone over, fumbling with the case.

"Lemme see that." Kimo grabbed the bedazzled phone and raised his eyebrows mockingly, then snorted. He prized the case off, then plucked a strand of wire from a nearby tackle box and used it to pop the lid on the slot. Malia took the phone, tossed the SIM card overboard, and initiated the factory reset.

"I ain't never seen a girl give up her phone before." He punctuated the comment with a dry chuckle, but Malia could tell he didn't think it funny.

"Well," she said, then swallowed. "It won't work where I'm going."

Kimo studied her with a grim look of hindsight on his older face. Clearly fighting his better instincts, he said, "No, kid. That it won't."

CHAPTER 4
BLOOD BLISTER

"**S**o, you *are* a runaway." Park shot her a snide look from across the table. "But I get it. Mom's dead. Dad's a pain in the ass. So, you ran."

Blood drained from Malia's face. She could see Park judging her, could feel the sting of her unspoken verdict: another spoiled, immature teen who thought she knew it all. "No! Haven't you been listening? It was only supposed to be two weeks, just some time away before college." Beneath the table, Malia looped the drawstring around her index finger as she spoke and tugged. She could feel the blood ballooning in the tip.

"People taking a vacation typically don't end up on a missing person's report."

"Fine. Whatever makes you happy."

Park eased herself forward out of the slouched position from which she'd been listening to Malia's tale. She placed her pen atop the pad and straightened it just so. Thanks to Malia's impromptu oversharing, the name of the boat captain, Kimo, appeared circled multiple times. "No, Malia. Nothing about this makes me happy."

"Could have fooled me."

Park ignored the comment and laced her fingers atop the table, as if to reset the conversation. She'd tossed aside the accusatory tone and asked, "How'd it happen?"

"How did *what* happen?" Malia raised her head and glared. She just told her how she got to Kaua'i.

"Your mom."

"You want to know how my mom died? Why do *you* care? You don't even know me."

"No. But I have a daughter."

Malia shot her a caustic look, wondering if it was true. And, if so, what difference it made. But rather than pick a fight, she answered Park's question as succinctly as she knew how. "Drunk driver." Park didn't need to know more than that. Didn't need to know the driver had run a red light, that her mother's car was found pinned against the guardrail three lanes over. That the injuries were so severe, Malia wasn't allowed to view the body. And she definitely didn't need to know that Malia never said goodbye before the crash—and was given no chance to afterward. A fact that had haunted her ever since. She tugged the drawstring ever tighter and stared, unblinking, as her fingertip swelled in violet. Could she pull hard enough to make her finger burst? Would she? Quite possibly if it distracted her from the pain of those memories.

"Parents worry. If something happened to me—"

"It was a hit-and-run with a stolen car. Lousy police never even caught him." Malia glared at Park as the familiar fury returned.

"If I wasn't there for my daughter ... I can't even imagine."

Malia relaxed the string and looked up.

"That's why I wasn't at Kalalau this morning." Park allowed herself an embarrassed laugh. Her eyes flicked in the direction of the mirror. She lowered her voice. "Helicopters scare the hell out of me. No way I'm going up as a single mom."

Malia laughed a short burst, with Park as much as at her.

"How old were you when it happened?" Park asked, again ignoring Malia's jabs.

"Seventeen. Last April."

Park's stony jaw softened as she rolled her empty coffee cup between her palms for almost too long. "Then it was just you and your dad. No siblings, right?"

"Yeah."

Park nodded. Being an only child was unusual in Hawai'i. Normally, she'd just let it be, but Malia could tell her role was to talk. And part of her didn't want Park to think her family weird.

"I always thought it'd be neat to have a little brother. But mom miscarried twice. Then they stopped trying. Subchorionic hemorrhage," she said, pronouncing it with the air of a med school professor.

Park's eyes widened as though surprised by the big words.

"Dad's an obstetrician," Malia said with a you-pick-things-up flick of the wrist. "He blamed himself for not making sure she was eating healthier or exercising more," she said, recalling a conversation over a Big Kahuna bowl of shave ice.

"And when your mom died—"

"He went nuts. Barely let me out of his sight. He wouldn't even let me ride the bus alone until senior year. Hardly let me go out with friends. And—"

"Were you abused?"

"What? No!" Malia recoiled, her face twisting in disgust.

"I had to ask."

"Sure, but—"

"You were all he had. He probably didn't want something to happen to you. Makes sense."

But something did happen, didn't it? She'd been arrested. Malia turned over her palms, noticing the indentations from the handcuffs on her wrists, and couldn't help thinking it was his fault. If he hadn't made it so damn impossible to ever want to be home …

"We haven't called him yet, since you're not a minor. But we can if you cooperate."

For two months, Malia struggled to ignore the torment she knew she was inflicting upon her father. It was one thing to disappear for two weeks. He may have even deserved that. But all summer? She had opportunities to leave the valley, to hitch a boat to town or hike out. Or to send word she was okay. But no. She'd get distracted, absorbed in the goings-on of the camp, and leave it for another day. And by the time she wanted to leave, it was too late. Trapped—until today.

Malia didn't wipe at her tears, but allowed them to flow freely as she nodded in response. Yes, she wanted Park to call her father. With all her heart she wanted him to know she was alive. Even more, she wanted to hug him and apologize for the heartache she'd put him through.

Park pursed her lips and set the cup down. When she spoke, her voice had taken on the cold inflexibility of case-hardened steel. "I will, but here's the thing." Malia looked up, wanting to ask what, but misplaced the words upon seeing Park's demeanor. "We've been here for forty minutes now and you haven't once asked why you're being questioned. You know who does that?" She didn't wait for a response. "Someone who's guilty."

"What? No!" Malia shouted. "I didn't do anything."

"Let's set aside the reason you and I both know you're here. Kaua'i County is one of the safest in the country. One point six. Know what that is?"

Malia suppressed her knee-jerk tendency to make a wisecrack and swallowed a retort about her daughter's GPA. Instead, she offered a minimal shrug.

"It's how many homicides we average each year. This isn't Honolulu; it's still a big deal when someone turns up dead."

Homicides. The very sound of the word rattled Malia, the heft of its syllables collapsing over her like a net, certain to ensnare her the more she denied its presence. *This is it*, she thought, cursing herself for believing for a single second that Park cared. *I'm not getting out of here.*

Park fixed Malia with a serious look and clasped her hands. "I'll cut to the chase. We know Inoke Duarte is dead, and you had a relationship with his killer—"

"No. I didn't. I ..." Malia stammered at the sound of Park's accusation. "How—"

"Never mind that. Where is Jordan?"

"I told you I don't know."

Park stared at Malia with the focus of a hawk for several uncomfortable moments, then shifted abruptly in the chair. Her tone took on the enthusiasm of someone planning a road trip. "Okay, let's assume you're telling the truth." She raised a hand to silence Malia's protest. "He must have told you something."

Malia scrunched her face in confusion, unsure what Park was getting at.

"Let's start again from the beginning and be as specific as possible. Don't leave anything out. Even the most innocent detail might be a clue."

Malia squeezed herself small as she struggled to swallow Park's command, already thinking ahead to memories best left forgotten.

CHAPTER 5
COPS & ROCKETS

Jordan cringed as the cacophony of utensils clinking against glassware swelled to an obnoxious crescendo. Beside him, HyperTap's acting CEO balanced atop a swank weatherproof sofa, the de rigueur class of rooftop furniture common to the Seattle tech set. He flailed his arms as he conducted the crowd in a chant. Jor-dy! Jor-dy!

Having led the weekly all-studio meetings for eight months, Jordan knew he'd be called upon to say a few words at the launch party. It would have been weird not to, but he never expected this. Never wanted it. As the puerile nickname sloshed from the roof of the luxury high-rise, Jordan couldn't help imagining those on the sidewalk forty stories below, craning their necks toward the roar of misplaced adulation. He sipped his drink and forced a smile as he endured the alcohol burn. Normally, the whiskey was merely a prop he carried to prevent being harangued for having empty hands. Tonight it was essential.

He undid the button of his sport coat and stepped onto the faux leather stage. Steadying himself alongside his boss, Jordan thanked him for the introduction, then motioned for the crowd to quiet down. Despite the thousands of hours spent working together, he barely recognized some of his coworkers without their customary T-shirts, flip-flops, and dogs. He cleared his throat, raised a single finger to the sky, and waited.

"A stellar benchmark for the genre," he said, swiping his finger downward, as if checking an item from an invisible list. The crowd cheered until he again silenced them.

"Intense and mesmerizing." Another air check brought even louder applause. After a few seconds, he made a show of licking his fingertip before holding it aloft again. It seemed all of the major gaming outlets agreed that *Cops & Rockets* was shaping up to be one of the hottest video games of the year, the must-have holiday hit. And everyone who worked on it had to know which review quote he'd repeat next.

"An all-time masterpiece," he bellowed, this time pumping his fist as everyone hollered and whistled in response. Given his boss's antics moments earlier, the crowd hardly needed additional hyping—but Jordan did.

"Brace yourselves if you haven't heard from any old roommates in a while. I got a dozen DMs from people begging for free download codes tonight—just in the time it took to order my drink!" Jordan looked to his glass for effect and shook his head. "Fucking Twitter."

From his perch atop the sofa, the string lights and propane fire pits lent a campfire intimacy to the party that Jordan found comforting, unburdening. One he missed, sorely.

He waited for the laughter to fade before continuing, his voice somber. "My whole life, all I wanted was to work in gaming. I doubt I'm the only one." A sea of nodding faces proved his point. "And I've dreamed of one day seeing my name on the credits crawl for a Game of the Year contender—"

"With a fat bonus check!" someone shouted from the back, spurring another round of cheers.

Jordan grinned through the interruption, convinced more than ever that he should speak his mind. To hell with the memo about not discussing former employees.

"But this isn't really my speech to give. I can't stand here and be feted for the work of another, the toil of he whose name I'm not supposed to mention," he said, dressing the phrase in air quotes. Across the rooftop, a pall descended as management mouthed silent warnings and plus-ones shook their bug-eyed heads. He sensed his boss stiffening next to him. "I know you all think I led us across the finish line— and maybe I did—but I got that baton with a massive lead." Jordan took another sip and grimaced. Then, not caring if he mixed sports metaphors, added, "Born on third, right?"

"That's our Jordy. Always deflecting credit." His boss clapped him on the shoulder, causing his knees to buckle. "But it's thanks to him we're here tonight. And to all of you too," he added. "But mostly Jordan." He laughed with the authenticity of a politician on the trail and guided Jordan down from their perch. His face morphed into that of a disappointed father as he wrapped his arm around Jordan and whispered a plea for him to give it a rest.

"But it was *his* game—"

"C'mon, man, we talked about this."

"Why isn't he here? So he quit? Big deal. He burned out, got sick. Wasn't like he jumped ship for another studio."

His boss pressed against his shoulder, as though guiding him to the timeout corner. "Jordy, let it go—"

"I don't get you," Jordan said, trying to keep his voice under control. "What about all that stuff with Pearl Jam's drummer. The one that didn't get inducted into the Hall of Fame. You said it was a disgrace. That he'd played on their most important tours and their two best albums. You said he'd earned the right to be included. How is this any different?"

"It just is."

"Not to me." He turned away, wanting to leave, but instead walked to the far corner of the roof where he could be alone.

Development on *Cops & Rockets* was a nightmare. Mismanagement, budget shortfalls, infighting, and unending overtime went unchecked for years. The resulting avalanche of shit claimed a fifth of the studio, including the lead designer and some of HyperTap's best programmers. Those who didn't outright quit took extended breaks for mental health. The industry had taken to calling it "stress leave." Jordan didn't begrudge those who left, even as their workload fell to him. Instead, he welcomed the opportunity to shine. But if he was to ever be the toast of a studio, he wanted it to be for a game he designed. Not a mess he cleaned up.

Jordan stared out across the inky waters of Elliot Bay, watching a ferry bound for Bainbridge Island as a slender hand, nails shining like polished gems, slid along the metal railing and stopped beside his. A woman in an off-the-shoulder, yellow dress leaned in with the grace of a sequined ballerina. She smelled like Paris, or so he imagined. He stopped short of tucking his shirt into his Dockers and straightened.

"Hell of a speech," she said, picking a speck of nothing from his shoulder. "I'd have loved to hear the ending."

Amused, Jordan stared at where she touched him, then cleared his throat. "You're ... not with HyperTap, are you?"

"Video games? No." She laughed, swatting away his comment like a silly thing. "I live in the building. Thirty-seventh floor." She paused, as if expecting a reaction, but Jordan resisted the bait. She introduced herself as Holly.

"It's a private party," he said, more serious than not.

"Does it matter?" Holly tugged her lower lip slowly into her mouth with teeth as white as starlight. Over her shoulder, he noticed one of the marketing guys watching him, flashing his eyebrows and grinning like an imbecile. "You look like you could use some company."

"I'm fine, really."

"Tall, dark, *and* brooding. My lucky night."

Jordan faced the bay, unable to keep from smiling.

"And dimples too. My, my."

Jordan dropped his head, blushing, and searched the gaps in the stone tile floor for something clever to say, a movie quote perhaps. He noticed her ruby-tipped fingers fall into view. A baited hook he couldn't help biting. Holly dragged her hand upward, brushing her dress ever so slightly, reeling in his gaze along her satin legs, the dizzying heights of the dress's hem, the waist he could so easily wrap his hands around. She glowed like a sunbeam, the shade of her dress made all the brighter against her tanned shoulders. His eyes locked on the dimple of her neck.

"I didn't expect HyperTap's big hero to be so mopey."

He snorted when he laughed, yielding to the celebratory theme of the night. "I'm Jordan."

"I know."

CHAPTER 6
THE DAWN OF A NEW SKYE

Daybreak colored the sky with flamingo daubs as Kimo edged the boat closer to shore. Malia knew the scenery would be stunning—every photo she'd seen promised as much—but no amount of Instagram scrolling could have prepared her for the unspoiled, primordial grandeur on display: the overwhelming scale, the lustrous stroke of sand and waterfall, the fluted verdant cliffs. Kalalau Beach appeared how the Earth was meant to be. Raw, jagged, and wild.

Her pulse quickened as she gazed beyond the side of the boat as one might a ledge prior to bungee jumping.

"They call it the Cathedral," Kimo said with reverence. "Most tourists think the cliffs look like church spires. Tell the truth, I always thought they kinda looked like spear tips."

Malia stared in awe of the cliffs towering nearly three thousand feet above the beach. Ringing the valley in a semicircle of knife-edge ribs, they formed an amphitheater fit for the gods. Mother Nature's pulpit, she thought.

She envisioned herself standing beneath those ridges cutting straight to the water's edge, walling her between the mountains and sea. Her legs trembled in time with the boat engine's vibrations as a bout of claustrophobia gripped her. Kalalau Beach presented the most majestic scenery she'd ever seen, yet Malia couldn't shake the feeling of it being a trap, a veritable prison in a postcard.

"Well, I can't get much closer without risk of running aground. I packed your duffel into a trash bag while you slept. It should keep dry during the swim."

Malia lifted the sack, appreciating the gesture, but struggled to wrap her arms around its amorphous shape. Yet, despite its awkwardness, the bundle suddenly felt inadequate for the adventure she'd flung herself into. It had been easy to focus on the lie at hand while packing, that she was going car camping with Jenna's family, but was a couple outfits, a sleeping bag, pillow, and handful of energy bars really enough for two weeks?

I didn't even pack a tent. What was I thinking?

"You oughta get going. This isn't exactly legal, ya know."

"Oh, I forgot—"

"Don't worry about it," he said, waving away her concern.

"Thank you." She wanted to say more but knew if she didn't leave soon, she might never go. She shook Kimo's hand, then swung her legs over the side of the boat. She paused atop the gunwale, sixty yards offshore.

"You won't be able to call for a pickup, but I'm usually moored at Kikiaola Harbor, down on the south shore. In Waimea. Maybe you make it there and I take you back to O'ahu. But, eh, no promises, okay?"

Malia brightened at the gesture. "The harbor in Waimea, but no promises. Got it."

With that she turned and heaved the bag as far as she could. "Here I go." She gulped a huge breath and shoved off.

Saltwater shot up her nose, startling her, but she didn't panic. Even as she plunged into unanticipated depths. She bent her knees and propelled herself from the sandy bottom, fighting the tug of water filling her hood as she shot upward. Malia shook the water from her face and let loose with a scream.

"Cold, eh?" Kimo asked with a toothy smile.

Malia shrieked a reply, spurring laughter from Kimo. She spotted her bag bobbing a few strokes away and was about to swim toward it when he called out to her.

"Hey, *wahine*. Come find me at the harbor when you done. I'll hold your phone till then—for safekeeping. You can pay me proper when you get back to O'ahu." Kimo shook his hand in the air, extending his thumb and pinky finger.

"*Mahalo!*" she yelled as loud as she could, thanking him for the ride. She threw him a *shaka* of her own, then turned and kicked after her bag.

The bag floated, but barely. Malia pushed it ahead of her, swimming an awkward sidestroke until she could touch bottom. By the time she dragged herself from the water, her sweatshirt nearly stretched to her knees and the shorts she'd worn over her bathing suit clung unpleasantly to her thighs. But she made it, thanks in no small part to the lazy summer surf. Malia dropped to her knees in the sand, emotionally weary but triumphant. The trepidation she experienced on the boat was already subsiding, yielding to the thrill of undertaking her life's first true adventure.

"I made it."

Malia rose to collect her bearings. From her research, she knew the beach stretched roughly a mile, angling from northeast to southwest.

She raised a hand to her brow to block the sun's glare shining over the cliffs and quickly spotted the waterfall that marked the far end of the beach. Knowing she had a long walk ahead of her, she untied the knot in the garbage sack and withdrew her duffel. It was damp, but better than the alternative. She dumped a puddle of seawater from the trash bag and shook it out, wondering how she'd dispose of it.

With her duffel slung over her shoulder, she set off along the beach, sticking to the water's edge. The beach slowly came alive as she walked. Backpackers emerged from their tents beneath the trees. Swimmers took to the water for a morning dip. Malia couldn't wait to meet the people here but suspected those she was looking for, the community of hippies her mother described, would be harder to find. They wouldn't be camped among the tourists along the beach.

Malia soon noticed a tall, pale man striding across the sand with an intensity at odds with the bucolic surroundings. He veered toward her, shouting with a precise German staccato. Growing up in a vacation hot spot made Malia quite skilled at identifying various accents from around the world. "What are you doing? Do you have a permit to be here? Coming by boat is illegal." Malia was taken aback. So much so she turned to see if he might be addressing someone else. Alas, there were only footprints and the sight of Kimo's boat shrinking into the distance.

"You must go," he said, stopping several steps from her, wagging his finger.

"What? No." She'd heard of people being a stickler for rules, but this was ridiculous.

"It is unfair. Many people wait months for camping permits. It is the only way—"

"Leave me alone," Malia said, brushing past him. She wanted to say more, to tell him these were her islands and that he should mind his own business, but she didn't. She'd always felt uncomfortable when her friends played the locals card, but she was irked all the same. Chiefly because she knew the guy never would have opened his mouth if she looked as tough as Kimo or one of Jenna's brothers.

"I hope I am here when the ranger tickets you!"

"Fuck off," she hollered over her shoulder. Malia immediately regretted her choice of words upon spotting a family up ahead, the mother tsk-tsking with her head.

Despite having just arrived, she already wanted to head up-valley. She needed to reset, to find the people she hoped would welcome her, and, if she were lucky, secure a place to stay—her lack of shelter was starting to weigh on her more than her duffel. She trudged onward, paralleling the water toward the streamside trail in the distance. Loose sand spilled from underfoot with each step, slowing her progress. And with every tumbling grain, so too did her confidence slide bit by bit. She'd nearly reached the far end of the beach when she spotted the lithe silhouette of a woman practicing yoga. A wisp of a figure, slender and flexible, she moved with a graceful power that drew Malia in. The woman shifted between warrior poses as Malia approached close enough to realize the woman was nude.

Malia halted, quickly looking away. She'd never encountered someone naked in public before. Even in the locker room at school, she and her friends did their best to remain covered up—and to avert their gaze when not. Despite her bashfulness, she couldn't help sneaking a glance, drawn by the simple beauty of the woman's purest form on display amid such a setting. The woman's hair plunged down her back in twisted, waxy dreadlocks. Beaded necklaces hung around her neck, dangling between her slight breasts. A dusting of sand on her knees was all else that adorned her bronzed body.

She shifted forward, a knee bent before her, one arm outstretched toward the sea and the other pointed *mauka*, at the mountains. A backlit tuft of armpit hair caught Malia's eye. She crinkled her nose reactively, then smiled as she recalled her mother's stories about her friends living off the land. Malia had never considered the possibility of her mom having gone *au naturale*, but her time in Kalalau was when she was younger, single. This yogi looked roughly the same age as her mother did in the group photo Malia carried: early twenties. Twenty-four, tops.

She transitioned to cobra pose, stretching her body prone atop the sand, pushing with her palms as she lifted her chin to the sky, balancing on the tops of her feet and toes. Malia kept a respectful distance, mindful of her shadow as the woman exhaled a tremendous sigh and shifted backward into child's pose. She folded forward over her knees, her head and torso lowered to the sand.

Perhaps sensing Malia's presence, the woman soon turned her head in greeting. "Another morning in paradise."

Malia nodded, then, upon realizing the woman's eyes were closed, blurted out the first awkward thought that come to mind. "Isn't the sand uncomfortable?"

The woman smiled cordially, no doubt sensing Malia's timidity, and opened her eyes. "You're soaked."

"Yeah. Just got here."

The woman sat up, resting atop her heels, and slowly blinked in the morning light. She stared at Malia's duffel, as if in a daze. "You hiked in with that?"

Malia glanced back up the beach, toward the man who had scolded her, and lowered her voice. "I got dropped off."

"Ah, I thought I heard a boat." She smiled a conspirator's grin. "Well, welcome to Kalalau." She closed her eyes, resuming her meditation.

Malia had the manners to know she shouldn't intrude on what appeared to be a beloved morning ritual, but was reluctant to pass on the opportunity to befriend someone who might be of help. And this woman, naked in the sand doing yoga, with her dreads and her hairy armpits and chill demeanor, seemed exactly who Malia was looking for.

"Um, this might sound weird, but I was hoping to spend time in the valley. Do you …" She trailed off, certain she was being ignored.

The woman's chest rose and fell as she inhaled deep and slow, eventually releasing her breath with a hissing echo of the lapping waves. Malia ground her foot into the sand, fidgeting, wondering how long she should wait for an answer. But with each passing moment, the gravity of Malia's situation accelerated. Since graduation, she'd focused on the why and how of her coming to Kalalau, had channeled her energy into finding a way to this far-flung corner of Kaua'i. And there she was. With no tent, little food, and only a clue where to go. She knew people lived hidden amongst the shadows of the valley, but what did she expect? A bamboo village with guesthouses? A concierge waiting to show her a room? To carry her bags? She recalled the various terms thrown about online: hippies, squatters, outlaws. Malia peered at the woman before her and wondered to which tribe she belonged.

Malia spotted a red-dirt hillside to the north. The Kalalau Trail climbed that slope, the first of several treacherous crossings on an eleven-mile cliffside trail. She'd read it was one of the most famous trails in the world—a bucket-list hike for global adventurers—but also one of the most dangerous. Her hometown hill, Diamond Head, was a stroll in the park by comparison. But even that left her sore for days. Hiking out along the Kalalau Trail alone, with its unrelenting climbs and perilous heights, was unfathomable to her.

She debated clearing her throat, a loud, distracting noise sure to get the woman's attention, but was spared the embarrassment. The stranger turned her palms to the sun, exhaled a final lengthy breath through her nose, and slowly opened her eyes. Then, with enviable posture, she crossed her legs beneath her and rose to her full height in an elegant motion, like a stork rising from a nest. She wiped the sweat from her brow and flipped her dreads over her shoulder. "I'm Skye."

"I'm Malia. Nice to—"

Before Malia could finish, Skye had wrapped her in an embrace, pulling her close, inhaling deeply, as if absorbing her energy. Malia hovered her hands near Skye's bare back, unsure how to react. "Oh, we're hugging. Okay," Malia said, adding in her mind: *Please don't be a weirdo.*

Skye tipped her forehead against Malia's and swayed ever so slowly, eyes closed, as if drifting upon Malia's life force.

What is she doing? Malia fought her instinct to tense up or to run away screaming. Instead, she aimed to match Skye's breathing, hoping the woman wasn't a mind reader.

"You hungry? I bet you're starving."

Malia slumped as her eyes saucered in relief. "Actually, I am a bit—"

Skye didn't let her finish. She grabbed Malia by the wrist and started toward the forest, breaking stride only to turn and say, "The guys are gonna love you."

***

Malia couldn't believe her luck. Not even ashore an hour and already boasting an invitation up-valley.

She followed Skye to where the sand lapped against a milo forest and colorful nylon domes pockmarked the jungle backdrop. Skye maintained a pace that belied her laid-back demeanor, walking with such a loping gait as to almost be a prance. But Malia noticed not everyone shared her admiration of Skye. Few of the permitted hikers returned Malia's smile as she strode past. Some made no effort to hide their contempt, blowing scorn and judgment across the steam of their titanium coffee mugs. Others glared at Skye with a blend of jealousy and disdain Malia had seen a thousand times in the halls of school, at the mall. Green glances lobbed at the pretty girls, the popular crowd, and the ones who got away with risks others only dreamed of. These hikers were no different—it was written in the way they scowled at Skye as she passed. Naked, dreaded, and lean, she was clearly one of the so-called Kalalau Outlaws. Malia hurried after her, meandering past the tidy campsites, spurred by Skye's impudence and the sense she'd been drafted by the winning team.

The sand yielded to dirt and they soon reached a junction uphill from the mouth of a stream. "The main trail crosses Kalalau Stream here. That's the way out when you need to leave." Skye pointed along the shore toward the red cliff face Malia spotted earlier, then jerked her thumb to the right. "This way leads into the valley."

"Why don't you camp at the beach?" Malia shrugged the duffel bag's straps higher onto her shoulders and glanced back at the idyllic setting.

"Too many mice. Plus, you need a permit. Don't worry. It's only a mile or so."

The valley trail skirted a crumbling orange hillside then plunged into the jungle proper. Skye danced over tree roots and bounded from rock to rock as though her bare feet had memorized every placement. Malia did her best to match her step for step, but the steady incline wore at her stamina as the awkward luggage tugged at her strength. Within minutes, sweat darkened her hoodie as her bathing suit began to chafe.

"How long have you been here?"

"Not long. A month or so."

Malia expected Skye to ask about her plans, but she never did. "So, what's it like?"

Skye tossed Malia a frolicsome smile, but said nothing.

"What about the guys?"

"What about 'em?" Skye hooked her hand around a narrow tree and swung herself over a boulder to a soft patch of ground. Her feet hit the dirt with a kiss.

"Are they ... *nice*?" Malia asked, trying to hide her panting.

"Sure, I guess. It'll be good to have another girl around, though." She faced Malia and scrunched her face in a sideways smirk. "Too much testosterone is never a good thing."

"Do you ever feel—"

"You should go barefoot, by the way," Skye said, interrupting Malia's question. "The thong on those flip-flops will rip your toe off on the downhills once it gets muddy." Malia considered her dirt-stained toes extending off the front of her slippers and shrugged.

"It's through here," Skye said. She pushed aside a towering fern, revealing a faint path that branched from the main trail.

Malia laughed nervously. "I'll never find this on my own."

"That's your cue," she said, pointing at the ground. "The two rocks flanking the tree root."

Malia struggled to make sense of Skye's clue. On a trail littered in stones, the two marking the entrance to camp were as nondescript as any other. "I'll need to wrap one in a ti leaf—"

"No way. The rangers would notice that in a second. You know we're not supposed to be living out here, right?"

"Yeah, but—"

Skye wrapped her arm around Malia's shoulders and gave her a friendly squeeze, perhaps sensing how overwhelmed she felt. "You won't get lost. Trust me." Malia fought the urge to recoil as Skye pulled her into a hug. She didn't mind Skye's touchy-feely nature but doubted she'd ever get used to having a naked stranger pressed against her. *At least she doesn't smell.*

Malia returned her attention to the rocks. She tilted her head this way and that in study and smirked upon noticing their arrangement alongside the tree root resembled a cock and balls. But the rising giggle hung in her throat as the image triggered an unexpected concern: what if the guys were naked too? It wasn't that she hadn't been with boys— Malia wasn't a virgin—but no way would she have come to Kalalau if it were filled with pervy weirdos. Still, she had to play it cool. Skye revealing the secret path to their camp was a big step, but it didn't mean she'd be invited to stay—or even want to.

"So, are the guys our age?" Malia asked, hoping she was right about Skye being in her early twenties.

"I dunno. Why?"

Skye's flippant response unsettled Malia. In her experience, people in their teens and early twenties were fixated on age. It unlocked your driver's license, drinking, college. The only people who acted as if age didn't matter were those too old to remember being young.

Malia had no time for a follow-up as Skye weaved quickly between trees much larger than those near the stream. Malia kept pace, blinded by the sting of sweat and exhaustion—and apprehension. Minutes later, Skye swept aside some shrubs, revealing a secluded clearing. "Home sweet home."

Malia's breath snagged like a fishhook on coral. The camp she'd dreamed of visiting, the host of her mother's most cherished memories, was nothing like she expected. Frayed, sun-bleached tarps of faded blues and greens sagged from every tree branch, as if the blanket forts she'd made during childhood sleepovers were left to molder. Flimsy tents squatted in the lower ends of these tarp tunnels, each streaked with dirt and mildew. Piled in drifts throughout the periphery were nests of discarded plastic jugs, bottles, and coffee cans.

The scent of forest decay and spoiled food hung in the air. A mouse scampered along a rope.

"So, whatcha think?" Skye wore a proud look.

Malia didn't answer. How could she be honest when she'd seen nicer homeless camps beneath a freeway?

She knew the reputation kids from Black Point had. Especially the ones who went to the Kamehameha School. She avoided undue snob-bishness by fiddling with her bag. Malia moved to set it atop a nearby table but feared it might collapse. She lowered it to the ground only to yank it back as a cockroach scurried toward it.

"Was it ... always like this?" she asked, struggling to picture her mother in such a sty.

Skye chuckled. "It grows on you."

Malia picked at her shorts as her skin crawled in disgust.

"So, where's everyone else?" Despite the nearby tents and several more visible in the distance, the camp seemed deserted. Not at all the buzzing collective of campers she'd expected.

Skye stuck her fingers in her mouth and loosed an ear-piercing whistle.

The tent nearest the firepit shook as someone startled awake with a grunt. "That's Darren." Skye dismissed him with a roll of her eyes. She whistled again, even louder, causing Malia to cover her ears.

"Eh, enough with da whistle!" The shout was gruff. Powerful.

"Inoke! I got someone I want you to meet." Skye pointed to a hammock Malia hadn't noticed hanging between two guava trees in the distance.

An exaggerated sigh and puff of smoke rose from the hammock. The man she called Inoke flung his legs over the sides of the hammock, straddling the Rasta-themed knitting, and sat upright. Malia's first impression was that of a bull, a hulking mass with a barrel chest and biceps that seemed an extension of his shoulders. He wasn't muscular so much as solid. His head appeared as round and hard as a coconut, with black, closely shorn hair. His chin bore an unkempt scruff that didn't quite form a goatee.

He wore black board shorts and the outline of the Hawaiian Islands tattooed on his chest, above his heart. Only Kaua'i was colored green, marking him a local. A quote she couldn't read was stamped in an elegant font along his neck.

"You find another stray?" Inoke narrowed his eyes, sizing Malia up, and took another drag of his joint. "That's two this week."

Malia half-stepped behind Skye's shoulder.

"This is Malia. She's gonna stay with us."

Malia whispered, "I am?"

Skye turned to face her. "That's what you wanted, right?"

"Um … yeah, but," she began, barely restraining her second thoughts, "I don't have a tent."

"No worries. My roommate moved out a week ago You can share mine."

"You sure?" It was all happening so fast. Too fast. "What if she comes back?"

Skye shook her head, causing her dreads to sway. "Most girls only stay a week or two."

They do? Malia only planned a couple weeks herself, but assumed she'd be an outlier.

"She can move in with me." Malia turned toward the drawling invitation and quickly averted her eyes. The one called Darren emerged from his tent, spindly and pale with bloodshot eyes and a toothy grin. He wore a scraggly, strawberry-blond beard several inches long with matching ratty braids that tickled his shoulders. Like Skye, he was stark naked.

"Man, get some clothes on before I beat yo' ass," Inoke said. "Ain't nobody want to see your tiny *ule.*"

Malia held a hand to her face, shielding her from the sight of Darren's bare ass as he ducked away. She forced a laugh, trying to mask her discomfort.

"Ignore him. I'm Inoke." He passed the joint to his left hand and extended his right in greeting, all the while maintaining a scrutinizing gaze. "Ain't nobody gonna come looking for you, are they?"

Malia glanced between them for a sign she'd misheard him, but they only stared back, waiting. That's when it hit her: he thought she was a runaway. "Umm, no. I just wanted to see this place before I left for college."

"You sure?" He arched his eyebrows high.

Malia nodded in quick, jittery motions despite wondering if it were true. She hadn't considered that there'd be a leader in charge of the camp—and wondered what, other than his muscles, made Inoke the boss.

"In that case, Skye's right. Move in with her. Nice to see a local girl checking this place out for a change." Malia looked to Skye for assurance she'd understood correctly, for some hint of pushback, but Skye said nothing. She simply cocked her head and smiled like *See, I told you.*

"Well …" Malia began, rubbing the back of her neck, unsure what to say. Was this what she wanted? To live amongst the filthy camp, Inoke's bossiness, and Skye's ever-present nudity? She wasn't a priss, but the camp seemed less a piece of hippie paradise than a refuge of last resort. But what choice did she have? Even if she wanted to leave, she'd need a day or two to prepare for the eleven-mile hike out—not to mention amass the necessary courage. She'd read there were several sections where a single misstep could cost a hiker their life.

Still, even as she considered leaving, Malia couldn't escape her mother's comments about how peaceful Kalalau Valley was. *Maybe things weren't all that different,* she thought. Maybe a place like this needed a ringleader like Inoke to keep everyone in line. After all, she did benefit from his ability to send Darren scurrying. And so what if it was a little dirty? At least the tarps would keep them dry in the rain. She turned in place, noting ways to straighten the camp, make it homier. But Malia couldn't recall her mother ever commenting on the camp itself. For Christina, it was all about the people. Her Kalalau *'ohana.*

"Can you show me your tent?" A hesitant step toward staying.

"Sure." Skye laughed a short burst. "I guess it's *our* tent now, huh?"

Malia followed Skye out of the central camp, ducking beneath the tarps as they beelined for the woods. Up ahead, about twenty yards, Malia spotted a blue tent. She was thankful to have found a place to stay, and a girl to share it with, but hoped some other girls showed up. And soon. She'd seen a smattering of other tents tucked into the woods during the hike in from the beach, but Skye said most were abandoned. Others, tucked further in the valley, belonged to loners best ignored. Nevertheless, Malia hoped it wasn't just the four of them.

The crunch of footsteps on dry leaves drew Malia's attention to someone making his way through the woods. Tall with wavy brown hair cropped short, dark skin, and a relaxed walk, he smiled and lifted his chin in that innocuous way guys do. Less a hello than an acknowledgment without commitment.

"Who's that?" Malia asked, pointing with her elbow.

"That's Tiki. Showed up last week. Kind of quiet."

Malia repeated his name to herself, assuming it had to be a nickname despite his Pacific Islander appearance. Local boys always had nicknames—the interesting ones at least. She fluttered a hand at him, no more than a butterfly's greeting, and looked away when he smiled back.

The tent door flapped shut, sealing Malia within a sour fog of mildew, stale smoke, and who only knew what. She held her breath and scanned for the source of the rot amongst the chaff of Skye's carefree communion with nature. Pinpointing it was impossible; her belongings lay heaped in drifts as if blown by the trades.

Malia didn't move for fear of touching the grime, didn't blink despite the odor stinging her eyes.

"Just push my stuff to the side," Skye yelled from outside the tent.

Malia mumbled her acknowledgment. *Where's a torch when you need one?*

Knowing she had no choice but to make do, Malia held her nose and extended her heel toward Skye's limp air mattress. She kicked it, plowing aside a variety of wrinkled paperbacks, crumpled towels, and a backpack's worth of camping paraphernalia. She lifted a ratty blanket by the corner, pinching it between thumb and forefinger, and tossed it aside. A circus of ants scurried about, energized by the light.

She flicked them one by one from the half of the hulking box tent she cleared. *My half*, she thought, finally releasing the initial breath she'd swallowed upon entering.

Malia scooched to the front of the tent. She unrolled her Thermarest, opened the self-inflate valve, and unfurled her lightweight sleeping bag. Kneeling alongside her duffel, she removed each item of clothing and folded them neatly atop her bed, quarantining her possessions from Skye's. She fluffed her travel-size pillow, then removed the photos of her mom from a Ziploc and propped them against the tent wall, safe behind her pillow. Within view. One, the snapshot of them sharing a birthday dessert. The other, the decades-old group photo from Kalalau Beach. Malia trailed her fingers across the smiling faces and sighed as a ticklish wave of euphoria washed over her. She blinked away the emotion pricking her eyes and filled her chest with an assuring breath. "I made it, Mom," she whispered.

Done unpacking, Malia changed into a dry swimsuit—a sports bra style top with boy shorts—and ran her fingers through her hair. They snagged in a knot. *Already?* She turned her bag upside-down and shook it, hoping one of her hair ties would fall free. "You gotta be kidding me." Malia heaved a sigh, knowing she'd have to do something or else her hair would be a bird's nest within days. It shouldn't be hard to borrow a scrunchie, she figured, but hated feeling so ill-prepared.

Outside the tent, Skye appeared to be half asleep in the hammock. Malia hesitated, then asked, "Uh, is there somewhere I can hang these?" She held out the clothes she'd swam ashore in.

Skye opened her eyes, then guffawed.

Malia looked around as if she'd been caught trailing toilet paper from her shoe. "What?"

"Are you really on your second outfit?"

"Yeah. Why?"

"Nothing. Nothing." Skye smiled, trying not to laugh, and exited the hammock.

"Why are you looking at me like that?" Malia crossed her arms and turned to the side, suddenly self-conscious. Not because of her appearance, though it was the least sexy swimsuit she had, but because she couldn't escape the sense that her every move was being scrutinized. From the German on the beach to the other tourists to how Inoke looked her over, and now this. Whatever *this* was.

"You're never gonna keep that thing clean."

Malia said nothing.

"And between the rain and sweat, you're gonna be wet the entire time. Think about that. Chafing, the constant dampness." Skye flicked her gaze at Malia's crotch ever so noticeably and sucked air through a toothy display of wariness. "It's awfully tight. Not good."

Malia shrugged, dismissing Skye's comments. She'd been going to the beach her whole life, had been in bathing suits from sunup to sunset and couldn't recall any problems. "I'll be fine."

Skye poked the bundle of clothes with the curiosity of a child jabbing at roadkill with a stick. "Suit yourself. Nothing really dries out here. But you can try hanging it from one of the ropes."

An orange cord stretched like a beam beneath the blue square of vinyl strung above their tent. Malia brushed the mold and dirt from the underside with her hand, then draped her clothing over the rope. She straightened her clothing the best she could as Skye watched with amusement. Malia adjusted her sweatshirt with a delicate tug and dialed up her enthusiasm. "Good enough. You mentioned something about food earlier?" Malia wasn't particularly hungry but was eager to see the rest of the camp.

"Yeah, sure. The garden's back past the firepit."

"Oh, I thought it was further up the valley."

"Community Garden is up that way. Near Big Pool. This one's closer." She waved her along, adopting the demeanor of a tour guide. "That's Inoke's tent over there. Watch your head." Skye lifted a tree branch out of the way.

"And whose is that?" Malia pointed at another tent staked amongst a growth of ferns.

"Also Inoke's." Before Malia could ask, Skye clarified, "It's, um, storage. Hence the zipper locks."

"Oh." Malia's voice sagged. "I thought we had neighbors."

"Others used to live out here, but the state scared most of 'em off. Probably better there's only a few of us now." She turned and winked. "Less likely to get caught. Sucky part is the farm kind of went to hell. Nobody really takes care of it anymore."

Malia knew better than to get her hopes up. The farm, she figured, was likely no more than a pair of scraggly fruit trees and smattering of wild herbs. She'd know soon enough.

The ground was mostly level, but the air was thick with humidity and insects and Malia soon bore a slick of sweat. She wiped her hands on her shorts and grimaced at the smear of dirt left behind.

"Dammit." Malia slapped a mosquito. Her third in as many steps.

"You'll get used to them."

"Doubtful." She swatted another on her neck. "Don't they drive you crazy"—her gaze drifted toward Sky's breasts—"especially being naked and all?"

Skye shrugged. A mosquito hovered near her face then alighted on her hairline. Skye's pupils rolled upward in acknowledgment. The mosquito speared Skye's scalp and fattened before Malia's eyes. Skye didn't flinch. "See? Told you."

"I hope I never get *that* used to anything."

If Skye heard her comment, she chose to ignore it. Just as she failed to answer questions about showering, passing the time, and several others Malia knew might sound petty, but asked anyway. They fell into an awkward quiet until Skye pushed between two gargantuan heart-shaped leaves, leaving them swinging in her wake like batwing doors. "We're here."

Malia could scarcely believe her eyes as she entered a sprawling grocery of jungle produce. Invisible from steps away were three taro ponds, each home to dozens of plants jutting shoulder-high into the air, leaning drunkenly in various directions, straining to support leaves the size of elephant ears. Fruit trees, many of them choked with vines and undergrowth, walled the ponds with rainbow battlements of passionfruit, banana, guava, mango, breadfruit, and papaya.

At once, the knot of incertitude in Malia's stomach vanished, dissolved within the sweet, tropical scent of her favorite fruits. "It's beautiful," she uttered, less a comment on how it appeared in the now than how it may have looked twenty years earlier, when her mom was there—and how it might look again.

Skye waded into a pond and grabbed a stalk with yellowing leaves. Despite the stagnant water and a scum that clung to many of the plants, the taro—or *kalo* as Malia knew to call it—looked surprisingly healthy.

"Gotta watch for the snails. They're hell on your feet." Skye lifted the plant straight out of the water, pulling a potato-like tuber from the soup. "This one's ready." She bounded back to the edge of the pond and handed the dripping plant to Malia. "We eat a lot of this stuff."

Malia inhaled its earthy scent as much out of instinct as curiosity. Despite having eaten plenty of fried taro chips and poi over the years, she'd never handled a fresh taro corm before. Life in the city didn't grant much opportunity for farming. Now she wanted to splash into the water and yank one out herself.

"Woah! The *liliko'i* are going off! Look at 'em all." Skye grabbed Malia by the wrist and guided her across a diversion channel that fed the ponds from a nearby stream. She plucked two canary-tinted passionfruit from a tree, tore a hole in the cork-like skin, and handed one over. Malia tucked the taro stalk under her arm, pried the fruit open, and slurped the airy seeds. Exquisite. She spotted another that had gone deliciously wrinkled and tore it from its bunch. The taste reminded her of the bakery, where the *liliko'i* jam was a popular request for buns and pancakes. By this time on a Saturday, about ten or eleven o'clock if she had to guess, she'd typically have served forty orders of cream puffs, most going to tourists unaware that *liliko'i* was simply what Hawaiians called passionfruit.

"You even have shampoo ginger," Malia said, squeezing a reddish flower head shaped like a pinecone. A slippery, sudsy, ginger-scented sap oozed onto her hand.

"As in *shampoo* shampoo?" Skye asked.

"Yep. Paul Mitchell has a whole product line using this stuff. *'Awapuhi.* The rhizome's edible too." Malia squeezed sap onto Skye's outstretched hand. Then, mindful of potentially sounding like a know-it-all, pointed out some bananas. "Any way to get them down?"

"Not ripe yet." Skye twisted her face as a debate appeared to play out in her mind. "I probably shouldn't, but ... " She shrugged. "What the hell. You seem harmless."

Skye led the way around the furthest taro pond then backed through a thicket of plants, revealing a second, smaller clearing lit by the late morning sun thanks to a window in the tree canopy. A throng of shoulder-high tomato plants, loosely tied to bamboo posts, stood basking in the warmth. "Most people don't know they're here—"

"I won't tell a soul," Malia promised, cutting her off. She stepped lightly to the nearest plant, placed her palm beneath a red globe, and lifted, relieving the vine of its burden. "May I?"

"Yeah, go ahead. Just one or two though."

Malia plucked the softball-sized tomato, blew away the forest dust, and bit. Warm juice dribbled down her chin as she grinned at the novelty. She took another bite, then another, savoring the freshness and silently giving thanks to the luck that led her to Skye. As she scanned this secret garden, she detected a secondary scent, something pungent. Skunky. She parted the outer vines and leaned in, discovering what appeared to be a number of marijuana plants sheltered behind the tomatoes. She'd never seen marijuana in person before, let alone in plant form, but the leaves were unmistakable. She counted a half-dozen plants, several bearing knobs of purple flowers. "Are those ..." she began, then gestured with her chin, reluctant to call them by name.

"*Pakalolo?* Yeah. Forget you ever saw it. It's Inoke's."

"Oh, I just—"

"I'm serious. Only Darren and I know it's here."

Malia was confused. Sure, marijuana was practically still illegal in Hawaiʻi, especially to grow, but she didn't anticipate secrets amongst the campers. "Not whatshisname? Don't you trust the other guy?"

"Tiki?" Skye shrugged. "He's only been here a week. Inoke shares when he wants, but these are his babies. He's got more, but hell if I know where."

Malia returned a puzzled look, but the calculus solved itself. The storage tent, the secrecy surrounding this other garden. The tomato blind.

Skye scratched a bug bite above her eye. "He's got a guy who comes in by boat every week or so to pick it up."

Malia nearly dropped her tomato upon realizing she moved in next to a drug dealer. She'd seen joints at parties in high school—even Jenna bragged about trying it—but the journey from smoker to grower was immense, and her dad was constantly warning her about Hawai'i being one of the strictest in the country when it came to narcotics.

Skye must have recognized Malia's reaction. "Forget you even know."

Malia bulged her eyes.

"Seriously. It's no biggie." She plucked another tomato and handed it over, like a mother pacifying a disgruntled child. "But that reminds me. Not sure how long you plan on staying, but his guy does grocery runs for the camp. Just let Inoke know if you need something. But be prepared for extra chores if you do."

Malia did a double take. *Need something?* It had to be at least twenty miles round-trip to Hanalei by boat.

"You think I'm joking. I don't know what you had in that Hefty sack you dragged up the beach, but you're a girl, right?"

Malia stroked the air beside her, gesturing from her chest to waist like a game show model. "Last I checked," she said.

"Then you're gonna need supplies. Toilet paper, tampons, condoms. That sort of thing."

"Oh, right. Nah, I'm good ..." Though Malia packed a roll of toilet paper and couldn't imagine having sex while camping—she shuddered at the thought—she'd forgotten to account for her period. "I think." She counted the weeks on her fingers and breathed a sigh of relief.

"Like I said, if you stay long enough to need anything, let him know."

"Right. The neighborhood drug dealer has a tampon service. Noted."

"Hey, I'm only trying to help—"

"I'm kidding." Malia said with a nervous laugh, taken aback by Skye's abrupt hardening. Malia bit the tomato, wondering how she'd last two days, let alone two weeks.

Malia had just spotted the phallic array of rocks marking the hidden path to their camp when she heard the scream. Not human, but no ordinary barnyard cry either. The kind of bloodcurdling shriek as easily felt in the bones as heard by the ears, and its intensity silenced the forest. An unnatural silence that would have curled Malia's toes if they hadn't already been clawing her sandals for traction as she lumbered down the trail with an armful of firewood.

Minutes passed before the honeycreepers and cardinals resumed their song, before she could will her feet in the direction of camp— and the source of the savage squeal.

She stepped gingerly with her senses on high alert. Five yards ahead, Inoke emerged from behind a tree, blocking her path with a curved knife in his hand and blood streaked across his shirt. Malia startled, nearly dropping the firewood.

"Gonna eat good tonight." He scratched the elbow of his knife hand. "You picked a good day to join us."

Malia tightened her grip on the bundle, clutching the wood against her torso as a shield, enduring the pokes and scratches. She retreated a half step, her gaze fixed on the blood dripping from the blade.

"Man, it's been weeks since I snared one."

Malia made a confused face.

"No horns, either. The ones with the horns? No fun without a cross-bow." Inoke dragged his teeth across his lower lip while shaking his head, as if recalling an encounter with the business end of a prior capture.

"I heard it cry," she said, trying to conceal her trepidation. She flipped through her mental repository of local fauna. *Horns? Did he kill a goat?*

"Yeah, grip slipped as I sliced its throat. Sloppy." He grunted, then spit in the dirt. "Should have expected her to buck."

Inoke gestured toward camp and began walking. As Malia fell in behind him, she caught sight of the kill hanging by its hind legs from a tree not far off the trail. She swallowed hard as the bitter sight of the goat's slit jugular and gutted abdomen spun into view. Worse was the tongue, hanging limp from its mouth, a droplet of blood refusing to fall.

"Poor thing."

Inoke looked back and chuckled. "Hey, you're not one of those PETA types, are you?" He thrust his arm and pushed lightly at the firewood. A friendly jostle. "I'm just playin'. Maybe you good luck, eh?"

Malia forced a smile.

"It didn't suffer. Just gotta let the blood drain, then I'll butcher it."

Inoke led the way to camp in silence as Malia struggled along behind him, her arms aching from the weight. She couldn't believe he didn't offer to help carry the wood and considered asking him to, but instead felt pride in his unwillingness to assist her. It made her feel at home; guests don't do chores.

And if this were going to be home, she'd have to accept the hunting. Malia told herself it was no different than the countless pig roasts she'd attended over the years. But was that true? She'd never heard a pig cry in pain; never tore into the flesh of an animal whose path she might have crossed earlier that day. The echoes of the goat's scream scratched at her like the splintery wood she hauled in her arms. Malia cringed, recalling the carcass hanging from the tree. Was it even edible? She'd never tasted goat before, never seen it on a menu.

Guess I'll know soon enough.

Once at camp, Malia added the wood to a pile she amassed beneath one of the tarps. It was her third scavenging trip that afternoon. Tiring work—and harder than she expected owing to the preponderance of vines and pandanus palms that choked the forest—but she eventually found a stockpile of dried branches perfect for a fire. To her amazement, it was already stacked in rows. She only had to lug it back to camp.

Inoke approached, wiping his knife with a towel. His brow furrowed as he inspected her haul.

"One or two more trips should be enough for tonight."

Inoke tilted his head in thought, as if troubled by the wood's presence.

"It should burn, right?" Malia asked, guessing at his concern.

"Where you get this?"

"Just off the trail, up-valley. Someone already piled it in a row." As she spoke, Inoke raised his head to the treetops and shut his eyes. "What? Was it for another camp? I didn't see anyone."

"This is Java plum."

"Is that bad?"

"Is it bad?" Inoke repeated, his voice squeaking with faux femininity. "Yes, Malia, very bad. That wood is a fence. For Community Garden. You tore it down."

"A fence?" She looked more closely at the brittle wood, noticing the ashen bark, the splintered cores. The wood had clearly been cut a long time ago; the fence might even have been older than her.

"It keeps the goats out. They hate the stuff."

"Oh, I ... I didn't know," she said, considering the possibility that her mother helped build the fence.

Inoke stomped away, balling his empty fist and squeezing the knife so hard the veins in his forearms popped. He muttered something as he went. Malia wasn't sure, but it sounded like *Skye's fucking stray*.

The greasy scent of grilled goat tugged Malia awake early that evening. She shivered as she emerged from the nap, her first decent sleep in over a day. The forest was silent, calm, in fading light. She wrapped herself in a black and neon sarong, as much for warmth as to conceal the hammock's fishnet imprint on her legs, then followed her nose to the campfire, wondering why Skye hadn't woken her.

Malia approached hesitantly and kept to the edge of the encampment, unsure she was still welcome. From behind a tree, she watched a bevy of glowing faces tuck into dinner bowls, their misshapen shadows dancing against the trees.

The group ate in quiet, like a tribe of strangers, emitting no sense of the communal cheer over which Malia's mother so often reminisced. Neighbors bound only by a shared jungle zip code, with Inoke lording over them; he alone in a proper camping chair as the others squatted atop boulders and a fallen tree. Inoke ate directly from the rough metal grill, ignoring the stewpot—or a plate. Goat or not, watching him chop and stab at the meat made Malia salivate. Yet she remained in the shadows.

A college-aged blonde sat beside him, her sunburn marking her as FOP: fresh off the plane. She picked at her food with the boredom of someone who'd sought a party and found a study group instead. Clockwise from her was the one Skye had called Tiki. He sat cross-legged atop a woven rug so decrepit it had all but withered into the forest floor. He glanced directly to where she hid but said nothing. He returned his attention to the fire as Malia released a held breath, admiring how the flames reflected like fireflies in his chestnut eyes.

Darren hunched atop a boulder to Tiki's left, his ragged goatee drizzled in soup. Another member of the inner circle. Behind him sat several men Malia didn't recognize. Grizzled and lean, all sinew and bones, they lacked both the starry-eyed softness of hikers on holiday and the youthful physiques of the others. These men reminded Malia of contestants on a survival reality show, slowly withering in the jungle as the world moved on without them. And by the look of things, they'd been there for years.

Rounding off the circle was Skye, her back to Malia, legs folded sideways atop a log draped with a towel. Even if Malia hadn't recognized her dreadlocks, she'd have known it was Skye; who else would have helped herself to Malia's hoodie? And that was all the invitation Malia needed.

She wasn't two steps from the shadows before all eyes were on her, orange-lit faces staring in concert, observing her with an indifference so chilling, she felt like a sacrificial offering called to slaughter. *At least I wouldn't die a virgin,* she thought, grasping for comfort in the absurdity.

Skye caught the shift in attention and turned. "There you are. Come sit." She brushed a leaf from the log. Then, upon noticing Malia staring at her sweatshirt, Skye hugged herself for warmth and said, "I was getting chicken skin. You don't mind, right?"

"No. That's fine," Malia lied, suspecting she'd have her own goosebumps before long. She rounded the log to sit as close to the fire as she could and nodded at the others.

The men on the fringe returned a blank stare that may as well been directed at the trees behind her. Darren raised his hand in greeting and shot her an awkward smile as he turtled inward. Noticing his eyes were no longer bloodshot, Malia couldn't help wondering if he was embarrassed from their initial encounter. Malia sucked in her lips, trying not to laugh at the memory of him naked, and caught a hint of a smirk from Tiki as she did.

"You hungry? Pass your bowl." It was Inoke, stealing her attention.

"Oh." She scanned the camp for dishware. "Where are the bowls?"

Darren shook his head slowly as one of the old-timers mumbled something dismissive.

"No bowl? How you gonna eat?" Inoke bulged his eyes for emphasis, piling a feeling of stupidity atop her sense of unwelcome. And it *was* stupid of her, she now realized, to show up with nothing but some clothes and a sleeping bag. No tent, no cookware, no food. She was at their mercy.

"Hey, Darren. Get her a bowl," Inoke said.

"Why do I—"

"Cause your tent right there. And who you think got the wood we cooking on tonight?"

"Thank you," she whispered, relieved he seemed to forgive her earlier blunder.

Inoke gave Malia a subtle nod as Darren tilted his bowl to his mouth and drained the dregs of stew before rising in a huff. He returned with a shallow wooden bowl, seemingly hand carved, and handed it over. "You'll need to rinse it."

Soot and dust coated the bowl, but Malia felt the others looking at her, could sense them judging her ability to fit in, preparing their verdict. She wasn't about to ask for a rag. The last thing she wanted was to seem too dainty. She grabbed a fistful of her sarong and wiped the inside of the bowl, then blew it clean. "No prob."

"Pass it down," Inoke said, extending his hand. He ladled in a mysterious broth with vegetables, then added a few pieces of goat. "Your first bowl of Kalalau stew."

"The meat's a treat. Don't get used to it," Skye said, and thanked Inoke. A gesture that seemed less genuine and more an act of tribute. "Have my spork; I'm done."

Malia dipped the utensil into the murky liquid and lifted a slick of greasy broth. A scab of tomato skin floated alongside an unidentifiable pulp. Possibly breadfruit. She sipped it, unsurprised when the dominant flavor was *gray*. She took another spoonful, this time catching a shred of meat along with some beans. She ate quickly, more out of hunger than desire. "It's good," she said, being polite. "What's in it?"

Fits of snickering surrounded her before a craggy voice in the shadows replied, "What's *not* in it?"

"Hey, Inoke, what in da stew?" Darren asked, dripping with phony curiosity.

"I dunno. What day today? I'll check my menu." The comment drew an inordinate amount of laughter. Malia smiled as if in on the joke but scanned the crowd, hoping someone would explain. Only Tiki seemed to notice her confusion. He raised his palms and shrugged in a beats-me manner.

Skye lowered her voice and leaned in. "It's usually kinda sour, but you get used to it." She then turned to Inoke. "That reminds me. Inoke, Malia found some ginger by the *liliko'i*. Maybe it'll add some flavor to the stew."

"That so?" Inoke said. All eyes locked on Malia.

"It's not as tasty as the stuff in the grocery store, but it wouldn't hurt." Malia felt her intestines squirm as she eyed her bowl of stew and added, "Though it might be better to infuse the *'awapuhi* stems in water to help with the inevitable stomachache."

"Get a load of this one with the fancy knowledge," Skye said with a snort. "She sounds just like you, Tiki."

Malia smiled shyly across the fire at him, wondering what Skye had meant with her comment. Tiki grinned back, head cocked in bemusement, enhancing Malia's curiosity.

The earlier quiet returned as Malia ate. Nobody spoke; nobody asked where she was from, what brought her to Kalalau. She knew times change, but wasn't dinner where people came together to talk? She struggled to believe the spirit of this valley could have shifted so drastically in twenty years. Skye's words echoed in her mind as she slurped the bowl empty: *you'll get used to it.* She was referring to the food, but as Malia stared into the pot, she wondered what else she'd have to get used to.

Or why she'd want to.

Darren tapped Malia's leg and offered her a crinkled joint, wisps of smoke rising from its smoldering tip. Malia recoiled ever so slightly and shook her head. "Uh, no thanks," she said, recalling her failed attempt at smoking a cigarette, how she wound up coughing for an hour.

Darren hooked his head as if nudging away a fly. Malia stared back. *What?* "Pass it to Skye."

"Oh, right." She pinched the joint nervously, nearly dropping it. Skye took it. Eyes closed, her body swayed like a sunflower in a breeze only she felt.

The joint made its way to Inoke. Its cherry ring flared, advancing along the paper as his barrel chest inflated. He exhaled a billowing cumulus and passed it to the blonde who'd unsurprisingly sprung to life with its arrival. Tiki refrained, citing a headache, and the rounds continued. The group settled into their collective highs after the joint completed a second lap, each person floating in suspended animation. Malia sensed Inoke studying her as though she were some long-lost bottle cast adrift in the sea, only to wash ashore on his beach. But it was she who struggled to decipher the message of her arrival.

As Malia sought refuge in the tendrils of campfire smoke, she noticed Tiki watching her with a gaze that begged to be matched. She blushed and glanced to her lap, but curiosity dragged her attention back. Before she could look away again, he stood and wiped his hands against his shorts. He reached a hand around the fire. "They call me Tiki." His accent sounded Australian, but not quite.

"I know," she said, recalling Skye's earlier mention. Malia rose to greet him in an awkward half-standing, half-sitting manner. He wore blue board shorts and a loose-fitting V-neck tee that accentuated his surfer's physique. Tiki's skin was smooth and his grip strong without being overbearing. But it was his smile that sent Malia into a trance. That relaxed, dimpled, ain't-no-bother confidence was as magnetic as it was reassuring. That someone as clean-cut as he could be at ease amongst the rough-hewn Outlaws suggested maybe Malia too could fit in.

"I'm Malia." It came out as soft as steam but was all the breath she had to spare. That the cutest guy in camp was the only one polite enough to rise to greet her was almost too much to believe. Her hand dipped and rose in his grasp, seemingly pumping air back into her. "I like your accent. Where are you from?"

Tiki tilted his head, as if surprised by her question. He released her hand. "Oh, that. I'm from—"

"Nah. Party foul." It was Darren. He spoke quickly with an erratic annoyance. His fingers paused amidst rolling another joint. "So harsh."

"I was just—"

"He's from Kalalau. Ain't you, Tiki?" Skye said, her voice silky and distant. Ethereal. She twirled her hands overhead in a manner that made Malia wonder what other drugs she might be on. "We're *all* from Kalalau."

Malia sat, deflated. "I just wondered—"

"Hey, *malihini*," Inoke said, calling her a stranger. "Not cool. There's only Kalalau. You want to talk about somewhere else, you go back to da beach. Ask da tourists."

Malia flinched, but the sting of Inoke's reprimand cooled upon sight of Tiki's breezy shrug. "So much for getting to know one another," Malia said beneath her breath.

"New Zealand," Tiki offered before anyone could interject. "I'm Kiwi."

Malia mouthed the word *Kiwi* in awe as she considered the odds, the distance.

"Nope. We're not doing this." Darren thrust a freshly lit joint at Malia. "Here. Take a hit, newbie."

It was bad enough having Inoke order her around, she wasn't going to suffer his underling too. Malia shot Darren her most menacing look, wanting to tell him off, but decided to make another effort to fit in. "Oh, what the hell." She grabbed the joint and quickly raised it to her lips, denying herself the chance to back down. She held the smoke in her throat but didn't know what else to do. Why hadn't Jenna taught her? Should she exhale through her nose or mouth? Swallow? Malia had no idea. She gripped the joint tightly, not wanting to drop it as she doubled over in a coughing fit, choking on the smoke.

"Oi! We ain't here to fuck spiders." The girl beside Inoke glowered at Malia.

Tiki burst into laughter. "What'd you say?"

The girl did a double take. "What do ya mean? You're Kiwi ain't cha?"

"Sure, but—"

"Isn't that an Aussie saying?" Darren asked, motioning to the blonde. "You're from Perth, right?"

"Australia, New Zealand, who cares?" Inoke said.

"Nothing but a bunch of roofuckers, you ask me," someone said, probably louder than intended. "Good surfers, though."

"We both say it, but it's definitely Kiwi. Brought over by the Dutch, I reckon. Anyway, no excuse for this one not to know it." The blonde jerked her thumb at Tiki, who chewed his lip with an intense interest as the others discussed the etymology of the ridiculous phrase.

Malia felt a slight tug on her sarong. When she turned, Skye wordlessly took the joint from her and continued the circle. A jug of water and sliced papaya soon emerged—and disappeared every bit as suddenly. The earlier silence that felt so awkward suffused the group like a fog creeping from the sea. And Malia sank into it.

She scanned the circle, from Inoke (the blonde's head rested on his knee) to Tiki to Darren and the others and wondered how much of their bluster wasn't just stupid male jockeying for a chance to impress the new girl. She looked to Darren beside her, imagining his dirty dreads and bloodshot eyes hovering over her as he pumped away. She snorted a little too loudly and turned. Inoke? Doubtful. Her gaze settled on Tiki. A fit, friendly outsider, just like her, only with a chiseled jaw and perfectly messed hair. Hot. But like a chameleon in the desert, he pulled it off with a confident nonchalance Malia found intoxicating.

She arched her eyebrows in thought. Anything could happen in two weeks.

The joint entered its second lap. Skye grabbed Malia's wrist as she reached for it. "Try not to wet it. Just inhale smoothly, hold it for a second, then exhale nice and slow."

Malia hadn't planned on taking another hit but wanted to show Skye she could follow instructions. She took a moment to enjoy the taste, then blew a cloud of smoke without coughing.

Inoke led the group in a slow clap.

"Nicely done," Skye said.

Malia blushed as her head began to swim.

"Damn, Skye. Keep teaching her like that and she'll be ready take your spot as the token cool chick when you go," Darren said.

Malia snapped to attention. Any hint—real or imagined—of the pot having hit her vanished, drowned in the cold water of his comment. She spun toward Skye. "You're not leaving, are you?"

Skye took a lengthy hit, at least twice as long as Malia's. As she did, Darren leaned over and said, "All the hot girls leave eventually." Malia ignored him, but he continued. "It's like Hercules with the apples. He couldn't leave without someone taking his spot—"

"You don't know what you're talking about," Skye said, shooting him a nasty look.

"Yeah, shut up, Darren," Inoke added.

"Skye," Malia said, struggling to contain the fear of being the only girl living in camp. "Are you leaving?"

"No way." She dismissed Malia's concern with a flick of her wrist.

Later that night, as Malia stared at the ceiling of their shared tent, she realized she might have believed her if only Skye had looked her in the eye as she denied it.

CHAPTER 7
LOST IN THE CLOUDS

Each night, Malia crawled ever earlier into the shared tent, her exhaustion mingling with boredom. For ten hours, she'd toss atop a too-thin air mattress, no position safe from the tree roots lurking beneath her hip. She woke every morning ready to burst and lay uncomfortably in the darkness, waiting till the safety of daybreak to relieve her bladder. Then, like a house guest not wanting to disrupt the calm, she'd settle into the silence of the slumbering camp and await the others to start their day.

Her third morning in Kalalau began no differently, except it wasn't only her bladder needing relief: she knew she couldn't hold her bowels forever, but it had been worth a shot. Malia had seen an outhouse during her daily trips to the beach with Skye, but it was a mile away. She made it in time, barely, sweating and clutching her stomach as she raced down the trail in a telltale gait. She thanked the heavens upon discovering the blessed remnants of a toilet paper roll beside the seat and swore to never again cut it so close.

Upon returning to camp, she found the dogeared Castaneda paperback she'd been reading tossed in the dirt. A recommendation from Darren, on loan from his surprisingly impressive library. She bent to retrieve it and stared at Skye, who lay naked in the hammock. Malia grimaced and slapped the book against her palm with a jarring *thwack,* generating a puff of dust.

Skye startled and waved at the dirt cloud. "Geez, Malia, what gives?"

"I was reading here," she said, unable to hide her annoyance.

"Sorry. Thought you went for a swim."

"Had to use the toilet."

"You fall in a hole?" Skye laughed, then added, "You must've been gone an hour."

"It's a long walk. Why's camp so far from the outhouse?"

Skye pressed her palms against the hammock and sat upright. "Outhouse? You hiked to the beach just to poop?"

Malia looked away, embarrassed, but unsure why. She'd never camped outside of a developed campground before.

"So, you've never gone in the woods?'

"But there's a toilet—"

"It's a mile away. What're you gonna do in an emergency? You can't always trust Inoke's cooking, ya know?"

Malia had been fearing that exact scenario for days. With any luck, she'd get through the two weeks without such a crisis. "But the sign by the toilet says, 'No make doodoo on ground.'"

Skye shook her head and dismounted the hammock with an ease that had thus far evaded Malia. Her voice was of an exasperated teacher, dumbing down the day's lesson for the class delinquent. "Haven't you ever been camping before? You dig a hole, go, and cover it with a rock so nobody steps in your mess. But not near a stream or the garden. Super important." She knocked Malia in the arm with her fist for emphasis.

Malia scrunched her face as she envisioned the landmines strewn throughout the forest. As far as she was concerned, the hike to the out-house was worth it. And, she thought, looking at the cover of the paper-back, it wasn't like she couldn't fit it into her schedule. *The Teachings of Don Juan*. Was that what she came here for? To sit around reading hippie books from the sixties? She knew better than to expect days of nonstop action—this was no adventure tour—but there had to be more than yoga and smoking weed.

"So, what's there to do around here?" Malia asked, wondering why her mother never mentioned being bored.

"Plenty of stuff."

"Like what? I get firewood, pick fruit, and fetch water," Malia said, counting each chore on her fingers. "Sometimes I look for those sunset shells everyone talks about."

"Sunrise. They're sunrise shells."

Malia rolled her eyes. "Fine. Sunrise shells. Or I go shower under the waterfall on the beach—"

"Don't do that. Goats piss in the stream above those falls."

"Great. Now I don't even have a place to bathe."

"There's Big Pool."

Malia held her palms up and arched her eyebrows, hoping Skye would realize she'd never shown her where it was.

"You've never been?"

"Nobody showed me."

"You know, for a runaway, you sure aren't very adventurous." Skye grabbed the paperback from Malia's hand and flung it onto the hammock. "C'mon."

Skye took a shortcut to the main trail and quickened her stride. Malia winced as she struggled to keep pace, wondering if the ache in her muscles would ever fade. She had to believe she was getting stronger—the daily hikes to and from the beach were the most walking she'd done in years—but her calves and hamstrings howled with every step as Skye bounded over rocks and roots, chewing up the distance with a graceful power that Malia couldn't help admiring.

Not far beyond the remnants of the garden fence she'd raided, Malia heard the unmistakable roar of rushing water. Skye turned from the trail, pushed through overhanging limbs, and waved Malia through. Judging by the proximity of the cliffs, the valley rear couldn't be far.

Skye led the way down a rocky embankment, where rainbows flickered in the stream's chilly mist. Malia held her arms out for balance, trying to ignore the view. Finally, they were there. Kalalau Stream cascaded in step-like fashion from their left, pouring into a boulder-lined pool shaded by guava trees. She gasped as her soreness vanished, taking her earlier annoyance with it. Malia smiled as a pair of yellow butterflies cavorted across the swimming hole of her dreams.

"Ta-da! Welcome to Big Pool," Skye said, easing herself into the water. "Tiki says the ancient Hawaiians used to get their water here and only bathed near the river mouth, but ..." She shrugged in acknowledgment that they weren't keeping with tradition. "No peeing, okay?"

Malia kicked aside her slippers and eased herself into the water, immediately sliding under. It wasn't only chilly, but deeper than expected. She hollered in surprise upon surfacing, recalling her plunge from Kimo's boat.

"Another wet swimsuit?" Skye shook her head, then added with a wink, "Darren's gonna be disappointed you didn't strip down."

"Gross," Malia said, splashing Skye. Then she asked, "Do the guys swim here too?"

"Of course. Everyone does."

Malia's voice hitched as she spoke. "Naked?"

Skye appeared as though she couldn't understand the question. "Well, sure. Why not?"

Her reply left Malia feeling cowed, naive. But since Skye brought it up, Malia decided to finally broach the topic of her nudity. "Can I ask you something?"

"Sure."

"No laughing, okay?" Malia pleaded with her eyes, hoping Skye would take her serious.

Skye made the sign of the cross, then winked. "Promise."

"Why naked?"

"Why not?"

Malia took a deep breath and sought a different angle of approach. "I get the thing about wet swimsuits, but what about a sarong? We're in a forest. It's dirty. There's bugs. I mean, don't you, ya'know, feel *weird*?"

Skye bobbed her head back and forth, conceding it wasn't always smooth sailing. "How do I put this? It's … well … liberating. Yeah. That's really all it is. Back home, we all wear these uniforms. To work, to restaurants, to go shopping. Dressing as we're expected. So once a year, I come here. Where I don't have to do any of that other stuff. Where I can just be me. Do whatever. Wear whatever."

"Or nothing at all," Malia added.

"Exactly."

"But you were the only girl when I got here. Don't you ever worry being naked around the guys all the time?"

"About …?"

Malia couldn't tell if Skye was being purposefully aloof or really that blind to what Malia was getting at. "About them getting the wrong idea." She lowered her voice. "Out here, alone. What if they got aggressive?"

Skye exhaled in an exaggerated aha manner and swam closer. When she spoke, it was with a seriousness Malia hadn't known her capable of. "Here's the thing about guys," she began, speaking as though they were back in the real world. "When I first showed up wearing my skirts and bikinis like you do, they were constantly checking me out. Making faces. Hitting on me. It was annoying. Then this gal, Lola, showed up. Probably in her forties, platinum hair down her back, lots of tattoos. You know the type. Always naked. I can't even remember her wrapping up at night. But the guys left her alone."

"Was she pretty?"

"Oh, that don't matter out here. Not to them. Some would screw anything that didn't put up a fight."

Malia's eyes bulged.

Skye touched her arm. "Relax."

"It's kinda hard when you say stuff like that." Malia stared at the water, not feeling any safer.

"You're missing the point. Once you remove the mystery, guys lose interest. They used to stare whenever I was bathing or doing yoga. But that stopped as soon as I went nude."

Malia twisted her face in disbelief. "I doubt that. I mean, look at you; you're beautiful."

"Thanks. But how sexy do I look hauling firewood? Or yanking taro?" Skye planted her hands on the rocks behind her and sprung from the water. Her thighs slapped against the boulders as the splash turned the river-polished lava rock from gray to black. "Look," Skye said, gesturing at herself. "Really look at me."

Malia raised her eyebrows.

"Not like that." Skye rolled her eyes.

Until that moment, Malia had avoided staring. If she was honest, Skye's constant nudity made her uncomfortable. But it didn't take long to see past her pert breasts and tattoos and notice the scratches and the bug bites, the dirt and bruises. Skye was lithe and beautiful from afar, but up close, as Malia now saw, her nudity was more *National Geographic* than *Playboy*.

"And the guys leave you alone?"

Skye slipped back into the water and glided across the pool on her back. Then with her arms outstretched and body floating, she said, "Nudity doesn't have to be sexual."

"So you think I should go naked?"

"That's up to you. Just be careful if there's booze around. If someone's getting drunk, I go to my tent. Trust me on that." Skye ducked underwater and swam to where the stream disappeared into grass and boulders. "But since you asked," she said, calling back over her shoulder, "your swimsuit does smell a bit funky."

"Gee, thanks."

"Told you nothing dries out here."

Malia stretched a strap to her face and crinkled her nose. Skye was right. The suit stank like a damp basement.

She'd first heard of skinny-dipping at a sleepover when she was younger, but that wasn't something good girls did—or so she believed at the time. But what if Skye was right? Ever since Malia arrived in Kalalau, she'd felt the guys staring, undressing her in their minds, especially Darren and the strays who wandered in for dinner. Inoke too, sometimes. But Tiki, the one guy she wouldn't mind checking her out, seemed a perfect gentleman.

One step at a time, she told herself. *It's just the two of us swimming.*

After floating for several minutes, Malia swam to the rocks. Facing the bank, she slipped the bikini straps from her shoulders. She took a deep breath, reached behind her, and gripped the clasp.

"Hey, ladies. Mind some company?"

Malia spun toward the voice in time to see Darren untying his drawstring. She froze in place, thankful he hadn't arrived any later. He tugged his shorts down with the ease of someone taking off their shoes, then let loose with a ridiculous yell as he cannonballed into the water.

He surfaced seconds later but stuck close to where he disrobed, appearing to enjoy his own private bath. "See?" Skye said. Malia paddled closer, wanting Skye to elaborate. "He thinks you're naked," she said, gesturing at Malia's bare shoulders. Malia had forgotten her straps were dangling underwater alongside her arms. To his credit, Darren seemed to intentionally avoid looking their way. Either that or he found a particular tree worth scrutinizing.

Malia slowly uncrossed her arms beneath the water.

Skye shoved off again, this time angling toward Darren as if to punctuate her point. "You'll get there. It just takes time. Right, Darren?"

"Huh?" he asked, oblivious.

Skye continued across the pool, then surfaced and whipped her hair back over her head, sending a spray of water in an elegant arc. She leaned against the bank and hooked her outstretched arms around the rocks, allowing her entire body to float on the surface, her breasts, toes, and face glistening in the sun, as relaxed as a house cat on a windowsill. Malia struggled to imagine herself ever feeling that free, that uninhibited, especially around strangers. The girl who'd happily donned the polyester uniform to her fancy, private Christian school for a decade? Impossible.

As for it taking time, Malia could barely see herself lasting another day. No part of her enjoyed spending day after day harvesting food, hauling firewood, and squatting over cat holes. Not to mention the bugs, sunburn, and inevitable rain.

"Isn't it tough living like this?" she asked.

"Cold feet already?"

"No, I just—"

"I'm kidding," Skye assured her. "The fact you're asking means you'll probably do well. Most people come out here dreaming of living off the land, all wild and free, and end up scurrying back to town within a week."

"They ain't got a clue how hard it is," Darren added, now paying attention.

"But you'll need to get better at entertaining yourself," Skye said, her tone bearing the echoes of summers long past when Malia's mother routinely offered identical counsel.

Chagrined, Malia touched her neck, subconsciously feeling for the beaded result of the craft days her mother once organized. The necklace had been lost to time, but time was what Malia had in abundance.

"And you can't be stupid. Nobody's gonna save you if you get hurt. People come for the freedom, but there ain't no help around the corner if you get into trouble."

"She's right," Darren said, mirroring Skye's laid-back posture across the pool. "People die out here. They drown, they fall. There's no room for mistakes."

Malia didn't know what to say. Part of her was thrilled to be rid of her father's curfews, to experience this place her mom raved about, but the risks never entered her mind. Now, she couldn't help thinking of that old movie cliche. The one about nobody hearing you scream.

"Don't get us wrong. The real world is harder. The pressure to earn money, to be popular, to look good." Skye shook her head with dismay. "Here, it's live and let live."

"Won't catch me sitting in a cubicle again. I did my time. I'm done," Darren said before disappearing underwater.

Malia stared up at the emerald cliffs towering above, encircling them as the current flowed around her. She shivered, not from the chilly water or the light breeze that rattled the palms, but from thoughts of her mom. And how she yearned to know if it was the bustle of Honolulu that made her miss this place, or if the trials of Kalalau had driven her to the comforts of being a housewife.

Kalalau Beach was quietest in the late morning, thanks to a high turnover and inbound hikers seldom arriving before mid-afternoon. But to Malia's surprise, the beach wasn't empty. From atop a small bluff she spotted a man sitting barefoot and shirtless in the sand, wearing a wide-brim safari hat, watching the waves. A smile bloomed upon her face as she realized who it was with a dollop of nervousness.

She'd hardly seen Tiki outside camp, and seldom without Inoke. But there he was, seemingly lost in thought, alone on the beach. Right where she normally practiced her yoga.

Malia considered letting him be, leaving him to his solitude, but quickly dismissed the thought. Did it have to be a coincidence? Maybe he was waiting for her. Tired of stealing glances across the campfire flames, she wasn't about to pass on a chance to get to know him, alone. Warming at the possibility, Malia slid-stepped down the sandy slope and went to him. She exaggerated the swing of her hips, twisting her foot in the sand with each step, dialing up her confidence. A little strut went a long way toward settling her butterflies. And judging by the way he straightened as he took her in, it had an effect on him as well.

"Want some company?"

"Sure." He moved his bag and patted the sand.

Malia tried her best to not flop awkwardly on the ground, and nearly managed. She left a polite gap between them and his eyes met the nearness of her body with approval.

"Nice day."

"Gorgeous day," she said simultaneously, then snorted. *The weather, Malia? Really?* She recovered quickly. "Don't normally see you outside camp. Not hanging out with Inoke today?" Malia arched her eyebrows.

"Nah. I was supposed to go into town with him, but he"—Tiki curled his fingers into air quotes—"had some things to take care of."

"You seem disappointed," Malia said, hating how the hat plunged his face into shadow.

"Not really." He was bad at fibbing.

"He go by boat?"

"Yeah, his buddy picked him up."

Malia nodded, remembering Skye's mention of groceries. Essentials. "Did you need supplies or—"

"So, how are you getting along?" he asked, changing the subject. "Sick of the place yet?"

Malia shot him a surprised look. "Am I supposed to be?"

He shrugged. "You tell me."

"You think I'm not tough enough?" Malia asked, giving him a playful nudge in the shoulder.

"I didn't say that." The corner of his mouth curled into a smirk as his gaze drifted over her bikini top, across her tanned belly, to the knot in her wrap, causing her stomach to backflip. "But you gotta admit, it's not for everyone."

Malia said nothing, unsure if he was implying she looked too delicate for the jungle or if he was referencing his own discomfort.

"It's just … reality doesn't always live up to our expectations." He pushed his hat further back on his head and turned. The sun painted his face in a golden warmth.

"Well, there is that."

"Camp's kind of a dump, isn't it?"

"It's not so bad," Malia said, wanting to not sound prissy. "Skye's tent doesn't leak, so at least I have that going for me." She punctuated the comment with a sarcastic laugh, not wanting to sound ungrateful.

"So, about that … Did you really show up without a tent?"

Malia crisscrossed her legs, tucking her feet beneath her and stretching the sarong across her thighs like a trampoline. "I hear guys like a girl who's spontaneous." She tilted her head, exposing her neck, awaiting his reaction. She'd never flirted so openly before but found herself thrilled by her unexpected sauciness. Like the first time she wore lingerie: emboldened despite the exposure.

"I'm serious," he said, but the spark in his eyes suggested he welcomed her daring.

"Honestly, I don't know what I was thinking. I just knew I had to see this place before …" She let the explanation go unfinished, unsure how much to divulge, wary of coming across as too sentimental.

"What's the hurry? Besides the obvious threats of overtourism, rising sea levels, and billionaires buying up the island."

"You always this cheerful?" Malia scooped sand as she considered how much to tell him.

She wasn't used to anyone in camp being so inquisitive. And most guys she knew only wanted to talk about themselves. The sand funneled through her fist, covering the hibiscus pattern of her sarong in a thin layer. She dragged a finger, doodling spirals in the grit as she opened up about how she couldn't wait to go to college, how lonely she'd been since her mother died, and her overbearing father. With admitted naivety, she confessed to having been so eager to get away, so caught up in her mother's rose-tinted memories, that she'd convinced herself she'd find a community of dozens with all the food and shelter she could ever need.

Tiki listened quietly and nodded when appropriate, then after a while, began to grin.

Malia swept the sand from her sarong and unfolded her legs. She turned to him. "What?"

"You had the look of someone deciding whether or not to share a secret."

Malia straightened, chilled by his prescience. "You noticed that?"

Tiki raised his palms and smiled. "It was kinda obvious."

"Geez. Remind me not to play poker with you." She shook her head. "Well, as a matter of fact ..." She looked away and took a deep breath. "I can't believe I'm doing this—"

"Ooh. Do continue." He rubbed his hands together mischievously.

"I've never told anyone," Malia said, sweeping her hair behind her ear.

"I bet I can guess. You're into guys with hairy feet. Is that it? The furrier the better—"

"What? No!"

"It's okay. I won't judge."

"No way. That's nasty." Malia leaned her head back, laughing at the sky.

"Phew. That's good to hear. I tried growing out my back hair once. Ya know, to get a good gorilla coat going. You wouldn't believe how hard that is." Tiki built upon his ridiculous story with tales of wearing peanut butter to bed and soaking his T-shirts in conditioner. "But you were saying ..."

Malia waved him off, laughing to the point of tears. "No. I can't," she managed, trying to catch her breath.

"Too late. No getting out of it." He licked his lips as he faced her. So close, mere inches away, she could nearly taste the salt on his tongue. "Go on." He gazed at her in a way so natural, so accidentally seductive, it melted the giggles away, and took her resistance along with it. He stretched his legs alongside hers. Darker than hers, unsurprising given what she was about to tell him.

She took a calming breath, forcing a straight face, then said, "My mom got pregnant with me when she was here."

Tiki looked as if he had a million questions, but said only, "Wow, a veritable daughter of Kalalau." He stared out to sea, thoughtfully at first, then a wry grin soon curled his lips.

"What?" Malia asked, unsure she wanted to know after the back hair shenanigans.

"I get it now. It makes perfect sense. You came out here cause you want a baby. Like mother, like daughter, right?"

"No way!" Malia laughed.

"Well, you've got plenty of choices. I'm sure Darren would be happy to accommodate you—"

"Ew, gross." She shoved him playfully, this time allowing her fingers to linger briefly on his shoulder as he teetered in the sand. Their eyes locked as he rebounded toward her. She could tell he enjoyed the attention. But whether he was attracted to her and just taking it slow, she wasn't certain. Still, those eyes. That smile. She bit her lower lip as her nerves did cartwheels in her belly.

Malia leaned back on her elbows, stretching out and showing off. Her sarong inched lower on her hips, emphasizing the expanse of her stomach. From her reclined position, she studied Tiki's muscular back, the ropes of his shoulders and neck, the bronzed skin funneling to his waist. Soon, he leaned back alongside her, elbow to elbow, hip to hip. His body brushed against hers. She thought back to his earlier comment and smiled. No, she definitely didn't want a baby. But she wouldn't kick Tiki out of bed if she were drenched in gasoline and he was on fire.

Malia stole sly glances out the corner of her eye as a shadow crept across the beach, stealing their sun. Big, puffy clouds hung scattered against the royal-blue sky. She arched her neck and looked up. "I hear cloud-spotting's pretty popular around here."

"Prime time entertainment in these parts." Tiki looked about the sky and shifted closer.

"A pineapple," Malia said, pointing to an oval-shaped cloud with a pointy top. She used her right hand to point, intentionally leaving her left splayed between them, craving the brush of his fingers against hers, the tickle of his arm hair against her skin.

"And that one?" Tiki pointed into the wind.

"An anchor."

"More like a sailboat to me."

Malia squinted in concentration, trying to imagine what he described. The shape transformed, shifting into something abstract. "Yeah, now I see it. Definitely a sailboat." She pointed out a nearby jumble of clouds resembling a child's drawing and declared it a car.

"Pretty slow for a car. My sailboat's gonna catch it."

Malia watched as the layered winds stretched, squeezed, and altered the vapor high above, but it was the rising energy between her and Tiki that most interested her.

"Boat coming through. Watch out." His voice sparkled as bright as the silver trim above. Tiki's boat sailed across the sky, closing in on her cloud car. Malia didn't blame the car for taking it slow. She too wanted to linger.

He made the sound of squealing tires. "Crash! Boat captain must have been drunk."

Malia stiffened, struck numb by his words.

He faced her, his smile melting into confusion. "What is it?"

She wanted to tell him it was nothing, to laugh and reignite the sparks firing between them. To say she was fine, that he reminded her of something. No big deal. Really. Malia wanted to assure him there was no need to worry. But her mouth wouldn't move. The magic rug had been pulled out when she was flying highest. She plummeted through the stratosphere; a vacuum of wind stealing her ability to speak. She heard the words *my mom* as if they'd yawned from a distant cave.

Understanding dawned on his face. "Oh. Oh no. I'm so sorry. I didn't mean …"

Malia's body trembled as her thoughts poured forth in unintelligible gurgles.

"Malia, I'm so sorry. I didn't know."

His remorse only made it worse. She was having her best time in days, laughing so much it hurt, and wanted it to continue. Wanted *him*. But not like this. Not now.

Her heart wasn't ready to let go.

CHAPTER 8
LEVELING UP

Jordan slapped the spinning business card and checked the last name for the fortieth time. "Holly McAdams."

"And whom may I say is calling?"

He swung his bare feet from the desk, smirking as he imagined Holly's reaction to such inelegant behavior. "Jordan Higgins from HyperTap Studios." It came out rushed, almost breathless.

Jordan wasn't usually so anxious, especially not after the first few dates, but Holly had an air about her that he found every bit as intoxicating as he did intimidating—and inconvenient. In their short time together, he'd come to see Holly as someone forever observing herself. As though her life was a live performance, and she alone had the power to demand a curtain call. That in and of itself wasn't bad—high standards should be applauded—but she expected the same caliber of anyone she allowed on stage. That's how he described her to a friend who asked about the pile of Nordstrom bags in his apartment. Even then, Jordan knew it wasn't a fair description. He initially thought the designer clothing, her mannerisms, and even her walk seemed coached, refined to a gleam before a full-length mirror. But the more he got to know her, the more he realized there was nothing about Holly that was an act. Cultivated and hard-fought, perhaps, but it wasn't an affectation.

He supposed it's what landed Holly in charge of the North American sales region for Seattle's largest pharma company. And judging by her condo, she did quite well for herself. She invited him up to her place two weeks earlier, after a long night of partying on New Year's Eve. A memory he'd taken to the shower every morning since.

"So, we've reached the calling-each-other-at-work stage of the relationship?"

He chuckled nervously. "Yeah, I tried your cell an hour ago, but—"

"I've been in meetings all day. But you should be flattered. I don't usually chat with guys I'm seeing while at work."

Guys. Plural. So many she needed rules. Like a game, he thought, glancing at the screen on his monitor. He considered begging off the phone. He'd text her later, he'd say. But no, he had news he wanted to share with someone other than his mom. *I'm in my mid-thirties, for chrissake!*

"Duly noted," he said, matching her flirty-yet-stern tone. "I've got news, if you're not too busy."

The tapping of manicured nails on a keyboard was her only response. Speaker phone. Jordan feigned interest in an email on a second monitor, hoping to wait her out, but he lost patience. "They promoted me to Lead Game Designer." The typing stopped. "I'll be reporting directly to the studio head."

"Jordan, that's fantastic. Hang on a second." He heard a door close. "Okay, I can spare five. Tell me everything."

"Well, the role won't be much different from what I did on *Cops & Rockets*, but now it's official. We've got DLC to ship each of the next two quarters, then I'll lead a pre-production team—"

"DLC? Pre-production? You're burying the lede, not to mention forgetting I don't play games. Tell me about the promotion."

I thought I was. He rubbed his brow. "It stands for downloadable content."

"What does?"

"DLC. They're like expansion packs."

"Great, I'll be sure to get some. What about your salary bump? Did you have to negotiate? I hope you didn't jump at the first offer." Her normally raspy voice vibrated with an excitement he hadn't heard before. "HyperTap's private, right? You should hold out for an ownership stake. Oh, please tell me you're at least in the bonus pool."

Jordan exhaled long and slow. "We'll talk compensation next week, but that's beside the point. This is the opportunity I've been dreaming of. I'll finally get to pitch my game!" As he spoke, he thumbed a design document he wrote back in college. Eighty pages, crinkled in the corners. It survived five studio changes and a trip across the country, gaining a questionable reddish-brown smear in the process, but otherwise remained intact with the name DRIFTWOOD stamped atop the cover page.

"I know what we should do," Holly broke in. "Let's celebrate. It's not every day my boyfriend becomes Lead Game Designer."

Boyfriend? Jordan was caught mouthing the word to himself as a coworker poked his head in to congratulate him. The promotion suddenly seemed secondary. He blushed and shooed the guy away as he tried on the new status, imagining himself introducing Holly as his girlfriend.

"He*llooo.*"

"Oh, sorry. Someone had a question. A celebration. Great idea. There's a Buffalo Wild Wings near your office, right? That works. Or, if you're up for something different, there's this GameWorks place nearby. Their burgers aren't bad, and they have unlimited games on Thursdays."

"Oh, that's cute. You gonna pick me up on your bicycle after you deliver your papers?"

The air escaped him like from a popped balloon. He squeezed his eyes shut and chomped his tongue for a three count. "Point taken. Sorry, I thought it'd be fun—"

"Let's do Shiro's. Say, five thirty. Why don't you get there early and get us seats at the sushi bar. Their *omakase* is to die for."

"Umm, sure. I can do that." He had no idea what *oma*-whatever-she-called-it was.

"Perfect. And I'll finally get to see you in that Burberry shirt we picked out."

Jordan sighed. He wanted to say he was fine the way he was, but refrained upon noticing the Spider-Man tee and Birkenstocks. He'd have to cut his afternoon staff meeting short to be on time. She'd come straight from work, no doubt dressed in heels, designer skirt, and low-cut blouse. He wanted to look like he belonged with her, that she wasn't slumming, but damn if it wasn't exhausting. Expensive too, he realized upon bringing up the restaurant's website. *What am I doing with her?*

"As you wish," he said, his tone deflated, expecting the movie reference would sail past her.

"Ha ha," she said playfully. "Perhaps you'd like me to call you *farm boy* from now on."

Jordan fist-pumped the air, barely constraining the urge to whoop.

"Okay, I better go. Be sure to get there early. They don't accept reservations for the sushi counter."

"I will," he said, beaming into the phone, abated by Holly's eagerness to honor his accomplishment.

"And Jordan, one more thing."

"Yeah?"

"The money is always the point."

CHAPTER 9
ALL SHE NEEDED WAS A PUSH

Her first few days in Kalalau passed with the monotony of a drum circle, an unrelenting beat of routine from sunup to sundown. Though the initial trip to Big Pool left her with plenty to chew on, the novelty of living off the land held little appeal. She'd grown bored with chores, the aimless wandering, the tedium of boiling water and foraging fruit. An inescapable film of sweat clung to her like a second skin. Stowaway grains of sand, ferried in between her toes, coated her tent and huddled like vagrants in abrasive drifts within her sleeping bag. If not for the horror stories she'd heard concerning the trail back to civilization, she would have hiked out days ago.

Then, as if a stone wedged within the narrow of an hourglass suddenly dislodged, the ensuing week tumbled away in high-speed delight, greased by a growing sense of belonging amongst the camp's disparate outcasts, of her expanded comfort within the valley.

Malia carved her tenth notch in the log outside her tent that morning, dreading the choice coming due. Her self-prescribed two-week deadline was fast approaching, and she felt powerless to halt the inevitable. Or was she?

After breakfast, she skipped her yoga routine to seek some elderly advice. She followed a game trail through a thicket of bamboo and across Kalalau Stream to a clearing she'd stumbled upon while out exploring two days earlier. A massive, gnarled tree—a koa, she believed—stood alone with bark like scaled armor and leaves the size of umbrellas. Malia affectionately named it *Tūtū*, the grandfather tree.

Tūtū stood far taller and broader than any tree she'd seen so far on Kauaʻi. A swing hung from its outstretched limb, a toy for the *keiki* who came to visit. Malia sat atop the weathered plank, straddling the single rope that ended in a knot beneath a hole drilled through the seat. She swayed in silent oblong orbits. A pendulum propelled only by her swirling emotions.

"What should I do?"

The tree didn't answer but the birds did, and in great choruses of gossip and laughter. A scarlet honeycreeper perched in a nearby shrub sang a tune that sent a shiver rippling across Malia's skin, its piercing staccato cadence a living replica of her mother's infectious giggle. A reminder of who wouldn't be awaiting her return home. Malia's biggest reason for coming to Kalalau, she now realized, was also her best argument for staying. At home, there was only her father; and she couldn't see him without thinking of *her*.

Malia kicked her feet lazily to get the swing moving and tightened her grip on the rope. Her fingers, so long and slender, looked different but simultaneously familiar. She hadn't noticed it before, so distracted was she with her teenage life, but they'd aged. The knuckles had grown more pronounced, wrinkled. Like her mother's, she thought. The observation reminded Malia of the days spent watching from the backseat of the family car, her mother's hands curled around the steering wheel, leading her "Mini Me" through the daily errands.

Growing up, Malia loved having her mom home every day, unlike so many of her friends whose parents were divorced or both worked. But, in hindsight, she couldn't help wondering if that's what her mother really wanted. Malia would sometimes catch her staring at the ceiling, lost in thought with a knife buried halfway through a papaya. Malia would clear her throat and tease, "Earth to space cadet. Come in space cadet." Now, Malia understood where those daydreams may have taken her. Here, to Kalalau Valley.

She wasn't certain, but Malia felt like she was finally beginning to see why her mother cherished this place. It wasn't just the natural beauty, or the people, or even the pace. It was the freedom. Freedom from worry, from stress.

Grades, money, social media, and popularity—none of it mattered in the jungle. And Malia never would have expected it, but she loved not getting a thousand texts a day from Jenna. Or feeling compelled to constantly check her mentions. Her father once said how glad he was to not grow up with a smartphone. Malia couldn't understand at the time, considering it indispensable. But now she got it. Now she saw it for the superficial distraction it really was.

She squeezed her eyes closed, torn between the trouble staying would cause and her reluctance to surrender what she'd only just begun to appreciate. "I feel like I just got here," she lamented.

"So stay." The response was as unexpected as the accompanying shove that sent Malia spinning. She kicked her legs and yelped as she leaned back, her lengthy hair glancing the ground as she swung past Skye like an off-balanced gyroscope.

The effort to slow down left her panting. "You know ... I ... came here to think," she said, regaining her balance. "Not to be made dizzy by some naked hippie."

Skye crinkled her nose. "I'm not a hippie." Then, channeling an elegant air, she batted her lashes and added, "I'm practical." Malia rolled her eyes as Skye chuckled at her own humor. "What's up? Missed you on the beach this morning."

Malia dragged the ground to stop. "I told my friend I'd only be gone two weeks. But ... I'm just starting to get it. It's like being here finally makes sense, you know?"

"Like I said. Stay."

"It's not that easy."

"Sure it is."

Malia snorted. "You've never met my father. It'll be a miracle if he doesn't send the Coast Guard looking for me if I'm not home when Jenna said I'd be."

Skye picked a weed from the ground and peeled slivers from the stem. "You're nineteen. And headed to college, right?"

"Uh-huh."

"Screw him."

"You're not helping." Malia kicked sideways. The rope coiled as she spun before slowing to a taut stop. She stomped her feet, refusing to release the tension, wondering if Charles really did miss her. Even a little. After all, he didn't ask for their arrangement any more than Malia did.

I was just the baggage he offered to help carry.

At first, but they'd come to love one another. Malia never thought of him as a stepdad.

He adopted me.

It was a long time ago. Things were different now. People change.

"All I'm saying is you're in a position to decide. You said you got into Mānoa but don't want to go. You got a scholarship to Berkeley, but your dad will start a war if you get on the plane. So that leaves two options: You go home to your part-time job and overbearing father, where you're miserable—"

"*Orrr?*"

"You stay in paradise." Skye arched her eyebrows, emphasizing the obviousness of the choice. "Anyway, it's only mid-July. What are you going to do for the next month at home besides wish you were here instead?"

"To be honest, I'm not even sure how to get home. I'll probably have to hitchhike." She added the last bit under her breath, knowing the hike out along the Kalalau Trail would land her on the opposite end of the island from where Kimo moored his boat—if he'd even be there.

Skye studied Malia with an invasive intensity, as though dredging her thoughts for an issue buried deeper.

Malia's gaze flitted back to the shrubbery, but the honeycreeper was nowhere to be seen. It was just her and Skye, and Malia couldn't help wondering if there wasn't a better ear to spill her emotions to. She took a deep breath. "My mother used to say it brought her peace just knowing Kalalau was out there, waiting for her. Someplace to go if she ever needed to restore her faith in the universe. Said her Kalalau family would always welcome her with open arms. I guess that's why I came. I felt, like, I don't know. That maybe I … needed a family." Sadness welled in her eyes. "But don't take this the wrong way—you've been great—but I needed to experience this place how my mom saw it, feel what she felt, and I keep waiting, but …" Malia lifted her feet, allowing the rope to unwind as her thoughts spiraled away.

Skye waited until Malia halted her spin to remind her that it had been twenty years since her mother was there. Kalalau changed. But not as much as she might think. "Why do you think I come back every year?"

Malia shrugged.

"For all the reasons you described." She raised a finger, delaying Malia's protest before it began. "Why not give it a few more days? Whatever you're looking for is here. I promise. But you can't wait for it come to you. You need to seek it out."

Malia leaned her forehead against the scratchy rope. Skye placed a hand on her shoulder, stroked her collarbone with a thumb. "Listen, I don't know the whole story about your mom. But you're still working through stuff. And maybe you're holding back. Like I said, I don't know. But one day you're gonna think back and either be glad you stayed and can tell your own daughter how wonderful it was, or you'll kick yourself for leaving too soon."

Malia closed her eyes as her head lolled to the side. Skye was right. They passed the moment in silence, then Malia sniffed back her emotions and faked a smile to lighten the mood. "You're just scared to lose me as a roommate."

"*Au contraire.* Someone's gotta watch over the idiots when I'm gone."

"Not funny," Malia said. She turned to punch her in the arm, but Skye had already turned to leave. She only made it a few steps before shouting over her shoulder, "Here comes one of them now."

Malia's eyes went wide as she sought to reconcile Skye's hint at leaving with the sight of Tiki's approach. She looked herself over and noticed the sarong was folded completely over her right leg to accommodate the rope. Her entire left side, save the bikini strings, was exposed to him. She shifted reflexively to cover herself, then thought better of it. Instead, she leaned away from the rope, arching her back, emphasizing her curves. She extended her legs high in the air and pointed her toes, hoping he'd take the hint and give her a push.

She hadn't caught Tiki alone since the day on the beach when everything was going so well—until the cloud crash. A literal hit and run. Around camp, at dinner or while doing chores, Tiki had acted as though nothing happened. She appreciated his discretion at first, thankful not to be teased by Darren or the others. But, as days passed without him asking if she was okay, Malia couldn't help wondering if she imagined the whole thing. If the heat rising between them was merely radiating from the sand; if the glimmer of attraction she thought she'd seen was only a product of him squinting in the sunlight.

Malia expected Tiki to turn and watch Skye go, to ogle her as she strutted past on her merry way, but he didn't. He barely acknowledged her. Not that Malia would have faulted him if he had. Skye had a look that could turn heads wherever she went. Dressed or not. But Tiki held course for Malia, a sight as suddenly pleasing as the feel of the rope clutched between her thighs.

"You found the swing." Tiki kept his voice conversational, but she sensed a discomfort in the way he paused beyond the tree's shade with his brow furrowing ever so briefly.

She wanted to ask if something was wrong, but knew better. Another unspoken rule of the valley: let people be with their thoughts.

"Didn't know it was so popular."

Tiki looked around as if unsure where to stand. His hand pressed a sling bag tight against his white tee. "I can come back."

"No. Not at all." Too eager, Malia knew. She offered a sheepish smile which seemed to burn away the fog clouding Tiki's easygoing demeanor. "What about you? You need privacy?"

Please say no.

Tiki bobbed his head to and fro, then shrugged. "Nah, it's okay. I mostly come for the sunshine. Only spot in the forest with a partial view of the sky." He looked upward as he spoke to where the morning's blue canvas was graying by the minute.

Malia nodded, then leaned back further still. She pumped leisurely to get the swing moving. She looked over her shoulder to him. "Mind giving me a push?"

He hesitated, only for a moment, but long enough for Malia's confidence to dip. Then he flashed a delighted smile and came closer.

Tiki stepped behind her as Malia swung backwards into him. She held her arms tight to her side, hands clutching the rope. Her breath hitched as he pressed along her shoulder blades, his fingers spread wide, sending a spark down her spine, a tingling reminder of how long she'd gone without contact. But he wasn't anything like the boys she dated in high school. Tiki was a man, possessing a strength and rawness that excited her. She closed her eyes, envisioning the dimpled impressions left by his touch, and swung higher with every push. And with every return, Tiki held his ground. He leaned back as she swung toward his chest, then his head, and higher still. His hands landed softly, lower on her body, with every cycle. His thumbs flicked over the string of her bikini, his palms splayed against her ribs. The touch was as scintillating as it was brief, and Malia leaned into it, craving to go higher, anxious to see how low his touch would descend, wanting to feel his hands on her hips, her . . .

"I haven't pushed anyone on a swing since my sister was a kid."

Malia kicked her legs askew and leaned into the rope to slow herself. *His sister?*

Her sudden movement sent her careening into a figure eight; she spun straight toward his outstretched hands, face-to-face. He leapt from her path to avoid being kicked. But as she swung by, she noticed a glint in his eyes, a spark of something serious. Attraction? Flirtation? Proof that in no way did he view her as a sibling?

Malia dragged her feet like an anchor, spinning slower and slower with every pass until Tiki snagged hold of the rope. She stepped from the swing, feeling dizzy, then met his eyes. "Thanks." Thoughts swirled as she locked her gaze on him. Thoughts of those hands on her again, pulling her close instead of propelling her away. The anticipation of his mouth against hers, the heavy warmth of his body atop hers. She licked her lips, feeling as she did on the beach, hoping he'd make the move, then recalled Skye's advice.

Don't wait for it to come to you. Seek it out.

A breeze fluttered her sarong as a raindrop splashed against her head. Above, billowing storm clouds had sunk the day into dusk. The birds, so cheerfully singing their approval only moments earlier, had gone silent. She heard it first, the drumroll of the rain bombarding the forest canopy. Then, within seconds, they were caught in a midday downpour.

Like mirrored images, they each raised their palms and looked to the treetops in wide-eyed surprise. Malia smiled as the rain flattened Tiki's bangs and splashed along his shoulders, soaking his shirt. Her chest heaved with excitement as she decided to follow Skye's instruction. She didn't come to Kalalau seeking a summer fling, but damn if she wasn't going to make it happen. Tiki smiled, unblinking, and didn't move. Knowing the rain would only add to the memory, Malia raised her hand, slowly, toward his waist, hoping he'd follow suit. She let it hover inches away as she channeled the courage to pull him toward her.

Her heart thumped within her chest as she lifted her head to his. Her eyes fell shut in anticipation. The bolt flashed an instant before its resulting thunder shook the ground, before the blinding light left her seeing spots, stealing the opportunity.

Tiki showed no sign of knowing that she'd nearly kissed him. He bore the intensity of a man needing to act, a primal urge to protect when she only wanted him to take—then take some more.

"We need to get back across the stream," Tiki yelled over the barrage. He tugged her elbow briefly, then let go as he led the way to the trail. Malia knew they had to get out of the clearing, away from the tallest tree in the forest, but stood frozen in place, cemented in the moment. "This way!" Tiki called from the clearing's edge as another thunderbolt splintered the sky.

Malia kicked off her slippers to avoid sliding in the mud and ran after him. His shoulder bag bounced with each step, as if weighted with a brick. But more interesting to Malia was how his shirt clung to him. Gone sheer in the rain, it revealed as much as it hid. The body she'd nearly pulled to hers seemed oh-so-much-sexier than Tiki's languid manner ever suggested—and she wanted to drag herself across every bit of it.

Tiki reached the stream first and waded into the swirling rapids, the water to his knees and rising. Despite living in Honolulu, Malia knew to be wary of flash floods. She hesitated on the bank, no stranger to the horror stories of hikers swept to their death.

"Grab my hand. I won't let anything happen!" He nodded with an intensity she found reassuring.

Malia brushed the rainwater from her face and took a halting step from the bank. A rock tumbled underfoot, but Tiki caught her wrist as she wobbled. She straightened and hiked up her sarong to keep it from snagging in the current. Not taking her eyes from his, she took another hesitant step into the rising water, encouraged partly by the strength of his grip, the confidence in his voice as he egged her on. But mainly it was the way he looked at her. Strength. Inspiration. A promise of more than just safe passage across the stream. She paused amidst the swirling waters, feeling her reservations and disappointments draining away, being swept out to sea on the current. For the first time since arriving, she felt wanted.

She'd gone to the swing feeling sorry for herself for having to return to her father and college and a life of what-ifs before fully uncovering the magic she sought. But Malia knew, rooted in place in that stream, that Skye had shown her the way. Her advice, murky at first, now shone as clear as a lighthouse in the void of night.

Malia resolved in that moment to stay, believing that Kalalau would reveal its wonders as long she was brave enough to take the first step.

CHAPTER 10
PACIFIC SILK

Malia turned on her side in an effort to block the blinding glare. It was no use. The sun perched too high, and the book's ivory pages proved as reflective as a mirror. Her head throbbed as sentence after sentence came and went without notice, her concentration ebbing like the tide. She tried shaking energy into herself, then lunged to the end of the paragraph she'd spent fifteen minutes rereading. She flipped to the next page with half-hearted intent only to discover it torn down the middle. The one after nowhere to be found. "Sorry, Katniss," she said, tossing the sun-warped copy of *Mockingjay* into the sand, "Peeta's gonna have to wait."

A day in the sand was supposed to be her reward.

For two weeks, Malia stayed true to her thunderstorm promise. She braved that first step, and hundreds of thousands more. Armed with a dog-eared guide to local plants and flowers she'd pilfered from Darren's library, Malia explored the valley from headwall to river mouth, bushwhacking along game trails and splashing up streams, getting a head start on her ecology studies as she tapped that wild Nāpali energy. She tended to Community Garden, rebuilt the fence she'd plundered, and bartered her way to a stockpile of dehydrated meals from hikers who'd overpacked—a feat that earned Inoke's respect, as evidenced by the care package she'd found one morning outside her tent: sunscreen, toothpaste, and four bags of *arare*, rice crackers. The jungle trails that so easily confounded her upon arrival had become as familiar as her cul-de-sac sidewalk. Yet still, something remained missing. Whereas her mother spoke of losing herself within the freedom of Kalalau, Malia felt simply lost.

She stared at the book beside her, wondering, wishing, unable to focus. The third book wasn't her favorite—the inability to rely on trusted companions too unsettling—but even if it had been, she doubted it could have held her attention.

Tiki.

Ever since their moment by the swing, his reluctance to leave Inoke's side had advanced from a mere irritant to a chronic condition. Malia's failure to get Tiki alone gnawed at her night and day. Even when he wasn't with Inoke, he insisted on going solo on his daily hikes. And everywhere Malia went, whether hauling wood, practicing yoga, or lying alone in her tent—especially in her tent—her thoughts drifted to that moment near the swing, to the caress that never came, the press of lips she'd yet to taste.

Worse was that she couldn't understand how Tiki and Inoke were friends. One a manicured, soft-spoken surfer type from New Zealand and the other a brooding drug dealer from the islands running an illegal grow operation on public land. She could see them tolerating one another. But friends? Other than being the only male Pacific Islanders in a corner of Kauaʻi crawling with tourists, it didn't compute.

Of course, she knew not everybody was who they claimed. Skye made that abundantly clear, ultimately copping to a life back in Chicago with a kid, a career in advertising, and an apartment overlooking the lake. Before leaving, she told Malia to think of Kalalau as a stage. "I come for a break from the grind. A character swap. Others, especially the ones running from something..." Skye sucked air through her teeth. "They're the ones you gotta watch out for."

Malia had been so preoccupied by her runaway thoughts that she hadn't noticed the hikers settling in around her. Normally, she'd be back up-valley, relaxing in the shade before the midday transition. Yesterday's campers had cleared out hours earlier and the new batch was busy staking out their turf. The fastest among them had already pitched their tents and spread out across the half-mile of sand.

Solos, couples, and small groups of friends drifted along the beach, snapping photos, swimming, and lounging about. Malia observed with blended curiosity and jealousy, proud but lonely in her independence. They'd come from all over the world to stride the beach in the same dream-addled trance, without a care. Or so it seemed to Malia.

An older couple entered her periphery. Leather skin with a sun-freckled patina, they reminded Malia of the retirees that choked the beaches at Waikiki. They laid their towels down not twenty yards away and smiled a hello. Then, without fuss, the woman slipped off her cover-up, the man his shorts, and together walked hand in hand to the water, naked from head to toe.

"Oh my God," Malia chirped, immediately averting her gaze from the bare bums. It only took a moment before curiosity got the better of her. She sat up, reaching for her book, and peered over the paperback like a spy, feigning discretion as she watched with a voyeur's fascina-

tion. The couple was hardly alone. To Malia's left, nearer the waterfall, two men propped a pair of collapsible chairs in the sand, angling
them just so at the sun. They doffed their trunks in unison with the
normalcy of a couple preparing for bed and sat to read.

Malia pulled the book close and tucked her knees to her chest, wondering if it was like this every afternoon. She had no reason to doubt
it, other than a reluctance to admit that Skye wasn't an outlier—and
that Malia wasn't as brave as she thought.

She remembered that day at Big Pool, when she'd almost gone skinny-
dipping for the first time but didn't. Why? Because Darren showed up?
A convenient excuse. She'd resisted going nude even while alone with
Skye. Malia had no clearer understanding of her apprehension then
than she had for her desire to try it now.

You can be whoever you want here. Skye's words.

What Malia wanted was to be as confident as her mother appeared
in the photo.

She dropped her head, then recoiled from the musty odor of her
bathing suit. It stank like a bath towel left to fester in a school locker.
When she stretched her legs, she felt the sting of sweat running along
her chafed bikini line.

"Should have listened to the hippie," Malia said with a snort.

She rolled onto her stomach and gave the book another try, but the
push-pull of her thoughts proved exhausting. By chapter's end, she
was covered in a slick of sweat and about to suffocate in the heat. She
marked her page with a stray strip of palm and sat up as the sounds of
cawing gulls and lazy conversation carried on the breeze.

The men had shifted from their chairs and now lay side by side on
a large blanket. Malia stared, initially to admire their physiques, but
her admiration quickly morphed into jealousy. They were probably
thousands of miles from home but completely at ease there, in that
moment, warming under the allover sunshine. She wanted to know

how that felt. *Needed* to. But they were older—and guys. It was easier for them, Malia thought.

Skye isn't a guy.

No, she wasn't. But that was Skye. Big city woman with a neon attitude and a back-the-fuck-up look.

Malia sighed, realizing she was nothing like Skye—and probably wouldn't ever be as tough as she liked to believe. She'd almost stood to leave when a nervous titter drew her attention. A girl, no more than a year or two older than Malia, gripped with a case of the giggles. Tall with the gangly limbs of a high jumper and long red curls, she bent into a squat and undid her bikini top. She covered her pale breasts with a single arm and scanned the beach with wide-eyed excitement.

This girl, who looked more stork than rebel, quickly yanked her bottoms off and sprinted to the water, no doubt hoping nobody would notice her if she ran. She hit the water with a slap and nearly tumbled backward in the surf. But she righted herself and dove through the coming wave. She surfaced in a fit of laughter and swept her arms upward, splashing the sky.

Malia watched her frolic for several envious minutes, perpetually shifting in her damp suit, trying in vain to ignore its mildew fragrance.

The redhead emerged from the water sporting an enormous grin. She jogged back to where she'd left her bikini with huge loping strides, laughing as her friends streamed from the woods, cheering and clapping their approval.

That sealed it. Malia locked her eyes on the horizon and wiggled her toes, reminding herself this was for fun. She took a deep breath, then bit her lip and tugged her bikini pants off.

Just play it cool. Nobody's even going to notice.

She reached behind her back and undid her top.

Malia fought the urge to cover herself, but the desire to swim proved too strong. Straining against every nervous fiber in her being, she stood.

Her knees barely bent as she walked, bracing for the slightest comment or laughter from anyone on the beach. But none came. It was as though she were invisible. Her skin, her sex, the body she'd been taught to shelter and conceal at all costs was fully on display and nobody noticed. That nobody seemed to care proved as shocking as the fact that she was actually doing it.

Thirty yards shrank to ten within a few exhilarating seconds. She willed her eyes straight ahead, held her breath for the cover of the water. She felt it on her toes. A wave swirled around her calves, her knees and thighs. She pushed further into the sea and dove. The electric silk of the Pacific glided over her skin, caressing her—all of her—in ways she never before felt. Every frothing bubble, every atom of sand suspended in the swish of the sea tickled her senses. No arms or legs. No head or hands or breasts concealed by cloth and straps and clasps. Only her, Malia as a whole, from head to toe. All woman.

New. Complete.

I never would have done this a month ago!

She squealed as she surfaced, delighting in the sensation, feeling more alive than ever. This, she realized, was the freedom her mother pined for. The freedom to be herself, to break loose and holler and cavort. To not be the type of person who sat on their hands because a dean asked them to.

Malia dove beneath the lolling summer swell without concern. She surfaced and swam the backstroke, exposed to the sun, the clouds, and God. She swam and danced until she couldn't manage another stroke. She'd drifted on the current a bit, but not far. She strode through the whitewater until she was back in line with her towel and book. Malia emerged onto the bare, damp sand—and froze.

Now what?

Unlike earlier, her back was to the ocean. Her nudity, her *exposure*, hit her like a thunderbolt. She crossed her wrists below her waist, shying as her stomach flipped. Malia willed herself to look up, to stare down any would-be gawkers. But nobody peered over the lip of their books, their travel mugs. Nobody lowered their sunglasses to peep.

Malia's heart swelled as she realized she'd cracked the Kalalau code, that *this* was the magical something she was missing. Then she saw it. Her puddled towel, laying discarded in the sand. Alone. As avoided as a carcass on the side of the road. Malia had no welcoming party. No friends waiting to tease or cheer her on. No one to snap a selfie with and provide her with a bedside keepsake of her own.

Photos.

Thoughts of her mother's picture kicked aside any lingering joy from the swim. Her mother and friends jubilant on the beach, taken mere steps from where Malia stood. *My Kalalau family,* she'd called them.

Must have been nice.

Malia arrived in camp that afternoon, towel draped around her shoulders, swimsuit wadded in hand. She marched past the firepit and, without breaking stride, dropped the dingy bikini into the flames, ignoring Inoke's exasperated eye roll and Darren's slack-jawed wonderment. Only one reaction mattered. Tiki slumped noticeably in disapproval. The color drained from his face, but he didn't look away. Nor could he conceal the undeniable glint of arousal in his eyes.

It was the look she needed, the green light to forge ahead.

Without bothering to dress, she emptied her tent and dragged it to a small rise nearby. Whatever reason Skye had for pitching it near Inoke's no longer mattered. For weeks, Malia had endured the midnight intrusion of a tree root beneath her hip, the seep of puddling rainwater. No more.

She lugged her bedding over to the tent's new position deeper into the woods and shook her sleeping bag free of sand. She inflated the air mattress extra firm, riding a wave of adrenaline, and nearly huffed and puffed herself dizzy inside the sweltering tent. She unzipped the sleeping bag into a square and tucked it under the corners. She fetched her books, her duffel, and the photos and stray pieces of camping equipment she'd come to possess. Each item dusted and placed with care. Despite the tent's earthy aroma, the task reminded her of the deep cleanings she and her mother performed on her bedroom before every new school year. Only it wasn't good grades Malia currently sought.

After admiring her tidy abode, she exited the tent and found Tiki standing nearby. "You left these on the line," he said, extending a pile of neatly folded clothes. Her sweatshirt and sarongs. He blushed, then added, "Though, not sure you'll need them."

"Thanks. Um, that's sweet." Malia took the clothes, feeling a flush of warmth in her face.

"So. Is this"—he gestured at the full sweep of her body—"your new look?" Malia could feel his discomfort.

"Maybe." She shrugged. "Unless it gets chilly."

"Or too buggy." Tiki released a short burst of nervous laughter.

"They never bothered Skye."

His smile faded. His voice sincere. "You're not Skye."

"Is that bad?"

Malia mustered every ounce of nonchalance she had in delivering the velvety retort despite growing acutely aware she was standing naked, in broad daylight, before a guy she'd yet to even kiss. She hugged the bundle of clothes to her, less so for modesty than to muffle her thumping heart. Her toes carved an anxious trench in the dirt as she wondered what he meant. Was she not as pretty? Too young? Too *nice*.

He grimaced in anguish, like someone bracing for an injection, but didn't answer. Tiki ran a hand through his hair, causing his bicep to jump. "Just be careful, okay?" He turned sideways, making to leave, then said, "I gotta cook dinner, but I can help you move the tarp tomorrow."

"Oh, okay." She'd forgotten about the tarp. Didn't care about the tarp. And was certainly in no mood for being careful. "Want to collect *liliko'i* with me?"

He looked confused.

"Tomorrow. Down along the campground trail. There's a bunch I can't reach." She spoke too fast, trying to keep him from leaving.

He bit his lip in consideration, then nodded with less enthusiasm than Malia would have preferred. "Sure. I can help for a bit."

"Great," she said, feeling herself flush. "Meet me after breakfast."

CHAPTER 11
TIME FLIES AT A STANDSTILL

Malia's mouth tasted of cotton. She'd never talked so much in her life—thirty minutes straight if she had to guess, which she did on account of the room lacking a clock—and not once did Park interrupt her. No comments or clarifying questions. Even as Malia reached for her water, Park remained silent, nurturing a bemused grin that sprouted over the previous minutes.

Malia reached for the glass and gulped the water down. It tasted sweet on her tongue, a stark contrast to the bitterness of having said too much. It wasn't until after Malia emptied the glass and made it clear she wouldn't be continuing her tale without prompting that Park set down her pen and spoke.

"So, you flashed this Tiki fella the goods, huh?" She smirked at the mirror beside her, as if sharing a joke with a hidden observer.

Malia let the comment slide as she grappled with the recollection, realizing everything could be traced back to that chance thunderstorm, her hand in his, wanting so badly to follow Skye's advice that she'd mistaken Tiki's heroics for something so much more. In reliving the memory with Park, Malia understood that the look Tiki had given her that morning aboard the helicopter was the same one he'd shown that day in the river. She swallowed deeply, but couldn't dislodge the lump in her throat, the feeling that it was still midnight in Kalalau and she was the only one in the dark.

"Anything come of it?" Park's eyebrows arched to her bangs as she awaited an answer. Malia gave only the slightest shake of her head in response as the pang of what could have been jabbed home.

Park scrutinized her, then switched gears. "Okay, so you met some hippies. And one convinced you that going naked was ... *safer?*"

"You wouldn't understand."

"Got that right. Seems you've conveniently left out one important detail."

"Such as?"

Park wrote a quick note in indecipherable script, then looked up. "Mr. Higgins, for starters."

"Who?"

"Really?" Park's tone was not only indictive, but carried the incredulity of someone being openly lied to, as if she'd caught Malia and this Higgins person lunching together just yesterday.

"Nobody used their last names. Hell, half the people out there go by their Instagram handles."

"And the other half?"

Malia rolled her eyes.

"I don't believe you."

"Suit yourself." Malia did her best to appear indifferent, but beneath the table she needed her hands to stop her leg from trembling. In her gut she knew Park was referring to Jordan—who else could she mean?

Park studied Malia as if the question had been a test. "I gotta admit, Malia, you're a lot savvier than most of the teens I deal with. I get some in here, older than you even, who can't function without calling home. You kinda remind me of myself," she added with a laugh.

"Is that bad?"

"Means I gotta stay on my toes."

Park retrieved a manila folder stuffed thick with papers from beneath the notepad. She cleared her throat and made a show of weighing the stack in her palm, bouncing her hand, pretending to strain beneath the heft. She yanked her hand away like a magician tugging a table-cloth. The slap of the files against the table echoed in the tiny room.

"Let's see how all this fits into your little story."

Park flipped open a file and dragged her index finger along the top page. Her burgundy nail polish was chipped at the edge and exposed a half-moon of naked piggy-pink growth along the cuticle. The sight reminded Malia of how her mother warned her to only start painting her nails if she wanted to do it every week. "Don't only paint them when you've got a date," she'd say. "Otherwise, when it grows out, people might think you're lonely."

Malia stared at the fingernail until Park folded it away. She bore a self-conscious look that suggested she knew exactly what Malia had been thinking—and the truth wasn't far off.

"We've received a number of complaints about you so-called Kalalau Outlaws."

"It's just a name."

"Really?" Park flipped the page. "People come from around the world to Kalalau. Then they go for a swim or walk in the valley and come back to find their stuff missing."

"Coulda been anyone."

"Since when do other hikers want to load their packs with extra gear before hiking out?"

Malia shrugged. "Well, it wasn't me. If anything, visitors were always wandering up into the valley, mooching off us."

"And you never took advantage?"

"I traded with them, sure. Homemade necklaces for leftover food or books they were done with."

"So, all those hikers took time during their vacation to file false police reports?"

Malia sighed. "Some theft happened. But little stuff, ya know? Like slippers or a water bottle. Or shorts off a clothesline." Her voice trailed into a whisper as she recalled the time Darren had returned with a sleeping bag, claiming he found it on the Free Table. Nobody believed him for a second, least of all Inoke. He grabbed Darren by the neck and bent his arm so far back, she thought it might snap. "Nothing expensive. That was the rule."

"Why's that?

"Inoke didn't want negative attention."

"Inoke?" Park perked up at the mention of his name, like a dog hearing it's going for a walk. The detective tapped her pen atop the pad. Twice her lips parted in question, only to pinch back in restraint. She scribbled a note, then flipped through the various complaints, reading them aloud: "Theft. Drugs. Indecent exposure." Park shot Malia a judgmental look and turned the page. "Why don't you tell me about the little ferry service your friends were running? Illegal landings, price gouging; you know boats are prohibited from transporting supplies or passengers to Kalalau, right?"

"You knew about that?"

"Oh, come on, Malia. We're not dumb. How else would your friends have gotten lawn chairs and coolers back there? Gonna hike 'em in on their backs?"

Park's sarcasm was bad enough, but Malia wouldn't abide her implying they were lazy. Living off the land was hard work, weekly supply drops or not. "If you knew, why didn't you stop it? And so what if a boat brought in supplies or took some exhausted hikers back to town now and then. What difference does it make?"

"It's illegal. Not to mention the hundreds of dollars they were charging."

"Cheaper than a helicopter rescue," Malia scoffed. "And besides, nobody forced them to pay. They could have hiked out; most were just scared."

"If someone was in trouble, your friend with the boat should have called 911. Search and Rescue would have—"

"What? Bankrupted them?" Malia leaned forward, her palms flat on the table. "Or was that the problem? The police need the money. You're mad 'cause they were moving in on your turf." Malia arched her eyebrows, having heard emergency evacuations could cost thousands of dollars. "No. Police only fly out for free when it's time to hassle people. Well, not *you* personally, of course."

Storm clouds descended over Park's face, but to Malia's surprise, the squall never came. After several beats, Park nodded self-assuredly, like a prizefighter whose challenger had managed to land a sneaky blow to the jaw. Park held her cool, but the gloves were coming off.

"And the drugs?"

Malia shrugged. "Weed's harmless. Besides, plenty of hikers brought their own."

"Really?" Park cocked her head to the side. "Sure doesn't look it."

At first Malia could only wonder what the detective was referencing, then Park stroked the side of her face, indicating Malia's bruises.

Malia shrank in her seat. Her voice lowered. "Pot had nothing to do with that."

"Enlighten me then. Tell me how you got a swollen lip. Tell me why your eye's black and blue. And don't say you went five rounds with a coconut tree."

Malia felt the color drain from her as she fought the urge to touch her injuries. She opened her mouth to speak but couldn't find the words. Not yet. The fight. Last night. It was too soon.

"No? Okay, tell me about Mr. Higgins then."

Malia looked up in confusion.

"Jordan," Park said, dragging the last syllable with frustration. "Did you really not know the name of the guy you were living with?"

Beneath the table, Malia again wound the drawstring around her finger. She tugged on it, feeling her fingertip balloon again, wondering how much Park already knew. Her mind reeled with images of the contest, the blow to her face, the swim back from Honopu. And questions. So many questions. But mostly, she wondered how the police found out. "How do you even know about—"

"Need I remind you where you are? You don't ask the questions. If you want any hope of being released—"

"Okay, okay. Jordan showed up a day or two after Skye left. He was nice. A hard worker. He wasn't a freeloader like ..."

"Tiki?" Park asked, and again her eyes glimpsed the mirror.

"What? No. Well, sometimes I guess." Malia studied Park's reaction. "Why do you look at the mirror every time you mention him?"

"Do I?" Park shrugged. "Guess I'm just anxious to hear what he's saying about you down the hall."

Malia's stomach twisted into a knot so tight she felt she might be sick. She pulled her drawstring noose tighter, gripping it like a lifeline back to her final moments aboard the helicopter. She searched her memory for comfort, recalling her attempt to coordinate a response, only to realize Tiki never agreed to say it was self-defense.

"Back to Jordan. The others must have been jealous. New guy shows up, ends up dating a pretty girl like you."

"That's not what—"

"But you *were* together, weren't you?" Park smirked from across the table with the confidence of a card shark. "Odd since you had a crush on Tiki. Or ... are you one of those girls who prefer to sample every-thing from the buffet?"

Malia leapt from her seat, sending it skidding backward as she slammed her hands down on the table. "It wasn't anything like that."

"Sit down, Ms. Naeole."

"I wasn't dating every guy in camp!"

"Didn't say you were," Park replied with practiced nonchalance.

"And my sex life is none of your business."

"I'll be the judge of that. Your job is to keep talking."

Malia remained standing, hands anchored against her hips, sending death stares across the table. Part of her knew Park was simply trying to rattle her, to get her to slip up and reveal something incriminating. She had to stay calm. To not allow Park under her skin. Malia under-stood this. She was nobody's fool. Yet as she bent to sit, she couldn't help wondering what it was that caused her to befriend Jordan when she had every reason not to. She dropped into the chair with a huff, leaving it askew out of spite.

"Good. Now, tell me about the day Jordan arrived. Was that after you showed back up in camp naked?"

Malia shook her head. "Before."

"But—"

"I didn't think it mattered."

Park cocked her head to the side and narrowed her gaze. "If I didn't know better, I might think you skipped over that part intentionally."

Malia bumped her knuckles along her ribs like mallets on a bronzed xylophone, counting the notes of her ribcage, expecting to play a full octave. Nothing but skin and bones, her mother used to say. Malia was always thin, but not like this. She pulsed her stomach in and out, marveling at the hollow beneath her ribs as she sucked her tummy in, nearly touching her belly button to her spine. A feat she found more curious than cause for alarm.

She returned her attention to the decorative kukui nuts pooling on the towel draped across her legs. After days of work, they were finally ready to be strung. She'd soon know if her instinct would prove true— that finished kukui leis in Kalalau would be as good as a debit card at the Island Mart. She'd collected them the day before Skye left. Back at camp, Malia asked Tiki if he wanted to help prepare them, figuring it a cute excuse to do something together. She gathered dozens of the cherry-sized nuts and, recalling her mother's instructions from long ago, shucked, punctured, and buried them in the ground so ants could devour the oily meat before it turned rancid. Then, yesterday, they boiled the hollowed-out nuts to kill the bacteria. She'd spent the morning polishing them one by one with a sandy rag, alone, disappointed by Tiki's lack of participation. Threading the nuts on fishing line was tedious work, but surprisingly therapeutic. The swoosh of each oblong nut along the monofilament signaled a small gift to the world, to herself. Proof she was still learning, contributing.

But what she wanted most was for Tiki to make a move.

Malia watched him read from across the firepit, studying the way his eyes snaked across the text, his habit of licking his lips when he turned a page. She'd nearly completed her third necklace and was running low on nuts when her grip slipped. The heavy-gauge needle shot through the side, stabbing her index finger. "Dammit." She sucked the trickle of blood from the wound, hoping it wouldn't become infected.

Inoke looked up from where he hovered over a pile of kindling. "Waste of time, you ask me. Whatever the tourists give you for 'em, they'd probably just leave behind anyway."

"Only waste of time I see is you tryin'a start a fire with wet wood." Malia stuck her tongue out, then quickly ducked as a stick looped through the air at her. "Hey!"

"You gonna give, you gonna get."

"You two mind? Some of us are reading," Tiki said.

Malia and Inoke exchanged a mischievous glance, then took aim at Tiki. She lobbed the damaged nut as Inoke flicked a lit match at him, toppling him backwards off a log. The trio fell into the kind of laughter that lazy summer days were made for. Days spent lounging about, talking story in the shade, listening to the gurgle of the stream as July slipped away.

She inspected the unfinished necklace as Inoke returned his attention to the twig teepee he'd built in the firepit. She strung another pair of nuts onto the strand, but soon found her concentration disturbed by the hiss of the sputtering fire, the murky scent of its spiraling smoke. Though she'd never been off the islands, let alone anywhere with seasons more distinct than rainy and dry, the damp-fire scent inspired made-for-TV thoughts of autumn on the mainland. Hillside palettes of rust and crimson foliage, crisp foggy mornings, pumpkins, and hot apple cider. *Won't be long now,* she thought, knowing in just a month's time she'd be off to college. As her thoughts snowballed from wool sweaters to winter hats, Tiki raised his chin, gesturing beyond the perimeter of the camp.

Malia turned, expecting to see a goat or one of the feral cats she'd seen evidence of, but was wrong on both accounts. A man stumbled forward, narrowly grabbing a small tree for balance as he strained beneath the weight of an expedition-sized backpack, its sides bulging beneath the straps like a holiday roast. He wore a collared plaid shirt, gray, sweat-soaked nylon shorts, and a pair of trail sneakers encased in vermilion mud. Clean-shaven and pale—too pale for midsummer in Hawaiʻi—with sweat dripping from the brown hair jutting from beneath his trucker-style ball cap, he appeared precisely the type Inoke loved to mock: a weekend warrior with more miles logged in the aisles of a North Face store than on the trail.

The guy didn't stand a chance.

Malia turned to gauge her friends' reaction as Inoke rose. He gripped the stick he'd been using as a fire iron and spoke first. "You lost, brah?"

The man considered the question. "I ... I smelled smoke."

"Trail's back that way." Inoke pointed with his stick. "Leads to the beach. Plenty of campsites there."

The hiker swayed forward as he unbuckled his hip belt in a daze, then shrugged the pack from his shoulders. It thudded against the ground. He surveyed their camp with eyes like saucers, his gaze darting between the tents, the men, and eventually settling on Malia. His eyes flashed with recognition briefly, as if she reminded him of someone. He turned away. There was something off about him; even Malia could sense it. In the way he kept his distance, his mouth shut. How he stared at their table, like a dog begging to be let in from the cold.

"This ain't where you need to be," Inoke said.

Malia shot Inoke a puzzled look, wondering what his deal was. *Is it the drugs? Is that what he's worried about?* Tiki, too, seemed surprised by Inoke's inhospitable tone. In all the time she'd been in Kalalau, she'd never seen Inoke send someone packing as soon as they arrived, especially not without first seeing what they might be willing to trade. Least of all someone this exhausted. Sure, they'd bust their balls, as Darren liked to say, but they weren't rude.

"Inoke, he's—"

Malia huffed as Inoke silenced her with a no-touch stiff-arm that quelled dissension. She wanted to say something. Had been there long enough, had earned that right. But before she gathered her nerve, the man shouldered his pack and made to leave.

"Sorry to bother you," he said, half turning to face them.

He lurched in the direction he came but didn't get far. His initial trajectory led him past Tiki's tent and toward the river, but he soon ricocheted the other way, bouncing from a pandanus tree before catching his heel on a root. He landed atop his pack, his limbs flailing in the air like an upturned turtle.

Inoke snorted in derision as the man flailed, "Stupid *haole.*"

Malia circled around to stand next to Tiki. "Something's not right," he said, watching as the man began unpacking his bag right where he fell.

"Is the trail really that hard? He looks crushed."

"With all that weight, yeah, probably."

Malia sidled a half step closer, pleased to see his concern. She sensed an intimacy building between them, stacking like kindling in wait of a spark, and sought to encourage it at every turn. Together they watched in silence as the man rose to his feet. He stumbled further in the direction of the main trail, then fell again. There, he worked to assemble his tent with the inertia of a boulder.

Malia turned to Inoke, wondering what he might do. "He's far enough. Leave him," he said, dismissing the interloper with a wave.

Tiki eventually returned to his book and Malia to her necklaces, but they were interrupted minutes later by the crunch of nearby leaves. The man paused at the edge of their camp, shirtless and barefooted with a thousand-yard stare. "Excuse me. Can you spare any food?"

This time, Malia resisted the urge to look to Inoke for approval. "Yeah, sure. Right here." She padded over to where they kept a pile of fruit available for late-night cravings.

"You ain't bring any?" Inoke asked.

The man cast his eyes at the dirt in obvious embarrassment.

"Awful big pack not to be carrying any food."

"I was ... I had the heavy gear." His voice trailed into a whisper as Malia stepped forward with a mango.

"No, Malia."

"He's right, Malia," Tiki said softly.

Malia bulged her eyes in disbelief. They'd never refused anyone food before. It was the whole reason the garden had been built in the first place. "We can spare it," she said. Inoke glowered back, daring her not to abide his command. She clutched the mango within her trembling grasp, refusing to give in, and gestured for the guy to take it.

The stranger bit his lip as his eyes darted from the fruit to Inoke to Malia and back. With obvious reluctance, he gave the tiniest nod before turning to retreat.

"Hey, what's your name?" Tiki called to him.

"Jordan," he said without facing them.

"Follow the valley trail another half mile or so. You'll find bananas," Tiki said.

Inoke held his ground in silence, arms crossed, clutching his fire stick like a club as Jordan strode off without a word. The situation was clear, even if the reasons weren't. He wasn't welcome, and he'd be well-served to keep his distance.

Malia watched him return to his tent. It was the first time she'd seen the group send someone packing—and she wouldn't let it happen again.

<hr />

"I'm gonna stop you right there," Park said, holding up her hand. "You were there a month when Jordan arrived?"

"About three weeks when he showed up. But really a month before he joined—"

"A month? Just like that?" Park held her palms up, awaiting an answer.

Malia sucked in her lips as her knee bounced, unsure what to say.

"No phone call home? No letting your father know you're alright?"

The shell of the all-business detective had shattered, hatching the disappointment of the parent within. Even if Malia had a valid reason for what happened, there was no use in trying to justify herself. Park would never understand.

She didn't even know if she completely understood it herself.

Shame settled on Malia like ashfall, dampening her ability to respond, numbing her mind.

"Oh no. You're not getting off that easy. This whole time I've been listening to you, I've ignored the fact that you ran away in early July." She slapped the table. "In July!"

Malia recoiled in her seat, causing the chair leg to screech across the floor.

"You told your friend you were going for two weeks. Do I need to tell you it's late August?" Park didn't wait for a response before heaping coal in her boiler. "And here I kept hoping you might surprise me and say you flew home for a week and returned. Or at least had someone call your dad. But you didn't do any of that, did you? Did you?" Park threw her pen down. It bounced and skittered onto the floor, echoing in the wake of her ire.

"I ..." Malia began. A false start.

She chose to ignore the excuses zinging around her mind like confetti-colored bouncy balls. After all she'd been through, she wouldn't resort to childish excuses. If she was going to say anything, she decided, it would only be the awful, pathetic, rat-fucking truth: she was selfish. Malia stared at her nail-bitten fingers as she spoke. "The days blurred together, like we were adrift in our own sea. I can't explain it. But it was like everything outside Kalalau—family, the news—it didn't exist."

"Didn't you miss your dad? Your home?"

"No." She looked up, her eyes beginning to water. "Think what you want, but no, I didn't. And why would I? My dad's the reason I left. It's his fault we never went to Kalalau as a family, why my mom never got to show me where I'm from."

"Malia."

"Nobody talked about family. Or home." Malia took a steadying breath. "Probably so we wouldn't feel so lonely."

"Knowing you were the only family he had left, you never thought what your disappearance might do to him?"

Malia slammed her eyes shut, trying to block the sight and sound of Park's haranguing, but there was no isolating herself from the truth. Not here. Not with Park's spittle showering her from across the table.

"Well?"

Malia looked up. "I need to pee."

"You've gotta be kidding." Park flung herself back in her chair with parental incredulity.

"I gotta go."

Park snorted. "Fine. But first you're gonna explain this complete disregard for your father."

Malia crossed her legs, pressing her thighs together. She opened her mouth, but no sound came out.

"Did he abuse you?"

She shook her head.

"Was he a drunk? An addict?"

"No! Of course not."

"Did he make you uncomfortable? Stare at you? You know, with you ending up naked on a beach, I have to wonder. A lot of girls end up promiscuous or in unhealthy relationships because they were molested—"

"Gross. Stop."

"So what was it?"

"I told you." She squirmed in her seat as her bladder responded to her psychosomatic urging. "I really gotta pee."

Park stared from across the table, smoldering with a disdain bordering on disgust. For a moment, Malia thought she might slap her. So much so, Malia flinched when Park abruptly stood, sending her chair spinning out from under her. The chair collided with the wall beneath the camera, adding a scuff mark to the collection. Park yanked open the door behind her, the one Malia assumed led to the observation room. "Make it quick."

Malia scurried to the door, but the clamp of Park's hand on her elbow halted her. She glared down at Malia from her elevated-in-heels perspective. "What you put your father through ..." The rest of her condemnation died amongst the vibrations between them.

Malia's lip twitched as she strained to hold herself together, if only for another second. She tugged the door shut behind her, noting the handle had no lock, the sink no mirror. *They don't trust me.* She tugged the sweatpants to her knees and sat upon the frigid, vomit-green toilet. Despite her immediate relief, the institutional callosity demanded harder thoughts. There were no good girls here. Like a blacksmith firing his forge with the bellows, Malia fed her angst by recalling the night she found the scholarship letter in the trash, soiled with Rorschach tea stains. He had no right, she thought, gnashing her teeth, recalling the barbs they hurled. No right at all. But no matter how many times she pounded her fists against her thighs or how loud the memories screamed in her mind, she couldn't drown the echoes of Park's reminder that she was the only family Charles had left. And likewise for her. Malia plunged her head into her hands and sobbed. Soft moans burbled up as her body convulsed, yet she couldn't wring herself of the guilt.

"I'm right here," she croaked, picturing her father alone and trembling at the kitchen table, wondering where she'd gone. "Please come get me, Dad."

CHAPTER 12
HALF PLUS SEVEN

The morning after she'd gone skinny-dipping, Malia walked the winding path through the milo forest, uphill of the hikers' tents. Great campsites with beachfront views, shaded by broad-leaved trees entangled with passionfruit vines. She arrived early, wanting to collect the recently fallen fruit before the animals got to them, not to mention the hikers clever enough to identify the canary-colored sweets. But also out of excitement. Anticipation. An irrational fear of having overslept, of missing her date with Tiki, kept her awake most of the night.

And when sleep finally did come to her, so did he. In her dreams, he wasn't bashful. Didn't keep his distance. He entered her tent where she lay stark naked, beckoning him. She felt the air mattress sag beneath his weight as he ran his fingers along her sides, tracing the curve of her hip, the softness of her inner thigh. Malia shifted in her slumber, rubbing her feet against one another, pinching the nylon bedding between her knees as her breasts swelled in want, in need of him. All of him.

Biting her lip, she stared at the darkened tent ceiling, wanting more than anything to make her dream a reality. And she knew how to make it happen.

She straightened her tent at first light, then set about deciding what to wear. She recalled how uncomfortable he seemed around her by the tent yesterday, resisting the urge to look—and not necessarily out of politeness. She also remembered how awkward it sometimes felt dealing with Skye's constant nudity—if only women's swimwear dried as quickly as men's. At the risk of retreating from yesterday's boldness, Malia tied a sarong around her bare waist, opting to leave something to the imagination. Her hair she pulled forward over her breasts, having read in a magazine what a turn-on the tease of a little side boob was for guys.

The sarong, purple with white palm trees, fluttered in a light breeze as she held the loose material in a makeshift basket. A carpet of kukui nut fragments crunched beneath her feet as she gathered the freshly fallen liliko'i. They were edible, but tart. She didn't care. They could ripen back in camp. For now, she merely needed a distraction, a task to keep her from looking too eager—or that he'd kept her waiting.

Malia had a dozen intact fruit gathered in the cotton bowl of her wrap when the sound of baby bleats called her attention. Up ahead, a family of goats pecked at the ground near a bounty of fruit. Malia drew up the rest of the sarong to keep from dropping her harvest. She reached for a rock, but thought better of it. She scooped a handful of kukui shells from the ground and hurled them at the goats. "Get outta here. Shoo!"

"Stop. You'll hurt them." The voice was small, childlike in its innocence, and scared.

To her right, peering from behind a tree, were a pair of twin boys, no more than seven years old. Their hair zigzagged in all directions. They wore matching blue shorts, rubber-soled reef shoes, and white tees bearing the crinkles of having been slept in. Malia loosed an aggrieved sigh, not wanting to share Tiki's attention with others. But she was in too good of a mood to ignore them. She bent to their height on instinct drawn from taking orders at the cafe. Kids loved it when you spoke to them directly. Made them feel special. And the parents ate it up— and tipped accordingly. "Nah, goats are tough. And the shells are little. See?" She picked one up to show them.

"Oh," one said without looking at the shell. Malia could tell he wasn't sold. His eyes dropped to her chest.

"Where's your shirt?"

"Why are you naked?" his brother asked.

Malia cocked her head to the side in a wouldn't-you-know-it manner and put her free hand on her hip. "Laundry day. I put all my clothes in the machine and forgot to leave something to wear." She smiled, hoping they'd catch her joke.

"Oh…" the boys said in unison, nodding until the one on the right grew suspicious. "Wait a minute. There's no washing machines here."

"Can you keep a secret?"

The boys' faces lit up. They nodded vigorously.

"It's a special machine that plugs into coconut trees. I made it myself."

Their eyes bulged, then they burst into belly laughs.

"This one time. My mom was doing laundry. And the phone rang. But then my dog—"

"His name is Buster," his twin interrupted.

"Buster got loose. And the water kept running. And the soap—"

"The bubbles were up to here!" the other one shouted, stretching his hand above his head.

"No way," Malia said, acting astonished. "That's crazy!"

"What are those?" one of the boys asked, pointing at the fruit.

"Passionfruit. Want me to show you how to eat 'em?" She didn't have many to spare, but anyone who hiked all the way in at that age deserved a treat.

"Hey, boys. Who you talking to?"

Malia turned toward the voice as a tall, middle-aged man approached. He followed his sons' gaze to Malia and stopped abruptly. "Oh, you're …" He seemed caught by surprise, then raised his hand to his curly hair as if to shade himself from the sun, but he didn't stop staring. "Looks like you lost your suit."

Malia smoothed her hair across her chest and angled away.

"Her clothes are in the wash, Dad."

"Ain't that a shame," he said, scratching the T-shirt stretched across his paunch. The man grinned with the air of someone having a lucky day that kept getting better.

"I better get going," Malia said, worried the dad was going to send the boys away and come closer. She let out some of the material bundled by her hip, causing a passionfruit to fall.

"But you were gonna show us how to eat one."

One boy picked up a husk already gotten to by a critter. "This one has ants!" He threw it on the ground, then wiped his fingers on his brother's shirt.

"Yuck, stop," the other one said, pushing him.

"Okay, okay. Here's one for each of you." To her relief, the father bent over his sons' shoulders, inspecting the fruit she'd given them.

Malia squatted, allowing her harvest to pool in her lap. "Hold it with two hands, with the stem pointing up." She tilted the fruit to show them. "And pinch just below the top like this." The fruit cracked evenly in Malia's hand, but the boys struggled. It wasn't yet ripe and the cork-like rind was resilient.

"Here, let me try," the father said, taking one.

"Roger? Boys? What are you … you … Oh." A shouty voice snagged their attention to a blonde-haired woman in hiking shorts and a baggy, long-sleeve shirt. She stomped past the family's tents and rounded the corner in a huff. She pumped her arms, twisting back and forth with each step.

"Look, honey, they're passionfruit. You were wondering if they were edible—"

"Boys, go to your tent." Her tone dropped like a piano off a moving truck. "Roger."

"What? No, they're—"

"Now."

Roger sighed. He contorted his face in apology to Malia, then turned and followed his sons. He made a weak attempt to steer his wife back to camp, but she shrugged his hand away.

"What's the matter with you? Those are little boys. Where do you think you are, walking around like that?"

Malia stood abruptly, causing her fruit to spill. Her instinct was to apologize and leave, and she might have a week earlier, but no longer. "Like what? I was just teaching them—"

"Look at you, strutting around with your tits out."

"Half the people here sunbathe nude. It's no big deal." As Malia stared at the woman, she noticed Jordan approaching from the waterfall carrying a dromedary bag. He paused within earshot but kept his distance.

"No big deal? You're tempting young boys. Perverting them."

"Oh, please." Malia rolled her eyes.

"And don't think I didn't see how you were looking at my husband."

Malia laughed and squared herself to the woman, mimicking her stance. Her heart raced and palms sweat, but she couldn't help questioning the current of jealousy streaming through the woman's remark. Sure, Malia was younger and certainly more fit, but was that all it took to trigger such hostility? Had she really become that threatening to other women?

"What a disgrace," the woman sneered.

The comment struck like a slap. "Congratulations. You hiked into paradise and got to show everyone what an uptight bitch you are."

"It's called being a mom. Yours must have been a real winner."

Malia's every muscle drew taut as the insult echoed between her ears. She wanted to scream in defense of herself, her mother, the memory, but could find no handle on her rage. She balled her fists, squeezing the halved passionfruit she'd been clutching until juice oozed through her fingers, wanting to claw and punch this woman for what she said. But she couldn't—wouldn't—give her the satisfaction. With her nostrils flaring, Malia chucked the halved passionfruit at the woman's feet, then turned to run. She managed only a few steps before colliding into someone on the trail.

She glanced to see who it was, then clenched her eyes shut and nuzzled against the bare chest holding her up, breathing in the summer rain scent she'd forever associate with him.

"What's going on? What'd you say to her?" Tiki's voice carried a presence not often heard in Kalalau. One hand cradled Malia's head as another rubbed comforting strokes along her back.

"Tell your friend to put some clothes on."

"You're here for what, three days? This place is in her blood."

"I don't need my boys getting any ideas." The woman's voice vibrated with exasperation.

"Then next time, take them to Disneyland. Come on, Malia; let's go."

The narrow trail made it difficult to walk two abreast, but Malia loved the feel of Tiki's arm around her shoulders, how her body snugged against his hip as he held her close. Her anger had run its course, and in his embrace, Malia felt almost glad the woman had said those words. No amount of picking fruit could have pushed her and Tiki together as fast as her verbal ambush. *Perfect*, Malia thought, except for her arm going numb from being pinned awkwardly between them.

"So, what was that all about?"

"I wish I knew."

"Really? By the way she was carrying on, I'd have guessed she caught you pissing in her Cheerios."

"Ew, gross." Malia immediately hated how prim she sounded. To cover, she forced a laugh. Then, with a mischievous tone, she said, "Well, not her cereal. But she might want to add a few more sugars to her coffee."

"Well played," Tiki said, chuckling. "Good thing I'm a tea man."

Malia brightened against him, enjoying the sensation of her head rising and falling against his side with his breathing. "But seriously, I appreciate you sticking up for me."

"Ah, don't mention it. Anyone woulda done the same."

"Maybe back in New Zealand, but not here." She recalled how Jordan stood in the distance watching, saying nothing, and had yet to decide how she felt about that.

"You'd be surprised."

"So, surprise me." She nudged him playfully with her elbow. "I hardly know you. Tell me about yourself."

"What do you wanna know?" He dropped his arm and turned to face her.

"Lemme think." Malia held a finger to her lips, regretting having jabbed her way out of his hold. And for what? She didn't even have a good question ready. "Umm ... Start with your nickname. Why *Tiki?*"

"That? It's cause of my research. Kind of a funny story, actually." He paused and gestured her forward down the trail. "Ladies first."

Malia took the lead as they passed the abandoned ranger station, wondering if he was being chivalrous or sly. She soon heard what sounded like him tripping. She glanced back in time to catch him leaping to pluck an orange from a tree. He landed with a thud, sporting a boyish grin. "I'm working on a master's in Pacific Islands Studies."

"Impressive," Malia said, continuing the walk.

"Thanks. Built a bamboo raft for my thesis. I had a theory about how early Polynesians may have traveled between islands that didn't have trees large enough for dugouts."

"I always wondered about that." Not really, but she wanted to seem interested.

"We know they had canoes for major trips, but—here." He offered Malia an orange wedge. "I tried a short trip. Proof of concept. Just Maui to Lana'i."

"That's really far. It took me all night to get to Kaua'i and that was on a powerboat." She bit the orange in half delicately. "You made it?"

Tiki snorted with practiced modesty. "Not even close. Raft came apart a half mile offshore."

Malia looked back, puzzled, trying to make the connection to his name, but found herself stuck on the image of him struggling aboard a disintegrating raft.

"Turns out I'm a better student than sailor. The knots slipped. Logs drifted apart." He sighed. "I couldn't face starting over. Not yet. So, I came here. Now they call me Tiki."

Malia licked the juice from her fingers and hazarded a guess. "As in *Kon-Tiki*, the movie?"

"Yep. First night around the fire everyone was smoking up, and I told them that story. Darren wanted to call me Heyerdahl, after the explorer." Tiki paused upon seeing Malia's confused expression. "Yeah, exactly. He wanted to spell it H-I-G-H-E-R. Get it? They settled on Tiki when they learned I don't smoke."

"Leave it to Darren to come up with a joke that only works in print."

Tiki's laugh, and the fact that he accepted the nickname without complaint, endeared him to her. Had it been her boat—her master's thesis, no less—that failed, she wouldn't have told a soul.

"Enough about me. What brought you out here?" Tiki asked.

"That's easy. Wanted a good tan." She twirled to face him, extending her arms as she did, causing the sarong to part like curtains in a breeze. It was sudden, an invigorating surprise even to herself, and sent her heart racing.

That's when he did it.

For the first time since she'd met him, he made no effort to hide his gaze. It didn't linger, but he definitely checked her out. Head to toe and back, just as she'd been hoping. "I'd say you got one." They locked eyes as Malia's anticipation heaved with each flash of his dimples; as did her temperature rise with every moment spent beneath the pressure of his piercing gaze. She wanted him—his kiss, his touch—and waited. The moment hung like a cresting wave refusing to break, building and building. Then gone. Tiki backed away. Oblivious? Timid? Chatty. "I told you mine; now you tell me yours."

"Ooh, pun intended I hope," she said, tossing a coquettish glance at his shorts. Something she'd never have done if not encouraged by the unrecognizable sauciness leaving her lips.

"Were you always so flirty?"

Malia raised a single shoulder and turned up the trail, questioning if she'd come on too strong. It was all so new to her, that boldness, that desire. The hunger. Like descending the stairs in a new pair of stilettos, she felt sexy as hell, but damn if it wasn't clumsy.

She didn't know what to say, or if even to speak at all.

As she walked, her tone turned pensive, wondering how much Tiki remembered from their cloud-spotting afternoon, and how much he may have inferred. But Malia found herself holding nothing back about her mother's death, the loneliness she felt, the despair. She'd so far kept her scholarship to Berkeley a secret, not wanting to come across as a showoff, but relished how genuinely impressed Tiki appeared to be when she explained that night in the kitchen. She continued past the valley trail, opting to continue along the main path along the cliffs.

As Malia bounded across the stream, Tiki asked, "But why Kalalau?" Only then did she realize he'd let her ramble uninterrupted, as if sensing she needed someone to vent to.

"Originally, it was to try and tap into my mother's spirit. Like, take a walk in her footsteps, you know? She used to talk about this place so much. Said her happiest memories were from here." Malia tore a palm leaf from a nearby plant and ripped it in strips as she went.

"Was that when she—"

"Got pregnant with me? Yeah. Early nineties."

"It's changed a lot since then."

"I wouldn't know." She thought it odd how matter-of-factly he said it, especially for a foreigner, but chalked it up to a figure of speech. Or a product of his research. "But when I got here, it was ..." A disappointing sigh.

"Not what you expected?"

"Not even close. I thought there'd be more people. More, I don't know ... camaraderie, I guess. It's okay. I'm used to it now. But I didn't expect that."

Tiki nodded, seemingly lost in contemplation, and, frankly, Malia was happy to let the topic drop.

They walked in silence for several minutes before coming to a promontory overlooking the sea. Massive boulders, worn smooth by centuries of rain and wind, dotted a breezy field. The grass, knee-high in spots, tickled Malia's skin as she led the way to the cliff edge. Tiki moved beside her as she stared into the Pacific over a hundred feet below, where the waves resembled mere ripples in a puddle. A pair of pelicans greased across the horizon, skimming the watery surface searching for a meal.

"Thanks again," she said, "for earlier, with that woman."

Tiki retreated from the edge and stretched out against a wedge-shaped rock. "Ah, you'll pay me back, I'm sure." Despite his confident smile, Malia could sense a shyness lurking behind the clouds mirrored in his eyes. But his posture, leaning as he did, relaxed and basking shirtless in the sun, appeared an open invitation. He wanted her, right? Of course he did. He's just shy, Malia told herself.

Don't wait for it to come to you.

Malia's heart raced. She'd never made the first move before, but couldn't risk having a moment's hesitation cost her again as it did by the swing. She stole a glance at the sky, checking for thunderstorms, then inched closer. She swallowed hard and reached a hand for his, mustering more of her newfound nerve. She dragged the back of her fingers over his shoulder, to his neck, and slid her hand beneath his wavy brown hair. Pulling him quickly toward her, she closed her eyes as his breath blew a whisper across her face. Her skin tingled as she moistened her lips and moved to kiss him, only to feel him pull away at the last second. His hands tightened upon her shoulders, gentle but firm, holding her at arm's length.

Malia shuddered with disbelief. Her mouth moved, tasting the unpleasant shock and embarrassment, but finding no justification to sink her teeth into.

"We can't." His tone flatlined, Malia powerless to resuscitate it.

She tried to speak, to demand an explanation. There she was, practically naked in a postcard setting, throwing herself at him, and it wasn't enough. Humiliation bubbled forth, choking off her words. She fought the shock for as long as it took for him to look her way. Only then did she find the strength to speak. "What is it? Do you have a girlfriend? Am I not attractive? I don't understand."

"What? No. God, no," he reiterated with the face of someone who'd stubbed a toe. The hold on her shoulders lightened. "It's just. We can't. *I* can't."

He's gay.

That must be it, she thought in a vain attempt to console herself. Malia slumped against the boulder beside him, disappointed. Tiki was the nicest, cutest guy in the valley, but if he didn't like girls, there wasn't anything she could do but get comfortable in the friend zone.

"How old are you?" His tone was sympathetic.

Malia eyed him suspiciously, wondering why he'd asked. "Nineteen."

For a moment, it seemed her response had satisfied some random curiosity—until he shut his eyes, shaking his head slowly, mumbling under his breath.

"What? Tell me." Her voice cracked with trepidation.

"It's nothing. Just ... half plus seven."

Malia bulged her eyes, demanding a translation.

"A thing I overhead in a bar. A rule." To his credit, Tiki had the decency to look embarrassed as he explained it. "They say you can't date anyone who's not at least half your age, plus seven."

"What? Who says this?"

"I don't know. *They.* But since I'm twenty-eight, you'd have to be at least twenty-one. Fourteen plus seven."

Malia pondered his comment, working through the calculations, then with a huff of disappointment asked, "So, you're not gay?"

"No. Why would you ... Wait. Is that why you thought I wouldn't kiss you?"

Her gaze fell to her lap, lacking an adequate response.

"Half plus seven," he repeated, as though powerless against a universal truth.

Malia snickered, unable to help herself. "That's fucking stupid."

"I think it kinda makes sense."

"Really?" Malia shoved from the rock, landing her hands on her hips. "So when you're thirty-eight and I'm twenty-nine, it'll be fine?"

"Yeah, I—"

"But that doesn't change when we were born. It's the same age difference."

"But—"

"And if you were seventy"—her lips moved quickly, silently, as she worked through the calculation—"you'd have no problem dating someone only forty-two?" She shot him a look of disgust. "Better still, if you were twelve, you could only date girls over thirteen. Half plus seven, right? How'd that work in middle school? You a big hit with the high school cheerleaders?"

Tiki raised his hands in defense, "Okay, okay, enough with the math."

"What's the matter? Too difficult for your *older* brain?" Malia backed away in protest, less hurt than frustrated. She couldn't help being young, no matter how eager she was to be older.

"For what it's worth, if I'd thought you were older, I would have kissed you days ago."

Her pride returning, Malia's anger melted before the warmth of Tiki's burgeoning smile. When it was clear she couldn't maintain her stony stance, she punched him lightly in the chest. "Jerk."

"Ow." He rubbed the spot.

"You have any idea how embarrassing that was?"

"I'm sorry." He cupped her hand between his. She felt a slight tug in his direction. She was sure of it. So certain, she'd nearly forgotten why she was mad by the time he said, "Forgive me."

Malia flushed as the butterflies in her stomach returned, fluttering on a gust of dizzying thoughts. Why was he holding her hand? Had he changed his mind that quickly? She looked up from their entwined hands to the faint scars and creases hidden amongst his arm hair. She'd briefly dated older guys in high school, but they were easy to figure out. Open books who only cared about themselves and sports—and getting in her pants. This was different. Tiki wasn't just older, but possessed an arresting maturity. As she struggled against her desire to try again, hoping he'd spare her the risk, his finger stroked the inside of her palm. The touch was as ticklish as it was arousing.

She placed her other hand atop his and kissed him, this time without hesitation. Her lips met his, first as a glance, then more firmly as they angled their heads the other way, as if by instinct—or practice. As though he'd been having the same dreams as she. Their mouths advanced and withdrew, synchronized, colliding, gulping hungry breaths before diving back for more. Finally. *Finally!*

Then, as Malia dragged her fingers up his arm toward his shoulder, he shot up from his seat against the rock, brushing past her. "I can't. It's not you, I swear," he said, stepping back quickly. "It's definitely not you."

Malia couldn't breathe, couldn't think. The cruelty of this consecutive rejection, more cold-blooded than the first, struck like a sledge to her midsection. She gasped as all the air within her vanished along with her strength. She reached a steadying hand to the boulder, her eyes wide and stinging, but she refused to cry.

Tiki looked over his shoulder, back toward the trail, and pivoted away, his fists balled so tight his veins pulsed and his neck tendons strained like piano wire. "Dammit!" He turned away again, shaking his head defiantly as if refusing to give in—but to what? His stupid rules? Society? She didn't know. He glanced again at the forest over his shoulder. Was someone calling him? He stepped toward her, clearly tormented by something she dared not guess. "I'm sorry." His eyes were red. "Please don't hate me."

He stomped angry steps across the grass, then launched into a jog. Malia stood alone atop the bluff, not a soul within sight, and with only the whispering grass to offer any sympathy.

CHAPTER 13
THAT NEW DOG SMELL

A blast of herb-scented steam fogged Jordan's glasses as he bent to retrieve the pan from the oven in Holly's kitchen. Unable to see, he fumbled while setting it atop her marble countertop and nearly spilled it in the process. It wasn't his first time cooking for Holly, but he was determined it'd be the first to avoid the garbage disposal. He lowered his fogged-over glasses and admired the spread of roasted shrimp and andouille sausage, the crisscrossed emerald spears of asparagus and shallot wedges. If he'd known how easy a sheet-pan dinner was, he would have begun eating at home years ago. Of course, his apartment wasn't nearly as well-equipped. "Thank you, Epicurious," he said under his breath, slipping his smartphone back into his pocket.

"You say something?"

"Oh, nothing," Jordan said, happy to see Holly already seated at the table. "You mind pouring the wine? I'll serve."

"Way ahead of you," she said, swirling a glass in the air. "After the day I had …"

Jordan paused to consider her comment, hoping she wasn't in another bad mood, only worn-out. She kicked her heels off beneath the glass dining table and leaned into the upholstered chair with a satisfied breath. Relieved, he took the plates from the toaster oven where they'd been warming and set about piling the food as artfully as he could, imitating the cook in the video app.

"It smells delicious. And no smoke alarm. Who are you and what have you done with my boyfriend?" she teased with what he'd come to recognize as her playful tone. Nobody would ever confuse her for jolly.

Jordan raised a hand to his chest, feigning insult. Cooking was never his forte, a failing dating back to soot-charred hot dogs and molten s'mores from his jamboree days with the Scouts. That he'd nearly sparked a forest fire with a marshmallow torch made him an early convert to freeze-dried vittles.

"I'm kidding. Besides, I didn't see you go into the freezer." Holly winked over her sauvignon blanc.

He aimed a spatula at her. "Hey, that package said fully cooked." It had been over a month since he served her spaghetti and meatballs, unthawed, and he'd yet to live it down. Despite the initial humiliation— and fear that Holly had chipped a tooth biting into the sauce-covered meatball—he'd come to relish the mistake. He'd always been jealous of couples with inside jokes. And now he was part of one. Six months and counting.

Jordan untied the apron and carried their dinners to the table. He set the plates down with a flourish and blushed as Holly oohed and aahed. "This looks amazing. And low-carb too." She forked a shrimp into her mouth and chewed, her face brightening with each bite. "You keep cooking like this, I just might keep you around after all."

The comment startled him. Jordan tolerated the ribbing, but her choice in phrasing couldn't have been worse. The days of him having time to cook were drawing to a close, and she needed to know. He swallowed his apprehension and spread a cloth napkin on his lap. "Well, this is a bit of a special occasion." He extended his glass across the table toward her. "Cheers."

She clinked her glass against his, then took a sip. Holly tilted her head, bewitching him with the simplest look. "So, what's up?"

Jordan sipped the wine, barely wetting his lips. "I've got good news. Well ... sort of."

Holly nodded for him to continue as she built a shish kebab of protein and shallot on her fork, but he found himself unsure how to begin. She'd made her impatience for long-winded explanations plenty clear in the past, routinely reminding him she only wanted the executive summary.

He took a deep breath. "My game got approved. We're making it."

She held up her hand as she finished chewing. She swallowed, then methodically dabbed her lips with the napkin before clearing her throat. "The seaweed one?"

Disappointment stabbed him in the gut, stealing his appetite. The fork fell from his hand, clanging against the china plate. "*Driftwood.* Yeah," he said, knowing he'd mentioned it at least a dozen times that month. "Kickoff meeting is on Monday."

"That's great. Congratulations. It's what you've been hoping for, right?" Holly shuffled around the table, still in her tight, knee-length skirt. She threw her arms around Jordan's shoulders and made to kiss him. He was slow turning to her, causing her lips to land awkwardly along the side of his mouth. "What's wrong? I thought you'd be thrilled."

"Oh. I am. Really," he said, faking a smile. He straightened in his chair and kissed her quickly—more of a peck than anything—and motioned for her to sit. "Just worried about the workload."

"What? Overtime?" Holly waved his concern away. "Welcome to my world."

He shook his head and inhaled through clenched teeth. "It's not that simple. Lead designer on a game like *Driftwood* means months, even years of overtime. And that's before we get to crunch. It breaks people."

"Aren't you being a touch melodramatic?"

"One of our former producers forgot his kid's name."

"Oh, please. That's not true."

Jordan shrugged, not quite conceding the potential hyperbole. "Point still stands. It's gonna be hell. And before we even get to development, I'll be traveling a ton. Scouting trips to the different environments. Weeks away. The arctic. Desert. A jungle."

"Tough life." She rubbed her fist against her cheek and taunted him with a pout. "Boo-hoo."

"Sure. It sounds great. I love camping. And part of me feels like doing backflips..."

"But?" Holly leaned her elbows on the table. She interlaced her fingers and stared over her polished nails, eyebrows raised. For years, he dreamed of designing a game of his own, forever waiting for the technology to catch up to his vision. And now, finally, it was possible—at a price. He never imagined what a rush it could be having a woman like Holly in his life: successful, confident, sexy as hell.

"But, now I'm with you," he said, unsure how it would ever work. "And I ..."

Holly's mouth fell open. He'd never before seen her genuinely speechless. "I'm flattered," she began, prematurely. She blinked once, hard, and in that instant Jordan got a glimpse of how she may have looked as a young girl, wishing upon a star.

Like a diamond in the sky.

"You can't let that stop you," she said. "I'm sure they'll make it worth your while. HyperTap's privately held, right? Did you discuss profit sharing? What about performance bonuses?"

He sank into the chair, deflated. It was the closest he'd come to saying he loved her—a step he'd been wanting to take for weeks. And she interrupted to ask about money.

Jordan reached for the wine, then decided on the whiskey she bought for his birthday. The soothing powers of high-end booze being yet another thing Holly introduced him to.

"Well?" she asked as he returned, swirling his highball. Money was the last thing he thought they'd be discussing.

"I don't know. I only saw the text before getting in the pool." Jordan brightened as he recalled the moment. "Was so jacked, I swam one of my fastest miles since college."

"So, you *are* excited."

"Of course I am. But we're not gonna see each other as much. And …" He motioned at the table, to her. "This is really nice."

"This won't change."

Jordan tried gauging her earnestness, but Holly could be as indecipherable as Faulkner. How could she not see how this would impact their relationship? For the life of him, he couldn't imagine someone like her waiting around for a guy like him. He stared at the mosaic of gristle and spice in the sausage coin, wondering if it wouldn't be better to break up now and save them both the trouble.

"How can you say nothing will change? I wouldn't even be able to focus; I'd be worrying too much."

"Worrying? About … me finding someone else?"

"Well." He couldn't believe it had to be said. "Yeah. Of course."

Holly's demeanor softened as her lips curled tightly upwards. Her eyes glistened and, for a moment, Jordan couldn't tell if she was about to laugh or cry. Then, before he realized what was happening, Holly was in his lap, her hand stroking his face.

"Then move in with me." She ran a fingernail down his throat and whispered in his ear, "That way, we'll at least see each other in bed."

With the sting of Tiki's rejection still palpable hours later, Malia hiked to Big Pool hoping the crystalline water could clear her muddied thoughts. Her reasons for remaining in Kalalau no longer mattered. Tiki's rejection only exacerbated the loneliness she felt the prior day on the beach after her swim. Still, she dreaded the hassle of going home. The hike out, the logistics of getting to Honolulu, the inevitable fight with her father. College. It was too much.

Lap after lap she swam, getting no closer to a decision. So she deferred to the leaves tumbling over the falls into the pool, counting the waxy green ones destined to keep her in place, deducting the wilted browns that would send her home. But unlike a lovesick maiden divining her beau's intent by the count of a daisy's petals, the jungle leaves flowed without end.

Like it or not, she had to make the decision herself.

Malia reached for her towel and caught a flash of movement in her peripheral vision. The sound of someone—or some*thing*—crashing through the brush soon followed. She squatted low atop the rocks and strained to listen over the rushing water.

Though she was fairly certain wild boars hadn't reached Kalalau Valley, the thought of coming face to face with one sent her pulse racing. She scanned the riverbanks for a climbable tree when she heard it again. The snap of branches, the heavy crunch of leaves. Definitely bigger than a goat. *A bear?* She rolled her eyes, scoffing at her imagination. She was more likely to encounter a Menehune than a bear, knowing the pygmies once called Kaua'i home.

Probably just coconuts falling, she assured herself. Then she saw it again: a streak of color in the trees. Bright red and moving. Slow, but certain. Assuming it was a lost tourist, she hollered, "The pool's this way."

The jungle fell still. Then a man yelled back, "Thanks."

Not recognizing the voice, Malia expected to see a wayward hiker emerge from the woods. She hurried into her sarong and sandals and recrossed the stream, in no mood for company. Especially from men. She hadn't gone more than a few steps toward camp before the crash of rockfall stopped her cold. The clattering and scraping preceded a thud, then an unmistakable cry of pain.

"Aaargh! Damn it!"

The voice was familiar, if only vaguely. *Jordan?* "Are you okay?"

No reply. Malia pushed through the massive ferns, following the sound of his cursing toward the rear of the valley. She clambered over fallen palms and koa trees like an ant making its way through a field of pick-up sticks. Her sarong snagged and tore, and she barely avoided losing her slippers in the gap between two fallen trees. "Where are you?" she yelled, resisting the urge to add, *And why?*

He grunted unintelligibly, sounding as annoyed as she. "I'm okay."

Relieved, Malia slowed her pace. No sense risking an injury of her own. She eventually found Jordan sitting at the base of the cliffs, cradling a badly scraped knee from which a trickle of blood coursed into his sock. Muddy green slime streaked his shirt. His face bore the chagrined look of someone who'd gambled away the rent money.

"You sure you're not hurt?" Judging by the chunks of rock strewn around him, he was lucky he didn't break something. Or worse.

He nodded but winced upon putting weight on his leg. He gritted his teeth and held onto the cliff for balance as he bent and unbent his knee several times. "I'm fine. Grip slipped, that's all. It's Malia, right?"

It had been four days since he first wandered into their camp and, despite Inoke's initial attempts to run him off, Jordan hung around. He kept his mouth shut, stuck to the fringe, and little by little, as his catatonic state faded and he proved himself willing to gather water and firewood without being asked, was welcomed into the fold—or at least tolerated.

Jordan picked up what appeared to be a loop of homemade cord. He draped it over his neck and stuck an arm through, wearing it like a bandoleer in an old cowboy flick.

"You made climbing rope?"

The corner of his mouth twitched with pride. "Why not?"

Malia stared up the cliffs, unable to see the ridge she knew shattered into spires several thousand feet above. Jagged pinnacles resembling a spiked crown more than anything traversable. She vaguely recalled a story in the papers from years prior about two boys who tried climbing down from the top. One died and the other got stuck on a ledge for days. By the time a chopper reached him, it had become the most expensive rescue in Hawaiian history.

"How high you going?"

"I heard there's an old path leading up the cliff—the back door. Goes to a visitor center."

"Lot of effort for a Coke, if you ask me."

He made a face to show he was in no mood for jokes. "There's a road that drops into Waimea town."

"Really? A guy I know keeps his boat there." Pangs of helplessness stabbed at her as she realized her ride home was so close—just over the cliffs—yet virtually unreachable. She stared at the rope incredulously, no more than palm fronds braided together. "And you're gonna climb it with *that*? I wouldn't trust that to support a bag of papayas."

"It's just in case I get ledged out and need to down-climb. Besides … it's stronger than it looks." He fixed Malia with a steady gaze, his eyes dark and bottomless, ready to swallow any further doubt. About the rope—or him.

"Sounds like suicide, ya ask me. Why not hike back the way you came in?"

Jordan wiped a smear of mud from his face. "It's good to have options."

"For … ?"

He didn't say. Only offered an evasive shrug.

If his goal was for her to think him mysterious, mission accomplished. But not in a good way. There was something off about him. She was beginning to understand Inoke's reluctance to allow Jordan in camp. Like Tiki had said, all that fancy hiking gear and boutique clothes, but no food. Who does that?

The one's hiding from something. Skye's words echoed in her memory. *Those are the ones you gotta watch out for.*

"How long you staying?"

Malia startled from the suddenness of Jordan's question. The fuzzy moss she'd been staring at snapped into focus. "I'm headed back now." She forced a smile to be polite. "Just came up for a swim. Glad you're not hurt."

Jordan nodded throughout her answer, waiting for her to finish. "No, I meant in Kalalau."

"Oh. That." She searched for somewhere to anchor her attention. "It's complicated."

Jordan arched his eyebrows and offered a supportive smile, like a teacher challenging her level of effort. But not like a hard-ass; one of the cool ones. She appreciated it, but it was a sensitive topic. And he was the newbie here, not her.

"You first. You've been walking around in a daze since you showed up. What's your story?"

"It's complicated," he said, not quite mimicking her tone.

"Nuh-uh. Start with the food. Seriously. You lugged that giant pack all the way here with nothing to eat. What gives?"

He slumped with a sigh, making like he was going to talk, then snapped the branch of a fern and ran his fingers down the stem, stripping the leaves from it in slow motion. "My partner had the food." Jordan looked up at Malia, his tone curt. "I had the heavier stuff."

"And where are they?"

"She turned back."

Malia wasn't surprised it was a she. Those freeze-dried camper meals weighed next to nothing. "Why didn't you go with—"

"This was supposed to be a work trip to research a jungle setting. For a video game I'm developing. Crafting, outdoor survival, that sort of thing." He balled the remnants of the fern in his hand and threw them at a boulder. "We had a fight."

There was a pitying finality to the comment. One she could relate to. And it suddenly made sense why he was here, alone and seemingly comatose: he'd been dumped. She thought it kind of cute given how much older he was.

"Sorry to bum you out. But you asked. Your turn," he said.

"Why, you need a new pack mule?"

Jordan didn't laugh. "I'm serious. You look like you've been here a while. Ever think of going home?"

Malia sighed. "Recently? Every day. It's what I spent the past hour doing." She squatted on a boulder and hugged her knees to her chest. "Soon, probably."

"Why's that?"

"Paradise ain't always what it's cracked up to be."

"Ah, you fell for the brochure."

"Something like that," Malia said. "I expected this whole Eden on Earth wonderland. And it took some searching, you know? To get past that initial awe. And it's hard work, living out here. But what I found … or thought I found … wasn't really any fun experiencing alone."

The recollection burned in a way she could tell Jordan could relate to, but whether because he didn't want to share or his own personal wound was too raw to disturb, he said very little. "Same with me. Not here, though … at home." Jordan turned from her and grabbed hold of the rocks. He kicked one foot into the mossy, weathered face, then reached for an invisible crevice overhead. Groundwater seeped from the rocks, shining like oil in the sunray. Malia held her breath as he climbed, gluing himself to the rocks like Spider-Man. Lean limbs and longer muscles. Not at all what she'd have expected from the guy that limped into camp a week ago.

He's done this before.

He jumped down with a morose look framed by his sweat-soaked bangs. "I checked everywhere along the valley perimeter for that old trail. This was my last hope." He tapped the face of his watch. "Had hoped the map on my watch would have had it, but no luck."

"Well, it's not like you gotta climb out. Probably been decades since someone went that way—"

"Not true," he said, lunging for a handhold. "Some high schoolers made it a few years ago. Took a few days, but..."

"But what? You think you got special *haole* powers that'll help you climb faster?"

"No, but I used to hit the climbing gym at lunch."

"Does this look like a gym? Forget it. Just hike out like everybody else."

"Like you?" He wore a droll expression as he waited for her reaction. Jordan must have sensed the storm building within her because he quickly added, "Darren told me."

Malia looked away, avoiding his judgment. As if he knew anything about her—or any of them for that matter. She turned back and snapped, "Well, at least I won't kill myself on the cliffs."

"The cliffs don't frighten me." Jordan bent to tie the lace of his sneaker. When he stood, his face was calm, but drained of color or any sign that he'd been exerting himself. "It's dying in this valley I'm scared of."

Malia sat cross-legged in her tent, reading the label of a freeze-dried meal. "Kung Pao chicken with new and improved Asian-style flavoring." She rolled her eyes and turned the foil-lined bag in her hands. "Just add boiling water. Great." She had managed to avoid camp since the fiasco with Tiki that morning and intended to keep it up through dinner. But she had to eat. And that meant fire.

As she considered the awkwardness of having to borrow a pot—assuming they weren't all in use—and wait around for water to boil while the others tucked into their stew, she decided to hell with it. She'd ignore Tiki, wolf down a meal, and retreat to her tent. Still, knowing she'd been rejected despite being the only woman in the valley had her feeling like a dented can of lima beans left to expire on an otherwise empty shelf—and needing to know why.

Malia wrung her hands, cracking her knuckles one by one as she replayed the scene in her mind: her clumsy attempt to make the first move; his silly rule about age; the fleeting perfection of the moment he kissed her back.

If only the memory ended there. But she'd never forget him pushing her away a second time. Leaving her standing there. Alone.

She wanted to take Tiki at his word. If he thought she was too young, well, she couldn't do much about that.

Maybe he really is gay.

She straightened at the sudden thought, recalling the guys she'd seen on the beach, sunbathing in the buff together. But Tiki? No, that's just something Jenna would have said to make herself feel better. If Tiki were gay, he would have told her. The more Malia thought about it, the more she felt there was something else. Yes, she was younger, but that wasn't all. She could sense it in the way he looked at her. When they kissed. Invisible reins preventing him from galloping to her.

The not knowing stung nearly as much as the rejection. It was time for answers. She rubbed suntan lotion into her face, then pinched her cheeks for a little color. In want of moisturizer and makeup, it would have to do. Instead of her hoodie, which she often wore on chilly nights, she doubled up her sarongs, tied two ends over her shoulder like a toga, then knotted the lower ends at the hip on the same side.

Malia didn't care about being warm; she wanted to show some leg.

Malia ladled vegetable stew into her bowl and sat at the far end of the log, diagonal from Tiki. Jordan squatted beside him, across from her. Inoke and Darren were in their normal spots. Ruby, Inoke's runner, was there too. A first. She hadn't officially met him and could only assume his nickname (if it were one) was owed to his scarlet beard. He must have brought his inflatable ashore while she was at Big Pool, she figured.

They each nodded their greeting, save for Tiki, who offered a meek smile dappled with embarrassment. A second's glance revealed the concern in his eyes, a need to know if she was okay. Malia angled away and adjusted the sarong so the hem slid up her thigh, allowing an expanse of skin to answer on her behalf.

Was she okay? No, he humiliated her. And it hurt to be around him, harder still not to steal glances in his direction. But she wanted him to see what he was missing.

They ate in silence until Jordan cleared his throat and said, "Hey, Malia, I forgot to ask earlier at the cliffs. Whatever came of you with that woman on the beach?"

Malia felt Tiki's attention on her and turned in time to see him shaking his head. He seemed to be telling her to let Jordan's comment drop. Was he jealous?

Jordan continued. "By the way, Tiki, that was nice of you to stick up for her."

"It was nothing."

"When was this?" Inoke asked.

"This morning, along the camper's trail," Tiki said. An annoyance crept into his voice as his accent softened. "Some mama bear got a bug up her ass over Malia going topless 'round her kids."

Inoke turned slowly toward Jordan like a tank's turret acquiring a target. "And you saw this?"

"Yeah, I was coming back from rinsing off at the falls. I'd gone for a swim—"

"And you ain't do nothing?"

"No, well, I —"

"What? You thanked Tiki, so it must have been serious. But it sounds like you just stood and watched."

Jordan stiffened in reaction to Inoke's accusation. "When you put it like that ..." He cocked his head to the side, appearing to choose his words carefully. "Guess I figured Malia had it under control. She seems strong."

Darren snorted. "Malia?"

"Shut up, Darren," Inoke commanded.

"Yeah, shut up, Darren," Malia echoed softly, hoping they'd drop it.

Inoke set his bowl on the rocks ringing the fire pit and leaned forward, resting his elbows on his knees. He stared at Jordan for several uncomfortable seconds. Nobody made a sound or moved, except Ruby, who stretched out against a rock as he tossed popcorn into his mouth.

Malia's stomach tightened. She hated the male drama, the posturing. Sure, it bothered her that Jordan hadn't come forward to help defuse the situation, but she barely knew him. Either way, he didn't deserve Inoke's ire.

"Why are you still here? Unless someone can correct me"—Inoke scanned the faces around the campfire for effect—"I'm pretty sure nobody invited you."

"He's here to do research," Malia blurted. "He's working on a video game. Set in a jungle or something."

"Like *Call of Duty?*" Darren asked.

"Didn't I tell you to shut up?"

"What? You gotta admit, it'd be pretty cool. Like, having hovercrafts storm the beach and helicopters with machine guns—"

Ruby tried correcting him. "That's *Battlefield*. *Call of Duty* has the—"

"Enough. Nobody cares about stupid games." Inoke took a steadying breath. "Research. Fine. It's a free country," he added with a derisive snort. "But we don't know you. And this here is my family. My jungle *'ohana*. And every night this week you come to my table, and you eat our grindz, and you smoke my *pakololo*. But then you see sister in trouble—"

"It's not a big—"

"No, Malia. It is." Inoke turned back to Jordan. "She a girl and you, a grown man, do nothing?"

"I thought—"

"You thought what? That it wasn't serious? Then why you thankin' Tiki?"

Jordan slumped forward. His hands trembled noticeably, causing the spoon to scratch along the edge of his bowl. Malia could feel Darren looking around the fire at each of them, fishing for a reaction, but she couldn't look away. For his part, Tiki remained quiet. Though he didn't focus on Inoke or Jordan directly, he wore the same scowl of concentration as Malia's father while playing chess.

The crackling flames were the only noise; their sunset glow flashed hot against the fire in Inoke's face. How such an innocent remark— Jordan's attempt to ingratiate himself within the group—could lead to this, Malia didn't know, but she would do anything for a return to the silence of her first meal in camp. Back when asking questions was a party foul and everyone ignored the newcomer.

"See, man, that's what I'm talking about." Inoke punched the palm of his hand, producing a solid thwack. Jordan flinched. "That's why I no trust you. People like you, scared to stand up to some tourist, wanting to stay out here with your fancy equipment. You got secrets. Biiiiig *haole* secrets."

"What do you want to know?" Jordan asked, his face as pale as boiled taro.

Behind her, Malia heard the crunching of leaves and the swish of branches. Then, a cheery voice she didn't recognize called out, *"Aloha, friends. We come in peace."*

A twenty-something couple strode into camp shouldering compact bags. They were fit, tanned, with blond hair and blue eyes and skin that shone in the firelight. They looked like models from one of the surfer magazines Malia used to read, leaning just so against an old Volkswagen microbus.

Inoke stood and clasped hands with the guy, his meaty bicep flexing as he wrapped his free arm around him in a bro hug. "What up, Fish? I's wondering when you coming back."

"Ah, you know. Never soon enough." He thumped Inoke on the back then stepped aside as his companion hugged Inoke warmly.

She waved to the rest of them. "Hi, I'm Lily. This is Fisher." She turned to Inoke. "You gonna introduce us?"

Inoke appeared a different person, unlike any time Malia had seen him in the five weeks she'd been in the valley. He went around the campfire, introducing each of them, his demeanor rising like a breeze as he made his way from Malia to Darren, around to Ruby and Tiki. Each rose to shake hands as they were introduced. When he got to Jordan, Inoke flapped his hand and said, "Don't worry about him. He's leaving soon."

Fisher and Lily smiled awkwardly at Jordan, clearly unsure how to take Inoke's comment. After a moment, Jordan lifted a hand in greeting and introduced himself.

"Make room," Inoke said to the regulars. Then, to Fisher, "You two hungry?"

Everyone shuffled around the fire as Malia scooted down the log. Her chest tightened as Tiki moved beside her.

"You just getting in?" Inoke handed Fisher a bowl.

"Thanks, man. Yeah, haven't even been by the tent yet. Didn't get on the trail till noon."

"You should have caught a ride in with Ruby."

Ruby nodded and tilted the bag of popcorn crumbs into his mouth. Kernel flecks sprinkled his beard.

"Nah, we enjoy the hike."

"Except when a certain someone oversleeps," Lily said, elbowing Fisher.

"You come from Hanakoa?" Jordan asked. He leaned forward as he spoke, giving off the vibe of someone desperate to fit in.

Fisher, Inoke, and Darren exchanged looks, then burst into laughter. Even Tiki chuckled a bit.

"I don't get it," Malia said. "What's so funny?"

"Hanakoa's a total mud pit."

"Worst campsite on Kaua'i."

"It's where the noobs stop halfway to Kalalau."

The comments came fast from all directions. Having never hiked the trail, Malia only knew what she'd read on travel blogs: that *National Geographic* called the trail one of the most dangerous in the world.

"I thought since you said noon—" Jordan attempted to explain.

"What's it take you guys?" Inoke asked his friends. "Five hours?"

"Yeah, if we're not hauling supplies. It's only eleven miles," Fisher said.

Lily passed the bowl to Fisher, who gestured to Inoke for a refill. Inoke tilted his hand toward the pot and Fisher helped himself. Lily wiped her mouth with the hem of her shirt and said, "I'll never understand it. You see these hikers with heavy boots and seventy-liter back-packs. Like they're setting out to climb Everest."

Darren laughed. "Sounds like Jordan." He hooked his thumb at him. "This guy showed up with a pack the size of Malia."

"And no food," Inoke added, the ire still simmering.

"Maybe that's why he won't leave. He's too slow to hike out in one day and knows Hanakoa's such a shithole, he'd rather stay here."

Jordan chewed his lip, flicking bitter glances at Darren as his face reddened.

"Either that, or scared of Crawler's Ledge," Fisher said, adding a play-spooky tone to his voice, like a troop leader telling ghost stories.

Ruby spoke up. "Hey, I'm glad people are scared of Crawler's. It's good for business."

Malia grew uncomfortable watching the camp pick on Jordan but needed to learn more about the trail. Particularly, its most notorious section. Despite Inoke's bluster about family, she doubted Ruby would give her a free ride back to Hanalei. And after seeing how they were acting, she was leaning toward hiking out sooner rather than later.

"I never hiked it. Isn't that section dangerous?" Malia asked.

The guys fought to hide their snickers as Lily put her hand on Malia's elbow. "It's really not that bad. The name scares people. They hear 'Crawler's Ledge' and assume they gotta go on their hands and knees or they'll fall to their death."

"It's like the ski resorts back in Colorado," Darren said. "Half the black diamond trails are named things like 'Intimidator' and 'Widow-maker,' but to be honest, most aren't any harder than the blues. They give 'em scary names so ski patrol doesn't have to work as hard. Same with Crawler's Ledge. The name keeps the masses away."

Malia wasn't convinced. "Anyone ever fall?"

Everyone scrunched their faces in thought. A murmur of uncertainty echoed around her.

"One. Few years ago," Tiki said.

"That's just a rumor," Inoke scoffed.

"No. It's true." Tiki stared at the fire as he spoke. His steady tone brooked no argument.

Fisher spoke next. "Crawler's no big deal. It's that red clay slope after it you gotta be wary of."

"Especially if it's raining," Lily added, waving her hands in front of her. "No way. Total death trap."

"Man, you start sliding there, you're done for. Three hundred feet." Darren whistled the sound of a bomb dropping. "Splash!"

"Look at this one," Inoke said, jerking his head at Jordan. "He's getting pissed."

"Really? Looks like he's gonna cry to me."

"Ha, I was right. He's scared of Crawler's," Fisher said, then quickly added, "Hey, man, don't take it personal. Plenty of people are scared of heights."

"Yeah, if you're a pussy," Inoke added.

Malia had had enough. "You guys are assholes, ya know that?" A stunned silence, then boisterous laughter from all around her. Jordan craned his head back and stared at the sky. His knees pistoned like jackhammers as firelight reflected in the sweat running down his face and arms. She recalled their earlier meeting and couldn't imagine anyone considering climbing the *pali* could be scared of a trail that dozens hiked every day.

Whatever it is, he's not afraid of heights.

When Jordan straightened, he didn't look scared or emotional, only cornered. But it reminded Malia of something her auntie once told her about a neighborhood dog that kept getting attacked. She said, "Some dogs give off a scent that only other males can smell. Weakness. And some dogs can't stand it." Malia considered Jordan's trendy haircut and high-tech clothes and realized he definitely had a smell to him, too: money.

"Fuck this," Jordan said, jumping to his feet. He threw the dregs of his stew in the fire and stalked off without a single glance to anyone.

The urge to follow him gripped Malia, but Tiki seized her wrist before she could rise from the log. His grasp was firm, but gentle. "The sooner he goes, the better," he whispered. "Trust me on this." Malia gritted her teeth and turned away, as confused by Tiki's comments as she was her reasons for wanting to follow Jordan.

CHAPTER 14
STORM WARNING

Malia flattened her hands against the beach, shoulder-width apart, and rose into a plank. Grain by abrasive grain, the sand lost its grip, falling free from her stomach, her thighs, and her calves. Minuscule irritants unable to maintain their hold. Warmth spread across her body from head to toe, like a blanket drawn in reverse, as the sun crested the *pali* and illuminated the lingering darkness of her thoughts, chasing away the shadows of Kalalau.

No birdsong or whistling kettles this morning; no helicopters or thundering surf. And Malia didn't care to wonder why. The riot that had raged in her mind for two days had been settled. It was time to leave. The serenity accompanying that decision brought her to the beach that morning. She'd spend the day resting, packing, and get an early start tomorrow. But first, one final yoga session in paradise.

Only a month ago, the pose was too intense. Her abs would scream out; she'd collapse within seconds. Now, strengthened by jungle living, she could hold the pose seemingly forever—if only her mind had developed a six-pack too. Logistical concerns penetrated her calm. Fears about the trail, finding a ride to town, and deciding when and how to contact her father topped the list. Though she knew a plane ticket was a mere phone call away—and would only cost her the shame of having to beg her father to pay for it—she could already hear the dim satisfaction in his voice: *If you can't handle going to Kaua'i on your own, how will you manage California?*

Malia brought her right foot forward and anchored her left in the sand, stomping out the imagined argument. She rose in a lunge and stretched to the heavens, palms facing in. Warrior one. She inhaled deeply, filling her lungs with the briny scent of the silvery Pacific, but the unwelcome whispering between her ears grew louder. Thoughts streaked by like the cars of a runaway train: California, majors, part-time jobs, dorm rooms, winter clothing, finals, semester breaks, visits home, wishing she'd never left. They kept coming, one concern after another, refusing to be ignored until Malia finally dropped her hands in a huff. A warrior fallen.

If she couldn't truly *be there*, she thought, then there was no reason to be there.

"So much for clearing my mind," she said, deflated. Reaching for her water, she noticed someone sitting alone. Brown hair, slim-fitting red shirt, an outstretched arm rested atop a crutch of sorts. *Jordan?* She hadn't seen him since he stormed off during dinner the night before last. But seeing him then, alone, she realized he might be the perfect companion for the hike out. She'd much rather hike the trail with someone who'd done it before. All the better if he could give her a lift to the south side of the island.

Malia wrapped the sarong around herself and went to ask him. After all, it wasn't like he had any friendships keeping him in Kalalau—and for a guy supposed to be doing research, she hadn't seen him with even so much as a notebook.

Jordan sat cross-legged in the sand, left eye closed and right cheek pressed against his arm, as if sighting down a rifle. His wrist rested in the crook of a forked tree branch protruding from the sand.

Without facing her and before Malia said a word, he spoke. "Storm's coming."

Malia shook the silly feeling from her mind and followed his gaze. She had to squint to see it, but a bank of charcoal clouds loomed above the horizon. Showers were an almost daily occurrence but seldom amounted to much during the dry season. She shrugged, figuring it not worth worrying about. "What's that you're doing with your arm?"

"Old maritime trick … I think," he said, turning to wink before pressing his face to his arm once more. He folded two fingers inward at a right angle, then shifted slightly and extended a third. "I'm measuring the height of the clouds over the horizon. The larger the gap, the closer the storm is getting. Theoretically at least."

"Where'd you learn that?"

"Remember that survival game I mentioned?" he asked, rising to stand.

Malia nodded.

"Well, someone has to figure out how to do all that stuff, right?"

Jordan, she began to realize, exuded a confidence she wasn't quite used to. She recalled the cliffs and his homemade rope, wondering if she too had underestimated him. A lone seagull cawed from afar, drawing their attention. "Maybe it'll miss us," she said.

"Unlikely. It's why the hikers cleared out. Some trail runners warned everyone yesterday."

Malia watched the clouds blooming like a bruise in shades of black and green. "Forecast said it wouldn't hit till tomorrow night, but the storm alert on my watch woke me up. Barometer's dropping fast," he said, tapping a graphic display on his watch. "Might only be an outer band, but it's early."

"Outer band? Like a hurricane?"

"Nah. If it was that serious, the rangers would have flown in to evacuate. Probably just a bad storm ... I hope."

Malia turned her back to the ocean, as if that alone would make the storm vanish. The tree line, usually polka-dotted with neon tents, sat empty. Her scalp tingled as the eeriness set in. *The missing birds? The lack of surf? No wonder there weren't any helicopter tours this morning.* The thought drew her gaze skyward, where the unscalable cliffs rekindled the claustrophobia she felt upon first seeing them all those weeks ago. A prison in a postcard.

"We should go. I was planning to ask if you wanted to hike out with me, but—"

"Too late."

"What do you mean?" Her voice peaked in urgency. "You heard that guy Fisher. It only takes five hours to hike the trail."

"Maybe for him. Took me over seven, and I'm probably faster than you. No offense."

Malia couldn't shake the feeling he might be exaggerating the situation to scare her. To pay her back for not sticking up for him with Inoke. But Jordan's attention was focused squarely on his watch—and whatever he saw had him concerned. Still, she wasn't about to give up.

"What if I run to get my stuff? I can be ready to go in an hour. I don't need much. Just a few things—"

Jordan shook his head sympathetically. "No time. Even if we got past the clay on red hill before it turned to snot, the rivers will be too high to cross."

"Rivers?"

"Well, yeah." He didn't need to elaborate. The vibration in his voice spoke volumes. It was clear Malia had absolutely no idea what she'd gotten herself into when she jumped off Kimo's boat. "If the storm is anything like the one that hit last year, then the stream at Hanakāpīʻai will be impassable. Hell," he said, shaking his head, "the whole coast might flash flood."

"So, we're trapped here?"

As if on cue, a raindrop splashed upon Malia's nose. She thought it might have been spittle from Jordan—the clouds were still so far away—but then felt another. She stretched her arms wide and waited. The purple tassels of her sarong fluttered lazily, tickling her ankle on a rising wind as minuscule droplets pecked her face. She stood stock-still, mesmerized by nature's sudden change of plans. The ocean calm gave way to chop as gusts sent their clothes flapping. Impact craters dotted the fine coral beach Malia was supposed to leave behind.

"We ought to get back. I'll think on the way," he said, and took off at a jog. "Come on."

Dejection welled within Malia as she trailed Jordan through the empty campsites, adorned only with forgotten footprints and preternatural rectangles of flattened sand, the foundations of hastily packed tents. Raindrops sizzled on the smoldering embers from an abandoned firepit. Practically every night, hikers would flock up-valley like moths through the darkening forest, drawn by the promise of fire, food, and weed. They came like frontiersman upon a trading post, ready to barter with rolling papers, half-spent cans of fuel, or a paperback they'd finished reading. But they didn't care about Malia and her friends; the hippie squatters were a novelty. Something to post about on Facebook, a story to tell at work.

How could nobody warn us?

Malia's chest tightened with a familiar heartache. She rubbed her itchy nose, allergic to the pain of being forgotten, left behind. But she couldn't allow the tears to flow. There was no time.

A turquoise ukulele lay inexplicably abandoned on the Free Table. Light and bright, she grabbed it on impulse. Something to cheer her up. Then, before strumming her first chord, something caught her eye. Large and white, poking out from beneath a tarp near the rocks.

Ruby's boat.

Malia led the way into camp, rain dripping from her hair, ankles and sarong smeared in the curry paste of mud and cinders. The rain persisted, but over the mile back to camp, they'd managed to outpace the storm's fury. They found the others encircling the table, playing cards beneath the tarp. Just another drippy morning.

Inoke looked up as Malia bent to catch her breath after the mile run. "Someone chasing you?" A toothy grin accompanied his sarcasm, which she'd come to accept was his way of being friendly. But his teasing nature vanished at the sight of Jordan. "You again," Inoke said.

"Storm's coming," Jordan said, ignoring Inoke's comment. "We gotta ready the camp."

Darren and Ruby exchanged bemused glances, then burst into laughter.

"He's not kidding," Malia said, her eyes shifting between the four seated. "The hikers already cleared out. They got a warning."

"It's probably just a bad storm, but—"

"But what?" Tiki asked Jordan, his tone a splash of cold water on the others' clowning.

"Barometer's been dropping all morning. Might be a tropical storm," Jordan said.

Tiki slapped his cards facedown as the tarp tugged on a gust of wind. Sideways rain speckled the table, briefly distracting him. He backhanded the air in Ruby's direction. "Why didn't you know about this?"

"I don't watch the news," Ruby said with a shrug.

"Fuck!" Inoke slammed the table with a fist.

"You worried about the *pakalolo?*" Darren asked.

"What you think?" Inoke glowered at Darren. "Was gonna flower soon."

"How many plants?" Tiki asked, but Inoke made a face like catching the smell of a bad fart and waved him off.

Malia took advantage of a lull in their bickering and turned to Ruby. "You can take us to Hanalei. The zodiac's big enough, right?"

Ruby nodded. He did so in a halting, unsure manner that didn't instill confidence, but Malia had to hope.

"Hold on. What's this *us?*" Inoke asked.

"There's plenty of room. I saw his boat—"

"*My* boat. Ruby works for me. And yeah, we got room. For a fee." Inoke looked at Ruby. "What you think? Supply and demand, right? Looks like demand pretty high right now."

Malia and Jordan shared a stunned look.

"Darren, you're coming. I got things I need you to do. We'll get Fish and Lily on the way out. That's five."

"Great, I'll get my stuff. Don't leave without me."

"I can take seven, maybe eight," Ruby said.

"So, all of us then. Right?" Tiki asked.

Inoke eyed Tiki with the scrutiny of a judge, scratching the scruff on his chin for several lengthy moments before coming to a decision. "Tiki, you come too. I got some guys I want you to meet."

"Cool."

"What about me?" Malia took a deep breath. "Please"

Inoke ran his tongue across his lips and grinned. "Yeah, okay, there's room. But I need to recoup my losses. Two hundred bucks. Payable at the dock. Except you." He pointed at Jordan. "Mr. Abercrombie pays triple."

Malia swallowed hard as the tarp snapped against its lines, billowing on the wind and slamming back into place, as if the tarp and trees might all come crashing down atop them. "I can't afford that," she mumbled as tears pricked the back of her eyes.

"I'm sure I can think of a way for you to earn passage," Ruby said, biting his lower lip, making Malia's entire body clench in disgust.

"Not cool," Inoke said, thrusting a finger in Ruby's face. He turned back to Malia. "One fifty or nothing; best you're getting."

"Well, I'm staying," Jordan said matter-of-factly. "I spent two weeks battling storms up in Alaska this spring. My tent will hold."

Nobody cared.

"I can't believe you," Malia said, glaring at Inoke. "This is how you treat me? What happened to your jungle 'ohana?'"

"Business is business. Nothing personal. Besides, you ain't my blood. I don't owe you nothing." Inoke laughed with a cocksure grin and flipped his cards over. "Full house. I win." He plowed a dozen sunrise seashells from the table and stuffed them in a pocket.

A hand landed upon her shoulder. "It's okay. I've got plenty of room," Jordan said. "The tent's built for expeditions."

Malia looked from Jordan to Inoke and back, scared to miss her opportunity to leave, but she couldn't help thinking of the choice her mother would have made, would have wanted *her* to make. Inoke, she now realized, was toxic. A poison soaking into the valley soil, killing the aloha spirit root by root.

"There's an ATM at the dock. I'm sure your daddy left enough in your account."

"Fuck you," Malia said. She turned to Jordan. "Thanks."

Tiki sighed and clutched his hair in obvious frustration.

"What's your problem?" Inoke asked. "I already said you can come."

An empty water jug skittered across the ground. "We gotta go. I don't like this wind," Ruby said.

Tiki stepped to Malia, causing her heart to skip. *This is it. Our sudden goodbye.* He turned his back to the others and whispered, "Don't do this. Get on the boat." She shook her head, her jaw set. "Don't worry about the money. I'll work it out with him."

"No," she said, softly at first. Then again, louder, "No way."

"Malia, you need to go. He said he'll take you."

"I don't want anything from him," she said.

"God dammit," Tiki yelled. He mashed his lips and dropped his head back in frustration. After a lengthy sigh, he said, "Then I'm staying too."

"What? Why?" Malia asked, whirling toward him.

"You're welcome to join us," Jordan said. "There's room for three."

Tiki nodded in acknowledgment of Jordan's offer but held focus on Malia. She could feel his exasperation, sense it morphing into frustration and worse. But why? She never asked him to stay. Wouldn't consider it after the way he embarrassed her. It made no sense. One minute he was pushing her away, fleeing into the jungle, now he wouldn't leave without her.

A flash of lightning paralyzed her thoughts; instantaneous thunder robbed her voice.

"Last chance," Inoke shouted, staring at Malia. "The boat or the Boy Scout. Your call."

Malia grit her teeth, knowing her best chance out of Kalalau was about to leave without her. Her stomach flipped as she wrestled to understand her decision to stay, but knew it was a choice she had to make. The right choice. If not on principle, then maybe for safety. She'd seen the growing surf, saw how small the boat was. Knew there was nowhere to come ashore if they got into trouble. Better to take her chance in the tent. She looked away, knowing she was rolling the dice like never before.

"Your funeral," Inoke said before jogging to his tent.

"Good riddance," Jordan said.

Tiki said nothing. He stood gripping the table with both hands as the others gathered their valuables and filed out. He stared through Malia, unblinking, his chest heaving. Without warning, Tiki erupted in a roar and swung his arm along the table, sending cards, water bottles, and fruit flying into the expanding puddles of mud.

Malia stood beneath the porous umbrella of a java plum as Jordan checked the tent's guy-lines and stakes. "One more for good measure," he said, and slammed a chunk of lava rock against an already-buried tent stake with surprising force.

Watching from nearby, she hugged her balled-up sleeping bag, the nylon membrane cool and soothing against her skin, and faked a trusting smile as her heart echoed Jordan's hammering. He circled around the front of the tent and touched her shoulder as he passed. "Don't worry. I pitched it under the oldest trees around. I'm sure they've seen worse storms than this."

Malia nodded nervously, then all but burrowed her rain-streaked face into the pillowy bag. Her pangs of doubt had nothing to do with the tent's placement. Nor did they involve Jordan, though it was essentially a stranger's tent she'd be sheltering in. No, her concern was Tiki. Namely, the way he stared at her after Inoke left. His eyes, as taut and piercing as a laser, burned with an unprovoked, incomprehensible resentment. It made no sense. Was it because she didn't leave? Sure, it was a rash decision—one Malia hoped she wouldn't soon regret—

but why should Tiki care what she did? Or was he angry because she was at the beach with Jordan? No. His temper didn't flare until she decided to stay … when he felt obliged to do the same. Malia tensed at the thought of Tiki appointing himself her reluctant protector. Of all the things she'd dreamed of him doing to her body, guarding it wasn't one of them.

I should have never kissed him.

But was that really the problem? She'd heard of guys acting like lost puppy dogs before, the kind you feed once and can never shake free. But Tiki? He didn't seem the type.

Jordan unzipped the tent and called her over. She gave the largely abandoned camp an anxious look, hoping it wouldn't soon be in shambles. She wanted to believe she'd be safe in the tent, but the sight of the playing cards laying in the mud made her wonder if the tight confines wouldn't pluck Tiki's strained nerves even harder.

Malia crawled into the tunnel-shaped shelter, followed by Tiki. Jordan backed in last and sat cross-legged at the head, encouraging his guests to stretch out. He wore the smile of someone excited to show off his new apartment. "I pitched it into the wind. Assuming it blows from the sea—"

"How can you tell? The ocean's a mile away," Malia asked.

"Digital compass." Jordan tapped his watch.

"Winds swirl in a tropical storm," Tiki said, his tone soaked in the annoyance of someone tired of stating the obvious.

Jordan's upper lip curled into a politician's grin. "We'll be fine." He reached between Malia and Tiki and unzipped a vent in the wall behind them. The tent inflated briefly, then settled with a sigh. Fresh air flowed across Malia's clammy skin, but did nothing to ease the suffocating tension.

She huddled tight, occupying as little space as possible, in deference to the larger men, but also out of respect for Jordan's tidily organized belongings. His clothes lay folded beside her, seemingly sorted by warmth. Multiple pairs of shorts, pants, shirts, and underwear. Brands she'd never heard of with reinforced patches and waterproof zippers, like those the survival experts wore on television. An array of electronics in oversized Ziplocs lay spread along the back wall. She spotted an iPhone, laptop, microphone, and several USB battery packs amongst the pads and pens.

"What's that?" Malia pointed at a neon-yellow chunk of plastic attached to a lanyard.

"Locator beacon." Jordan adopted the silvery voice of an infomercial narrator talking about asbestos. "If you or your loved ones are caught in a storm, find a clear view of the sky and send an SOS."

Tiki snorted. "We call it yuppie 911. No offense."

"Boss wanted me to take a sat phone, but those things weigh a ton. The beacon was a compromise."

"Would it even work out here?" Malia asked, then turned toward the sound of Tiki's foot twitching against the seam of a sleeping pad, scraping back and forth.

"On the beach it should. Just needs a clear view of the southern sky. But this close to the equator ..." He raised his palms in a shrug.

Malia placed a heavy hand on Tiki's ankle. "Can you stop? That scratching is gonna drive me crazy." He startled ever so slightly, as if woken from a daze, then folded his foot beneath his other leg. A gust of wind buffeted the tent, pelting it with a thunderous downpour.

The trio stared at the ceiling, wide-eyed and silent, in mutual awe. Malia was no stranger to torrential rains, neither at home in Honolulu nor here in Kalalau, but the intensity of the current squall reminded her of those early trips through the car wash as a kid. How she used to hide in the footwell, convinced the blasting water and monstrous brushes would shatter the windows, claw through the roof, and eat her alive. And how her dad always promised she'd make it out the other end.

She dragged a shaky finger along the skin of the tent which, unlike the glass and steel of her father's Honda, bowed under the lightest touch. The howling wind italicized the narrow shelter as rain pummeled the fabric mere inches overhead. The swelling roar rendered conversation impossible; she could scarcely hear the voices within her, shouting and doubting such a flimsy structure was any match for a tropical storm.

At least we're dry.

"I've got a dozen guy-lines anchoring it. She'll hold," Jordan hollered over the din as though reading her thoughts. Suddenly, something slammed against the tent roof. The monstrous shadow suggested massive talons. It scratched at the tent as if trying to rip its way in. Then it vanished, blown into the ether.

Malia felt the color drain from her as she strained to resume breathing.

"Just a palm frond," Jordan shouted. He shifted closer so as not to yell. "We'll be fine. Trust me."

She wanted to, but how? This wasn't her father swearing her safety. It was Jordan. A stranger resembling a little boy on his first backyard adventure, all innocence and smiles. The disturbing dejection he wore since arriving was gone, replaced with an excitement that only intensified with every gust. Whereas Malia sat praying a fallen tree didn't crush them where they lay, Jordan wowed with awe at the sound of every snapping branch.

Stormy darkness settled over them as the heart of the storm roared around them. She scanned the shadows of the veiled tent, hoping someone had thought to grab some food, when she spotted Tiki glaring at her. She tried ignoring him, but the effort was exhausting. After several excruciating moments, she turned to him and made a face: *What?*

"You shouldn't have stayed."

"And you should have left," Malia replied as a crack of lightning strobed the tent. In that moment, Tiki's eyes flashed toward Jordan and back to her. Did he not trust her alone with him? Is *that* why he stayed? Or was he jealous? She wanted to mouth the question, but Tiki abruptly rolled his back to her in a snit.

And I'm the one who's too young?

She tried making sense of their predicament but struggled to corral her thoughts as the world outside their cocoon tore itself to shreds. Malia closed her eyes, wishing it away, hoping the tent would hold, but there was no escaping the ruckus painting visions in her mind. Portraits of trees and limbs thudding against the soggy ground; of tarps and tents cracking like whips; of torrents of rain spilling over the banks of their taro ponds, cascading into camp.

Despite the sticky mugginess, Malia coiled within her sleeping bag, twisting it around her legs and arms and in search of comfort. Protection. Anything to armor her as well as that old Honda did.

CHAPTER 15
NEW RULES

Malia woke, gasping for air in the oven-like confines of the tent. Sweat soaked her scalp. The nylon sleeping bag lay glued to her skin. Her muscles ached, yet after taking quick inventory of her limbs and vitals, she closed her eyes and thanked the heavens. *I'm alive.*

How much time had passed, she didn't care. One minute Jordan sat extolling the merits of his Swedish-made tent, sometime later she imagined the heaviness of an arm draped across her. In her sleep, she welcomed the security of that heft, the comfort it brought. Even if only in a dream. But now she was awake, and the squeeze of that protective embrace hadn't vanished. Malia rolled just enough to see over her shoulder and bit down on her lip to stifle a gasp. Tiki, still asleep and curled in behind her, had his arm across her side, hand dangling near her ribs. His thumb brushed the underside of her breast.

So, this is how it feels to wake up next to someone.

Malia sighed with bewildered contentment and sank into his cuddle, choosing if only for a moment to ignore the voice of reason shouting in her head. She didn't care about intent, or how it might confuse their relationship, or whether or not this moment signaled the start of that very something she'd been craving. She survived a tropical storm. She deserved this, this feeling of safety. Protection. With him. Ever since their walk along the campground trail, Tiki sheltering her tight against him, she'd craved more. More of his scent, his strength. His affection and attention. She cozied herself against his warmth, losing herself in the wonder of what it would be like waking up beside him every day. But as she lay there, motionless beneath his arm, she grew ever more certain he had a girlfriend. His spooning in behind her had to have been a habit born of living with a lover—and she, merely a stray utensil tossed into the wrong drawer. Malia aimed to put the thought from her mind, to instead focus on this stolen gift of happenstance.

Then she felt it, hard against her backside.

She wanted only to snuggle against him, to relish the moment, but couldn't wipe the thought of his erection from her mind. She shifted slowly, easing some space between them. Tiki yawned and shifted his hand to her hip, halting her movement. A spark ran though her as his unconscious grasp pulled her close.

We can't, she thought, wanting to avoid the embarrassment of him waking up to realize he'd been caressing someone he'd already twice rejected.

Malia squirmed away, causing his hand to gracelessly fall upon the mat as she turned to face him. Tiki came to slowly, perplexed, like someone drugged and dragged to unknown whereabouts. He blinked the sleep away, squinting at the sunlight penetrating the tent. With a yawn, he adjusted the bulge in his shorts. He turned in time to see Malia barely constrain her giggle. Recognition seemed to wash over him, coloring him as red as a pomegranate. "I-I'm sorry. I was sleeping."

"Not all of you," she said, her lips curling into a vampish grin. Though the closest thing to brothers she had were Jenna's family, Hollywood had taught her plenty about morning wood.

"It wasn't you. I swear."

"Gee, thanks."

"No. That's not what I meant—"

"Uh-huh, sure," she teased. Malia knew it was uncontrollable but enjoyed seeing him squirm.

He shook his head good-naturedly and sat up. But as Tiki looked about the tent—Jordan was nowhere to be seen—she could see the moment fading, swept clean by the recollection of what they'd endured. Recalling his irritation over her decision to stay, Malia crawled through the interior door to the vestibule and pulled on her slippers. Other than a watery streak on the ground cloth, the tent was miraculously dry. Recalling the tempest that hammered the tent, she braced for the worst and unzipped the exterior door, only to be assailed by millions of glistening water droplets as bright as a death ray. Malia shielded her eyes and stood, blinded by the sunlight reflecting from every surface.

She didn't need her eyes to gauge the destruction. The soaked-clay stench of mud and compost, of pooling campfire grease and water-logged books told the tale. With each step, her feet sank into the mire, wringing a gallon of rainwater from the valley floor. Their carefully strung tarps now dangled from the boughs of trees, twisted and torn. Rain-carved ruts, ankle-deep and flowing unabated, crisscrossed the camp. Darren's tent lay deflated and limp, the poles snapped in thirds. In the distance she could see that Inoke's storage tent, where he cured his bud, didn't fare much better. A fallen palm split it in two; a week later and he'd have lost an entire harvest.

Malia scanned the area where she'd pitched her tent. The wind-whipped jungle barely aligned with her memory of the place, as if the storm were a prankster rearranging furniture while she were away. She swatted a mosquito from her forehead and spotted her blue ukulele poking from beneath a fallen palm frond, but everything else had vanished. Her clothesline, her hoodie, and worst of all, her tent. Malia released a hoarse cry and gazed skyward. And that's when she saw it. Seemingly intact, but upside down in a tree. Her tent, its half dozen stakes no match for the storm's wrath. She gulped the dank forest air as a chill danced along her spine; if not for Jordan, she'd have been inside when it took off.

She stared up at the tent with its unzipped door dangling like the tongue of a panting dog, wondering how to get it down, when something crumpled underfoot. There, caked in mud but otherwise unmarred, was the photo of her and her mother, neon plastic spoons aloft above their icy birthday tradition. The sight of it brought a flash of relief—shoved aside a moment later by a surge of panic.

"Where's the other one?"

A pang stabbed at her heart. "Oh no, oh no," she said, repeating it over and over in sync with her pounding heart, fearing the one possession she couldn't bear to live without had disappeared. Malia scanned the ground, her eyes flicking every which way in alarm. She swept aside branches and heaved yellowed, wind-whipped fronds from her path, frantically searching. To no avail.

The photo of her mother amongst her Kalalau friends. The only copy. How many nights had Malia stared into their eyes, wondering which, if any of them, were her father? "How could I forget to take it?" Bile stung the back of her throat as a staggering sense of abandonment squeezed at her core. She'd never met her father, only knew he was from California, yet despite all the questions and uncertainty, that photo was proof of her existence. That she had come from somewhere. But with her mother dead and that visual evidence gone, Malia felt cut loose, floating out to sea in a fog of anonymity. "What was I thinking?"

"You weren't," Tiki said as he circled past. He perched himself atop a boulder near the flooded campfire, his feet folded uncharacteristically beneath him as if the ground were *kapu*. Malia opened her mouth to shout, to drill understanding into him until he grasped what she'd lost. "Don't worry. I'll help you get it down," he said, softening in sympathy but oblivious to her true pain.

Before she could respond, Jordan pushed through a thicket of ferns and dumped an armload of bruised bananas on the ground. "Well, the garden's trashed. We can salvage some fruit, but the taro's flattened and tomatoes are goners."

Tiki smacked the side of the boulder. "Fuck!"

Malia and Jordan exchanged a look. Jordan shrugged it off, but Malia couldn't. She wanted to shout too. Or cry. Why should Tiki be the only one who got to act upset? Sure, it was her idea to stay. And for some reason, he followed her lead. But they were safe. They'd find food. Rebuild. Hike out or flag down a boat or helicopter. After all, Malia thought, Search and Rescue would definitely check to ensure no tourists were stranded.

"Look at us." Tiki swung his arms, gesturing around the ruins. "Look at the camp. All this water. The mud. The road to Hanalei's probably out. Landslides, flash floods. This corner of Kaua'i barely stays open after a normal storm. The rivers will be impassable, the trail a death trap—"

"It's not all bad," Jordan said.

"You hear yourself? With your fancy tent, talking Malia into staying. Causing me to have to—"

"Hey, don't blame me for you getting stuck here too."

Tiki brushed her off, then turned to Jordan, who was already busy stacking stray items from camp atop a log. "What are you smiling at?"

"Just thinking how many people would kill to have this place to themselves."

"Bugger off." Tiki leaned his furrowed brow in his right hand. Then, after several tense moments, he glared at Jordan and said, "We shoulda let Inoke run you out when we had the chance. Then we wouldn't have—"

"Stop it. It's not his fault—" Malia cut herself short upon seeing Tiki jump to his feet, his stance wide and hands up in defense. He sidestepped his way behind the boulder as if preparing to be charged by a wild animal. She turned to see Jordan holding a knife at least ten inches long from handle to tip. The blade was as black as coal, with a hooked end and the serrated bite of a barracuda. The kind of knife that could saw through bone as easily as it could split a coconut.

"Whoa, whoa. Calm down." Tiki pushed against the air in front of him as Jordan approached, locked in a fifty-yard stare, whispering an indecipherable plot as his fingers drummed against the knife grip. Tiki bent quickly, picking up a broken tent pole from the ground and brandishing it in defensive posture. "It's cool, man. I'm just frustrated. I didn't mean nothing by it."

"Jordan, don't!" Malia yelled.

Jordan snapped to and looked from Malia to Tiki and back, appearing as confused as someone emerging from a surprise spell of hypnosis. "What?" he asked, and then, seeing Tiki wielding the pole, realized the cause of their alarm. "Oh, the knife." He let out a boisterous laugh. "Sorry. I tend to tunnel a bit when I get an idea. A necessity when working in a busy office."

Before Malia could realize his intent, Jordan bent alongside a fallen tree, splintered at the trunk, and sawed the log free. The knife made frighteningly quick work of the task.

"Hey, Malia. You mind pacing out the distance between those trees?" Jordan said, pointing to two narrow kukui trees nearby. Unsure of his intent, she shrugged and did as asked. She walked a straight path between the trees, counting her steps, heel to toe. "Twelve."

He raised onto his toes and looked across to Malia. "Size seven?"

"Huh? Oh, my feet? Size six."

Jordan cracked a slight smile. "Cool. Thanks." He laid the knife down on the freshly cut log and flipped it end over end, counting as he went, then cut again. "Left it long, for overlap. In case we want to add on." He dragged the log to another downed tree of similar size and cut a twin. "Can you grab the cord from my tent? It's in the vestibule."

Malia looked to Tiki, seeking his assent for reasons she couldn't quite state. Allegiance? Guilt? He fluttered a hand at her, whether to encourage her to leave him alone or to bat away the idea of repairing the camp, she couldn't tell. Regardless, it wasn't in Malia's nature to sit idle while others worked around her. She retrieved the homemade rope and tested it with a yank. The strength of the braid surprised her.

Jordan dragged the logs to the trees she paced out and held their ends up. He measured the width of the tree with the knife, which had a ruler etched into the blade, then sawed a notch from each log. He lifted them into position, sandwiching them around the tree. Facing Malia, he instructed, "Hold them up like this. They're not heavy." She cradled the logs in her arms as Jordan tied them in place.

"You can let go."

Malia relaxed her grip ounce by ounce, expecting the logs to fall, but they didn't budge.

"Just gotta lash the other end in place. Then we'll have a place to sit while we plan the layout."

"Layout?"

"For the new camp," Jordan said, kicking aside the notch of wood he'd cut free. Malia picked it up and rubbed her fingers across the grooves of its fresh-cut edge. She inhaled the sawdust aroma, filling her lungs with birdhouse memories. Her dad in his denim carpenter's apron, Malia in the safety goggles too big for her ten-year-old face. Their first father-daughter project after the adoption was official. Myna birds moved in days later, waking Malia with their morning song. So happy they were, she and the birds. Them in their new home, and Malia with the satisfaction of having helped build it.

Jordan lashed the other end of the logs to the tree and backed away to admire his handiwork. "Ladies first," he said.

Malia looked at the bench, as suspicious as she was impressed. She ran her palm across the smooth bark, noting how perfectly the logs fit together, with nary a gap between them.

"Go on. It won't fall." Pride danced in Jordan's excited eyes. "Promise."

Malia eased herself down, thinking of those birds taking their first hesitant step through the hole she'd drilled all those years ago. Building the bench couldn't have taken fifteen minutes, tops, she noticed. Amazing.

"I'll shave it flat once we get the food situation settled."

She looked to Tiki, hoping he might come sit next to her. But he only turned away, acting indignant. "I like it," she said. Then, sensing it wasn't enough, she added, "It's perfect."

"Couldn't have done it without you," Jordan said, then twirled the knife on his index finger like a gunslinger before sheathing it alongside his hip.

By the time Malia tied a knot in the bulging trash bag, they'd been at it for hours. Dusk was closing in and every inch of her ached. Scrapes and blisters marred her hands, and the mud-caked sarong clung to her legs like damp denim. But absolute exhaustion wasn't what stopped her cold. Nor was it the mass of waterlogged garbage trailing like an anchor behind her.

She'd gone back and forth between her tent, the camp, and the wreckage of the garden a hundred times that afternoon. Inspired by

Jordan's vision for a new and better camp, she darted like a humming-bird between flower-laden balconies, swooping from one task to the next. While she salvaged fruit, Jordan sawed a thicket of bamboo. As she piled fallen palm fronds, he dredged the firepit. And while Malia cleaned out the flooded tents of those who deserted them, Jordan constructed a camp to call home.

That first bench he lashed together hours earlier now faced another across the new firepit, dug out and encircled high with a wind shield of lava rock. The area they so laughingly called the library now boasted an improved table, modest shelving, and a bamboo enclosure in the shape of a lean-to. And somehow, on top of all that, Jordan found time to balance each of the sodden books atop newly strung clotheslines, their pages fanned out to dry.

Malia gazed upon the camp, speechless, refusing to budge an inch lest the vision shatter. Finally, thanks to the storm and their tireless toil, the camp approached the expectations set by her mother's doe-eyed recollections. The shambles, the bullshit, all of it gone. Replaced by something befitting the indelible impression this place had left on her mother.

"Not bad for a day's work, huh?" Jordan called out, breaking her spell.

"It's a-amazing," she stammered, watching him wince as he stretched his back, rubbing his side. A bead of sweat coursed its way down his chest, disappearing into his waistband.

"Well, I wouldn't go that far. Still gotta finish the roof. And the shelves need straightening. But it's serviceable."

Malia could only look on in admiration—of the camp, of him.

"Here," Jordan said, handing her a stainless bottle. "You earned it." She took a swig of water. It was warm but refreshing. She downed half the bottle then offered it back, but Jordan refused. She turned to offer the rest to Tiki, forgetting she hadn't seen him in hours.

"Is Tiki—"

"Went for a walk." Then, in reaction to Malia's frown, he added with a what-can-you-do shrug, "He helped out a bit."

Malia nodded, withholding her judgment. But whether or not Jordan knew the full story between Malia and Tiki or was just being charitable in his assessment of Tiki's lack of help, she couldn't tell. Turning away, she noticed her gathered fruit arranged in a bowl. A centerpiece atop their new table. The drama of the storm and her exhaustion mingled with that simple touch of home was nearly too much to shoulder. Memories of a day long ago pricked her eyes, but she didn't weep. She lacked the energy.

"I'm gonna rinse off and hit the hay. Tomorrow, I'll build some fish traps. Maybe some snares too. See if we can't get some meat."

Malia was so absorbed in her memories, it barely registered when he offered to take the trash with him on his way to the beach. She handed it over without a word, transfixed by the promise of having the new-and-improved camp to herself, even if only for a few minutes. It was so clean, even the air seemed refreshed with the scent of moss and the faint whiff of sea salt. But despite her exhaustion, the pull of the fruit bowl proved irresistible. She dragged a finger around the edge of the calabash, smiling at its wobble, recalling rainy days spent around the kitchen table at home. Her mother, always with a cup of jasmine tea and crossword. Malia with her favorite Minnie Mouse glass of strawberry Quik, a pad, and flip-top box of Crayolas. Time and again she tried drawing the family fruit bowl, only to be disappointed by the unremarkable results. Oranges, plums, and passionfruit. "They're just circles," she complained, balling up her artwork. "They all look the same."

"Why don't you try this side?" her mother said and spun the bowl, rotating a banana and strawberries into view one stormy afternoon years ago. "See, honey," she said later that day while hanging Malia's coloring on the refrigerator. "Sometimes we just need a little help to see things differently."

Malia looked about the camp, grinning at how such a simple lesson could be so easily forgotten—and how her mother's wisdom never ceased to turn up when she least expected it. "Guess I'm not past needing that help," Malia said to herself. At long last, she had the images she'd imprint on her memory, the visions she'd recall years later, in her own future daydreams, of a tidy, welcoming camp she called home.

The next morning, Malia found Jordan sitting cross-legged in the dirt, surrounded by a pile of palm fronds and twigs. Tiki perched atop his boulder nearby, wearing the look of someone refusing to give Jordan the satisfaction of using the furniture.

"What's that?" she asked after saying her good mornings.

"Fish trap. There's hot water for coffee," Jordan said, pointing. "Found some instant in Darren's tent."

That there was coffee was no big deal. They'd rarely gone without. But the simple act of retrieving a clean mug from actual shelving lent an unexpected sophistication to the moment. Malia never would have imagined a tropical storm could be a blessing, but not twenty-four hours later, the camp was better than ever—and she was on the upswing as well.

She dipped a mug in the pot, spooned in some coffee crystals, and gave it a swirl. All the while, she studied Jordan's activity with the fascination of an anthropologist studying a primitive culture.

Using his thumbnail, Jordan split the palm leaves lengthwise into narrow strips, then spread them on the ground several inches apart. He sliced small buttonholes into each and wove the sticks through the holes, over and under, perpendicular to the fronds, in a checkerboard pattern.

"Looks like a net," Malia said. "I thought you were making a trap."

"I am." He rolled it into a cylinder. "It's essentially a minnow trap, but bigger. For freshwater prawns."

Tiki snorted, drawing a cross look from Malia.

Jordan gathered the sticks and moved to sit beside her. He stabbed them one by one through the webbing nearest the mouth of the trap at an inward angle. "These will keep the fish from escaping," he explained.

She ran her fingers across the lattice, expecting it to buckle, but it held strong. *I should have known,* she thought, watching him clamp the tail of the trap shut like someone who'd done it a hundred times.

"Shame we don't know where Inoke's friend stashed his rods," Tiki said, emerging from his stupor.

"Wouldn't help. Stream's too muddy for fish to see the lure," Jordan said, not looking up from his task.

"I meant for the ocean. I've seen some *ulua* near the rocks. Goat fish too."

Jordan appeared intrigued by the suggestion. If for no other reason, Malia believed, than for a chance to engage Tiki. "I was planning on spear-fishing once the waters calmed, but that'd be even better. You got any ideas where they camped?"

Tiki sighed. "Not a clue."

"I can look for it," Malia offered.

Tiki snorted. "How? By wandering the valley? You'll never find it."

Malia shot Tiki a dirty look. "At least I'm trying to help," she said under her breath.

Jordan cleared his throat. "Hate to say it, but Tiki's probably right. Best we get the traps placed. Then I'll rig up some snares. See if I can't catch us a goat."

"You got a permit?" Tiki asked.

Malia and Jordan turned to one another in surprise, then burst into laughter. She expected Tiki to join in—after all, nothing they did was technically legal—but Tiki's seriousness didn't waver.

"What? You gonna narc on us?" Jordan said with a chuckle.

A glint of insult flashed across Tiki's face as he stood and shouldered his bag. "Aw, I'm just takin' the piss. Good luck with the trap."

"Where you going?" Malia asked, wishing she could take back the laugh if it meant he'd stay.

"Gonna look for some fruit—"

"I've already picked the garden clean," Malia said.

"Yeah, I know," he said without slowing his stride.

Malia stared after Tiki for some time, cradling her coffee for comfort, wondering where he went every day—and why he never invited her. She replayed the prior hour in her mind, searching for any hint of him wanting to be alone with her, but reading him was as impossible as reading the leaves of a tea bag. One thing was certain, though. Her thirst for him was proving nearly as distracting as her hunger for food.

"Whatcha think?" Jordan asked, setting the finished trap in her lap.

"What? Oh," she said, picking it up. "It's, um, light."

"The prawns, or fish if we're lucky, will swim through this end," he said, pointing. "And get stuck inside the wider part. It's like a funnel."

Malia turned the trap end over end, puzzling over Tiki's daily walks. He always took his bag—but she'd never even seen him open it. But more than that, she thought of their time in the tent yesterday morning. His arm over her. The warmth of his body against hers. She knew it was foolish, but she wanted to believe him awake, desiring to hold her as much as she craved to be held.

Jordan continued his explanation. "They shouldn't be able to find the narrow exit. Especially against the current. Just gotta attach some cord. Figure a few hours in the water ought to be good."

Malia gulped her coffee down, surprised by the sudden promise of food. "You think we'll have prawns for dinner?"

"Yep. What do you think I ate those first few nights before I was allowed in camp?" Jordan winked, then started off down the trail, toward the stream. Malia followed in silence to the water, where Jordan tied one end of the cord to a tree and the other to the center of the trap.

"My dad used to have a trap like this, back in Delaware. His was metal, of course. He'd toss it in the estuary on the incoming tide to catch bait fish. We'd yank it six hours later." Jordan smiled at the memory. "There'd be forty or fifty fish in there sometimes. Too bad we don't have any Wonder Bread. They love that stuff."

"So, is that where you learned all this? From your dad?"

Jordan looped the rope around a tree. "Nah, he left when I was ten. It's amazing what you can teach yourself from books."

"I'm sorry."

Jordan shrugged. "What about you? Your pops take you camping and stuff? That why you're out here?"

Malia snorted. "Definitely not. His idea of roughing it is staying at a Best Western. Mom said she used to be outdoorsy, but I never saw it." No sooner had she answered than she felt the dull lifelong ache of having never met her birth father. Her mother had always taken credit for Malia's so-called free spirit, saying she got it from her. *Along with your good looks*, she'd add, delivered with a playful hip-bump. But which of her qualities were owed the stranger who helped make her? What might she have learned from the man whose genes she shared? Would he have taught Malia how to fish or make fire? Did he know how to build a shelter of bamboo or pluck prawns from a stream? Would her life at Kalalau been easier if she'd known him? If she hadn't wound up the daughter of a big city doctor?

The muddy water cascaded thick and brown over a fallen log, as unclear as the life she tried imagining. She wondered if that "cute boy" had ever loved her mother; if he'd have still gone home to California if he had known Christina was pregnant? A dangerous game, asking herself all those what-ifs, but Malia couldn't stop her slide. Marriage? Her mother's career? Malia's entire life would have changed.

Would we have stayed in Hawai'i?

Would he have done the grocery shopping?

Would he have gone to the store that day in Mom's place?

Malia chewed her lip as her stomach plunged into a double boiler of intrigue and repulsion. For over a year, she'd believed—even said as much—that she'd sacrifice anything to have her mother back. A figure of speech, perhaps, but never before had she considered what that entailed. She recalled the suffering in her father's eyes when she told him it should have been him in that car wreck. Did she mean it? Was she really the type of person who said such things?

"I've always loved the outdoors. Hiking, climbing, kayaking, anything. In college, I used to nag my swim coach to let us train in the lake near campus." Jordan laughed at the memory. "But games were always a close second. Super Nintendo, PlayStation. That's what's so great about the one I'm designing. I finally found a way to blend my passions."

"Uh-huh," Malia said, distracted by her regrets. Her only experience with video games was visiting a high school friend's house, only to sit there, bored, while he shot aliens and yelled into his headset. "I mean, no offense, but games are kind of a waste."

"A waste? Tell that to the tens of thousands of people making them. Gaming generates over two hundred billion dollars a year. There's hardly a person on Earth who doesn't play these days."

"I don't."

"Congratulations. Your trophy's in the mail," he spat sarcastically, and yanked the knot tight against the trap. He reared back and flung the basket into the water, farther than necessary.

Malia watched the trap sink, taken aback and unsure what to say. She hadn't expected him to be so sensitive.

"People are always like, 'Film is art. It matters.' Big deal. The gaming industry eats Hollywood's lunch."

"Guess I just thought they were for kids. I didn't realize how big it was."

"It's fine. Comments like that just tick me off, that's all. Take my game, *Driftwood*, for example. I've been wanting to make it for years. But now I got this whole studio relying on me. People with families, bills to pay. They're trusting my vision. It's a huge gamble. And yet there's always people coming up to me, saying shit like, 'Oh, you work in gaming. My kid loves games. He should come help you.' As if we just sit around playing *Minecraft* all day."

"So, why did you stay? Not to be nosy, but I haven't seen you doing much research. And it sounds like you could have afforded the boat ride."

Jordan threw his arms up in frustration. "Money? Really? What is it with you women?" He stomped several steps away in frustration, kicking up the stench of drying mud.

You women? Malia tried not to take it personally, figuring she must have touched a nerve—and that her earlier guess of him having broken up with someone was probably right.

A veil of resignation descended over Jordan. "It's a means to an end. This stuff around camp the past two days? The building, the survival skills. That's what I love. I thought after the game shipped, I might move to Montana. Put the city behind me. But a simple life doesn't come easy. Not when you have student loans to pay. In America, it's almost like the more off the grid you want to be, the more money you need. And don't get me started on working for the Park Service or some feel-good conservation job—"

"What's wrong with that? I plan to go into conservation," she said, not mentioning that her mother's ecology research was what brought her to Kaua'i twenty years prior.

"Better marry rich then. Or, better yet, hope for an early inheritance. Society's spoken: park rangers, naturalists, environmentalists—only suckers go into those jobs."

"They're important—"

"You're not listening. Of course, they're important—"

"And I'm not a sucker," she said, crossing her arms.

"Well, unless you want to be broke your whole life, forget it. They don't pay. And there's the rub. You gotta make your money elsewhere first. Probably abusing the very land you want to save." Jordan kicked a rock into the stream. "But let's say you follow through. By the time you're ready to make the jump, you'll be too old or too soft to be of any use out in the wild."

"Sounds like you got it all figured out. Got everything you wanted," Malia said.

If he heard her, he didn't show it. Jordan stared at the stream, muttering beneath his breath. "Broke and lonely, or rich and miserable. Take your pick."

***

Smoke spiraled into the still air as the ukulele's dulcet notes led a sizzling accompaniment to the fire's crackle and pop. Malia leaned into the bamboo backrest, as untroubled as smooth jazz, strumming once-forgotten chords as she awaited dinner on the third night after the storm.

A dozen freshwater prawns, some nearly the size of her hand, lay skewered atop the grill. That Jordan's trap managed to feed them wasn't nearly as surprising as his ability to scrounge up the makings of a chili-citrus marinade.

She closed her eyes and hummed as she played, allowing the tangy aromas to carry her back to Oʻahu, to barbecues at Makapuu Park with family and friends, to heaping piles of *kālua* pork and teriyaki chicken, coconut rice and mac salad. The few prawns they had couldn't hope to satisfy her hunger, not like those remembered gatherings where she'd always eaten till she burst, but there was nowhere she'd rather be. She finally had the tranquility she sought—and wasn't about to let anything sour her final days in the valley.

Tiki approached dragging a java plum limb, its branches raking the ground behind him. He knelt to saw it into firewood with Jordan's survival knife, then looked up sporting a puckish smirk. "Too bad plums aren't in season." He poked a prawn with the knife as though it might bite and said, "I hear their seeds are antidiarrheal." Jordan looked up, at first without reaction, but when Malia giggled at Tiki's teasing, Jordan immediately joined in. A welcome sign the prior days' tension was behind them.

"Ha-ha, wiseass," Jordan said in jest. "Keep it up and there'll be no dinner for you."

"Somebody say dinner?"

Malia's stomach knotted as Darren stepped from the shadowy approach to camp. She exchanged furtive glances with Tiki and Jordan, whose corduroy brows mirrored her own.

Darren's legs and hands were streaked with mud, his arms a mesh of scratches. He looked exhausted, but otherwise in good spirits. "Whoa. I like what you've done with the place. Some serious Swiss Family Robinson level shit." Malia watched with an unsettling mix of pride and disappointment as Darren took in the camp's table, benches, and shelter. The construction wasn't perfect. Much sagged, the shelves weren't perfectly square, but it held—and it was theirs. Just as Malia had dreamed it could be. But if she had her way, she'd have been long gone before Darren, Inoke, or any of the others threatened to muck it up.

"You did all this in what? Three or four days? Damn, Tiki. I gotta say, after hearing about your raft, I didn't think you had it in you."

Tiki pushed an awkward hand through his hair. "Actually, it was Jordan."

"Get the fuck outta here. For real?"

"Tiki and Malia helped," Jordan said.

Darren scrunched his face as he inventoried the new configuration, causing Malia to say, "We took down your tent. Hope you don't mind."

"It stank," Jordan spat.

"That so?" Darren tossed his pack on the table, muddying a spot Malia had just cleaned. She sat bone straight as he stalked the camp, prodding the furniture, tugging the lines, giving everything a shake and a rattle. A sadistic smirk accompanied his tour, like a drill sergeant intent on finding something to fault. He stopped near the fire and plucked a prawn dangling loose from a skewer's end. He blew it cool and tossed it into his mouth. Chewing with a smile, Darren reached for another when Jordan grabbed his wrist. "One is all you get."

"What do you mean?"

"There's not enough."

Darren wrested his hand free. "Dude, lay off. I just spent all fucking day picking my way across a landslide—"

"A landslide?" Malia interrupted. "I was gonna hike out soon. School starts next week."

"You?" He snorted derisively. "No chance. I've been hiking this trail for years and barely made it. Unless you've got a death wish, you'll have to catch a ride with Ruby."

Malia's spirit collapsed as the word *landslide* caught in her throat like a shrimp tail. Landslides were common on the islands after heavy rains, but always elsewhere, no more than a detour on the way to school or the beach. But there was no detouring around a fractured cliffside. She stared at the blood-laced scratches and bruises on Darren's legs, envisioning a brown scar on the emerald *pali*. As if Mother Nature herself scooped at a mint-frosted cake, the trail disappearing within a devil's food canyon. Malia sank into the bench, perspiration pimpling her cheeks. Finally, after weeks of highs and lows, she'd helped forge the Kalalau of her dreams. And it was the storm that made it possible. She hated to think she might be once again reliant on Inoke and Ruby, especially after the way they acted when fleeing. But she had to stay positive. After all, she couldn't think of a better place to be trapped than here. So long as Darren didn't ruin it.

"When are Inoke and Ruby coming with the boat?" Malia asked.

Darren shrugged. "I dunno. Maybe a day, maybe five. Anyway, I'm starving," Darren said. "Haven't eaten since leaving Kapa'a."

"Then you should have brought some food," Jordan said. "Isn't that what you told me?"

Darren rolled his eyes. "Whatever. I'm getting some fruit."

Jordan crossed his arms and puffed his chest, his face set in stone. "Garden's off-limits. We're rationing. You can have some rice and coffee since it was in your tent."

"You went through my stuff?"

Malia tensed as Tiki approached the two men, whether to choose sides or play referee, she wasn't sure. Nor could she predict where his allegiance lay, if he had any. Tiki lifted the skewers from the grill where they'd begun to char. He divided them between three plates.

"So, everyone eats but me?" Darren asked, scowling.

"We earned it," Jordan said. He thanked Tiki for his plate and circled around the fire to sit. He faced the group and eyed each of them one by one, commanding their attention. "I've given a lot of thought to how the camp needs to be run. I put off saying anything, but since Darren has shown back up unannounced—"

"Hey, man, I was here before you—"

"And you left," Malia interrupted. Then, under her breath added, "Hardly did anything anyway." Darren shot her an ugly look and Malia flipped him off.

"She's right," Jordan said. "But that's gonna change. Everyone take a seat."

Malia and Tiki picked up their plates and sat opposite one another. Darren made like he'd join them, then snorted and leaned against a tree several yards away. Jordan rolled his eyes, but didn't comment.

"I don't care how the camp was run in the past. From now on, there are rules," Jordan began.

"What kind of rules?" Darren asked, his hoarse voice streaked in disgust.

"For starters: no work, no eat. Firewood, fishing, gardening, cleaning, there's always stuff to do. If you can't think of something, ask. No more lounging around, getting high all day, letting other people to pick up the slack."

"I worked," Darren protested.

"Good. Then we shouldn't have any problems. Another thing is food. It needs to be hung."

"Man, this ain't Montana," Darren said. "There's no bears."

"You have any idea how much mouse shit we had to pick out of the rice?" Malia stifled a laugh. It was only three tiny pellets, but she wouldn't stop Jordan from driving the point home. "Food gets hung. Got it?"

Nobody said anything.

"Tiki? Understood?"

"Aye, aye, captain my captain," he said, then pulled a prawn from the skewer with his teeth.

"Malia?"

"No problem here."

Jordan arched his eyebrows at Darren, awaiting an answer.

"Man, I didn't risk my life getting here so some wannabe Boy Scout and his gal pal can tell me how to camp."

"Scouts. Cute," Jordan said, rising to stand. "Here's a reference you'll appreciate. Unless you want to end up like Piggy in that copy of *Lord of the Flies* you left behind, you'll fall in line." He glared at Darren, as if challenging him to refuse ... or worse.

Malia was stunned by Jordan's threat and, judging by his narrowed gaze, so was Tiki. But that wasn't all. There was something about Darren's comment that unsettled her. She couldn't tell if he were merely suggesting they were ganging up on him or if he were hinting at something Malia herself had yet to notice. She and Jordan spent a lot of time together, repairing the camp, setting the fish traps—they now had four—and repairing the taro ponds, not that Darren could possibly have known that. Still, it was natural for her and Jordan to bond. He'd taught her so much this week, but ... *He's just a friend. More like a teacher than anything*, she told herself.

Malia noticed Tiki studying her, his face twisted in consternation.

With Darren staring quietly off into the forest, Jordan clapped his hands. Like magic, his stiff, aggressive posture vanished. Friendly, cool Jordan was back. He scooped some rice into a bowl and drizzled his plate drippings atop it. When he noticed Malia watching him, he gave her a knowing look. He had it under control. Don't worry. He extended the bowl toward Darren. "Here. Eat."

Darren snatched the bowl, but instead of thanking him, said, "You're crazy if you think Inoke's gonna listen to you."

"And you really don't know when he's coming back?" Tiki asked.

Jordan released a frustrated sigh.

"Man, I ain't his keeper. He's waiting on some equipment he ordered. After that, I guess." Darren snorted. "Can't wait till he hears Jordan's rules."

"They apply to everyone," Jordan said.

Darren chortled. "Oh, okay. Don't say I didn't warn you."

Inoke bore Jordan's presence like a toothache before the storm. But now? His rules would torment him like an abscess demanding a root canal. But that didn't matter. Not anymore. Malia needed Inoke to return—it was her only chance of getting to college on time—and if it meant having to pay her way off the island, so be it. Still, the thought of his and Jordan's inevitable clash soured her stomach.

On her plate, the prawns sat curled in submission, speckled with bits of pepper and orange zest. It sure beat Kalalau stew. But this wasn't about food. Inoke welcomed her into the camp, stuck up for her. And they alone were from Hawai'i.

And he's a local. The only one with Kaua'i in his blood. That mattered.

Malia grimaced, unable to ignore the fact that Jordan did more to improve the camp in four days than the rest of them ever had. Inoke may have more claim to the land, the *'āina*, than the others, but where was his *aloha*? Did he love Kalalau like they did, or was he merely using it? She didn't know. Worse, she'd be powerless to solve their differences anyway.

Though Inoke's return meant she'd have a chance to boat out of there and make the start of school, part of her couldn't help hoping his return would be slow in coming.

Malia shook the rinse from the mug and set it upside down alongside the near-empty jar of instant coffee. She gave the camp a quick once-over, intent on prolonging its tidiness. She returned two unburnt logs left out overnight to the wood stack and gladdened as a gecko scampered out in greeting, its throat fluttering excitedly. Malia fancied it had come to thank her for its new home. "I like it too," she said.

Weeks of going barefoot numbed her to the rocks and splinters of the trail. Her lengthy gait made quick work of the mile-long trek, swallowing the distance in surefooted strides. But today she seemingly floated above the mud and sticks, buoyed by the promise of having Kalalau Beach to herself. She hadn't the time nor energy for yoga since the storm but was eager to get in a few more sessions before leaving. She ran, pumping her arms with anticipation, as though only speed could keep the realized dream from expiring.

"Hey, Malia, wait up." She nearly stumbled as she turned at the sound of Tiki's voice. He jogged after her, his hair bouncing atop his head.

She slowed to a brisk hike, allowing him to fall in behind her.

"Heading to the beach to do yoga?" he asked.

"Yep. And you?"

"Mind if I tag along?"

It wasn't like Tiki to make small talk—or to seek company while walking the valley—and she couldn't help wondering if there was something there after all. She led the way in silence, aware this was the first time they'd been alone since the afternoon in the tent, when she woke in his arms. Twenty minutes later, they reached the red-earth cinder hillside near the mouth of the valley.

"Listen, there's something I want to talk to you about."

"I figured." Malia came to a sudden stop and extended her hand behind her, halting him. Further up the slope to their left, a tribe of goats stood silhouetted against the azure sky. Two bucks spun off and faced one another.

"I can tell you're still mad," Tiki said.

"Shh. About what?" She kept her eyes on the goats.

Tiki stepped lightly alongside her and whispered. She glanced his way long enough to tell he wasn't going to take no for an answer. "That day on the cliff. You'd have every right to be."

Malia sighed. "Am I mad? No. Hurt. Embarrassed. Confused? Yeah, that too. But I'm not angry." Then, softer, she added, "Disappointed."

In Tiki's silence, she sensed him beginning to understand. Without taking her eyes from the goats, she asked. "So, what's it you need to say?"

"It's about Jordan. You've been spending a lot of time with him lately—"

"We're friends."

"Is that all?"

"I would know, wouldn't I?"

"Of course. It's just that Jordan …"

Malia turned to face him. "Dontcha think it's a little late for jealousy?"

"It's not that." He ran a hand over his face. "Listen. Jordan doesn't know what he's dealing with. And things might turn violent when Inoke gets back. You need to keep your distance from him."

"But that's not—"

"I know you don't want to hear it. Especially from me." Tiki paused, slowing the tempo, cushioning his tone. "I don't want to see you get hurt. I care about you." His eyes shone with sincerity as he licked his lips, buying time, then continued. His words fell upon her ears like coins in a wishing well, rippling through the darkness of her uncertain thoughts. Jordan's age. His purpose. Tiki's suspicion of him. Every sentence vanished into the murky abyss of her mind. *Tiki cared.* It was a wonderfully awful sentiment and Malia dared not guess how to take it. She felt his arm around her shoulders, hugging her against him as he did that day by the beach. The day he came to her defense. Malia's body flushed with warmth. She didn't want him jealous, only to want *her.* Here, now, and later. To start something they could continue after Kalalau.

"I wish I could tell you more. But you need to stay away from him. He's playing with fire."

Malia's heart plummeted faster than a hot air balloon without fuel. Tiki wasn't a jealous suitor, but an overbearing brother. Another man telling her what was best for her. She spun away from him. "God! What is wrong with you?" She stormed her way up the crumbling hillside toward the goats.

"What? I just don't want to see you get hurt."

"Last I checked, it was you who trashed the table. You're the one who lost his cool. Not him."

"I lost my temper. I'm sorry—"

"It's not all you lost. I'm done listening." She glared at him, her heart pounding. "I came to Kalalau dreaming something idyllic, hoping to capture what my mom experienced. And it was a dump. And everyone was so aloof. But I met you, and you were this ray of sunshine that brightened everywhere you went. So I stayed. I liked you, Tiki. I really liked you."

He reached for her hand, whispering her name. She pulled it away. "No. I can finally taste the magic of this place. And it's not because of you, or Inoke, or Darren. It's all thanks to Jordan. So, don't tell me he's dangerous. Or that you care. Because I don't."

Tiki adjusted his bag and looked downcast. When he spoke, his voice had the slow, deliberate tone of someone left with no choice. "Fine. But be sure to ask Jordan about that tan line on his left hand."

Malia turned her back on Tiki as two male goats reared on their haunches. The birds, the harem, even the wind paused as they charged headlong at one another.

. . . turn violent when Inoke gets back.

She braced for the impact, just as she now dreaded Inoke's return, and winced as the bucks slammed their horns in a thunderous collision. The clash echoed like gunshot across the valley, stealing Malia's breath. She knew it was coming, that senseless brutality, and was powerless to stop it.

In Kalalau, there could be only one alpha.

CHAPTER 16
STARBOARD SOLITARY

Jordan stood beneath the mizzen sail, rehearsing his vows as his wind-whipped linen suit concealed a shake in his legs. He held typewritten notes snug in his palm. Arial size six. As impossible to read as problematic to have … *and to hold.*

He clenched his jaw, imagining Holly's reaction if she caught him with a crib sheet. She wouldn't interrupt the ceremony or make a scene. No, that wasn't her style. She'd wait until later and deliver a critical hit when he least expected it. A comment about his inability to memorize a few words on the most important day of his life. She'd probably throw in a jab about how video games had rotted his brain. Of course, she'd deliver the barb with a smile and play it off to her friends as a joke, that she herself thought it kind of cute. But inside, she'd fume.

And maybe she'd be right. If he needed to memorize a script, as opposed to coming up with an earnest message of love and devotion from his heart to her ears, then he had no business marrying her. Jordan crumpled the paper and dropped it overboard. He watched it struggle to stay afloat in the yacht's wake, then continued staring long after it vanished into the Salish Sea.

A chorus of oohs and aahs broke his trance. Jordan turned toward the commotion in time to spot an orca spy-hopping off the port side of the *Lady Madrona*. A calf surfaced moments later, sending the guests into a tizzy.

Her guests. All four of them.

The maid of honor, Brianna something or another, a friend from Holly's sorority days, flew up from California with a plus-one. Beside her stood Holly's boss, Ally, and her husband Craig. Jordan met them once at a happy hour in Belltown, at a nouveau dive bar with beer keg urinals and twenty-dollar martinis. Ally seemed likable enough; quick to laugh, easily impressed. Craig worked in finance and referenced companies by their stock tickers in casual conversation.

The couples, strangers prior to their arrival on Orcas Island, now traded phones and position along the gunwale as they sailed past one of the hundred rocky islets in the archipelago. Watching them hastily post the photos to Instagram, Jordan couldn't help thinking how much his sister would have enjoyed the whales. And his parents. His grandmother, aunts, and cousins too. He knew he'd never hear the end of it. *How could you get married without your family?* they'd demand. *Family is what weddings are about.*

With time, they'd forget. Forgive. They'd understand the wedding wasn't about him. It was for Holly.

So he told himself.

Earlier that spring, atop the roof where they'd first met, Holly and Jordan sacrificed a bottle of Prosecco in honor of his moving in. Two glasses down, in what Jordan later realized was as much stipulation as confession, Holly detailed her wedding dream. Without warning or segue, she described reading an in-flight magazine a decade prior. The article's author, fresh off a sailboat wedding in Washington State's San Juan Islands, splashed sun-kissed praise across five high-gloss pages. "I was barely out of grad school, single and dreaming of one day getting married, but already fearing this burden of obligation. That article freed me." Holly shook her head in wonder. "Reading it made me feel so light, like I could have climbed out onto the wing and floated home myself."

She tore the article from the rag and ferried it through life ever since, through every move, every relationship. Like a get out of jail free card she'd cash to dodge the trap of familial expectations.

Jordan knew he needed to cut her some slack. Together, they'd arranged the wedding of her dreams, but she paid the price long before ever meeting him. After losing her mother to cancer as a teen, Holly went to live with her father and his wife—and their two kids. Nice girls, but half sisters in every sense of the term: half her age, half her height, half a care in the world. She confined herself to their finished basement, coming and going as no teenager should. Three years later, Holly left for college. And on the way out, she scanned the house one final time. Past the drifts of toys, over the couch where she ate her meals, alone, to the portrait-lined walls, where not a single photo of five hung. Not one of her.

Some women dream of being married in the church where they made their first communion. Others hope to ride off in a horse-drawn carriage, feted by every family member and friend they ever knew. Holly yearned to be wed at sea, thousands of miles from home. Where space was at a premium and the photos would be for her walls alone.

Jordan gripped the transom for balance, knowing he should focus on his vows. Still, he struggled to swallow his family's absence. No matter how many times he told himself that Holly would have done the same for him if it were she who grew up ensconced within a loving, close-knit family, he couldn't ignore the hurt this inflicted on his mother. Not to mention how stupid he felt having just met his supposed best man. He should have worked his frustration out that morning. Swimming always set Jordan's mind right; he intended to hit the lake near their inn to calm his nerves. A mile or two in the water was all he wanted, but Holly insisted there wasn't time. Between the group breakfast and appointment with the photographer, she said he'd be cutting it too close. "Weddings require sacrifice," she said without a trace of self-awareness. "Besides, I don't want you smelling like pond scum on my wedding day."

The opening chords of "The Wedding March" trumpeted from tinny waterproof speakers and Jordan unclenched the rail. Together, he and the guests faced the steps leading below deck as a photographer backed his way into view, sprinkling white rose petals in his wake. He positioned himself beside her friends.

A five-zip shutout.

Does anyone even know I'm—

Jordan's thought vanished as Holly emerged inch by inch from the cabin. A veil of beaded lace and flowers failed to conceal her proud smile, tight-lipped as usual. Her eyes flashed back and forth, seeking the camera, judging the light, angling her neck and chin in a way only models and angels know to do.

Plus-One elbowed Jordan in the side, causing him to release a held breath. He waggled his eyebrows as Holly, with help from the wind, swept her veil back over her head. Terrified of tripping over a floor-length train and falling overboard, she chose a shimmering satin dress cut at an angle below the knee. A symphony of Swarovski beads and lace embellished her decolletage. She advanced slowly, her every step a shutter-worthy pose. Holly didn't spare a glance toward her guests. Her focus was perfection—and that reality always match her expectations.

It's why Jordan was barefoot despite the cold. Why the guests were a handpicked friend and coworker. Thin and beautiful in their own right, but not more so than Holly. No wrinkles allowed—on clothing or otherwise. They completed the catalog promise. A *Vanity Fair* spectacle she'd covet forever.

They turned to face the captain who, during last night's dinner, joked about having married sixty-nine couples that year. "And at least half are still together," he said.

Jordan couldn't help replaying the comment as he stood there, on the verge of the ceremony, wondering on which side of the coin they'd land. He plucked at the rear of his boxer shorts and shifted his frigid feet. Of all the people aboard the yacht, he alone really knew Holly. Yet even though they'd lived together for five months, he'd yet to achieve the level of familiarity he always imagined with a wife.

"The groom has prepared his vows."

Holly turned to Jordan with expectant eyes. Flanking her, the friends she'd rarely ever mentioned stood in judgment, draped in plain coral. The maid of honor clutched the bouquet, bearing the look of someone mentally writing their Yelp review before finishing the appetizer course.

"It's been almost a year since you first approached me, plucking me from my doldrums. That's a nautical joke, by the way."

"I appreciate it," the captain said amidst polite laughter from the other men. Holly cleared her throat.

"And I've been on a rocket ship ever since. Holly, you've opened my eyes to so much. To great food. To art. And to the magic of ironing one's clothes." Another chuckle. "You've introduced me to the finer things in life, but none finer than yourself. You, who expect so much of yourself, have taught me to aim higher. And I have.

"I stand here today in awe, not just of you, though"—his eyes traced her from head to toe and back—"you look positively stunning. But I've even surprised myself." Jordan paused to lick his lips, slowing his pace, knowing he was being driven on by the crop of his racing heart. He pulled the ring from his pocket.

"It's only thanks to you that I'm here, with you by my side. You've taught me how to be a better man. One deserving of you. And for that,

I love you. I thank you. And with this ring I promise to honor you as my wife, every hour of every day from now till eternity."

He slipped a platinum diamond ring onto her finger. Her eyes glistened and her chest heaved as she stared at the ring, then she delicately dabbed her eyes with a lacy handkerchief. *I've done it. She's speechless.* But as quick as his relief surged, his thoughts ran aground on a more sobering realization. For he knew, as with the opening hours of a video game or book, he'd set an expectation she'd calibrate her hopes against for the rest of their lives.

Jordan's heart pounded in his ears as he stood wondering if he could maintain the level of acquiescence required to stave off her disappointment. He'd changed so much since meeting her, all in an exhausting effort to please her. Could he keep it up? Could he continue processing his every decision through the mill of Holly's judgment? He wondered as Holly took the ring—his ring—from the maid of honor. A seagull soared past, cawing in the salt wind as she began.

"For as long as I can remember, I've dreamed of this moment. Of being here, on a day so beautiful, surrounded by great friends"— she beamed in Brianna and Ally's direction—"and standing beside someone who loves me like you do. Jordan, you make me laugh when I need cheering up. You know just how I like to be held after a long day. And you're not afraid to push me when I need a shove." Jordan's heart raced faster and faster as she dabbed the corners of her eyes. He sensed her building to the promise, to the *I do.*

"I love what we have. You've made my home and my life complete. You were the missing ingredient, the Chateaubriand to my Bordeaux," she said, pausing to appreciate her own cleverness. Jordan grinned, knowing he was supposed to. "And with this ring, I thank you for being my perfect pairing."

Jordan glanced at the ring, titanium per his request, and took Holly in his arms to deliver the first kiss of their married lives. And when their lips met, all the prior stress and frustration leading up to that moment vanished. *Pinch me,* Jordan thought, only then allowing himself to fully believe she'd said yes.

Later, during cake, an otter popped its head above the water and floated, staring at Jordan. "Aw, he's so cute," Holly said, wrapping an arm around her groom. When Jordan faced her, she said, "You're not so bad either."

She pecked him on the lips. Immediately, the guests began clinking their stemware, demanding another kiss. He decided he'd give them, these strangers at his wedding, what they wanted. Jordan pulled Holly tight as he pressed his mouth to hers, breathing her in, tasting her love and affection, seeking to lose himself in the moment.

The photographer's shutter whirred around them, snapping photos from every angle. And Jordan leaned into it, giving her again what she craved. He cradled Holly in his arms, dipping her low in a kiss, her bare shoulders over the railing, her veil floating in the breeze. Holly stiffened her lips, perfecting the pose, the moment in time. She held her breath, sucked in her stomach. The consummate shot. The one that'd be framed on the wall, sent in cards, and "Pinned" by thousands of adoring brides-to-be.

For the rest of their married lives, his every action would be compared to the image of him in this moment. *Sink or swim. Heads or tails?*

Holly tapped to be released as soon as the photographer's camera stopped firing.

"Got to hand it to you, Jordan. Those vows were beautiful," Bob said. "You should write cards for HALL."

"I know, right?" Ally said as Jordan masked his puzzlement. "I started crying when you said she made you a better man. That was so sweet."

This was what he hoped for. What he knew Holly demanded.

"It's true though, isn't it, Jordy?" Holly said, nuzzling against his side. She kissed his cheek, then turned to her friends. "He's still a work in progress, but you girls know I love a challenge."

CHAPTER 17
ANONYMOUS TIPS

Malia rolled the empty cup between her palms as her thoughts swam in the bead of police station coffee oscillating at the bottom.

At some point when discussing the storm and ensuing rebuild, her time with Detective Park had gained an air of catharsis. Reluctant at first, Malia had soon thrown herself into the adventure of her unmapped story, charting her footsteps through that week, uncovering buried treasures and hidden dangers alike. Such as Tiki's hint concerning Jordan's tan line.

She'd forgotten that detail amidst the roar of her emotions that day on the cinder hillside. But lost in the act of reliving her experience to Park, his vague warning flowed as clear as a mountain stream. It wasn't the first time the gift of a patient audience helped her recount once-forgotten details. Malia tunneled into the foam cup's vacancy as the smell of burnt coffee reminded her of afternoons spent clinging to a cheap vinyl chair across from a grief counselor.

For days following her mother's death, Malia endured streams of sympathetic well-wishers arriving on her doorstep, arms laden with homemade food and empty promises to be there if she needed anything. Most inquired about her father, shaking their heads with such pity over the difficulty of losing a spouse, of having to raise a daughter by himself. "It's good he has his work," most said, as if reading from identical scripts.

They were sorry for her loss, each and every one of them. And the funeral was always, in their words, *a beautiful event*. But not a soul offered advice on being a girl without a mother.

The ensuing loneliness, that disappointment in her father and neighbors and anger at the world, blotted out her memory of the service. Gradually, thanks to counseling, the fog lifted. The details returned. From the way her dress clung as she walked to the church lectern, to the mascara-smeared Kleenex she clutched in the receiving line, to the soul-eating pain of placing her lei of orchids and *maile* atop the cremation casket. The space to talk, uninterrupted and without judgment or the pressure to be strong, helped her heal. To remember. To forgive. That was her first brush with therapy. And Malia felt that relief once again, there with Detective Park.

Malia unhooked her feet from behind the chair legs and set the cup down, no longer needing a distraction. Instead, she needed a bed. Between the lack of sleep and the hours spent talking, she was exhausted.

"We'll take a break soon," Park said following Malia's second yawn. "I've got some calls to make."

Detective Park untucked the pages from behind the pad and flipped backward through the unfurling yellow paper. She dragged a finger across each page in a squiggle that twitched with the energy of a polygraph needle, tossing Malia occasional glances as she scanned her notes in reverse. It wasn't long before the corner of Park's mouth hooked in a coy smile. She looked up, tapping the page.

"What?"

"I know you don't want to hear it," Park said, "but I'm relieved to learn this Tiki fellow knew he was too old for you. Nice to know there are still some honorable men in this world."

"That doesn't speak well of your coworkers."

Park flinched ever so slightly, but recovered quickly. She glanced at the one-way mirror, then said, "I meant outside the force."

"Yeah, well, it's stupid if you ask me." Malia cringed at how whiny it came out and thought Park appeared ready to say as much too, but the older woman politely closed her mouth before commenting and dipped her head. A subtle acknowledgment of Malia's unrequited crush.

"Let's talk about why Tiki stayed behind."

"What else do you want me to say?"

"Sounds like he thought you were in danger."

"Me?" Malia bulged her eyes.

"Tiki sensed the potential for violence. Maybe he was worried about you getting caught in the middle?"

"Jordan wouldn't hurt me. And neither would Inoke."

"Really?" Park arched her eyebrows. She made a show of tapping her lip.

"He didn't mean it."

"Inoke?" Park's entire face perked up.

Malia knew they couldn't dance around the topic anymore. It was why she was there. She nodded solemnly.

"Tell me about last night."

"It was self-defense," Malia said, finally blurting out the words she'd shared on the helicopter with Tiki.

Park flipped to a clean page of her legal pad. "Explain."

Malia's split lip cracked anew as she opened her mouth to respond. She tested the puffy wound with her tongue, unsurprised by the fresh taste of iron. Malia blotted the trickling blood with her fist, then lowered her hand beneath the table and rubbed it clean against her sweatpants, half-expecting to feel the gritty Honopu sand against her skin. She closed her eyes to think and to avoid Park's expectant gaze, but in the darkness there was only her, alone with the blood, the horror, the crushing weight pinning her against the frigid midnight sand.

She didn't know where to begin. Tiki was right. There was no room for both men in that camp.

Across the table, Park's demeanor shifted. Seconds earlier, she resembled a student who'd been told whatever came next would appear on a test. Now, lines of worry creased her face as Malia fumbled to form an answer.

"You gotta try, Malia. We know Jordan killed Inoke—"

"How?" Malia's voice cracked. "How do you know any of this?"

Park tented her hands and paused. "Anonymous tip."

Malia ran through the people there: herself and Jordan, Tiki, Inoke, and Darren. Jordan had a locator beacon back in camp, but she couldn't imagine him summoning the police on himself. Ruby was there too. He and Darren could have taken the Zodiac to town while she slept. Or maybe they found Fisher. He could have run the trail. It was unlikely given the landslide, and so late, but if anyone could have done it, it was him.

As she rummaged her mind for other explanations, a ray of light parted her confusion. "Wait. So, you know I'm innocent? You know I didn't help kill Inoke."

"I never said you did—"

"Then I can leave, right?"

Park took a deep breath and glanced at the one-way mirror. "You're here because we need your help. We believe you know where Jordan went—"

"What do you mean? He's in Kalalau, isn't he?" Malia's lips tugged sideways in distrust.

Park flipped through her notes. "When you encountered him trying to climb the cliffs, he mentioned Waimea town. Is that where he went?"

"I don't know. Don't think he ever found a way up the cliffs."

"Which is it? You don't know or aren't saying?"

"I don't know. I don't know. What is this?" Malia's pulse quickened as her attention flicked around the room, to the mirror, the camera, and back to Park. "What are you implying?

"How can we know he didn't hike out in the night, that you're not intending to meet him up north, in Hanalei?"

Malia slapped the table. "I told you. I don't know where he is. Last night wasn't supposed to happen. It was just a competition to settle a stupid argument. Nobody was supposed to get—" She refused to say it. Uttering the word—*murdered*—would make it real. "Nobody should have died." Malia turned sideways on the chair and hugged her knees to her chest. What if they couldn't find him? Would they blame her? Hold her responsible? A tiny island like Kaua'i wouldn't let a murder go unpunished. Especially of a local—even if he was dealing drugs. They'd charge her as an accomplice or an accessory or whatever it was they called the criminals on television. Malia paused at the unexpected reminder of home, of watching true crime shows as a family.

She looked to Park. "I want my dad."

Park said nothing, her eyes locked on her notes.

"You said we'd take a break. I told you everything I know. I haven't seen Jordan since last night. Since before we"—her voiced faded to a wisp—"buried Inoke."

"Let's say I believe you. Jordan disappeared and you don't know where to. Fine. But there's more you're not telling me."

"Like what? What else do you need to know?"

Park leaned back in her chair, making it clear the questioning was far from over. Twenty, thirty seconds passed in stifling silence before Park finally rocked forward once again. "Tell me what you know about Holly McAdams."

Malia's face twisted in confusion as sweat trickled down her back. "Who?"

"Jordan's wife."

CHAPTER 18
CAVING IN

Malia closed the book with a thwack, bored by its unremitting backstory and her reluctance to while away another afternoon doing nothing. The days spent improving the camp rekindled her love of staying busy, of having a project, a goal. But with the roof thatched, the tarps restrung, and the garden tidied, the only thing left to do was wait. The sooner Inoke returned, she thought, the faster she'd hitch a ride out with Ruby. Seven weeks in Kalalau Valley would have to suffice—classes started next week.

"I'm going to the beach. Anyone wanna come?" Though she said it aloud, an open invitation to the group, she faced Jordan as she spoke. As much by chance as intent.

"I'll grab my spear," he said. "See if Tiki's right about the *ulua*."

Tiki stood and chucked a mango stone into the firepit. He retreated to his tent, disapproval evident in his heavy strides. Malia and Jordan exchanged now-familiar shrugs, having grown accustomed to his constant brooding. Tiki had barely said a word to her in the two days that passed since their blowup near the goats. Another painful incentive to leave.

"You coming?" Jordan asked Darren, an obligatory offer laced with an uninviting tone.

"Nah. You two have yourselves some fun." He said it with a ribald smirk that Malia found obnoxious, but, as it came from Darren, was easy to ignore. Not a day passed without him insinuating that something was brewing between her and Jordan. Sure, they spent a lot of time together since the storm, rebuilding the camp and gathering food, and she enjoyed learning from him. But, as far as anything sexual between them ... Malia shrugged the idea off. They were friends, practically coworkers at this point. Also, Jordan was too old—a good bit older than Tiki, she guessed. And she was leaving soon. End of story.

Jordan grabbed his spear from where it leaned against a tree. The spear was as long as he was tall, a tree branch he whittled smooth around the campfire. He'd tied a length of orange rope—paracord, he explained—to one end for retrieval, and to the other he lashed three wooden spikes. The points jutted out in a triangular pattern like tines in a fistful of forks.

They hiked in silence to the beach, where Jordan led the way westward across the sand to where the receding tide exposed a jumble of rocks. It was the first time Malia had been that far down the beach, let alone close enough to the water to see around the headland. For all the times they discussed the Kalalau Trail snaking its way northeastward from the closer end of the beach, she'd never considered what lay in the opposite direction. Never heard it mentioned.

One look was all it took to understand why. For as far as Malia could see, there were only cliffs and ocean. Rolling indigo ruffles lapping against rock walls smeared in a palette of reds and pinks. The sun hung above the horizon, setting the cliffs ablaze, as if to warn of the infernal dangers lurking beyond Kalalau Beach.

The dread she experienced upon arriving—that fear of being imprisoned between mountain and sea—rushed through her with a shudder. Especially now, knowing a landslide had effectively cut off the only overland route out.

Clad in rubber-soled reef shoes, gray hiking shorts, and polarizing sunglasses—better to see the fish, he explained—Jordan stood motionless atop the rocks, an arm-cocked, spear-holding, silhouetted statue. "Normally, I'd be snorkeling with a hand spear," he said as the Pacific lapped around him, ebbing and flowing as though exhausted. It had given its energy to the storm; Malia's, to its aftermath. They were both drained. An hour passed as Malia sat watching, thinking. Of everything and nothing.

"Hey, come here." Jordan jerked his head to the side for emphasis, not taking his eyes from the water, the tip of his spear hovering motionless inches above the water.

She brushed the sand off and hiked the sarong up as she waded into the shallows.

"There, between those rocks."

"What?"

"You'll see. Reach in."

Inky, dark water swirled between the boulders, concealing whatever Jordan wanted her to find. She bent to the crevice but straightened before dipping her hand.

"Don't trust me?"

"Should I?" Malia's gaze darted between Jordan and the underwater mystery. Curious, but wary of crabs and sea urchins, she reached toward the water and hesitated as Jordan's wry smile reminded her of the pranks Jenna's brothers often played. Efforts to amuse themselves through her friend's torment. "It better not be something gross," she said, hoping he wasn't tricking her into gripping a sea cucumber.

"It's not," he said, holding three fingers up. "Scout's honor."

She frowned, thinking of Darren's comment, but said nothing.

Sand danced amid the sloshing water as she submerged her hand. Malia flinched when something clicked against her fingers, light and delicate. But harmless. She groped blindly until she pinched a shell between her fingers and drew it to the surface. Dripping with water, the scallop boasted the same banded strawberries-and-Creamsicle vibrancy as the sky. Malia had never before found a sunrise shell. "It's gorgeous," she said, bumping her finger along the shell's wavy edge.

"Told you these sunglasses were great." Jordan acted humble, but his pride shone through.

She returned to where she'd been sitting and held the shell in line with the horizon as the sun continued its descent. Jordan soon joined her, tossing his spear aside, saying he'd try again tomorrow.

Lacking Tiki's surfer physique or Inoke's bulk, Jordan had the skinny-fat build common amongst Malia's former teachers. He sat with a slight hunch, his shoulders rolled awkwardly forward, as if permanently stuck over a keyboard. But despite that image, Malia couldn't help thinking he belonged in Kalalau. Perhaps more than any of them. So what if he worked in video games or arrived overburdened with gadgets and no food; he was smart and knew how to survive. She was surprised to find herself admitting it, but damn if that didn't make him a bit sexy.

She scratched a mosquito bite on her shin as Jordan broke the silence. "What's the first thing you're gonna eat when you leave?"

"Ooh, lemme think." She searched her mind for the best answer, rejecting options one after another, from sushi to ramen to barbecued chicken. She wanted to be honest, but classy. Mature, but original. Jordan hummed the *Jeopardy* tune as Malia squinted in thought. Her mind ventured to the food trucks along Oʻahu's North Shore, the crispy piles of garlic shrimp she loved to eat tails and all, but the dazzling splash of colors over the horizon induced a detour. "Shave ice," she said, warming at her decision despite the chest freeze it always induced.

"No cheeseburger?"

"Dessert first." She looked to her shell as she pictured a mound of snowy shavings, the sunset-tinted syrups soaking in, the drizzle of sweetened cream and macadamia nut topping. Her mouth watered at the image and, for the first time since her mother's death, her heart granted her the memory of their birthday tradition without tears. That awareness ushered a smile to her lips. Afraid to dwell for fear the pangs of loss would return, she hurried to keep the conversation going. "What about you? And don't say a hamburger."

"Why not?" He laughed. "I'd kill for a bacon double cheeseburger. Side of fries. Wash it down with a vanilla shake and a beer. I haven't gone this long without an IPA in years."

As he spoke, Malia noticed a scraggle of gray hairs amidst the brown tuft of his chest, as foreign to her as the IPA he referenced. Whatever that was.

"Passed a burger joint in Kapaʻa on the way here. Looked pretty good."

Malia shrugged, having never been.

"Guess your shave ice won't be long now. Still leaving when Inoke returns?"

"That's the plan," she said. "Assuming Ruby doesn't try ripping me off."

As they chatted, the sun dropped into the ocean. Malia hoped to spot the green flash, that rarest of optical tricks, but like so much that summer, it too remained elusive. The clouds that shone moments earlier in sunset hues turned ashen. She watched their approach, having long sought comfort in those celestial puffs. To Malia, they concealed the emptiness of the horizon, helped her forget Hawaiʻi was alone in the middle of the ocean, out of sight and mind from the rest of the world. Clouds shrank the sky, the earth, yet bolstered her significance.

"I'll miss having you around," Jordan said.

They faced one another with matching nervous smiles. Malia could tell she wasn't alone in sensing the air change between them, as if the electrons bonding their friendship had split and coalesced into something volatile. Explosive. *I'm such a nerd*, she thought. Blushing, she returned her attention to the dusky sky, wondering if it might rain.

"Shame the sky's not clear. Was hoping for another star show tonight," he said. "There's so much light in Seattle. And most of the year it's so cloudy. We rarely get to see more than the Big Dipper. Sometimes the Pleiades, but that's about it."

Malia thought for a moment, orientating herself on the island, then pointed over her right shoulder, to the northeast. "Too early for them now, but they'd be over there in the winter. We call them the Makaliʻi. The Seven Sisters. Their appearance signaled the start of the harvest season in ancient times."

Jordan sat in silent contemplation for several moments. When he spoke, his voice carried the heft of a ponderous whisper, as though his thought had sailed the ocean on a breeze to Malia's ears. "They say we know more about the stars than we do the sea."

She twirled the sunrise shell in her hands slowly, as if within its grooves was the key that unlocked the universe. But the only truth was its darkening features warning her that a hike back without a flashlight held little appeal. "I'll need a few puffs on some of Inoke's good stuff to debate that one." She popped to her feet and turned to give Jordan a hand standing when she spotted a hole in the base of the cliff. "Whoa, is that a cave?"

"You hadn't seen it?"

"Hadn't been down this far." Minding the signs warning of rockfall, Malia jogged past the opening. Nearly as wide as their camp and high enough to stand in, the cave floor was carpeted in soft sand and pockmarked with miniature craters from dripping groundwater. The air smelled faintly of iron and moss, but sweeter. Her eyes adjusted to the dim lighting as she followed the wall of the cave to where it tapered at the rear, and wondered if the bats she'd seen along the beach would return. She'd nearly rounded the end when a hand landed upon her hip.

She stiffened in surprise, clamping down on the seashell, but only briefly. Malia turned her head slowly, peering back over her shoulder at Jordan. She gazed at him in the shadowy silence of the cave, translating the unspoken question of his touch as he spread his fingers wide against her, brushing over the edge of the sarong, tickling her bare skin. Her stomach fluttered in response. Her breathing quickened.

And when Jordan dipped his head, repeating that mute invitation to join him, her response came at once. Malia licked her lips, feeling a surge of warmth rush through her, and refused to deny herself the pleasure she craved. Yes. She didn't know it hours or even minutes ago, but she absolutely wanted this. To celebrate the camp they'd built. To cap her summer holiday. To vanquish the rejection that still burned inside her.

I need this.

Malia closed her eyes as his fingers climbed along her back and swept her hair aside, exposing her chest. His thumb glanced her nipple as he cupped her breast, sending a spark of anticipation rippling through her. She raised her mouth to his, wanting him to take her. And he did. But softer than expected, more delicate. He kissed with a gentleness she wasn't accustomed to, as though she were a fragile keepsake that could be easily damaged. And as they kissed, he dipped her backwards, slowly guiding her to the ground like a princess who'd fallen fast asleep in his arms. "You're so beautiful," he said, but his quiet compliment was all it took to shatter the spell. She'd envisioned this moment, this romance, for so long. But not with him. From Jordan she needed some-thing else—something fierce.

She stepped from his grasp and in one swift motion pushed him to the ground and promptly straddled him.

A quick study, it took only an instant before the whites of his eyes shone with a lust rivaling her own. At once, their hands clawed as one at the knot binding her sarong in place. Together, they grunted, fumbling in the dark, before he peeled through the layers to her opening. She shifted forward atop his stomach and groped for him growing behind her as he cupped her breasts, pinching her nipples. Malia arched her back, moaning in delight, squeezing his erection in her hand, willing him to pinch harder.

Jordan shifted to suckle her, but Malia pushed him back down with force. She didn't need any more foreplay. "Protection?"

Jolted from the heat of the moment, his face bore the mix of embar-rassment and disappointment.

Malia deflated. *So much for the Boy Scout always being prepared.*

"I've had a vasectomy. I'm clean."

Malia rolled her eyes, thinking of course he'd say that. But could she believe him? She'd always been more scared of getting pregnant than catching something. But wouldn't a guy with a vasectomy be more likely to have a virus? Jordan bucked slowly beneath her, grinding her inhibitions down as she deliberated, sparking a wildfire of frustration that raged through her from head to toe—burning mostly somewhere in between. Her subconscious, perhaps knowing how badly she wanted this release, recalled the sunrise shell hidden from sight amongst the rocks. *Don't you trust me?* he had asked. She did. And had the souve-nir proving she could.

She bit her lip and clawed her nails down Jordan's chest, as if in warning. "Okay," she said, nodding along to encourage herself.

Malia threw her wrap to the side, then shifted off of him. She tugged his shorts below his knees and straddled him once again, her back to her stand-in lover. She took a hungry breath and lowered herself onto him, free of guilt or shame. And in a moment she'd never forget, within a cave at the edge of the world, she gasped as her excitement echoed throughout the convenient darkness, delivering on her anticipation. It wasn't the man she wanted, or how she fantasized it to be, but it was what she craved. Malia rose and fell atop him faster and harder in the throes of desire, driving him into her further, deeper, filling a void that had ached inside of her for weeks.

Malia shuddered with a chill despite the arm draped over her. She scooched backward, half-asleep, cozying against the body behind her just as she had after the storm. She tugged the sarong to her chin for warmth and breathed in his earthy scent, committing it to memory as she melted back into the sand, satisfied and secure in the comfort of what transpired. Finally.

This is nice.

"Are you cold?"

That voice?

"You want to head back?"

Her eyes widened with surprised recollection. Jordan.

She cut off a gasp midbreath, hoping he didn't feel her startle. And if he did, that he wouldn't realize she was thinking of Tiki. "What time is it?" she asked, hoping nobody would still be awake in camp.

The glow of his watch cut through the darkness. "Nine thirty."

Malia nodded as she sat up, realizing she'd fallen asleep. She brushed sand from her legs and arms. Jordan had pulled up his shorts while she slept.

"Here," he said, handing her a flashlight as they readied to leave the cave. "You carry it. I'll follow behind."

Thirty minutes later, they reached camp. And in all that time spent walking, she had yet to make sense of what she'd done—or why. Was she over Tiki? Would she ever be? Malia stood apart from Jordan, unsure what to say. She'd never before had sex with someone she wasn't in love with—or at least hoped to be. Would he try to kiss her good-night or invite her to stay with him? Or was this better left as a one-night stand? So many questions. Zero answers. Why didn't anyone ever tell her random hookups would be so hard?

"Thank you." She blurted it out, an honest sentiment, but immediately regretted how awkward it sounded.

"Yeah, well, I try." He swung his head and chuckled, flashing a modest smile. He gestured in the direction of his tent and said, "So, do you want to—"

"I'm really tired," she said, avoiding the trouble of saying no—or telling him what took place had almost nothing to do with him.

"Sure. Of course."

"It's just—"

"Shh," he said, putting a finger to her lips, smiling. "No need to say anything. It's okay. Hey, by the way, I think you left a photo in my tent the day of the storm. Bunch of people on a beach."

Malia swooned with surprised relief. Her mouth fell open; her initial attempts to speak failed to produce anything remotely intelligible. It was nice to find the muddied photo of her and her mother sharing their annual birthday treat, but that one wasn't rare. She had the file on her computer, her phone, stored in the cloud. But the one of her mother from the nineties, in Kalalau with her friends … irreplaceable.

"It must have gotten stuck in my sleeping bag when I came over. I thought I'd lost it forever."

"Well, you didn't," he said. "Figured it had to be yours. You look just like one of the—"

"My mom. I'm surprised you could tell with that hat she had on."

"I was gonna say one of the guys."

Malia's hand darted to her mouth as her skin tingled with excitement. All this time, she'd suspected one of the men in the photo might have been her birth father, but she'd never noticed much resemblance. That Jordan thought one of them looked like her was exhilarating, even if only a guess. She glanced in the direction of Jordan's tent, torn between wanting the photo back right away and not wanting to stretch their tryst into anything more.

"Is something wrong? You look—"

"Uh ..." She bit at a torn cuticle, thinking. "It's just. The photo ..." Malia took a deep breath, unsure how much to reveal. Should she admit she was a Kalalau love child? That her mother took the secret of her birth father to her grave? That the man Jordan thought resembled her might be the father she never met—and that part of her was terrified to know which one—and even more scared of him being wrong.

"How about I hold onto it. Say ... till tomorrow night?" He smiled with a flirtatious glint in his eye as he posed the invitation.

"Okay," she said, relieved to defer to another day. "See you tomorrow."

Returning through camp, Malia wasn't surprised to see Darren awake, sitting by the embers of a fire long left to die. "Somebody got laid," he said, sing-songing his teasing.

She harrumphed her disgust and hurried to her tent, hoping to avoid any further questions—or encounters. Malia wiped her feet outside her tent, unzipped the door, and crawled inside. She remained kneeling, hand on the zipper, when Tiki approached.

Shit.

"Not like you to miss dinner. Everything okay?" He paused, seeming to lose his train of thought in the forest floor. "Do you need ...?"

Need? I'd been needing something for weeks. Now you ask?

"Wasn't hungry," she lied. Malia didn't want to hurt Tiki's feelings—and wasn't going to risk souring the night by arguing. Least of all with the one she'd been thinking of the whole time.

"You were with Jordan?" he asked.

Since he seemed to know the answer, she said nothing.

He dragged a hand across his face. "Malia," he said, drawing her name out in exasperation.

"No, don't do that."

"What?"

"The *Maliaaaaa* thing. You can't expect me to—"

"What do you want me to say?"

"I don't want you to *say* anything." She took a steadying breath, hating that it had come to this. "If I can only be your friend ..." It was Malia's turn to struggle to finish a thought, distracted by the realization it would take a lot more to get over Tiki. And his constant watching out for her didn't help.

Tiki opened his mouth to speak. She could see the jealousy, his desire for a second chance dancing in his eyes, in the way his jaw quivered, yet he said nothing.

His silence stabbed at Malia's heart, but she refused to show it. She straightened her shoulders and bit back the sob building within her. "You know how I feel." Then, because she didn't know what else to say, added, "And summer's nearly over."

Tiki said nothing. Just stood there holding his breath, his fists balled at his side, but not in an angry way. Like someone fighting their temptations—and struggling not to lose.

"Good night, Tiki." Malia zipped the tent closed but didn't move. Didn't breathe. She posed frozen in the dark, holding back her emotions until Tiki's footsteps faded into the distance.

CHAPTER 19
BEACHED

Malia wished the monk seal to be alive. She waited, hoping it would move and render any question unnecessary. When she finally asked, Jordan didn't answer. Whether he didn't know or was lost in thought, she could only guess. They sat side by side, dangling their legs over the lip of a short bluff, watching the seal in silence. She'd never seen a monk seal outside an aquarium before. Never before seen any endangered animal in the wild, for that matter. Yet, there it was. Twenty yards away.

The creature lifted its head and belched, causing Malia to giggle. The scratchy grunt, no doubt stinking of fish, rode the wind as the seal looked at Malia. It rolled its neck and resettled, head down in the sand, surrendering to sleep, to staying in Kalalau ... indefinitely, Malia thought with a trace of jealousy.

Jordan sat closer than he might have two days earlier, but not near enough to be awkward. Or presumptuous. There was a friendly ordinariness in the air between them that pleased her. Adulthood, perhaps.

"They're named for the thick fold of skin around their neck. Like a monk's robe."

Jordan tilted his head and squinted as he watched the seal, as if trying to visualize what she'd said.

"In Hawaiian, they're called *ilio holo I ka uaua*. It means 'dog running in the rough water,' though I can't imagine why, given how lazy this one seems." She forced a laugh, hoping not to sound like a braggart. It was too bad Tiki wasn't there. If any of them could have explained the origin of its Hawaiian name, it was him.

Nevertheless, the creature's stillness reminded Malia of Jordan standing atop the rocks, holding his spear like a statue, scanning the low tide waters. In Hawai'i, surf and tide reports were as much a part of the daily news as sports scores and politics. She recalled the three-quarter moon illuminating their stroll back to camp, of how her mother said the moon held as much power over people and their cycles as it did the tides. It lifted some up, dragged others under.

She watched Jordan out the corner of her eye, wondering if the coming full moon had swallowed his tongue.

Jordan interlocked his fingers and twisted his palms to the sea in a stretch. He bent an arm overhead, pressing a hand against his elbow, then repeated the motion on the other side. He'd come to the beach to swim, or so he said as he followed Malia out of camp. At first, she wondered if he hoped to have her in the cave again—or right out in the open. Would he think if she was up for it once, she'd be down again? Would she?

The low whine of a motor drew their attention. And moments later, a small inflatable boat came into view. She spotted a man riding high in the bow, leaning over a tarp, another in the rear with his hand on the tiller. The boat turned toward shore and she gasped. Inoke and Ruby had returned.

"Look who finally came back." Jordan stood. "So much for my swim."

Malia heard the gravelly annoyance in his voice, noticed the color fade from his face. And who could blame him? Inoke left and Jordan stepped up and made the camp his. Something Inoke wouldn't take lightly. But that was for them to figure out. Ruby's return meant she could leave. Classes were soon starting, and she wasn't about to miss them. Even if she had to empty her bank account to pay them for the ride.

She jogged toward the water, yipping with her growing eagerness, and met them as the boat's rigid hull scraped along the sand. It was all she could do to not throw herself into the boat for fear they might return to town without her.

If Inoke noticed her eagerness, he didn't acknowledge it. He leapt from the inflatable the moment the boat glanced the shallows and charged ahead like an invading force. He grabbed the bow rope and tugged the boat onto the sand as Ruby tilted the outboard out of the water. With the boat ashore, Inoke rolled back the forest-green tarp, exposing a bushel of sealed orange Home Depot buckets. He yanked two from the boat, setting them on the sand, then barked at Ruby, "Stop fussing and unload. We can't drag it while it's full." Inoke stacked the buckets in pairs around him, a blaze-orange fortress containing who knew what.

"Need a hand?" Malia asked, approaching from behind.

Inoke turned and smiled, then saw Jordan following behind her. The spark of his eyes hardened into coal. "Still here, huh?"

"Thriving," Jordan replied.

Inoke's gaze shifted back and forth between Malia and Jordan, as if trying to isolate the correct piece for a jigsaw puzzle. Malia didn't need long to guess what was on his mind. She could see it in the crease splitting his brow, the way he worked his jaw, as though chewing through a burnt piece of steak. She didn't know how it was on Kaua'i, but plenty on O'ahu chafed when catching local girls with mainlanders. That Jordan was older, in his thirties she guessed, would only make it worse. She'd heard the stories, seen the fights. It wasn't as bad as it used to be, but tourists who hit on the wrong girls went home with souvenirs they didn't want. Black eyes. Concussions. Sometimes worse.

For Jordan's sake, she could only hope Inoke's intuition wasn't so keen. After several seconds, his demeanor relaxed and he said to Jordan, "Good. Then you won't mind helping."

Malia hoisted two buckets and passed them to Jordan. Judging by the speed at which everyone worked, Malia wondered if Ruby planned to leave right away for fear of being ticketed. With the trail closed due to the landslide, it wasn't hard to imagine rangers on the lookout for people boating in. She scanned the sky for a helicopter but saw none.

Before Malia could ask, Ruby hoisted a massive backpack from beneath the tarp. The pack, every bit as large as the one Jordan hauled into camp, bulged with so much gear its zippers were split open in the center. Ruby set it on his knee, then, while bending at the waist, slipped his left arm through the shoulder strap and humped it onto his back.

"What's that?" Malia asked, a pit forming in her stomach.

"My stuff." Ruby shot her a look as if to ask *What else would it be?*

"Come on, let's hide the boat," Inoke said.

Jordan waded into the water and heaved himself against the transom, shoving alongside Ruby as Inoke tugged from the front. Once on dry sand, Inoke barely avoided being run over by the boat surging on the strength of Ruby and Jordan's efforts.

"But I need to go," Malia said, weak-kneed in the shallows as the men plowed the boat across the beach. But nobody paid her any mind. Least of all Inoke, who urged the others on under a shower of profanity, as if driving a mule train. The boat, Malia's ticket out of Kalalau and only means of reaching college on time, disappeared into the milo forest. Infused with panic, she willed herself to move and nearly toppled the buckets as she raced after them. When she caught up, Malia crashed against the boat as Inoke and Ruby dragged the tarp across it, weighting it in place with lava rocks.

"Should have bought the bigger tarp," Inoke said.

"It's fine," Ruby replied, content to leave the motor and pointed tips of the pontoons uncovered.

"The hell it is. Might as well write SOS in the sand," Jordan said, drawing curious looks from everyone else. He dashed about, gathering fallen palm fronds and spreading them across the bow.

Jordan's comment took Malia by surprise. She hadn't considered signaling for help. All this time, she'd considered them on their own, forgotten. Ignored. Nevertheless, she didn't want to get anyone in trouble, least of all herself. She turned to Ruby and did her best to sound casual. "So, Ruby, are you staying long? I was hoping to catch a ride into town."

Ruby shrugged. When he opened his mouth to speak, Inoke cut him off. "Why you want him to leave so fast? We just got here."

"Classes are starting—"

"Ooh ..." Inoke said, grimacing as if he'd watch her stub a toe. "Shoulda thought about that when I offered you a ride. Guess you'll have to hoof it."

"I can't." The words stung her throat as if she'd swallowed a jellyfish. "Darren said ... a landslide." Malia's chest tightened as the vacuum of her despair stole her ability to breathe. *He doesn't care. Nobody cares.* She put a steadying hand to her chest, gulping for air, but could get none down. She needed to leave, and could only hope Inoke would change his mind after learning of the landslide. That notion helped her gain the slimmest of footholds on her rising panic.

"Darren? Where is he?"

"In camp. Probably." The pressure gripping her lungs had migrated to her head. Deep in her brain, the mention of Darren's name sparked a flash of insight with the permanence of a firefly. A flicker of recognition: Darren couldn't wait for Inoke to return. To tell him Jordan's new rules; to no doubt squeal about them sleeping together. Inoke wouldn't stand for any of it, but she was through caring.

She needed to get home—no matter the cost. She cast a glance at the boat, the tree canopy, and wondered if it was visible—and if she couldn't help the police spot it if the need arose.

"Give us a hand," Inoke said, returning down the beach to the buckets. He took two in his right hand, one in his left. "Be careful."

Jordan hesitated before grabbing any. "What's inside? Food?"

"Eh. Something like that."

Jordan frowned in response, his eyes flicking from Inoke to Ruby and back. Malia could sense him debating whether or not to help, even as he yanked four buckets by their handles.

Ruby buckled his pack's waist belt and likewise grabbed two buckets in each hand before starting toward camp. Malia grabbed one with each hand and, judging by their weight, figured them to be weighted down with rice or canned food.

Inoke motioned with his chin toward the valley. Malia fell in between Jordan and Inoke on what felt like a forced march.

She looked to the monk seal as she strode past, the buckets bumping against her calves with every step, and wondered if it too had ever beached itself somewhere it couldn't leave.

The hike back to camp was the most exhausting since the day she first followed Skye with her duffel bag. It wasn't fatigue or mud that wore

Malia down, but dread. The swinging buckets with their unknown contents banged against her calves and knees, drumming a constant, bruising cadence as she marched to the gallows, where her dreams of getting to college on time would terminate.

She wanted to believe the deans would be reasonable. That maybe they'd even find her story of being stranded on a deserted beach charming. But opportunities like hers didn't come often. What if they gave the scholarship to someone else? Someone who knew better than to ride out a tropical storm in a stranger's tent—and wouldn't her father love it if they did. Malia squeezed the plastic handle in anger, pinching it against the metal loop so tight the bucket ceased to sway. She wanted to scream and smash it against a tree like a piñata, spill its contents across the forest floor. Better still, if they wouldn't help her, she'd signal for a rescue—and if it meant them all getting ticketed, so be it. She'd give Inoke and Ruby one more chance to boat her out of there; otherwise, she'd take matters into her own hands.

Ruby dropped the buckets upon reaching camp. They hit the ground with a thud deeper and more solid than Malia anticipated. "You've been busy," he said, nodding at the improvements as Inoke loosed an impressive whistle. He set his buckets down atop the bench seating and gave the backrest a hearty shake. He arched a single eyebrow in approval. He ran his palm along the covered table, bumped his knuckles across the bamboo roofing. Malia noticed a new tattoo on the back of his neck. A tribal design that disappeared beneath his shirt collar. He'd gotten a haircut too, a tight fade climbing to a black buzz cut. Malia clawed the ground with her toes, her calves and thighs straining against the frustration of knowing that while she rode out the storm and its aftermath, Inoke was off getting pampered.

"You do this?" Inoke said, casting a sideways glance at Jordan.

"Malia and Tiki helped. But yeah."

Another whistle and a hint of a smile. *Great*, Malia thought. *Inoke likes it so much, they're never gonna want to leave.* Just her luck.

Inoke continued to inspect the camp, taking inventory of the tents, noting the placement of Jordan's, Tiki's, Darren's and Malia's. Of Inoke's two tents, only the one he'd slept in survived. Barely.

Malia watched him take it all in. She licked her lips, then said, "A tree fell on your other one. Tore right through it. Storm destroyed your—"

Inoke raised a hand, halting her explanation as he pondered the destruction.

"Mine wound up in a tree," she added softly, wanting to show he alone didn't suffer damage.

"What about the garden?"

"Wrecked. We cleaned it up, but …" Malia let the thought die, knowing the garden was in bad shape.

"The tomatoes? My … plants?" Inoke flicked a suspicious glance at Jordan before turning back to Malia.

Malia twisted her face sideways and shook her head.

"Damn it!" Inoke yelled, pounding his thighs. It seemed more out of frustration than anger. Like someone who expected bad news but felt obligated to react to it anyway. The outburst drew Darren and Tiki from their respective tents.

Tiki ran a hand through his hair as he emerged. His eyes appeared bloodshot and dull, like he hadn't slept in days. Malia watched him tying the drawstring on his shorts, unable to help imagining him lying awake thinking of her. She took a half step away from Jordan. She hadn't slept much either.

"Hey, welcome back," Darren said. He swept his frizzled dreads behind his head and twisted them in an elastic. He clasped Inoke's hand in greeting, leaning at the waist, and thumped him on the back. Darren darted his gaze from Malia to Jordan and back again. He flashed a toothy grin and nodded slowly, seeming to cherish the moment. He had the look of a teacher's pet ready to rat out those who misbehaved for the substitute teacher.

"You take care of that thing we discussed?" Inoke asked Darren.

Tiki crinkled his brow as he studied them.

"Nah, man. I couldn't. The plants—"

"So whatcha been doing? Just lying around?"

"Shit. I wish. This one"—he jerked a thumb at Jordan—"got me hauling firewood, fetching water, yanking taro every day. Said nobody eats if we don't work."

"That so?" Inoke asked Jordan. He tilted his head to the side and spit.

Malia swallowed hard. Fucking Darren couldn't wait, could he?

"Seems only fair," Jordan said, matching Inoke's stare without wilting, exhibiting a bravado she didn't anticipate. Whether Inoke would respect Jordan's confidence or take it as a sign of aggression, she had no idea. But one thing was certain: Jordan was working without a net. Even without Darren and Ruby for backup, Inoke had over eighty pounds of muscle on him. Not to mention over a century's worth of bad blood toward mainlanders acting like they ran the place.

Inoke's eyes narrowed to slits. In quick flicks of attention, he regarded the bench seating, the improved tarps and shelving. His lips curled in the corner. "Yeah, that's fair. I got you."

Darren did a double take. Malia could tell he was hoping Inoke would tell Jordan off—or worse. Malia didn't like it one bit, because she knew, as calm as Inoke was now, any hint that she and Jordan had hooked up would be like a match to gasoline.

But it was a one-time thing, that's all, Malia told herself. And she could deny it—all of it.

Really? And how would I explain what Darren had seen? What did he see? Her hair was forever in tangles; her sarong always a wrinkled mess; she'd gotten no hickeys. So what if he'd seen them say good-night, caught her on her walk of shame. *Shame? Fuck shame.* And fuck Darren. All of them. She wanted her photo, and wanted out of Kalalau. The sooner the better.

"Hey. Inoke. Malia tell you about her and Jordan?"

Malia's breath caught in her throat, but she pretended not to notice.

Inoke didn't respond. Not at first. Instead, he and Ruby set about sorting the buckets as Darren continued. Nice and coy, like a sadistic nurse peeling back a bandage as slowly and painfully as possible.

"She and Jordan *really* got to know one another after you left."

"Here. Put these with the others," Inoke said, handing Ruby two buckets. He turned to Darren. "Yeah. And?"

"Fishing. Repairing the camp. Long walks on the beach." He smiled at Malia, who only wanted to shut him up. Tiki came forward, stiff with coiled energy, but said nothing. And Jordan, despite being the center of Darren's story, appeared indifferent. As if he had no idea the danger sleeping with Malia had put him in.

"You shoulda seen them last night—"

Malia stared daggers at him, her tongue clenched between her molars, ready to drag her nails across his face if he said another word.

"Whoa! You got the solars," Darren said, interrupting himself as he rushed to Inoke's side. Malia went slack, drained by the hour's roller coaster of emotions.

"Man, I was dreading you making me haul in car batteries." Darren raised a spotlight from a bucket as though lifting a baby from a crib. The lamp contained multi-colored LED bulbs with a small panel mounted on its back.

"Another lamp in that one." Inoke pointed. "Figured we'll need at least two given the tree cover."

"Awesome," Darren said, rotating it as he recited a salesman's list of product specs. Wattage. Burn times. Nothing Malia cared about.

"Looks expensive. Where'd you get the money?" Tiki's tone was one of cheery curiosity—and completely at odds with the return of his chess-player's scowl.

Inoke said nothing, choosing instead to return Tiki's scrutiny with a hard, suspicious stare. She knew Tiki often passed the joint without partaking at night after dinner, but the presence of drugs never seemed to faze him until now.

"Aw, here we go," Darren said, breaking the tension. "Hello, my beauties," he said, tilting a freshly opened bucket for them all to see. Marijuana seedlings, a half dozen by the look of it. Inoke was expanding his business.

"How many you bring back?" Tiki asked.

Ruby counted aloud as he pointed from bucket to bucket. "Fourteen … fifteen … twenty plants or so. Enough to replace any damaged in the storm." He then withdrew shade netting and a five-pound bag of rice from another bucket. All the while, Tiki and Inoke continued to survey one another with silent skepticism.

"Those lights are trouble," Jordan grumbled, low enough for only Malia to hear.

Malia shot him a questioning look: *Why do you care?*

He replied through a clenched jaw, keeping his voice down. "Can't risk the attention."

Malia swatted a fly hovering near her face and pondered Jordan's words. Did he think he'd be guilty by association if Inoke were caught? No, that wasn't it. There had to be something else. But why would he care if a couple of drug dealers attracted attention? And was there really any chance the police would notice a few grow lamps in the jungle?

Ruby approached somewhat awkwardly, his eyes downcast as he offered a bag of rice to Jordan. "My contribution."

It was only when Jordan reached for the food that Malia noticed it. A pale band of untanned skin on his finger—exactly the kind of mark a wedding ring would leave.

Recalling Tiki's comment, she snuck a second look to confirm what he apparently knew all along. The leathery chestnut tan of Jordan's hand had all but encroached on the wintered, indented skin, but not completely. He'd clearly been wearing a ring until recently. Malia's pulse quickened as she realized she probably slept with a married man. The vasectomy. The lack of condoms. It all made perfect sense. But whether he'd taken the ring off in effort to pretend to be single or because of a recent separation, she had no idea.

One thing Malia did know was that she was on her own finding a way out of there. Even if meant scratching the damn SOS in the sand herself.

CHAPTER 20
FLIGHT CHANGE

Jordan slumped onto the bed, his frustration running neck and neck with exhaustion. Another holiday weekend come and gone, sacrificed to the lords of game development. He flexed his toes in the tan carpet of their bedroom. A mass of identical fibers matted together in a sea of uniform blandness. Not unlike the year's worth of days since his game was green-lit.

Holly grunted something unintelligible and rolled over, facing him, eyes closed. Asleep. Or pretending to be.

"No wonder they quit."

She shifted again, but said nothing. She tugged lightly against the duvet, but his weight held it in place.

"The whole country's at the beach," he told the floor. "Barbecuing, camping. Not us. It's goddamn Memorial Day, but Jordy was needed at the office." Half the studio was there too, crunching as if they were on the home stretch, even though the game wouldn't release for two years—at least. "We're gonna fucking lose 'em all over again."

Holly's lips smacked as she chewed the sleep in her mouth. "But you're home now," she said, her voice ethereal. Whether to Jordan or someone in a dream, he couldn't tell.

"Yeah. Thanks for waiting up." A stupid comment. He told her not to wait for him when he called at seven while his Hot Pocket heated in the break room microwave.

She scrunched her face. The sarcasm clearly penetrated her sleep-addled brain—and stung.

"It's fine. Keep sleeping." He leaned forward and shifted some of the comforter out from under him. Holly nuzzled closer. "Miss me?"

Jordan waited for an answer he knew wouldn't come. The past few months had gone exactly as he feared when she invited him to move in. *So much for seeing one another in bed.* Holly was an early riser, regularly on calls with East Coast reps long before Jordan woke. He worked late most nights, waiting until the last minute to update the next day's hit list for the programmers. He knew most were smart enough to figure out what needed to be done, but the others? Solid programmers, all of them, but he wondered if the younger ones could find their way home without Google Maps. He sighed. *Enough! Leave it at the office.* He turned to Holly, hoping for acknowledgment.

"No. Probably didn't realize I was gone."

She squinted against the band of light crossing the bed. He'd left the bathroom light on, the door cracked. "What's that supposed to mean?"

He sighed. "Nothing. Just feeling pissy. How was the picnic?"

"Fine. I only stayed an hour. They served hot dogs." She made the scrunchy face again. "Did you eat?"

"Microwaved something." Jordan pulled his shirt off and tossed it toward the hamper. He missed. "So, what'd you do all day?"

Holly propped a pair of pillows against the headboard and sat up, abandoning any pretense of sleep. She wore an oversized nightshirt that revealed her left shoulder. "Planning." She managed a coy smile, made cuter by her tired look.

"Really?" he asked, playing along. Holly invented secrets purely for the thrill of spilling them.

"Uh-huh. A trip," she said, her voice rising playfully, popping with her pronunciation.

Jordan manufactured the pleasantly surprised expression she craved, even as his stomach tightened into a knot—and it wasn't the Hot Pocket.

"Well … our anniversary is coming. And. I. Thought …" She walked her fingers upward along his chest as she spoke. She tapped his chin in time as she hammered each word home. "A seven-day cruise to Hawai'i would be a perfect way to celebrate."

His breath sliced between his teeth, escaping in a whistle. Jordan sank into the memory foam topper, forgetting to mask his disappointment. How many times had he explained that he'd be traveling all summer for work, scouting environments for the game, researching survival scenarios? Come autumn, he'd be even busier. A week in September aboard a cruise ship? Impossible.

"I thought you'd be excited."

"It sounds nice, but September is—"

"Our anniversary."

"I know. But—"

"Our *first* anniversary."

"Maybe I can get away," he said. Then, realizing she might get the wrong idea, quickly blurted out the first thing that came to mind: "For a night or two. We can go to Vancouver. Take a long weekend."

Holly flopped her hands in a huff against the covers.

"Babe. We've been over this. You know these next two years are gonna be crazy."

She said nothing.

"It'll be worth it. That's what you said. Remember?"

"I never said anything about forfeiting my anniversary."

"Hey, it's my anniversary too. Don't you think I want to get away? Besides, nobody's asking you to forfeit—"

Holly snorted. "You got that right." She spun her back toward him. "I'm going. With or without you. I waited my whole life to get married. There's no way I'm not celebrating my anniversary. Least of all because of some stupid video game."

"Better opt for trip protection then. Shame if you had nothing to celebrate." He didn't mean it. The thought of leaving her never once crossed his mind, but he refused to allow his livelihood—his lifelong passion—to go undefended.

Holly bounced herself lower on the bed, slamming her head atop the pillow in one swift move. "Turn off the light. I've got a call at six."

Jordan spun his feet to the floor, snatched his pillow from the bed, and beat a path for the living room. A cruise to Hawai'i? No way. He had hoped to keep the hours reasonable until the final months. At least until they released a beta. But no. The game was too ambitious. The staff too small. If *Driftwood* was ever going to see the light of day—if they had any hope of outrunning their burn rate—overtime was inevitable.

And vacations, or having a life, would have to wait.

Jordan unfastened his seatbelt and got out in stiff, robotic movements. He hoisted his backpack from the trunk and set it down with a thud as Holly rounded the car beneath the Alaska Airlines sign.

"Airport's not too busy for a holiday," she said.

He looked around. Did people often fly on Independence Day? He didn't know.

"I'll miss you."

"Yeah. Me too." He shifted his stance. The pack teetered against his knee, then rolled, turtling on itself in the July heat. The waistbelt and shoulder straps reached for him like stunted limbs, its belly stuffed with two thousand dollars' worth of tent, sleep system, clothes, and cookware. Not to mention laptop, camera, and assorted gadgets. The best gear he ever owned. Helpless on the sidewalk.

"You'll call when you get to Anchorage?"

Jordan nodded. Then, sensing Holly wanted more of a response, he added, "As soon as I get settled."

"Well"—she breathed deeply—"I guess you better go." Holly kissed him. Briefly, but long enough for him to savor her scent: sexy and brash. She dove in for a hug and he met her embrace with a yearning that surprised even him. He wrapped his arms completely around her, pulling her tighter, closer than usual, minus the times in bed. He held on too long without shame.

Holly placed her hands against him and arched away. "What's wrong?"

Jordan bit his lip, embarrassed to say, but knew if he hadn't wanted her to ask then he shouldn't have worn his sadness so openly.

In the month following his night on the couch, Holly hadn't mentioned the cruise a single time. At first, Jordan believed his message had gotten through. That though she'd never admit to being selfish, she'd do the next best thing: act like it never happened. But, as days turned to weeks and his schedule grew ever busier, his earlier concerns sprouted anew, like weeds in an untended flower bed. Chief among them, that Holly would get so used to him always working, she might question if she needed him at all.

"Talk to me," she demanded.

"I miss you."

"It's only one week."

"No." He shook his head. She wasn't listening. "Already. We hardly see one another. And now I have these trips. After Alaska, it's straight off to Death Valley. I'm exhausted just thinking about it."

"We'll get through it."

"I feel trapped. On the one hand, this is everything I ever wanted. To develop my own survival game. To travel." He laughed sarcastically. "Kind of ironic, huh? It took being promoted to finally get time to go camping again. Only now, I'd rather be home. With you."

"That's sweet. But you don't need to worry. I'll be fine."

Jordan bit his lip to avoid initiating a fight. He puzzled over her comments, wondering how she possibly could have interpreted what he said as a sign of him worrying about her. "It's *us* I'm concerned about," he eventually said, lowering his voice as a family in matching Mickey Mouse ears wheeled their suitcases past. Behind him, automatic doors opened and closed repeatedly. Swoosh-clank. Swoosh-clank. Like a robot working a wad of chewing gum, ready to devour him next.

"Jordan." She tilted her head to the side. "This again?"

He recoiled ever so slightly. *Again? Hasn't she noticed the funk I've been in the past two months?* "If it were just one or two trips, I'd be okay. But then I have to scout a jungle location too. Costa Rica, I guess. Maybe Brazil." He sighed. "I don't know."

"What about Hawaiʻi?"

"What about it?" he asked, hoping she wasn't about to bring up the cruise right before he left. As he cautioned himself against overreacting to any mention of their anniversary, a siren squealed short and loud. "Move your vehicle. This area is for loading and unloading passengers only." The cop rolled by slowly, checking out Holly as he went. The siren blipped again, and the cop repeated his order, this time at the owners of a nearby sedan. Jordan watched as a man kissed a woman goodbye. He'd meet her in Phoenix on Saturday, the guy said before jogging back to his car.

"Well?" Holly asked, fishing for a response. "Aren't there jungles—?"

"Come with me," Jordan interrupted, blurting out the brainstorm that struck like lightning only feet away.

"To Alaska? No way."

He laughed, shaking his head. Jordan couldn't believe he had hadn't thought of it before. "No. To Hawai'i. You're right."

"I am?"

"I just remembered an article in *Outside* about this valley on Kaua'i. It's got beaches and waterfalls and all sorts of fruit. The photos were incredible."

Holly crossed her arms and looked away. Her go-to move when she needed to compose her thoughts. When she faced him, he saw the determination that no doubt won her so many promotions at work—and so few friends along the way. "You expect me to go camping instead of a cruise?"

"You'll love it. We'll hike in—I'll carry the gear—and you can lounge on the beach while I work. Besides," he said, flashing a toothy smile, "after all the penguin suits I had to rent for those charity galas you like dragging me to, isn't it time I get to see you in a pair of hiking shorts?"

She repeated herself, her tone as flat and dull as the sidewalk they stood upon. "You want me to help you research your video game?"

Despite her lack of enthusiasm, hearing her say it aloud made Jordan vibrate with excitement. He'd never considered it before, but now that the idea was out there, it seemed the perfect solution. "Yeah. It'll be great. If it's the trail I'm thinking of, it's supposed to be one of the most beautiful in the world."

"And the rain and bugs—"

"Overblown. Besides, I'm pretty sure it's the dry season. What do you say? We can go later this month."

"I don't know." Holly looked like she'd eaten a lemon, but wasn't saying no.

"I'll tell you what. We spend a few days in the valley, at this Kalalau place I read about, then we'll spend three nights at a resort. Your pick."

Holly massaged her forehead with small circular motions as he gave her the hard sell. He spoke of atomic sunsets and Milky Way skies, of towering cliffs and trees dripping with exotic fruit. Sensing her uncertainty, he knew he had to bring out the big guns and appeal to her competitive side. "Cruises are so ... ordinary. Think of the pictures. The two of us. Alone. In paradise. Your friends will be so jealous."

"Okay." Holly nodded reluctantly at first. She took a deep breath. "We'll do it." Her tone dripped with discomfort, but whether at him or her own unfamiliarity with compromise, he couldn't tell.

A resurgent warmth raced through Jordan as he ingested her words. This bite of generosity she'd fed him was a first for him in their relationship. Energized, he grabbed his hulking pack with a single hand and yanked it onto his shoulder as if it were stuffed with feathers. He pecked Holly goodbye, then kissed her again slower. He turned and entered the airport, already thinking about the night he'd return home. The hunger he'd have for her. The things they'd do.

CHAPTER 21
A BAD TRIP

The volatility evaporated along with the men as Inoke and his crew tended their garden and Tiki and Jordan went to the beach in search of dinner. Malia appreciated their ability to set aside tensions when there were tasks to be done but knew there'd be plenty of downtime soon enough—and that idle hands were the most dangerous of all.

Malia hadn't time to worry about that. She needed to build a fire. Partly out of boredom, true, but she mainly wanted the practice. Scratching SOS in the sand might snag the attention of an observant helicopter pilot, but it would probably take a bonfire to attract a passing boat.

She placed two parallel logs in the firepit. Railroad tracks to nowhere. She fluffed a pile of kindling with her hands and let the sticks tumble loosely, mounding between what she'd taken to calling the heart logs, a malaprop gleaned from Jordan's fire-building lesson. *Hearth logs,* he'd called them. And heart logs they became, for no reason at all. She drizzled lighter fluid atop the kindling—cheating, but nobody was keeping score—and set the yellow plastic bottle aside.

A small flame licked the lower twigs, soon scaling the assembled pile, building to scarlet peaks, charring the sticks to candy apple embers. When the fire settled into a steady flame, she moved two additional logs into position. One as a bridge across the earlier two, the other propped over the flames. She held her hair, bent low, and blew until the bridge log caught.

She leaned back, warming as much from satisfaction as the heat, debating whether to erect an even larger one on the beach—or to give Ruby one more chance.

"They letting you build fires now?" It was Inoke, leading Darren and Ruby back from their work in the garden.

Annoyed as much by the comment as their intrusion, Malia said, "Not like it requires a Y chromosome."

"A why what?" Ruby asked, his freckled face a ruddy blend of confusion and ugly.

"She means you don't need a pair of balls to strike a match," Tiki called out good-naturedly from the opposite direction. He carried a spear in one hand and a fish that nearly dragged the ground in the other. His hand cupped its gills as he beamed with boyish pride. It suited him quite well, Malia thought. Jordan followed behind, cradling his bulky fish trap.

"Whoa, nice catch," Darren said.

"Shame Jordan didn't show up sooner," Tiki replied. "He carves a mean spear." Tiki offered a peacemaker's smile to Malia, who felt herself relax, glad he and Jordan returned in time with the others.

Jordan hoisted a four-inch prawn from the trap for all to see. "Tonight, we feast!"

Inoke stomped past Ruby toward the table and snatched a small, crocheted bag he'd set beside his backpack earlier. No sooner had Darren and Ruby come forward to ogle the fish—an *ulua*, Tiki said—than Inoke called out, "I, too, come bearing gifts for our *hui*."

Malia and Jordan exchanged a wary glance.

Inoke rummaged inside the bag and withdrew a small knot of plastic wrap. Though it appeared empty to Malia, Darren rushed over, taking it from Inoke with the most excitement she'd ever seen from him. He clamped his lower lip between his teeth as he carefully teased a blue pill from the bag's corner.

"What is it?" Malia asked, craning her neck to see around Ruby.

"My first call home in months," he said, holding up a cloud-shaped pill imprinted with the word *Skype*.

"I don't get it," Malia said.

"Ecstasy," Tiki said, now standing beside her. Then, so sarcastically she could practically hear his eyes roll, "Great."

That Tiki, who never partook in the nightly dessert joints, recognized the drug caught her by surprise. "Is that true? It's really ecstasy?"

"Well, I can't guarantee what they cut it with, but yeah, it's X. Just a sample." Inoke clapped Darren on the back. "Thought who better than Darren to test my new product."

"Good enough for me." Darren held the pill between two fingers, admiring it as if it bore the scent of a forgotten love. "I know I should wait till after I eat, but—" He shrugged and tossed the pill into his mouth. He swallowed it dry, then rubbed his tummy like a child who'd scarfed the last cookie.

"I didn't forget the rest of you. Gonna be a while before my babies flower, but this ought to hold us over." Inoke unfurled a Ziploc baggie containing over twenty pre-rolled joints.

Tiki mumbled something under his breath, then approached Inoke, dipping his head to talk in private. Malia couldn't hear them, but whatever he said caused Inoke's jaw to tighten.

Malia tried to eavesdrop—the camp was no place for secrets—but Jordan intercepted her. He kept his back to the others and talked into his trap, speaking in hushed tones, pretending to discuss the prawns. "This is bullshit. It's bad enough that boat could be spotted from the air, but now grow lights and hard drugs—"

"It's only one pill," Malia said, wondering if it weren't time to heed Skye's warning about drinking.

"For now. And since when does Ruby stick around?"

Malia said nothing, her thoughts tugged aside by the peculiarity of Jordan's concern.

"He's getting sloppy. And judging by the amount of plant clippings I picked up, he's got a hell of an operation. Police are bound to be onto him. One flyby with a thermal cam and we're all screwed."

"Couldn't the cameras detect us too?" Malia asked, figuring their bodies gave off more heat than plants.

"Shh. Keep your voice down."

"Fine," she hissed. "But, honestly, drugs or not, I don't care. I just need to go home."

"I know what I'll do," Jordan said, lost in thought. "I'll slash the pontoons tonight. Then I can roll the boat up, hide it. Nobody will ever see it then."

"Don't you dare! Didn't you hear me? I need that boat to—" Malia flashed her eyes in warning.

"So, how many you catch?" Inoke reached around Jordan's shoulder, plucking out one of the larger prawns. It wriggled in his grasp, clawing the air in slow motion.

Jordan shrugged. "Fifteen or so."

"Really? You two look like you're having serious talk about the shrimp, but you ain't count them yet?"

"I was saying how nice it'll be to have rice again," Malia said.

"But maybe we should conserve it for nights we don't have so much fish," Jordan added, somewhat stilted.

Inoke studied them with such pinpoint focus that Malia's stomach tightened, convinced he wasn't buying it—and part of her didn't care. She'd cover for Jordan only insofar as he didn't jeopardize her getting to college on time.

Malia excused herself to tend the fire, and one by one everyone dispersed to their afternoon tasks. Tiki cleaned the fish, tossing the guts into the flames, where they sizzled and smoked, suffusing the camp with the alkaline tang of salted iron. Inoke peeled the prawns while Ruby gathered extra firewood. Darren was the only one who did nothing, sprawled out atop the bench, no doubt waiting for the high to kick in. Malia had never tried ecstasy herself but heard enough from the EDM kids at school to know it could be unpredictable, which to her seemed a good enough reason to steer clear. Some described it as living in a rainbow, with every cell of their body vibrating like a tuning fork at the slightest touch. But others likened their trip to feeling like some crazed Frankenstein's monster born of caffeine and testosterone. Given how sloth-like Darren was in his unaddled state, she figured he'd be on the ground, reciting bad poetry to the trees, in no time.

Normally, a midafternoon feast would have attracted hikers wandering the valley, but with the trail closed, they were alone. And though Malia wasn't hungry, she hoped getting food into Darren would mute whatever effects the pill might have on him.

The seafood grilled up fast, and the group soon leaned into their meals, devouring the catch in silence, but Malia could sense it wouldn't last. Across from her, Darren ignored his meal, engrossed in the feel of the stick she'd set aside for tending fire. He dragged it across his skin, rubbing its scratchy bark against his arms and neck, purring as he did. The stick was the length of his leg and as thick as his wrist. Every so often, he'd use it as a poker, jabbing the rocks or the logs in the fire, but he also nearly stabbed Inoke's leg. Then, playing keep-away with Inoke, nearly poked Tiki in the face with its soot-smeared point. Jordan stared from across the firepit, picking fish bones from his teeth, shaking his head in disgust at Darren's tomfoolery.

"Darren, no. Give it to me," Tiki commanded.

Darren knelt between Tiki and Inoke, clutching the yellow bottle of lighter fluid Malia forgot to put away. He held it sideways over his head, flying it through loop-the-loops like a boy with a model airplane. He hummed a tune as he flew the bottle until switching to airplane noises.

"Yo, man, you're dripping that shit everywhere." Inoke shifted his feet and backed away as lighter fluid trailed down Darren's arm and onto the stick which lay propped against the fire ring.

"Come here, man." Tiki wrested the lighter fluid away and set it out of Darren's reach. He bulged his eyes at Malia, knowing she'd left it out. She mouthed a reluctant apology, one she didn't feel she owed anyone, and was happy when Tiki returned a look that made clear his annoyance lay with Darren, not her.

Beside her, Jordan mumbled invective beneath his breath.

"You say something?" Inoke asked, still riding the annoyance of Darren's sloppiness.

"I said the fucking idiot's gonna burn the whole forest down." Jordan spoke with a volume incongruous to the setting. "This is why we shouldn't have drugs here. Or grow lights. Or a boat. Any of it."

"You're nice. I like you." Darren leaned his face into Tiki's, staring into his eyes from inches away. Tiki tolerated it for a moment, then nudged him away.

Jordan's scowl hardened. "This is ridiculous."

"Man, why don't you shut up?" Inoke said.

Across the fire, where a third of the *ulua* sat crisping atop a cast-iron pan, Darren climbed to his feet in fits and starts, like a limousine making a K-turn on a one-lane road. He gripped the stick and twirled it overhead, trailing a small ball of flames from the end.

"Sit down, Darren," Ruby said, leaning against a log behind Inoke.

Darren rounded the benches toward Malia and Jordan, swinging the stick like a wannabe fire dancer as he gripped the seatbacks for balance. Then, stopping just beyond Jordan's reach, he said, "You're a jerk. Jerk, jerkety, jerk." He thrust the fiery stick with each repetition like a rapier. "Ever since you showed up …" He looked away, distracted, and swayed. He wobbled, not like a drunk, but as though the fire had struck up a soothing melody. Then he snapped to. "You suck."

"Me?" Jordan glared at Darren, then looked around the circle as he spoke. Malia could tell he was weighing something heavy. "I'm the jerk? You all wanted me to starve. Wouldn't even talk to me. Wouldn't even let Malia give me a goddamn mango."

"Thought you were a NARC," Inoke said, shrugging it off. No harm, no foul.

The entire group startled at Inoke's admission, not least of all Jordan. "Why would you think I—"

"He's no NARC," Darren said, interrupting Jordan. "He's an asshole." He thrust the torch at Jordan, who swatted it away. Though seated, Jordan's bouncing knees showed he wouldn't take much more abuse. Malia held her breath and scooted further down the bench, wondering if he'd just leave again, like that night weeks ago. She looked to Tiki for support, but he appeared distracted, lost in thought.

Darren retreated, stepping sideways, crossing one foot over the other, moving like a concussed athlete doing agility drills in quicksand. He did a little spin and swung the stick in a figure eight, trailing dusky ribbons of smoke. "You need to go," he said, presumably to Jordan. But it was he who went. Darren stumbled past the table and out toward the trail, moving with the conviction of a butterfly on a breezy day.

"Somebody better get him," Ruby said, scoffing at Darren's behavior. Nobody moved.

Darren approached a guava tree. He rubbed his back against it, giving himself a woodsy massage, reminding Malia of bears in a toilet paper commercial. "This is the best tree. I love this tree," he said amidst small moans of pleasure. After a few moments, he stopped abruptly, distracted by a shinier, newer passion. Without veering, Darren headed straight for Jordan's tent.

"No, no!" Jordan stood. "Get away from my tent."

Inoke clamped a hand on Jordan's shoulder as he rose. "Yo, Darren, get back here."

Ignoring Inoke's command, Darren danced nearer to Jordan's tent. To the music of the wind. To the birdsong. Who knew? But, while attempting what could best be described as a pirouette, he stumbled. Maybe on a tree root or his own bare foot. Or simply from dizziness.

"Whoopsy," Darren said as he fell to the ground in laughter, tossing his impromptu torch straight into the open vestibule of Jordan's tent. The door hung rolled like a loosely folded newspaper. A perfect firestarter ready to be ignited.

"Fuck!" Jordan broke free of Inoke's grip, hurdled the bench, and dashed as fast as Malia had ever seen someone move. He was at the tent in two, three seconds tops. He kicked at the fire, but the flames were already creeping along the walls, chewing the material in an incandescent, all-consuming arch. Where there was once tent, soon there was nothing. The fire ate it in giant bites. Flaming nylon dripped like molten ore onto the ground in an unceasing seep of destruction.

Jordan rounded the tent—he kept the area around his tent clear of leaves and sticks—and unzipped the other door and hurled his gear from the tent. Sleeping bag, pad, some gadgets he kept in a plastic bag. A stuff sack came next, right before he tumbled from the tent choking on the smoke. The flames crept along the ceiling, repelling his attempt to duck back inside. He screamed in agony and slapped at his neck where fragments of the dripping tent had scalded him.

Still, Malia turned away, looking for water, but knew it was too late. The tent was a total loss. When she turned back, Tiki stepped beside her. Together, they watched as scarlet embers floated on fire-borne currents, parachuting harmlessly to the ground as ashen bits. Whether in shock or because they knew it was pointless, nobody came to Jordan's aid.

Jordan backed away from the ruins, burying his mouth and nose in the nook of his elbow. The heat and smoke were all consuming, and whatever still lay in the tent had no chance of being rescued. It disintegrated, hardly leaving a sign of its existence other than the disfigured poles and perfect tent-shaped outline on scorched dirt. Jordan scanned it from tip to tail and continued his gaze ten feet further to Darren, who observed the destruction with a bleary-eyed expression of wonder.

And in an instant, Jordan rushed forward and unloaded a vicious right hook that hit Darren square in the face. Whether the crunch Malia heard was Darren's jaw or Jordan's knuckles, there was no telling. But Darren was unconscious before ever hitting the ground.

Darren lay sprawled in the dirt, his arms folded awkwardly beneath him, blood trickling from his lip. Whether knocked out, asleep, or worse, it was impossible to tell. Malia stood transfixed by the replay looping through her mind: the ferocity of Jordan's punch, the sight of Darren's body crumpling like a marionette cut from its strings.

Nobody moved. Not for a second, maybe two. Then the levee broke. Inoke and Ruby burst from their collective shock and crashed over the bench seating. They charged to their friend's aid with Tiki close behind. Malia's legs propelled her forward, as if dragged along on their current. Jordan shifted from foot to foot, standing over Darren's limp body with his fists balled, ready to strike again. She tried to shout, whether to stop him or to call Inoke and the others back, she wasn't sure. There was only her adrenaline-fueled need to scream, and she did, but the tremor in her throat rendered her words incoherent.

Inoke closed on Jordan and shoved him in the shoulder, sending the smaller man stumbling backwards. "You like throwing punches? Let's go!" Inoke yelled. The whites of his eyes blazed with hatred, and Malia knew there was no stopping him. He rushed Jordan again, slamming into him like a bull charging a gimped matador. Jordan was knocked skyward, his breath escaping in a haunting gust as he flew onto the flaming wreckage of the collapsed tent. "Get burnt, asshole."

Jordan screamed in terror as he landed atop the melted wreckage. He slapped at the flames singeing his arms and licking at his shorts as molten nylon clung to his skin. Fire rippled along the remaining shreds, consuming the material inch by inch, devouring everything in its path. Jordan kicked at the skeletal remains of the tent somehow still standing, knocking the aluminum poles over, clearing a path to retreat. He knelt in the dirt on the far side of the smoldering moat, coughing on the fumes and smoke as Inoke and Ruby advanced, smirking like cats who've cornered a mouse.

Malia clutched at her throat in horror. "Leave him alone," she gasped. Nobody noticed.

"Guys, relax!" Tiki yelled.

Malia snapped around as Tiki came forward, his gaze focused on the other men. He appeared taller, his jaw more pronounced. The Kiwi-accented surfer drawl Malia had grown so accustomed to had vanished, replaced with the tone of someone accustomed to giving orders. "Inoke, enough."

Inoke and Ruby faced Tiki with expressions bearing equal parts curiosity and surprise. "This don't concern you, Tiki," Inoke said as Ruby's eyes flicked between the other men.

"No more violence."

"You choosing sides?" Inoke asked, his tone accusatory. He curled his lip in a snarl and stepped toward Tiki, rolling his head from side to side, cracking the joints of his neck.

"Not at all," Tiki said, turning himself sideways to Inoke. "But if you send this fool to the hospital, you'll end up with cops all over the place."

Inoke considered Tiki's warning, then disregarded it. "Too late for—"

"Jordan, no! Drop the knife," Tiki shouted, extending his hand in a calming motion.

Jordan stood beside his salvaged backpack, clutching his survival knife.

Tiki stepped toward him. "Don't do anything stupid."

Jordan ignored Tiki's warning and eyed Inoke with a possessed look. Malia's gaze shifted from the glint of the blade to Jordan's wounds— red, raw, and seeping—and felt powerless to do anything.

Inoke spun back to Jordan, his eyes flaring in a surprised show of alarm.

"It's over, Inoke. The camp's mine. Time for you and your band of losers to gather your shit and set up somewhere else."

"Man, you better shut up," Ruby said.

"Or what, Ruby?" Jordan asked, pointing the knife at him. "Inoke's using you. He sits out here, getting high and partying, while you risk your ass going back and forth in the boat every week. For what? So you can get bossed around by this piece of shit?" Jordan jerked the knife at Inoke for emphasis.

"Yo, fuck you," Inoke said.

"I'm so sick of this," Malia yelled, her frustration boiling over. All the posturing, the macho bullshit. The drugs and the threats and the constant selfishness. *Some hippie paradise this turned out to be.*

Jordan held a sadistic look in his eyes, clenching the knife as the burns blistered upon his arm. Before him pooled the ruins of his tent, the shelter that protected Malia from the storm. She stared unblinking at the destruction despite the chemical smoke hanging over the camp in acrid clouds, reeking of plastic as soot floated in the air like hell's pollen. Jordan had saved his bedding, his backpack. But everything else—his clothes, the cord and tools he made—succumbed to the flames. *Everything.*

"My photo," she said with a gasp, suddenly remembering Jordan was holding onto it until later that night. The keepsake she was so relieved to know hadn't been lost in the storm now lay amongst the charred ruins of the tent. She envisioned the heat curling the picture's corners, bubbling the gloss, turning that faded Kodak print to sepia, then yellow, and finally death. She pictured the flames erasing her mother's handwriting from the back, the note she'd scrawled now incinerated. "For My Sweet Malia," she'd written. "May the magic of Kalalau shine within you always."

The photo? The note? In ashes. Along with any hope of ever knowing who her birth father was.

Malia's nostrils flared as her fury rose. She stormed past Tiki, ignoring his attempt to reach for her, hoping to find a tattered shred of the photo amongst the ashes, but the residual heat and fumes were too strong, her odds of success too long. She unleashed a rumbling shout as loud and as visceral as a volcanic eruption, casting the entirety of the valley under the shadow of her grief—and rage. Malia pointed at Inoke, knowing if he hadn't given Darren the X, the fire never would have happened. "You talk about family. That we're your *'ohana*. Bullshit!"

"He ain't family," Inoke said, gesturing with his chin at Jordan. Behind him, Darren moaned and rolled to his side, rubbing his face.

"You don't care about this place, this 'āina. Or us. You're just using it, using everyone. Anywhere else you're a nobody."

From her left, Jordan gave a derisive snort. Malia whirled on him before Inoke could respond, eager to unload on every one of them. "And you shut up. I don't know what your story is. Or what happened to your wife, but you should have taken a hint and left weeks ago."

"Left?" Jordan sounded indignant. He gestured toward the others with the knife. "I saved this camp. Remember? No, they're the ones who ought to leave." He shook his head, glaring at Darren. "Asshole burnt my tent."

"So what? He's high! It was an accident. There are other tents. You didn't have to start a fight," Malia hollered, exasperated, unable to contain what had really set her off any longer. "And you could have given me back my photo yesterday," she said, glaring at him through her smeared vision, hating herself for not having demanded it back when she had the chance.

There was so much more she needed to get off her chest. About Jordan, about Inoke, everyone. She opened her mouth, but only a hoarse cry escaped as she slumped forward in exhaustion. Malia watched the smoke tendrils rising from the tent as a hand landed upon her shoulder. Her breath hitched, knowing at once it was Tiki's. "And you," she said, her gaze climbing along his arm to his shoulder, to the regretful face that only made it worse. If only he'd ignored her like the others, hadn't tried to make her feel welcome, or safe. If only he'd lied and said he was in a relationship.

If only she hadn't sensed the passion she so desperately wanted to feel from him in the flash of their second kiss. Then, perhaps, she would have left weeks ago as well. And none of this would be her problem.

She steeled herself against Tiki's charms and looked away, knowing any attempt to speak would spill the tears she'd somehow managed to hold back.

Malia stepped from his grasp and turned to Jordan. "You can have my tent. I'm leaving tomorrow," she said, and bent to grab his sleeping bag. Then, as much for her sake as anyone else's, she added, "We'll sleep head to foot." Malia led the way to her tent, her certainty growing with every step that tomorrow, no matter what it took, even if it meant burning down the whole forest, she'd be going home.

CHAPTER 22
BAD MATH

"**A** burning tent? Wonderful." Park drummed her pen against the table, searching the ceiling for restraint as she gathered her thoughts. Malia combed anxious fingers through her mass of hair and waited. Whether real or a trick of the mind, she smelled smoke in the strands. A reeking reminder of the ugliness of that night.

"This is what really ticks me off. They claim to love the land, to be its protector. Isn't that what your 'Outlaw' friends like to say?" She added finger quotes and snorted with disdain. "That they shouldn't need permits because they're caretakers?"

Malia shrugged, not knowing how to respond. Below the table, her fingers sought the comforting tug of the drawstring in her lap and again twisted it tight.

"Bad enough with the squatting and the illegal ferry service. Not to mention the garbage. You have any idea how much crap DLNR has hauled out of there over the years?" She gave Malia no time to respond. "But now we've got arson and Schedule One narcotics? This is how you chose to honor your mother? By living amongst delinquents?"

The shame of Park's judgment stacked atop Malia's existing guilt with surprising force. Her heart ached from the pressure, as if that woman, as slight as Park was, had jumped atop her chest with both feet. "I had nothing to do with it," was all she managed.

"No? You got involved with a man twice your age. After everyone out there told you he was bad news."

Malia's fingers fell open; the drawstring went slack. *Twice my age? No, that can't be.*

Park drew her brow in tight as she studied Malia with such intensity one could all but hear Park mentally erasing every redeemable trait she'd found in the girl. "Unprotected sex in Kalalau. Gee, wonder where you picked that up from."

Malia swallowed hard, struck silent by Park's audacity. The pain in Malia's chest doubled as her shaking leg made the slipper to slap like a fishtail against her heel in panic. *How dare you. How dare you bring my mother into this!*

"Well, if him being thirty-seven doesn't bother you, then maybe you'll care that nobody's heard from his wife in weeks."

Malia's body froze stock-still as bile scorched the back of her throat. Park arched her eyebrows. A wisp of a smile graced her lips in reaction to the immobilizing effect the news achieved. Malia could only look away, unsure what to say, how to feel.

"You have any idea the risk you put yourself in?" Park paused only briefly for an answer. "Of course you don't. You're just a kid—"

"You sound like my dad."

Park clasped her hands together atop the table. Her fingers were slender; one could even call them bony. They bore the spotted creases of maturity. Mom hands. Malia again focused on the chipped nail polish, this time recalling how her own mother's nails had always been perfect. Freshly painted. Cuticles trimmed. But she didn't have to raise a daughter alone. Unlike Park. Unlike her father.

"If I sound like your dad, it's only because I know what it's like to have a daughter who thinks she's all grown up—"

"I'm nineteen." Malia's voice was soft, not combative. Just stating a fact, not a correction.

"Legally an adult. But you've got a lot to learn."

"Like what?"

"When Tiki first told you about Jordan's tan line, you didn't know what he meant, did you?"

Malia looked at her lap, embarrassed for not having realized it until later. Of course, it was dark in the cave the night they had sex. But no, she didn't understand until it was too late. Nor was Malia sure she would have cared. It was easy there in the interrogation room to wish she'd never befriended Jordan, let alone slept with him. But that night, alone with him? She just wanted to feel something. To be wanted.

"Is Jordan really thirty-seven?"

Park nodded.

Malia swallowed the lump in her throat. "And ... his wife is really missing?"

"Her name is Holly McAdams, and we have reason to believe she may have come to harm."

"He never mentioned her." Malia turned sideways in her chair, angling toward the wall. She pulled her feet onto the seat and hugged her knees close. That she was suddenly old enough to have slept with a married man startled her even more than the fact that she had.

Park cleared her throat, no doubt wanting to continue, but a knock on the door drew their attention. Sergeant Kahale poked his head inside. He glimpsed Malia's way then turned. "Detective? A moment in the hallway, please."

Park pulled the door closed behind her and flapped the neck of her blouse for air. She needed to stand, to get out of that room. Few interviews exceeded fifteen minutes, forty tops. The three hours spent cooped up in that box without a break was nearing a record. "Give me a minute," she told Kahale as he started down the hall.

Park leaned against the door, rubbing the small of her back as she tried to square what Malia described with the ever-present awareness that her own daughter, barely four years younger than Malia, currently sat at home, alone, in an apartment across town. Other than being selfish and a bit naive—what teenager wasn't?—she found little fault in Malia's story. The girl wanted an adventure, a chance to find some meaning during a difficult period in her life, and got caught up with the wrong crowd. Park knew it could happen to anyone. And *that*, more than anything, was what upset her. With an ex-husband on the mainland and her schedule so crazy, she couldn't be certain her own daughter wasn't getting into worse scrapes of her own.

"Detective," Kahale called out, "everything all right?" His tone was respectful, but she knew time was ticking. Kahale had been none too pleased about the head start Jordan had before they got the helicopters airborne.

Park wiped her palms dry on her suit pants and made her way to where Sergeant Kahale and Detective Bynum stood out of voice range, waiting. They'd been observing the interview, most of it at least, and could probably sense she needed a break. Either that or they had an update for her. That Bynum wasn't assisting in the recovery of the victim's body concerned her.

"So, what do you think?" Kahale asked, cutting to the chase.

Park rubbed her forehead. "Tempted to believe her. I don't think she knows where he went."

"Or maybe she's covering for him," Kahale said. "I wouldn't put it past her. Young girl. An older guy. They can get pretty attached."

Bynum dismissed Kahale's idea with a curt shake of his head, earning a wry smile from Park.

"I'll keep her talking." No sooner had the words left Park's lips than she wondered when she last spent an entire morning listening to her own daughter. She shook the thought from her mind. "Malia said he knew about the old back door trail up the cliffs. He clearly did his homework. We know he's good in the jungle, and with all that gear, smart money says he's still out there."

Kahale spoke up. "I'm telling you, he either hiked out in the night and is somewhere up north as we speak—"

"Isn't the trail washed out?" Park asked, interrupting him.

"Yeah," Bynum said. "But if that stoner Darren was able to make it through, then our guy definitely could have—or at least felt comfortable attempting it."

"*Orrr,*" Kahale said, not completely letting the interruption slide, "like I said, he's still in the valley, hiding."

Park nodded in agreement. "And if he ducks into a cave when he hears a chopper, even the sensors won't pick him up." The three stood in silence for a moment, contemplating what that might mean. Kalalau Valley was over two square miles in size, with countless places to hide. Anyone who knew anything about the Nāpali Coast knew it had a long history of attracting people who didn't want to be found, dating back to the famed "Koolau the Leper" who, in the nineteenth century, avoided banishment to Molokai by hiding amongst the cliffs of Kalalau Valley.

And a cop died trying to flush him out, Park thought with a chill.

"There's another possibility," Bynum finally said.

Park and Kahale exchanged curious glances before Kahale took the bait.

"The sea."

Park turned to Kahale, whose brow was nearly as wrinkled as his shirt. "The inflatable was still there when you landed, right?"

"Yep. But too heavy for one person to budge."

Park arched her eyebrows at Bynum.

"I didn't say anything about a boat."

"You're kidding, right? You think he swam for it?" Park asked rhetorically. The northwest coast of Kaua'i was essentially one continuous cliff, battered by shark-infested waters with few places to come ashore. Park never measured it, but figured it had to be at least ten miles from Kalalau to Polihale, the next accessible beach to the southwest.

"Me? No. Just saying it's not impossible—"

"For someone with a death wish," Park said somewhat flippantly. Her choice of words reminded her of how Malia described Jordan near the cliffs—and how he said dying in the valley was what he feared most. She pushed the thought from her mind. "Best we keep our focus up north and continue searching the valley."

"We've got officers stationed at the end of the trail and in Hanalei. Also, I got someone atop the overlook, in case he manages to climb out."

"Thanks, Kahale. Good work."

Bynum stiffened and looked away, straining to keep his objections under wraps. She respected his willingness to cover all the bases, but they were a small department—and he was the junior detective. She couldn't risk manpower on the improbable. She flattened her tone, trying to reengage with him. "Any word from the dad?"

"Left a message but haven't heard back."

"We'll keep you posted if we learn anything else," Kahale said, smoothing over Bynum's curt response. "Just have to keep her talking for now."

"Think we're making a mistake," Bynum said.

"Noted," Park said, refusing to debate the matter. She left the men and headed down the hall toward the vending machines, figuring she and Malia could both use a little refreshment.

"Hey, Park, interview room's this way," Bynum called out with a chuckle.

She froze in the hallway, her back to him. "Getting a Coke, if you must know," she said through gritted teeth. Then she turned and added, "But how 'bout taking a shower, Bynum. You smell like roadkill."

For ten minutes, Malia debated getting up to the use the bathroom, to pee and gulp some water from the faucet. But she stayed put, legs crossed beneath the table, sawing the drawstring back and forth through the waistband. There was comfort in the noise. When pulled fast, it whirred with the sound of the surf falling back to the sea; when dragged slower, it resembled her father's snoring. And even that was a worthwhile distraction from her guilt. Inoke, Tiki, and even Park seemed to know Jordan was bad news. But only she chose to ignore it.

Malia began a countdown, telling herself she'd get up to pee if Park wasn't back in twenty seconds. She slowed her count as the numbers dwindled, suddenly afraid to leave her chair without permission. By the time three became two became one, Malia knew she wouldn't budge. Park returned as Malia resorted to counting down fractions, leaving the door ajar as she placed two cans of Coke on the table. A reward for good behavior. Malia was about to comment on her thirst when her breath lodged in her throat. In the hallway, a flash of turquoise shorts caught her eye. Tiki.

Park followed Malia's gaze, then pushed the door closed with a silent thud. Jailed again. Malia accepted the Coke without comment, her mind racing with disbelief that Tiki was already done. For most of the day, she'd forgotten that in another room, probably as cramped and stale as hers, he was telling his side of the story. She no longer worried about what he told the police, or if he might sell her out. She only worried if he was okay, or if they were going to deport him.

"So, let's get back to your version of events. Was there any more fighting that night between Inoke and Jordan?"

Malia shook her head, recalling the sounds of Inoke and Ruby's mockery from the campfire, their teasing of Darren. She kept watch inside the tent, senses drawn tight, bracing for further violence, but it never came. Jordan's retreat had placated the other men.

"So you stayed in the tent? The two of you? All night?"

Malia could tell what Park was hinting at and made a sour face, sorry she'd ever mentioned that night in the cave. Malia never anticipated describing her sex life to an adult; least of all to a cop. "I tossed his sleeping bag into the tent. He climbed in without a word."

"But it was only dinnertime. And he must have had, what, second-degree burns? Surely you must have discussed what happened."

"There was nothing to say. Jordan tended to his burns. He had a first aid kit. I had a book. The end." Of course, that wasn't entirely true, but it was close enough. Between the hours spent reliving her summer and the sight of Tiki in the hallway, Malia couldn't focus on Jordan. Nor did she believe Park needed to hear any further tales of self-pity, how she spent the night staring at the surviving photo of her mother, how she'd wished she'd gotten on the boat when given the chance.

CHAPTER 23
A GENTLEMAN'S WAGER

Malia wiped the sleep from her eyes and reached for the tent zipper. Just another morning in Kalalau—hopefully her last, she thought. Then she saw it, the empty sleeping bag beside her own, and the memories rushed in: the fire, the fighting, Jordan spending the night in her tent. She stared at his unzipped pack, wondering where he'd gone. She listened for the telltale sound of a urine stream soaking the ground litter, but heard only silence beyond the nylon wall. Despite the presence of his bag, she suspected he'd left. Either to slash the pontoons or because he invented a way to drag the boat to the water and set off in the night. Light and fast. To seek medical attention for his burns, perhaps, or to escape Inoke—or to even rat them out to the police. The why didn't matter. Only that he may have stolen her way out of Kalalau.

"No. This isn't happening." She stared, marinating in the acid sting of his subterfuge, at the spot where he should have been asleep. It was barely daybreak. Malia took off in a sprint, hoping to catch him before he cranked the motor. She'd jump aboard and demand he take her with him. That's what she'd do. If she hurried.

She'd barely crossed camp before a voice called to her from the dim predawn light.

"Going somewhere?"

Malia jerked backward a half step, like a dog hitting the end of its chain.

She scanned the camp but saw no one. Was she hearing things? She nearly convinced herself the voice was a trick of her imagination, a prank of the breeze now sending her neck hair on end. Then she saw him, Jordan, sitting cross-legged atop the table, peering from the indigo shadows in the direction of Inoke's tent. He clutched the survival knife in his right hand; its polished blade lay propped atop his knee. His bandages fallen loose, the weeping white swath of his burn wounds shone against his summer skin like the pith of a peeled orange.

Her lips moved, but she said nothing. Nor did he repeat himself. He simply sat there, unflinching, staring with his bloodshot gaze, crazed and undeterred as if carved of stone. She wanted to speak, but what does one say to a gargoyle?

She backed away, circling to escape his field of view. And as she went, widening the arc of her path little by little, Malia found herself drawn within the orbit of Tiki's tent. Of course. He'd be able to help. If not with her need to leave, then at least in preventing another fight—or worse.

Malia knelt silently beside Tiki's tent and raised her hand to knock against its pole, but hesitated, realizing it was her first time there. Nearly two months in Kalalau and she'd never come this close, never seen inside his tent. That she was visiting now, because of Jordan, was bittersweet. She slumped, recalling the day atop the overlook—and the spark she felt when he briefly kissed her.

Throw another log on the fire of what could have been, she thought, then bristled at her mind's own phrasing.

She whispered Tiki's name, but heard nothing. "Tiki," she hissed again, urgent and louder. When he didn't reply, she shook the pole.

"Who's there?" His voice was frantic, on guard. She heard a brief commotion.

"It's me. Let me in."

He seemed to release a held breath. "Okay. Gimme a minute," he said, his voice trilling with adrenaline. From outside the tent, she heard bags shifted, zippers pulled, and space cleared. She nearly gave up waiting when Tiki unzipped the door, wearing a pair of nylon track pants and a tank top. He invited her in. Aside from his bedding, the tent was empty save for some beach towels and stuff sacks, the clothes she'd seen him in dozens of times, and a few water-stained paperbacks. No different than her own, save for the scent. The tent held an enticing blend of leather and coconut that loaned a sense of security to the space. An aroma she could get used to.

"What's up?" Tiki asked, his head tilted in curiosity.

"It's Jordan. He's got his knife, and this crazed look. Like he might …" The sentence slipped away as she caught sight of Tiki's shoulder bag, laying partially unzipped and half tucked inside his sleeping bag. He followed her gaze and pulled the covers over it without a word, as if concealing dirty underwear.

"You were saying?"

She pried her eyes from the lump, wondering what she'd seen. It was black. Bulky. She'd nearly lost her train of thought. "He's just staring at Inoke's tent. In some sort of trance." Malia wiped her sweaty palms against her wrap as violent guesses flooded her mind. "I think he's planning to hurt someone."

Across the piled navy-blue nylon of his sleeping bag, Tiki watched with a curious expression. Whether he too was struck by her sudden presence in the tent, finally after all these weeks, or waiting for additional information, she could only guess. Malia chewed her lip as a third option came to mind: that Tiki was upset over her sleeping with Jordan and might not help.

Knowing she couldn't undo the past, she prodded him. "Well, can you help?"

"Sure. I'll talk to them. But I'm not really sure what you expect me to do."

"I don't know. I need to get home. School starts next week and …" She gazed up at him, hoping he'd understand she was out of options. "I asked Ruby, but he wouldn't help. And it's not just school. Last night scared me."

Tiki nodded attentively, care written in his features. Still, he said nothing. Outside the tent, a thrush sang its morning greeting.

"Can you help?" The look on his face suggested he'd need convincing. "We can take the inflatable. Or maybe you can help me hike out. Just till I get past the landslide—"

"Malia."

"Or we can wave down a tour boat. Or signal a helicopter."

Tiki rubbed his forehead and squeezed his eyes shut, like someone bracing for an oncoming migraine.

"You planning to use that on someone, eh, *haole?*" It was Inoke, his voice loud, unwavering. Malia's and Tiki's eyes met in alarm, then they faced the tent door in unison. Outside, a commotion followed by another shout: "Whoa, drop the knife, you crazy fuck."

Tiki raced past Malia, pushing through the unzipped door in a flash. Malia's heart pounded in her ears. She hurried after him, exiting the tent in time to see Jordan shift into a knife-fighting stance.

"Time to leave, Inoke," Jordan said, moving toward him.

"I ain't goin' nowhere," Inoke spat, his tone defiant despite retreating stride for stride with Jordan's advance.

"That prick's still here?" Darren said groggily, emerging from his tent. His left eye was black and puffy. Dried blood spackled his nostril and upper lip. Ruby appeared seconds later, rushing to Inoke's side.

"Enough!" Tiki yelled, getting between Jordan and Inoke, spreading his arms in each direction. "Drop the knife."

Jordan shook his head, nostrils flaring, and took another step.

"I said drop it!"

The pounding in Malia's head melded with the shouted threats, the volleyed profanity. Blood drained from Jordan's face as he clenched the knife in a white-knuckle grip, biting off the distance between himself and Inoke, who stood flanked by Ruby and Darren, the two yelling and gyrating like crazed backup singers, drowning out Tiki's attempted refereeing.

Malia screamed for them to stop, but she was invisible, held hostage within the ruins of her Kalalau fantasy. Not by land or storm, but by these selfish men who didn't care about the valley, the 'āina. And they certainly didn't give a shit about her or her roots in this place. She groped a tree for balance as the gravity of the situation buckled her knees. She wanted to cry. To curl up in her childhood bed and bawl her heart out, to wish it was all just a bad dream. But in that wish, an echo penetrated her mind. Not of her words or anyone else's but of her heart. And how she felt the night her father forbid her from going to California for college. She refused to surrender what she'd earned. So she got a job, saved enough money for airfare, books, and whatever else she needed. She didn't need his help, his permission. And she'd be damned if she needed Jordan's or Inoke's either.

Malia straightened, realizing she still might hold a ticket out of Kalalau too. She sprinted to her tent and returned not a minute later clutching Jordan's locator beacon.

"STOP!" she yelled, this time leaving no doubt to the power of her voice.

She stepped forward, holding the beacon for them all to see. It wasn't much larger than an old flip phone, and one by one, the men's attention locked onto the device, their anger melting first in recognition, then alarm, as if she held a detonator capable of blowing the camp sky high.

"No, no, no, Malia. You don't want to be playing with that," Inoke said, more warning than request. Of them all, she knew he had the most to lose, and wouldn't hesitate long before wrestling it from her hands. After all, he was the one running a grow operation in a state park, dealing drugs across the island.

"Put it down." Jordan's earlier wide-eyed stare had focused into a menacing laser.

Tiki rushed to her side and placed a hand over the device, obscuring the buttons, easing it down and away as he watched Jordan out the corner of his eyes. She expected Tiki of all people to support the idea. "Why?"

He said nothing, but she could see in the droop of his eyelids, the sag of his jaw, that the answer lay just out of reach, one he couldn't share. One she might not even believe. He angled his back to the others and leaned in. So close she could see the pillow lines in his face. It was the look he gave her all those weeks ago when he sided with Inoke and told her not to give Jordan the mango. He'd asked her to trust his judgment once before. And she didn't. Now he was asking again.

She moved her thumb along the beacon's hard plastic surface, feeling for a button. Any button. Tiki squeezed her hand, pinning it in place. "Inoke, she just wants to leave," Tiki said. "Hop in the boat and take her to Hanalei. Problem solved."

"But don't come back," Jordan added quickly.

"Screw you," Inoke said to Jordan. Then, to Tiki, "I told you, man. The boat stays. We're not going anywhere while he's here. Not again." He jerked a thumb toward Jordan.

Inoke wasn't bluffing, and Tiki's grip on the beacon was such that Malia couldn't move her fingers, let alone send an SOS. Though frustrated and confused by Tiki's surprise resistance, it was Jordan she was most angry with. Her blood boiled as she looked across the camp as he stood, clutching the knife like a stubborn fool. "Just go! Leave! Nobody wants you here."

"Can't do it."

"The valley's huge. Go somewhere else. Build another camp. Just for you." Malia's voice cracked as she pleaded.

"Yeah, why not *ʻōkole*? It'd be nice having something bigger than a goat to hunt." Inoke slashed his hand across his throat.

The taunt sent a chill down Malia's spine as she recalled her first day in the camp, the squeal of the slaughtered goat, the blood dripping from Inoke's knife. Unlike the gangs in Honolulu, she'd always believed Inoke and Ruby were more bark than bite, despite their muscles and intimidating appearance. Now, she wondered if it was only through their restraint that Jordan hadn't already lost more than his tent.

"Inoke. Please. I need your help."

She stared at him, hoping he'd sympathize with her pleading, trusting in those moments that stretched to the horizon that he would see her as a sister in need and come through for the *ʻohana* he once claimed them to be. To his credit, Inoke didn't look away, didn't shy from the pain in her eyes, the truth of her necessity. In time he ran a hand across his face and sighed. "Okay."

"You'll take me?"

"Gimme a minute," he said, raising a finger, "It's not that simple." Inoke waved Ruby and Darren into a huddle, where they stood, heads bowed, conspiring in hushed tones. Every few seconds, one of them would look at Jordan, who had since lowered the knife. He at least appeared willing to hear Inoke out. Though how it would solve her problem remained to be seen.

"All right, all right. How 'bout we settle this with a bet," Inoke said, facing Jordan.

"I'm listening," Jordan said.

"You think you're chief. That you deserve to stay in this camp? Then earn it. Prove we can trust you not to rat to the police."

"Man, are you deaf? Ever since you brought that boat ashore, all I've been saying is we need to be careful. I don't want the police here anymore than you do."

Darren elbowed Inoke in the side. "You were right, man. He does have secrets."

Inoke ignored him. His jaw stiffened as he stared at Jordan, sizing him up. After several tense moments, he said, "As much as I'd love to pummel your ass right now, I've got a business to run. So, I'm gonna give you one chance. Drop the knife and beat me in a contest."

"What kind of contest?"

"Traditional warrior games. Like during Makahiki."

Malia scrunched her face in confusion. "The harvest festival? What are you talking about? It's not November—"

"Just the games," Inoke said, cutting her off. He pointed at Jordan. "Best of five in a set of challenges."

"I've no idea what you're talking about, but I'm listening."

"Of course you don't, *haole*," Darren said, poking his head out from behind Inoke's shoulder.

Malia shot Darren a dirty look. "Do you?" She gave him a second to answer, then said, "Didn't think so."

Inoke continued as though he didn't notice the interruption. "Ancient warrior games held every winter. During a season of peace. We'll put Tiki in charge. You win and we put all this behind us. Wipe the slate clean. No more trouble."

"And if I lose?"

"We don't ever see you around here again," Inoke said, sneering. As if it were that simple.

"What if I refuse to play?" Jordan asked, voicing the very question Malia had been wondering. Tiki too, given his reaction.

"I'm giving you a chance to live in peace. I don't have to. But if you turn it down ..." Inoke rolled his neck side to side, flexing. "Knife or no knife, you gotta sleep sometime, brah. And there's three of us ..."

"And only one of you," Ruby added, finishing Inoke's threat.

As the men stared one another down, Malia spoke up. "How does this help me?"

"Tiki boats you to Hanalei once Jordan clears out."

"You're assuming I lose," Jordan said, then under his breath, "Cocky fuck."

Tiki's grip on the locator beacon relaxed as Jordan lowered the knife, seeming to agree. Still, Malia couldn't trust it would end this easily. Her familiarity with the Makahiki, celebrated every year at the Kamehameha School, was enough to know Jordan stood little chance against Inoke's size and strength. Not to mention his pride. Inoke must have believed it too, else he wouldn't have suggested it. Still, she couldn't imagine this would be the end of their fighting. *Not my problem. I'll be gone,* she told herself.

"It's settled. There's a full moon tonight. And low tide's late. We'll hold the games at Honopu. Meet on the beach at nine," Inoke said. "Tiki, you study Makahiki?"

Tiki nodded with hesitation.

"Good. Then you and Malia select the games. But keep it interesting. Don't go picking all the pansy ones."

"Great. Somebody at least wanna give me a hint so I can prepare?" Jordan said.

Tiki exchanged a sideways glance with Inoke before speaking with a foreboding tenor impossible to miss. "Rest up. And conserve your strength. You'll need it."

"Gee, thanks."

"Another thing. No knives. I'm serious. But bring a spear. Both of you." Then, perhaps sensing Malia's unease, Tiki turned and slid his hands up to her wrists, cradling them loosely with a ticklish tremor. He met her eyes and said in a low but firm voice, "I know what you're thinking. For once, trust me. No beacon. Whatever happens tonight, I promise to get you home by tomorrow."

CHAPTER 24
HOTSPOT

Malia stood facing the sea, waiting for Inoke and the others. It was her first visit to the western end of Kalalau Beach since the night in the cave. She didn't glance Jordan's way, not wanting to risk a flash of recognition, or worse, a remark. Instead, she looked skyward, where the tug of the rising moon drew her memory to their discussion of the Makaliʻi. Jordan knew them as the Pleiades, he said, one of the few constellations able to shine through the Seattle gray. In Hawaiʻi, their winter arrival marked the traditional start of the Makahiki season.

She wondered if she'd even notice them in California.

The night's stars hung like breadcrumbs above the ocean, marking the path westward. Honopu Beach lay over a quarter mile from Kalalau, hidden beyond the headland. The going was treacherous, even at low tide, as there was scant beach at the base of the cliffs, only a jumble of fallen rocks—and the ocean's constant tug. Malia leaned into the rocks for balance as she picked her way along the jagged coast, hoping the basalt cliffs above didn't choose that moment to crumble further. The going was slow and nerve-wracking in the semi-dark, but she trusted that if Darren could make it, then so could she. Still, she stumbled twice, tripping on the shifting rocks, falling into the swirling waters, scraping her knees and hands. Reef shoes would have been ideal. Or a pair of flippers and a body board. For as calm as the seas were, the current's pull was an ever-present reminder to hurry: high tide would force them from the rocks and into the water for the return. And even a short swim could prove deadly along Nāpali Coast.

Finally, after thirty minutes of treacherous scrambling, they reached Honopu Beach. Her every muscle relaxed as her toes touched dry sand. She bent over, hands on her knees in relief. "I vote we never do that again."

"Someone remind me why we couldn't do this at Kalalau?" Jordan asked. He trudged past her, carrying his spear as instructed.

"Honopu's sacred. They call it the 'Valley of the Lost Tribe.' Legend has it ancient royals were buried above those cliffs," Inoke answered, pointing inland, above a weathered hillside.

Malia looked at him, mouthing the words *lost tribe*, wondering if he were making it up to spook Jordan. Real or not, it added to Inoke's sense of ceremony. Which, as far as she could tell, seemed the only reason they were there.

"Also where they filmed *King Kong*," Darren said. He affected an eerie tone and waggled his fingers overhead, like someone trying to scare a child. "Welcome to Skull Island."

"Really? Not computers?" Ruby asked.

Jordan rolled his eyes. "There were no green screens in the seventies."

"Oh, I thought he meant the remake."

Darren trudged past. "They're both remakes. They filmed OG Kong in the thirties."

"We gonna stand around talking movies or we gonna do this?" Inoke interrupted. "You two find us some wood and build a bonfire near the arch. Here." He tossed Darren a lighter.

Malia had no idea what arch Inoke was referencing. She followed the others up the beach toward the low rumble of a waterfall, figuring she'd help gather kindling. Honopu, for all the trouble they spent getting there, seemed only a smaller Kalalau. Then she realized the blackness towering in the distance wasn't sky, nor the valley head-wall, but rather a colossal ridge splitting the beach in two, bearing a massive hole in the center. Malia craned her neck to take in the scale of the formation, so large it could easily fit several homes stacked atop one another beneath it. And in that moment, on a dank, salty breeze, she smelled the history of this place. A scent of the forgotten, where humans had ceased to belong. Goose bumps dotted her skin as Malia imagined those long-ago people, their lives, customs, and burials.

"Pretty incredible, huh?" Tiki paused beside her, admiring the arch. She took it all in. The arch, his presence, his scent. "Well, the faster we get this over with, the quicker we get back," he said.

Despite having been around Tiki much of the day, she'd resisted the temptation to ask about his promise for fear of jinxing it. But with midnight only a few hours away, tomorrow was fast approaching. And she couldn't help wondering how he planned to deliver. But, like a falling coconut striking a tree root, her thoughts skipped sideways, not toward home, but to the future. Would she ever return to Kalalau, give it a second try? Or would she spend her years pining for what might have been?

And end up just like her mother.

The realization slammed home, caroming out of nowhere. For two months she'd been chasing a memory, measuring her every moment against the rose-colored fondness that blossomed in her mother's recollection. Malia had come to Kalalau hoping to experience what made it so special to her mother. But was that even possible? The people, the norms—they were gone. Left to history. "That's why she never came back," she whispered. Twenty years was so long. "A lifetime."

Her mother, one of the smartest women Malia knew, must have known she couldn't relive the past. "I'm such a fool." Her voice cracked, torn between embarrassment and relief. But it wasn't too late, she thought, seeing Tiki jog after the others.

She followed the budding light of the bonfire to the arch, where an unease settled over the group. Jordan stood alone, wearing surf trunks, fresh gauze over his burns, and a scowl. Whether anxious to begin or having second thoughts, Malia couldn't tell. Inoke prowled the sand beyond the fire, back and forth, psyching himself up as Darren and Ruby whispered amongst themselves. Nearest stood Tiki, whose face shone in the firelight, inspiring a flashback to Malia's first night at Kalalau. To the night, he alone rose to introduce himself. Two months later and he was still a step apart from the others. He dipped his head to her. It was time.

"Let's get started," Tiki said, lifting a small, orange stuff sack. "This bag contains the names of several traditional Makahiki events. Inoke's familiar, I'm sure—"

"Damn straight."

"Uh-huh." Tiki faced Jordan. "Malia helped me choose the events, and she'll be helping referee. She's the only other noncombatant who's seen these games played, so don't give her any shit."

Malia straightened with pride as the others looked on, clearly impressed. Then, surprisingly, Tiki extended his hand, inviting her to join him before the group. Malia blushed as she came forward, placing her hand in his as he guided her to his side. Whether his gesture was purely ceremonial or meant something more, she didn't know.

Tiki presented the bag to her and nodded. And for a moment, she forgot what she was supposed to do, so distracted was she by his unexpected touch. His proximity. He jiggled the bag with an easygoing smile, snapping her to. She reached in, gave the scraps of paper a swirl, and withdrew the first event.

"*Haka Moa*," she said, regathering herself. "Chicken fight."

Jordan gave a disgusted look. "Isn't that what drunk couples play in the pool?"

"It's the game where you end up on your ass," Inoke said.

Malia rolled her eyes, then tossed the paper into the fire. Using her heel, she dragged a circle in the sand as Tiki explained the gist of the game. She gave the fire a wide berth—God knows they didn't need a repeat of last night—and made a ring wide enough for her to lie end to end three times.

Inoke entered like a showman, scissoring his legs as though kicking up and over an invisible rope. Jordan entered the ring with less enthusiasm, but either intentionally or by coincidence, avoided stepping on the line Malia had trenched. He puffed out his chest for effect, but Malia knew the odds were stacked against him. Upon Tiki's instruction, the two clasped their right hands, keeping their elbows bent as if preparing to arm wrestle. Their grip was tight, muscles flexing, but Inoke's forearms were twice the size of Jordan's biceps. And though Jordan was taller, height was no advantage here.

"Now, grab your left foot with your left hand and balance—"

"This is ridiculous," Jordan said.

"You don't like our traditions, you can leave."

"On the count of three, fight. The first to be knocked down or fall out of the ring loses."

"One, two, GO!"

Jordan immediately strafed Inoke's position, hopping sideways in effort to budge the larger man from the center. Despite Jordan's rapid leaps, Inoke need only pivot in place, barely lifting his foot from the sand to maintain position. Darren and Ruby hollered encouragement at Inoke as Jordan continued to sweep around Inoke, flirting with the boundary Malia had trenched. But Inoke's balance was impeccable, his stance resembling a post around which a tetherball swung wildly. And the ball could only go so far before taking a pounding. Jordan had nearly orbited Inoke when the latter yanked him inward, pulling Jordan off off-balance. As fast as he pulled him in, Inoke thrust outward again, shoving Jordan in the chest, sending him toppling like a ragdoll.

"Ass in the sand. Told you," Inoke said before turning to fist-bump Darren and Ruby.

"Point to Inoke," Tiki said, standing on guard to see how Jordan took his first loss.

Inoke strutted toward Jordan and extended a hand to help him up, only to pull it back with a mocking laugh as Jordan reached for it. "Psych."

"Real mature," Jordan said, rising under his own power.

Malia shook her head, unimpressed. The games usually ended without incident, but even at school she'd seen her fair share of sore losers—and sorer winners. The nature of the games sometimes brought out the worst in people, especially alpha males. Inoke and Jordan were as similar in temperament as they were different in physique—and Malia could only hope they got through this without anyone getting hurt.

She allowed Jordan to brush himself off before drawing the second event. *"Kukini."*

"Shit," Inoke spat as soon as Malia spoke. "Why you go and add that one?"

Jordan's gaze flicked from Malia to Inoke and back, his eyes gaining a faint glimmer of confidence.

"This one's a footrace. A sprint down the beach," Tiki said, eliciting a nod of approval from Jordan. Tiki dragged a line in the sand outside the circle. "You'll begin here. I'll draw another down the beach a way. Malia will start when I get in position."

Tiki grabbed a flaming stick and marched off into the shadows cast by the arch. If she had to guess, he was probably fifty yards away. Not far, but long enough in the sand. She instructed the men to line up. Jordan did a few high knees, sprinting in place, as Inoke stood, hands on his hips, giving him the side-eye. On Tiki's mark, she took her place a few steps in front of the men, feeling like one of the girls in those drag racing movies. She raised her arms in the air, playing it up. Jordan dug his toes into the sand. Inoke leaned forward, his arms ready to drive off the line. "Get set." A pause. "Go!"

Jordan and Inoke burst forward, an explosion of grunting and flying sand. Jordan sped past Malia, appearing to sprint as fast he could. Inoke, despite an energetic start, had slowed to a jog within a few strides. He throttled down to a walk by the time he passed Malia, chuckling to himself.

Darren rushed forward, concern etching his face. "Everything okay, bro? You pull a muscle?"

Inoke laughed. "I look like a runner to you? Just saving energy." Then, to Malia, "He wins this one. Keeps it interesting. But you better not let it get *too* interesting."

Malia didn't know what to say. Did Inoke think she wanted Jordan to win? Was he asking her to cheat? To only draw events that favored Inoke? She considered the remaining events and, believing he held the advantage in all of them, said nothing. After all, the games were Inoke's idea.

"I win," Jordan said, walking back with Tiki.

"No shit."

"The whole thing. You never crossed the line. That's a forfeit in my book."

"What kind of *haole* logic is that? My muscle cramped."

"Yeah, right." Jordan turned to Malia. "That true? He pull up hurt?"

Malia didn't know what to say. She wasn't a liar—and definitely no cheater—but knew if she wanted to get through the games peacefully, then she had to do something. There was no way Inoke would accept a forfeit. She glimpsed Tiki watching her, eyebrows arched, like a judge impatiently awaiting a jury's verdict. "He looked hurt to me. Probably should have stretched—"

"Bullshit," Jordan said, swatting the air between them.

"You callin' her a liar?" Inoke said, stepping forward.

Malia rushed between them, extending her arms. "The score's tied. That's all that matters. But, going forward, failure to complete an event means disqualification. Which means you lose the bet." She looked each man in the eyes, demanding their understanding.

"Let's go. Tide's coming in. We ain't got all night," Inoke said, turning away.

"Gimme a minute," Jordan said, still breathing hard.

"No rest for the weary. Draw it, Malia."

Jordan kicked sand at the fire, muttering under his breath.

Malia ignored him and went to Tiki, who greeted her with a baffled smile. "Why the new rule?" he asked.

"I don't know. I . . ." She bit her lip. When she continued, she did so in a whisper. "Felt guilty about lying."

Tiki's lip curled in a ribald smirk. "You're sexy when you're honest." He rounded her quickly and held the entries between them, sporting a mischievous grin. Malia felt a nervous tickle in her face and plunged her hand into the bag, trying to resist the urge to sneeze.

"*'O'o ihe*," she hollered. "Spear toss."

"We'll throw from the finish line," Tiki said. "It's like javelin, but for accuracy. You each get one throw. Whoever comes closest to the center of the circle wins. The fire should help you aim."

Darren carried Inoke's spear to him, then leaned in to talk in secret. Tiki noticed it too, but when Malia asked him what he thought they were talking about, he dismissed it as nothing to worry about. Only he did a lousy job of appearing to believe what he was selling.

"Jordan goes first since he won the sprint," Tiki said. "Grab your spears and follow me."

Jordan took his spear from where he'd propped it against the rocks. Other than one of the tines having been broken off the end, it looked as solid as the day he carved it. Inoke's spear seemed longer, and tapered to a single, deadly point, but wasn't as straight. Malia wondered how well it would fly, or if he'd practiced.

"We better take cover behind the arch, just in case," she suggested. Though she didn't really care if Darren and Ruby followed her or not.

"They ain't gonna reach the circle with those flimsy-ass sticks," Darren said.

"One of those sticks speared your dinner last night." She'd said it out of annoyance, only to realize the truth in the statement. Sure, Tiki had been most successful fishing with it, but why did she assume Inoke would win? He was stronger, but what if it came down to equipment? A pit rose in her throat as she realized Jordan could take the lead. And if he won—and Inoke felt he might lose—then there was no guarantee Inoke wouldn't play dirty ... or involve Darren or Ruby somehow.

The sound of a spear drew their attention. A faint whistle rising, approaching, slicing the air with stealthy, deathly precision. Then the plunk of it impaling the sand. It didn't reach the circle, let alone the fire, but it wasn't far. Malia wondered when she should check their marks, holding her breath, listening for the all clear. She'd nearly left the safety of the rocks to determine a victor when she heard the second throw. Not a whistle, but sounding like the flutter of a bird with a broken wing. No more than a sad stick tossed in the sand, well short of the target.

Malia ran to inspect the first toss. It was Jordan's, as she feared. He'd stuck the landing barely ten feet shy of the circle. The three men approached soon after, Inoke carrying his spear, which he snapped over his knee upon seeing Jordan's, glowing like a sundial in the moonlight. "Fuck this. I'd have won if we had the same spear."

"Best of five, right?" Jordan asked, a smarmy grin on his face. He knew damn well it was, and couldn't pass rubbing it in.

Tiki extended the bag to Malia and arched his eyebrows. *Make it count,* he seemed to be saying. She reached in, plucked the first scrap she felt, and unfolded it slowly. Tiki's handwriting. *"Moko—"* She stopped short, the syllables lodged in her throat. She turned her back to the others, facing Tiki alone, and hissed, "Why is this in here?"

"What's wrong?" He squinted as he read the note. "It's just the dart sliding game. What's the big deal?"

"No," she huffed. "That's *Moa Pahe'e.*"

Knowing she had to act, Malia turned to drop the scrap into the fire only to have Inoke pluck it from her grasp. He read it aloud, mumbling to himself, seeming to not understand Tiki's writing. Then his demeanor morphed as the translation registered. A mischievous smile crept across his face as he began nodding. Exactly what Malia feared.

"Well. You gonna tell me or you gonna fake another excuse?" Jordan asked.

Inoke looked up, grinning with the cockiness of a classroom cheat who'd seen the test answers, milking the moment for all he could. Malia reached for the paper, but Inoke was too quick. He turned it around for all to see. *"Mokomoko."* He thrust the note at Jordan's chest, shoving him backward into the rocks. "Bare-knuckle boxing."

Jordan lay sprawled against the rocks, motionless, groaning as the collision rolled through him. Upon standing, he rotated his wrists and bent and unbent his elbows, testing them. Jordan looked to the rocks—they weren't sharp—then turned to Inoke. "Nice shove. Cheap shots part of your ancient traditions too?"

"Fuck you."

Jordan snorted, curling his lip in a condescending sneer. "Bare-knuckle boxing? Seriously? You played this shit at school? Thought these games were supposed to be peaceful—"

"They-they-they are," Malia stammered, feeling as if called upon to defend a failed group assignment. Only it wasn't her screwup. "It's a mistake. *Mokomoko* wasn't supposed to be included."

"But it was. And we're doing it." Inoke scanned the group, eying them one by one. He had the look of someone measuring how far he could go without being stopped. "Know what? Screw this. Give me one reason I don't beat your ass right now." Inoke strutted forward, fists balled, and arms pulled back.

Jordan backpedaled, reaching as if by instinct to his waist, where his knife had often been sheathed. Empty. Panic flooded his face as Tiki grabbed Inoke in a bear hug.

"No fighting," Tiki shouted.

Inoke squirmed within Tiki's grasp, but without conviction. For now. Malia knew with one storm of emotion he'd be free. "Oh, yes we are." Inoke flicked his chin at Ruby and Darren who, until then, had been idling nearby like rubberneckers on a freeway. They came forward, angling toward Jordan.

"No, not like this. We're here for a traditional contest, not a street fight," Tiki said before yelling, "Back off, Ruby."

Inoke erupted from Tiki's grasp, thrusting his elbows wide and shaking him off. He spun to face Tiki. "What do you care?"

"I'm trying to protect you."

Inoke snorted. "From him?"

Tiki glanced at Jordan, then, with a tone that could pacify a bear, said, "What if he really is a cop? You want that on your record?"

Jordan rolled his eyes, easing his posture. "I already told you. I'm not a cop."

"Exactly what a cop would say," Darren said.

"Fine. I'll do the mocha-whatever it's called. Let's just get it over with."

Malia was relieved to see Inoke calm down but hated the way the contest was progressing. She didn't see how Jordan could win against Inoke, which meant they'd need a fifth event—and hated to think what other accidental surprises lurked within the bag. She was exasperated. By Jordan, by Inoke, by the entire situation. If only she'd drawn a different event, they might have been done already. She pivoted to Tiki and threw her hands up in frustration, making it clear she expected him to fix this. "This is on you," she said, knowing if he didn't find a way to corral this, Inoke would beat Jordan senseless—or worse.

Tiki glanced about, scratching the back of his head. He bore a pained look and, unlike his usual demeanor, made no effort to hide it. He took an exaggerated swallow, then looked to Malia and nodded quick, shallow dips of assurance. *It'll work out*, he seemed to be saying, but she needed more. She crossed her arms, reluctant to test the depths of his plan.

"Okay. I didn't intend to include this event. I'd rather we draw another—"

"Too bad," Inoke said.

"You done?" Tiki sighed. "But since that's not an option, we'll use a points system. Points will be awarded for strikes to the head and for dodging."

"We don't need a knockout to win?" Jordan asked.

"Like you could," Darren said, drawing laughter from Ruby and Inoke.

Tiki shut them up with a look. "No knockouts. Just points." Then, stepping closer to Malia, he whispered, "This should keep it safe."

Malia wasn't sure how a points system would solve anything. Of all the Makahiki events, she'd never seen this one performed. Teachers spent their time breaking up fights, not encouraging them.

"Alright. The bout's to seven," Tiki said.

"Nine," Inoke countered, and punched his fist. "I wanna enjoy this."

Malia shot Tiki an uneasy look. "Seven," he said sternly. "More than enough time to have your fun."

Jordan turned and kicked at a stick, sending it flying as he walked toward the ring.

Malia reached out to Tiki before he fell in behind the others and tugged his arm. "I don't like this," she said. Tiki nodded, conceding as much. "You'll break it up if it gets out of hand, right? Before it turns ..."

"Yeah. Sure," he said, unable to mask an obvious annoyance. He squinted as he studied her, his brow drawn tight, as though the words he needed to say were hidden amongst the amber flecks of her eyes. The crisp line of his lips sagged. "You care about him, don't you?"

"What? No," Malia said, leaning away in surprise. Then, upon reflecting on the insecurity within the waver of his voice, an understanding bloomed within her: Tiki was jealous. She entwined her fingers over the top of his. "Not at all." She stared at him with an intensity that sent a tingle down her legs. "Honest." She squeezed his hand for emphasis, wanting to feel his reaction, but commotion stole the moment.

The sight of Inoke prowling the ring as Darren and Ruby hyped him from behind clawed at Malia's nerves in a way she couldn't describe. She grabbed Tiki's arm and pulled him close. I've got a bad feeling—"

"It'll be fine," he said. He then hooked his head toward the others. "Let's get this over with."

Inoke had taken his shirt off and stood pounding his chest, thumping the tattooed islands above his heart, psyching himself up and no doubt trying to intimidate Jordan. Unnerved by the display, Malia held her breath as Tiki motioned for the two competitors to join him in the center. Jordan, of average build, looked downright spindly next to Inoke's bulk. And judging by the look in his eyes, he knew to be scared. She'd seen it before. On tourists about to paddle into surf they had no business being in; a window to the sliver of their brain that knew being on vacation didn't make them invincible.

But when did that ever stop them?

Tiki repeated the rules, adding that points would be deducted for leaving the ring. He chopped the air between the men to start the bout, then backed away. He'd barely gotten out of the way before Jordan dashed forward with a lightning-quick strike, connecting with Inoke's jaw. Jordan retreated as fast as he struck. "Point!" Tiki yelled, extending an index finger on his left hand, keeping his right hand balled.

Inoke kept his fists up and his head back, seemingly caught off guard by Jordan's quick reach. He sidestepped forward, faked with his left, then threw a wild right hook that Jordan easily ducked beneath.

"Dodge. Two-zero, Jordan."

"Come on, Inoke. Kick his ass," Darren yelled.

Jordan and Inoke circled the ring, eyes locked on one another, staying out of arm's reach. Tiki moved along the ring's perimeter, avoiding the fray as Malia struggled to watch. Again, Jordan quick-stepped forward in attack, but his back foot slipped in the sand; the punch sailed wide. Inoke seized on the opportunity and unleashed a mighty overhand punch that clocked Jordan in the mouth. Malia turned from the sound, not wanting to see any blood. But when she looked back, Jordan appeared to have absorbed the punch well enough.

"Ain't so quick that time," Inoke taunted.

Jordan backed away, massaging his jaw as Tiki extended his right index finger. Two to one. Inoke burst forward with surprising quickness and unleashed a combination of wild left-right jabs. Jordan bobbed his head in a flurry, narrowly avoiding damage.

"Two more for Jordan."

"Second one hit," Darren called out.

"Four to one," Tiki reiterated.

"You're blind," Ruby said.

"He missed. Just like he's gonna miss being in charge," Jordan said, shooting Ruby an arrogant smirk.

It was in that moment, as Jordan took his eyes off Inoke, that Inoke's right hook landed. Fast. Vicious. It struck Jordan's face with the sound of rockfall. Malia yelled in horror at the spray of blood, the crunch. She covered her face with her hands as her stomach lurched, but she couldn't not look. She spread her fingers wide, enough to see Jordan kneeling in the sand, head slumped.

Just stay down, she wished, hoping he'd take the knockout. She knew he didn't want to give up the camp, but it wasn't worth this. Inoke came forward, hands at his sides, as if believing he'd already won. Tiki had scored the point for Inoke, evidenced by the two fingers extended on his right hand, but otherwise seemed as if he too thought the fight was over.

That's when Jordan spun to his feet and threw a fistful of sand. The fine grains erupted like a cloud, coating Inoke's sweat-soaked face. He hollered in distress, squinting at the pain as he clawed at his face. "You cheating bitch, I'm gonna kill you!"

"Not cheating," Jordan said, panting. "Gamesmanship. You move pretty good on that injured leg." Jordan spit into the sand, then lunged forward, not waiting to increase his lead. He cracked Inoke in the nose. Five-two. Inoke raised his arms in defense, still blinded by the sand, as Jordan jabbed again. Another left, a glancing blow. He wound up for a right hook, but Inoke lowered his head and charged him. Though backlit by the fire, Malia could see the rage in his bloodshot eyes as he crashed into Jordan. He drove through him like a tackling dummy, slamming him to the ground. Inoke knelt over Jordan, pinning him beneath his tree-trunk legs as he unleashed a barrage of punches, pummeling Jordan in the ribs and face. Jordan flailed in an attempt to block the abuse, to protect his head, but the efforts were feeble. Inoke beat him unmercifully.

"Stop him!" Malia screamed.

She snapped her head toward Tiki, only to see that Ruby had a massive arm wrapped around Tiki's neck, holding him in a choke-hold of sorts while Darren wrapped himself around Tiki's thighs so he couldn't kick free. "Get off me," Tiki coughed, thrashing about in attempt to get loose, like a fish struggling to find water. But it was no use. He was powerless to escape their grasp.

Jordan moaned in nauseating gurgles as Inoke tattooed him in one-two combinations that landed like twin sledges. The brutality roiled Malia's stomach. She turned to vomit, to wish it away and flee, but knew she had to do something. If she didn't stop him, Jordan would die.

Without a plan, she raced forward and threw herself atop Inoke's back, trying to catch one of his arms, anything to slow the assault. Inoke bucked like a rodeo bull beneath her. She clung to him the best she could, shouting for him to stop, but he was out of control, swinging his arms and head. He whirled from his kneeling position, smashing her in the face with his elbow. "Yowl!" She cried out in agony and tumbled into the sand. The taste of iron flooded her mouth. Hot tears blurred her vision.

Malia lay in shock, biting back sobs of pain, building the energy to scream.

"Oh God! Shit, Malia. What are you doing?" Inoke, still on his knees, turned to the sound of her yelling. He appeared dazed, confused, like a sleepwalker unsure where he'd woken. Malia opened her mouth, snapping the webbing of blood and mucus that spanned her split lips. She needed to scream—from pain, from desperation—but her lungs refused to function. She stared at Inoke in shock, unable to move. To speak. Or to warn him as Jordan rose to his feet behind him.

Understanding flashed on Inoke's face. Whether from the horror in Malia's eyes or from the shifting tenor of Tiki's shouts, he bore the look of someone aware he'd made a grave mistake.

The point of the spear burst through his chest beneath his left nipple, its scarlet tip emerging with gruesome ferocity. Blood spurted from the wound like shaken soda, spraying Malia's sarong with gore. She stared at that splintered peak, thinking of how it resembled a new island emerging from Inoke's tattooed archipelago. Inoke arched backward grotesquely. Then as quickly as he'd been run through, the spear vanished. The vicious tug felled Inoke forward across Malia's feet.

And for one fleeting moment, before Malia could scream, before she scrambled out from under him, there was only the sound of the crackling fire, the murmur of the sea, and the wheezing of blood and air sucked by a gaping wound ... then the sound of Jordan sprinting for the surf.

Malia wiped at the tears streaking her face, wishing Park would say something to distract her from the image of that spear-tip volcano rising amidst the gurgling blood. It would haunt her forever, that vision. That demonic sound of rending cartilage and muscle. She swallowed a sob and looked up, eying the detective, whose pursed lips were the only sign of her discomfort. Malia's head pounded with every heartbeat. The drumming reminded her of the morning's helicopter flight and her conversation with Tiki. She was supposed to say Jordan acted in self-defense. Those were the words she'd instructed Tiki to use. But why?

Out of fear she might be complicit? To protect a friend?

Friends don't leave you with a dead body.

She replayed the fight in her mind, fast-forwarding to when she leapt atop Inoke. What came next was a horrific blur, save for an image impossible to forget. Worse than the killing, the blood, and the aftermath was the madness she'd seen churning in Jordan's eyes right before he killed Inoke.

He could have run. He didn't need to yank out the spear. Inoke might have lived.

Malia trembled in the chair, recalling that look of hate-filled desperation. She hugged herself for comfort, but found none. Park extended a hand across the table, her fingertips barely reaching Malia's arm. The sensation of Park's motherly touch, stroking her skin, sent Malia over the edge, ushering in a new wave of tears. "He didn't have to..." The weeping made it hard to speak. "Didn't need to kill him."

"And you never saw Jordan again?"

Malia shook her head so hard it hurt.

"He never said where he might go?"

"No," she said, pleading. "You've got to believe me."

CHAPTER 25
THE PAST RESURFACES

Steam billowed from the institution-green porcelain as Malia plunged her fingers into the faucet's scalding flow. She winced, cranked the temperature down, then cupped the water to her face. Park had sent her to collect herself, telling Malia to calm her nerves after reliving the horror of Inoke's death. But with every splash of water, she could only picture herself back on the beach, scrubbing away the blood. Could feel the stickiness of that phantom splatter clinging to her, coating her ankles. Could see the droplets in midflight, the spear tip emerging from Inoke's chest with every blink. She had blood on her; of that there was no doubt. Maybe not in the folds and creases of her skin or amongst the roots of her hair, but on her hands. Certainly on her hands.

The torrent disappeared down the drain as a memory bubbled to the surface—Tiki helping her across the stream. Her decision to stay.

The first domino. No, she couldn't. She'd relived enough for one day: Park had wrung her dry.

Malia had to get back. Freshening up shouldn't take so long. She gripped the bare aluminum doorknob and took a deep breath, hoping Park had seen the truth in her testimony.

Sergeant Kahale sat beside Park. His doughy face framed beneath a slick of black hair, he regarded Malia with a soft, almost apologetic smile lacking the manufactured intensity it bore that morning. "Like your clothes," he said good-naturedly. An olive branch to which Malia didn't know how to respond. She didn't know why he was there, only that she hoped it meant she could leave soon.

"Sit," Park said, motioning to her chair. Malia caught a whiff of salt air as she rounded the table and wondered if he'd spent the day at Honopu, working the crime scene, tending to Inoke. She caught herself scrubbing her hands against her sweatpants and clutched the thick cotton material in her fists. "Sergeant Kahale informs me that while our two accomplices have remained tight-lipped, your account of last night's events corroborate that of our other witness."

Tiki.

"I must congratulate you on your memory. Your account was one of the more thorough we've heard."

"Does that mean you're letting me go?" Malia asked, suspecting Kahale had been watching the entire time.

"You didn't let me finish." He ran his tongue along his teeth. "You were very thorough, but we need the rest of the story."

"I told you everything," she said, heat vibrating in her throat. "There's nothing else."

Park leaned forward, tenting her fingers. "We need to know what happened after Jordan ran."

Malia gripped the underside of the chair as her toes clawed against the slippers, bracing to prevent being dragged back into that nightmare. Her free hand slid toward her ankle, expecting to feel him there. Inoke. She massaged her shin through the sweatpants, but it was no use; she couldn't soothe away the sensation of him collapsing atop her. Couldn't escape the sense he'd be alive if she'd only gone home sooner.

"Something wrong?" Park questioned, a single, pencil-thin eyebrow arched.

Malia looked at her lap. What could she say? That she felt Inoke's bulk against her legs, crushing her? That her skin tingled with the phantom trace of his blood coursing over her. She tried to answer, but only managed a hoarse groan.

"You said Jordan yanked the spear out. And Inoke fell. What happened next?"

Park shot Kahale a short, curt look before reaching across to Malia. She placed her palm down on the table, as if comforting an extension of her. "We know this is traumatic, Malia. But it's important. Only you know what you saw."

Malia's gaze flicked back and forth between the two officers, the shut door, the blank walls. She could no easier escape that room than she could what happened. She swished her tongue around, wetting her mouth with Park's sentiment. Where to begin? She tried recalling how she got Inoke off her—he must have weighed over two hundred pounds—but the rest of the night occurred in snippets, fragments of memory spliced together like jump cuts in a movie trailer.

"Start with Ruby and Darren. What did they do?"

"They were yelling. We all were. Calling Inoke's name. Screaming it. We were scared. Even Tiki." Malia looked across at Park and Kahale. Neither spoke. Park held her pen, angled just so above her notepad. They expected her to continue. So Malia told them what she remembered. That Darren and Ruby came running over. They rolled Inoke onto his back—that was how she got out from under him—and Darren pressed his hands over the wound, to stop the wheezing, to silence that awful noise. "Ruby took his shirt off," she said with a shudder, "and tried stuffing it into the wound."

"Would that work?" Park asked Kahale. He raised his palms and shrugged. "And Tiki?" Park asked Malia.

"He came back dripping wet. I think he chased after Jordan, but I guess he couldn't find him. It was dark."

"Even with the full moon?"

Malia's turn to shrug.

"When were you sure Inoke was dead?" Kahale asked.

She weighed the question in her mind. Was he implying that Inoke wasn't? That they made a mistake? No, that was absurd. She'd seen the spear, felt the lifeless weight of him atop her. *Dead weight.* "Darren tried CPR. Tiki told him to stop. Said Inoke was dead."

"And after Tiki pronounced him dead, what then?"

"Tiki suggested they bury him to keep the birds and crabs off him until morning since we didn't have a tarp."

"Did you help?"

Malia shook her head, ashamed.

"Why not? Did Tiki tell you not to?"

"I ... My sarong was soaked. He ... Tiki ... Walked me down to the water ..." Her voice cracked. "So, so, much blood. After I washed it, he told me to sit by the fire. I couldn't stop shivering." She turned to Kahale, recalling the way he regarded her that morning. "I couldn't get the blood out of my sarong, so I burned it. That's why I had no clothes. It was my last one. I wasn't going around naked for the fun of it."

Kahale dipped his head in understanding as his cheeks reddened.

Park cleared her throat. "Did anyone suggest calling the police? Reporting the murder?"

"Yeah, of course. Everyone. Darren wanted to take the boat back right away, but Ruby said it was too dangerous. It didn't have running lights. They planned to get help in the morning."

"And what did Tiki say?"

"He agreed with Ruby. Said Honopu was too small to land a helicopter at night. I guess 'cause of the cliffs and the arch. Said the body wasn't going anywhere."

"What did you want to do?"

Malia didn't answer. Not right away. She sat with her eyes closed for several moments, then explained that by the time the shock had worn off, they had already finished piling rocks atop Inoke. Then it was time to swim back. The tide had started coming in. The waves were small, but the current strong. She had to drag herself through the water, holding onto rocks, as if trying to swim and crawl at the same time. It would have been impossible even in small surf. Fighting the current was exhausting. "It was after midnight by the time we got back to Kalalau. I looked for Jordan's locator beacon—"

"But you didn't use it," Park stated. "Why not?"

"It was gone. Jordan's backpack, his gear, the beacon. Everything but his air mattress, which he probably didn't have time for," she added with a shrug.

"My team discovered his backpack earlier, along with the beacon. He smashed it." Kahale eyed Malia as he said it, studying how the news hit her. She gave him nothing.

Park turned back to Malia. "So, Jordan raced back to the camp, and what? Instead of taking his gear, he hid it?"

"I don't know," Malia said, growing uncomfortable with the way Park still seemed to suspect her of being in Jordan's confidence. "Maybe he stashed it earlier. I didn't see him all day."

Kahale looked to Park. "Sounds like he might have anticipated not returning to camp."

"Or that things might not go well for him at Honopu." Park tapped her lips in thought.

Malia didn't like them talking past her. And as she watched the two discuss the size of the valley and location of other known squatter camps, a thought occurred to her. "Wait a second. If Jordan destroyed the locator beacon, then who called the cops?" Park and Kahale stopped talking and faced one another. They exchanged nonverbals for several moments. When it became clear that Kahale was content chewing the inside of his cheek, Park spoke up, ignoring Malia's question. "You've been helpful today, Malia. We appreciate that."

Park's abrupt change of topic confounded Malia, but she was thrilled to hear what sounded like a wrap-up comment. "So, is that it? I'm done?"

"Not yet ..." Park said, drawing it out. "There's something you should know."

Malia braced for bad news, having no idea what. *Dad? Oh, God, please let him be okay.*

Kahale had the look of someone about to say they hated this part of the job. He took a deep breath. "We've recovered the body of Holly McAdams."

If they think I'm Jordan's girlfriend, then they might believe I had some-thing to do with—

A chasm yawned in Malia's stomach, threatening to tear her in two. She didn't know Holly. Never heard her name outside that room. Yet, learning of her death with the recollection of Jordan's murderous attack so fresh in her mind left Malia queasy. Now she knew why Kahale had come. Not to send her home or hear what they did with Inoke's body, but because he had to be certain Malia wasn't involved. She recalled that morning, in camp, when Kahale stood outside her tent, confi-dent she and Jordan were "shacking up." *Darren.* Malia glimpsed the one-way mirror out the corner of her eye, wondering how much Kahale had heard. If he'd been listening, doubting her all along.

She placed a hand on her knee to steady its shaking. The truth was on her side, she told herself. It would set her free. Wasn't that what her father always said? She sighed inwardly, wishing he was there to help. God knew she could use his wisdom now.

"We received a call the other day from some fishermen about a body off the coast of Barking Sands. Down current from Kalalau. Our guys retrieved what was left. Sharks didn't leave us much to go by." Kahale paused, as though expecting a response. Not wanting to appear squeamish, Malia forced the image of a waterlogged woman ravaged by teeth and claws from her mind, only to wonder if not reacting increased their suspicion. She wanted to look innocent, to show she wasn't hiding something, but didn't know how. She crossed, then uncrossed her arms as her gaze wandered the room as if tracking a wind-whipped helicopter with nowhere to land.

"Based on depredation, the medical examiner said it had been submerged at least three weeks. Maybe longer," Kahale continued. "We checked the dental records against those of women listed missing in Kaua'i County—"

"Including yours," Park interrupted to say. Her demeanor bore the return of her chiseled disapproval.

"The lab kicked us back a match today. Holly McAdams."

"Jordan's wife," Park added.

Malia didn't need reminding. Holly's name would be burned in her mind forever.

"We believe Jordan Higgins is responsible for the death of his wife," Park said, yanking Malia from her tainted memories. "You're lucky to be alive."

Park's words hit like a cannonball to the gut as she considered the person she welcomed into the camp, the man she sheltered with, learned from. Defended! The hours spent alone with him, trusting him. How many times had Tiki warned her? How could she have been so blind? Jordan was a murderer. Killed his wife. Killed Inoke.

It could have been me.

Malia shook her head in refusal as her heart raced to the point of exploding. "No, he wouldn't hurt me. He—"

"He killed two people, Malia."

"Maybe she slipped after turning back? Everyone says the trail is dangerous."

"Malia"

"Or got caught in a rip current?"

"Malia."

"Or maybe it was suicide?"

Park drew her eyebrows in tight. "Are you defending him?"

"What? No-no-no," Malia stammered, alarmed. The excuses weren't for Jordan. They were for her. For her sanity.

"We have a witness who says she saw the couple near one of the overlooks on the trail. We just got off the phone," Kahale said. He kept his tone level, factual. "She'd seen our alert on Facebook. Said she remembered them yelling at each other. That Holly shouted for him to take his hands off her."

"That sound like an accident to you?"

Nausea accompanied Malia's recollection of the day he stumbled into camp. His catatonic, almost feral look. A stark contrast from the guy she saw rebuild the camp, and the one who fought to take it over.

"We believe he intended to hide in Kalalau Valley to escape arrest," Park said.

"He probably thought if he got in with one of the camps out there, he could evade us indefinitely," Kahale added.

Malia shivered, thinking back to when she first met Inoke. "You find another stray?" he'd asked Skye. Malia never understood why

Skye vouched for her, but she realized Inoke had the same concerns as her father had regarding unknown cats. You feed one, it stays. You feed two, the whole neighborhood goes to shit.

"Malia, you know as well as anyone, better than us even, how hard it can be to find someone out there. Especially if they don't want to be found. You can save us a lot of trouble—and the taxpayers of Hawai'i a lot of money—by being one hundred percent honest with us. If there's anywhere you think he may be hiding, you have to tell us."

Malia bit her lip, trying to hold back her tears.

"A cave, perhaps?"

She shook her head.

"What about the cliffs? You mentioned him trying to find a trail out."

"Tell us where he is, Malia." Kahale's voice rang like a funeral bell. "Now or never."

Malia felt the penetrating power of the camera staring down at her, the chill wind of the air conditioner on her face as sweat trickled down her back, heard the sound of heavy footsteps in the hall. She wanted out. Out of the room, the police station, off the island. To be anywhere but there, trapped at that table. The thudding grew in volume, proximity, coming to take her away. No. It was her heart pounding in her ears, the rising fear and angst boiling into a crescendo as she realized that despite an entire day spent confessing everything she'd said and done, they still didn't believe her.

She slapped her sweat-soaked palms on the table and leaned forward, desperation shrieking like a teakettle. "Why won't you believe me?" she cried out. "I've told you everything I know!"

CHAPTER 26
A DIVERSION OF DREAMS

"Hey, stand by the trail sign. We'll get a photo before we start."

Jordan doffed his headlamp and instructed Holly to do likewise. He enabled the flash on his phone, then looped an arm over her shoulders. No easy task given that his pack hung from his back like an overtired kindergartner—one only slightly more cooperative. He pulled her close. "One, two, *Kalalaaaau*," he said, drawing it out as the camera froze the pre-dawn moment. From the screen, Holly stared with a level of interest often reserved for jury duty. Jordan chewed his tongue to avoid sighing, then masked his disappointment behind saccharine enthusiasm. "Come on, you call that a smile?"

"At this hour? That's all you're gonna get." Holly turned to read the sign, adding not quite under her breath, "Can't believe you woke me up in the middle of the night to go hiking."

What he suspected was that she couldn't believe he'd resisted her effort to call him back to bed. Two hours earlier, back at the resort,

Jordan exited the shower and found her standing in the middle of the bedroom, loosely wrapped in the duvet, backlit by a dim, amber lamp. Holly dragged her teeth across her lower lip, tugging it seductively as she trailed her fingers beneath the comforter, glancing her breasts. He'd nearly thrown her on the bed, taken her there and then, and said screw it to the research trip. But he didn't. Not because he'd grown bored with married sex or because work came first, but because Jordan sensed something was missing from their lives.

At least from his.

His time in Alaska reminded him how much he enjoyed being in the backcountry, the one thing he needed to be truly happy. But the days were lonely. All his life, he dreamed of seeing the Aurora Borealis in person, and he finally got to, only to realize experiencing nature's magic meant nothing if he couldn't share it with Holly. Back home, everywhere he turned, friends and coworkers careened toward messy divorces, so many citing a lack of shared passions. His life had changed so much since meeting her, moving in together, getting married. He needed her to fall in love with the outdoors to reclaim a little of his old self, and could think of no better way to make that happen than by hiking one of the most beautiful trails in the world.

"Sun will be up in twenty minutes," he said, leaning a hand against the sign, a weather-beaten warning about loose rocks and narrow tread bolted head-high to rusting poles. He hoped it wouldn't scare her off. "Come a few hours from now, when that heat is beating down, you'll be glad we got an early start."

"Uh-huh. You're the only person I know who'd leave a four-star villa to traipse around the jungle."

Jordan wore the comment like a badge of honor. And when Holly appeared to shrug off the sign's ominous warning, he stepped past her, leading the way. "Then let's get traipsing," he said as he tapped the start button on his GPS, a Garmin do-everything adventure watch he bought before Alaska.

From the outset, the trail lived up to its reputation as being every bit as challenging as it was scenic. Every step delivered them higher into the darkness lurking beyond the reach of their flashlight beams. The tread was little more than a jumble of clay-coated boulders, slickened by groundwater or dew, interspersed with a tangle of roots. A veritable staircase from hell, carved by nature, built for giants. But strenuous as it was, the ruggedness only served to inflate Jordan's belief that this would be a special weekend, a turning point in their young marriage. A chance that Holly might, if he played his cards right, not only better understand the man she married a year ago, but perhaps discover something in herself.

One thing Jordan needn't worry about was Holly's fitness. The small fortune she spent on Pilates and yoga memberships never went to waste. Nor did she hesitate to join him in jogging the stairs of their high-rise when he suggested it as a way to train for the trail. Muscle tone wasn't everything when it came to hiking, but what she may have lacked in endurance, Holly more than made up for with stubbornness. Or, what she'd call determination. Still, Jordan knew it was important to keep an eye on her, to not get pulled too fast, too far by the allure of their destination.

Some forty minutes later, soaked in sweat, with the purple dawn of daylight finally rendering the headlamps unnecessary, Jordan's watch beeped. One mile down, ten to go.

Holy shit, that was tough.

He rested a foot atop a fallen palm and leaned against his bent knee, waiting, stretching, as he sucked lemon-lime electrolytes from his hydration bladder and brushed aside the thousandth strand of spider silk that crisscrossed the trail. Holly's sky-blue shirt shone through the gauze of humidity. She wasn't far behind. Jordan felt weird saying he was proud of her, like something reserved for small kids whose abilities were being obviously tested. But what other word was there? He *was* proud. Of both of them. They'd arrived at this point in life from different directions, their paths wholly separate, but crossed they did and there they were. And for the first time since that rooftop party two years prior, he finally felt the arc of their trajectory bending to the pull of his own gravity.

"This is brutal," Holly said, stopping beneath Jordan on the trail. She stretched her back and wiped her forehead with a handkerchief. Her skin glistened beneath beads of sweat as her face bore the crimson of exertion. Glops of clay coated her shoes and socks, spackled her legs in ochre-tinted tiger stripes. Pinpricks of blood and grated skin marred her knee.

"Looks like you fell. Need a Band-Aid?"

"I'm fine. I tripped, that's all."

"Okay, well, let me know if you change your mind." Jordan grabbed his phone, told her to smile. Its camera was slow to focus in the shade, missing Holly's eye roll. But Jordan caught it—and it stung.

They ambled downhill to Hanakāpīʻai Stream, the first of three wet crossings and as far as the public were allowed without a permit. He suggested they take as much time as needed before pushing on, as trip reports described the climb out of Hanakāpīʻai Valley as the toughest, steepest mile of the entire trail. Guaranteed to make or break Holly's desire to continue. And though Jordan had game-planned scenarios for treating a case of the jitters on Crawler's Ledge, it hadn't occurred to him until then that they might not make it that far—and then what? Turn around? Go on without her?

No, he needed to get her to the end. It was his only option—their only hope.

To pass the time and take advantage of the lack of digital distractions, Jordan steered the conversation to past vacations, specifically his visits to National Parks. He raved about the views and solitude, the wild grandeur. There was really nothing else like it, he explained.

Responsive at first, Holly eventually fell quiet as discussion yielded to introspection ... or blank silence. Jordan couldn't tell which. The next three hours passed as the trail rose and fell en route to Hanakoa Valley, just beyond the halfway point.

He undid the straps and shrugged the pack from his shoulders upon reaching the rest area at Hanakoa Stream. The bag hit the lone picnic table with a thud, teetered momentarily, then fell drunkenly to the dirt. Holly all but collapsed onto the bench opposite him as the sodden ground squished underfoot and mosquitoes ascended to greet them. With gunslinger quickness, Jordan slipped a bottle of bug spray from a mesh side pocket and offered it to Holly. Experience taught him the easiest way to ensure someone swore off camping forever was to send them home covered in bug bites.

Holly sprayed her legs and arms, then pulled a chocolate chip Cliff bar from her pack and tore it open with a vengeance. Jordan opened an energy bar of his own as Holly stared in the direction of a tent pitched awkwardly amongst the cobbles. "How are your feet? Any blisters?" he asked.

"Fine."

"Need a refill?" He shook the bite valve of his water hose. "I can dig out the filter."

"No thanks." Holly scanned the area from one direction to another with a slow sweep of her head. Jordan waited patiently, smiling like an imbecile, hoping for her attention to again perch on him. Other than some orange trees and a trail leading several miles to a waterfall, the area held slight appeal. No more than a way station for those too exhausted to continue. And if not for the table and nearby stream, they wouldn't have stopped. Holly's eyes locked on a sign pointing upslope to a campsite, causing Jordan's stomach to clench. It was barely ten o'clock in the morning. They couldn't pitch camp now. No matter how tired she might be. It would be a wasted day. And chances were, if they stayed the night there, she'd want to hike out in the morning.

"Man, that outhouse smells like sunbaked dogshit," Jordan said, exaggerating the offensiveness.

Holly chewed the insides of her cheeks and said nothing.

"Hardest part's over. Only four miles to go."

"People camp here?" Her tone suggested less repulsion than abject confusion.

Jordan looked around as if noticing the nearby tent for the first time. "Probably slower hikers who got a late start. Another reason to hit the trail early. We can take as long as we need. I know it's kinda nasty here, but I don't mind resting longer if you want."

Holly crinkled her nose. "No need." She shoved the empty snack wrapper into a side pocket of her pack and extricated herself from the picnic table. "You coming?" Her tone was breezy, and her posture showed little sign of the grueling seven miles they'd covered.

He floated to his feet, spurred by her desire to keep moving. "Why don't you take the lead? Set the pace for a while." He motioned her ahead. "Once we get out of this hanging valley, the scenery is really going to open up."

She shrugged her agreement and moved in front, immediately setting a faster pace than he anticipated.

Jordan fell in behind her. His thighs and calves burned with the strain of carrying the bulk of their gear, but the sight of Holly charging up the trail was all the motivation he needed. He matched her pace, following the mesmerizing sway of her ponytail. And with each step, the peacefulness of the trail melded with the earthy scent of the forest, encouraging him to once again dream of change—and the shape their lives might take once his game released.

And by the look of things, she was starting to dream it too.

The trail leveled off to a gentle cinder path, and the ensuing mile passed without effort as the underfoot gravel crunch provided a hypnotic pendulum of sound. Hiking would never be Jordan's favorite outdoor sport—it lacked the adrenaline and demands of kayaking and climbing, neither of which he'd had time for in years—but he always appreciated how conducive a long hike was for thinking. And he'd been thinking a lot in the hour since Hanakoa.

"I ever tell you about my aunt and uncle in Vermont?"

Holly turned briefly. A faint look of surprise adorned her face, as though she'd forgotten he was there. "Not sure."

"They started hiking together in college. Every weekend. Been together over forty years now."

"Huh."

"Said long walks were the key to their marriage." Jordan recalled the advice his uncle gave him when younger. That all those Dear Abbys of the world liked to say how important communication was to a marriage, but they never told you how to do it. The key, his uncle believed, was to go hiking, because out in the woods, there wasn't anything to do but talk. And that was important. Jordan laughed, remembering his other advice. "He also said to make sure I had plenty of money and as few kids as possible—preferably none. My aunt used to conk him on the head when he said stuff like that. Guess she didn't want me thinking they didn't like children."

Holly maintained her steady pace. "Two out of three's not bad."

A painful sigh lodged in Jordan's lungs. It was true, they were child-free and wanted for nothing, but that was the easy part. Hell, they'd each checked those boxes back when they were single. He couldn't tell if Holly's comment was for laughs or meant to be as dismissive as it seemed. "I remember him saying it didn't matter where they went, or how far, as long as they had enough time to walk and talk. My aunt called it the daydream engine. It's why they left Boston. They wanted to live closer to the trails."

Holly snorted. "Sounds a bit extreme."

He held his tongue, clenched between molars, and willed himself to remain positive. *She doesn't mean it,* he told himself.

Up ahead, the forest canopy parted, revealing an expanse of blue sky. They were nearing the cliffside portion of the hike. With any luck, the scenery would help sell her on the allure of spending more time outdoors. After all, if a photo were worth a thousand words, the views ahead had to be worth twice as many.

He psyched himself up and asked, "You think you'd ever want to try that? Take weekly hikes. To talk. Plan our future."

Holly looked at him, her upper lip hooked in a confounded sneer. "We're talking now, aren't we?"

Up ahead, the trail hairpinned away from a small overlook affording an unobstructed view westward along the coast. To Jordan's surprise, Holly stepped from the trail without prodding and withdrew her phone for the first time that day. He held back, enjoying the sight of her snapping one photo after another. No selfies, only panoramas; an observation nearly as jaw-dropping as the scenery.

Jordan took care not to crowd her. Though fringed with rocks and knee-high shrubs, the viewpoint was barely larger than the couch he stood upon the night they'd met, after he wobbled his way through a celebratory speech. "Amazing, huh?" He could as easily been referring to the course his life had taken since the party, but directed the compliment at the one-hundred-eighty-degree view.

"You showed me photos online, but …" She let the sentence hang, no need to elaborate. As a game designer, he knew how poorly even the most magnificent images faired when stacked against the real thing. And nowhere had he ever seen blues or greens like this. Jurassic canyons carpeted in jade, plunging from heaven to sea. They stood perched hundreds of feet above the Pacific, its whipped-cream froth dancing atop the rollers, but it was Holly he couldn't take his eyes from.

"Are those people?" she asked, pointing across the next valley. "Wait. Is … is that *the trail?*" Her voice hinged in disbelief as she took a photo of the distant cliff face and zoomed in on the image. Jordan didn't need to look at the screen to know it revealed hikers clinging to a narrow ribbon of trail above the ocean. He intentionally avoided telling her about so-called Crawler's Ledge for fear she'd back out. And now that it stared them in the face, he expected her to put up a fight. Or at least demand to know why he hadn't warned her. To his delight, Holly pursed her lips as a spark of adventure fluttered in her eyes.

"You're actually enjoying this, aren't you?" he asked.

A stray hair fluttered in the breeze as she angled toward him, her face glowing in the morning sun. "Why so surprised?"

"Well, you did try to talk me out of it this morning."

"Guess I didn't realize how pretty it'd be." This was high praise coming from a woman who would downplay a private performance by the London Philharmonic. It took getting used to, this reluctance to allow herself to be properly impressed, but Jordan had come to learn any praise from Holly was a sign of intense pleasure. It wasn't that she was a cynic like so many of his coworkers whose default setting was derision, nor was she an impossible-to-please snob. Holly merely preferred to keep her reactions understated, honest. An adherent of the philosophy that said if everything was special, then nothing was.

"I'm relieved to hear you say that."

"Why's that?"

"I missed this." He gestured in a languid, swooping movement, taking in the trail, the landscape, their boots and packs. "Back when I first moved to Seattle, I spent almost every weekend in the mountains before the job became all-consuming." Holly tilted her head quizzically as Jordan released a nervous chuckle. "And ever since the Alaska trip, I've been hoping we could do more stuff together. Like this. But if you hated it, then ... I don't know." He shrugged his shoulders to his ears. "Part of me didn't want you to come, thinking it'd be easier to live with the dream than the rejection."

Holly scratched her cheek and stared past him as though instructions on how to respond were written in the sky. She opened her mouth to speak, but only breathed further uncertainty. Finally, with too much hesitation to offer any assurance, she straightened her shoulders and said, "No, this is fun. We can do it again."

Jordan sucked his lips, knowing all too well she was placating him. Yet, he could tell in the way she watched out the corner of her eyes that she knew there was more going unsaid. And Jordan didn't wait for her to ask.

"So, one of the things I've been thinking about—"

"During the hike or ... before?"

"Both. Today, but also for a while." He inhaled, searching for courage in the alkaline tang of mineral soil and sea breeze. The time was now. He had to lay his cards on the table. "I feel like I lost track of what was important in life. And well, the city, the job at the studio, the stress ... I don't think it's for me."

Holly recoiled as if tasered. "What are you saying? You want to change jobs?"

"No. Well, yes. But ... maybe once my game releases, after the bonuses come in, what if we move? Get out of Seattle. Head to the mountains. Maybe I'll get a job with the Forest Service or open a guiding company, taking people into the backcountry. With your business skills and my—"

"Whoa, settle down Indiana Jones. I said I'm enjoying the hike. There's no way I'm running off to open a mountain lodge." She shook her head in cartoon style, as if to wipe what she'd heard from memory. She cinched her pack's shoulder straps and started toward the trail.

Jordan tugged her wrist. "Don't walk away. We need to talk."

"There's nothing to discuss." She flashed to her wrist then back to him. He relaxed his grip but didn't let go.

"How can you say that? Can't you see how miserable I've been?"

"So, this is real? You want us to abandon our careers—ones we spent our entire adult lives building—and move to the sticks?"

"I want us to be happy."

"I am happy!"

"Could have fooled me," he said under his breath, thinking of all the nights she spent answering emails in bed, the weekends spent scowling at a spreadsheet. His overtime came in cycles, mostly during crunch. For Holly, it was a lifestyle. Control. Order. And whenever he suggested she leave it at the office, she'd lash out, ridiculing his ignorance when it came to finances. "I'm just saying there's more to life than a luxury condo and two-hundred-dollar haircuts. We can have it so much better. We can escape the stress—"

"Oh, please."

"We can take it slow. Maybe start with a summer cabin."

"I can't believe I'm hearing this. What makes you think I would even consider risking our future security over something so stupid?" Her exasperated tone reached a pitch Jordan didn't believe possible.

"Because I'm asking you to." He softened his voice and slid his hand down to her palm, trying to lace his fingers within hers. "Just consider it. Okay? It wouldn't be for a couple years. Maybe by then—"

She pulled her hand away. "No fucking way."

"So, that's it?" he asked. It didn't matter what he wanted. Probably never did. It was about her. Always and forever. And he'd been a fool to think she'd ever change—he saw that now. "After all I've done. All the hoops I've jumped through. You wouldn't even let me have my mother at our wedding! I bent over backwards to become the man you wanted, and you won't even consider this? Won't even try it?" He rubbed his temples in an effort to soothe his throbbing head.

"So it's my fault? Because I plucked you out of your college dorm lifestyle and showed you something better to spend your life on? No, you're not guilting me with this bullshit." Holly turned to go.

Jordan grabbed her again. His face vibrated as he compressed his anger into something palatable. Gritting his teeth to the point of pain, he spoke slowly, lobbing solid words that landed in thuds. "Just consider it."

"Let go of me," she yelled just as the hikers they'd seen earlier rounded the bend into view. Two women with bookend looks of concern and condemnation on their face.

"Are you okay?" one asked Holly before shooting a threatening glare at Jordan as he released his grip.

"I've got everything under control. Thanks, ladies," Holly said, stern faced.

The moment the women were out of sight, Holly emitted a caustic biting laugh of condescension. "Do you honestly think I married you so I can live like some hick in the mountains? I mean, really. Come on, Jordan. The video games were bad enough. I tolerated it because you made good money and, apparently, the internet dorks think you're a celebrity. But this? If you want to go build tree houses and spend the rest of your life eating granola, go ahead. But you'll be doing it without me."

Jordan's jaw stiffened and his nostrils flared as Holly's rejection drove a stake through his love for her. "And to think I wanted to spend the rest of my life with you."

Holly stepped closer, thrusting her face under his chin, so close he could feel the fire in her eyes. She poked him in the chest, driving her intentions into his shattered heart. "I am *not* gonna let you drag me down."

"Get out of my face," Jordan said, and shoved her away, harder than he intended, and without a thought to where they stood. Or to the consequences.

Holly's heel struck a rock, and she stumbled. Her pack, though filled with the lightest gear money could buy, shifted her center of gravity, drawing her backward through a web of plants as if they weren't there. In the moment it took him to realize what happened, to make sense of the sheer terror on her face, he'd forfeited the chance to do anything about it.

"*Nooo!*"

Jordan reached for her, but it was too late. His fingertips grazed her ruby-tipped nails, the first part of her he'd ever seen, now the last he'd ever touch. Gone. He dropped to his knees and peered over the edge. A cloud of dust erupted on the slope, all but concealing the bouncing purple flash of her backpack. If she screamed, he couldn't hear it over the sound of rockfall. He watched, trembling, as one boulder after another tumbled after his beautiful wife, cratering the water hundreds of feet below, disappearing beneath the waves without a trace.

Gone.

He brought his quivering hands to his face, ground his palms into his eyes, blotting out the sight, the memory of her expression. The horror. The awareness. The accusation.

She's dead because of me.

The world held still. Silent. Until shattered by the sound of Jordan vomiting himself empty.

Jordan wiped his lips and hocked the remaining filth from his mouth. Below him, lace-trimmed turquoise waves sloshed against the cliff-side, erupting like geysers with the regularity of a metronome. Wave after wave, they exploded in clouds of froth, like down pillows shredded in two, their feathers free to fly again.

He'd seen the boulders tumble. Saw Holly bounce from the sloping cliff. But that water. The sea foam. It looked so soft. *Could she ...* He didn't risk asking it aloud, not wanting to jinx it, but yes, there had to be a chance she survived. The weekly Pilates, the yoga. She was fit. Flexible.

Jordan ripped the phone from his pocket in a panic, knowing there was little time to waste. He mashed the screen, dialing 911. He was on the trail, before Crawler's Ledge, and needed help immediately. His wife. She fell, he'd say, keeping to the facts. Tell them only what they needed to save her. There'd be time for specifics later.

It never rang.

No bars.

He stared blankly at the screen in a moment of confusion before remembering the warnings: no cell service along the Nāpali Coast. "Dammit!" he roared, spiking the phone into the dirt. It splintered and bounced over the edge. Jordan balled his fists, trembling with panicked energy as his digital lifeline plummeted into the abyss. Guilt and despair tugged at him, drawing him toward the edge, toward her, a siren whose song he couldn't shake. He resisted, but only barely. He had to get out of there. For her sake. For his. But his legs refused to move. The shock of his predicament had been slow in coming, but now rooted him in place.

What to do?

What to do?

What to do?

The Garmin beeped, distracting him from his moroseness. Eleven o'clock. He tapped the stop button on the watch, freezing it just beyond seven miles, and stared at the digital breadcrumb trail marking their route. His mind wandered back along the LED scrawl, replaying the hike in reverse: their argument, the scenery, the final preparation that morning at the resort. With a flash of recognition, Jordan recalled packing a locator beacon. He could still save her! He hurriedly undid the straps and shrugged off his backpack. He had stored the electronics down low in a blue waterproof ditty bag, to keep them safe. He just had to—

"Not here," he said, knowing he'd need to tell the rescuers what happened. He had to get someplace safe. Where a helicopter could land.

The trail's endpoint at Kalalau Beach was closer, and the hardest climbs were already behind him. It made no sense to turn around. Jordan yanked on the pack, cinched it tight, and took off at a run. He'd signal for help at the beach, then tell them where she fell once the helicopter arrived. If only she could stay afloat or cling to a rock, she could make it.

The steady crunch of gravel underfoot was a balm for his overwrought mind. And though the heat and prior miles had sapped his energy, Jordan couldn't afford to stop. He'd rest later. Once Holly was safe. He followed the trail as it rounded a narrow valley. From there, the path hugged the cliffside, climbing out of view along a ribbon of rust-tinted cinders and chunky basalt better suited to goats than humans. The urgency of his mission propelled him onward with no concern for the scenery or the terrain; his only care was to call for help. He merely had to navigate one final ascent past the infamous Crawler's Ledge, then he'd be home free for a miles-long cruise down to Kal—a snag of his toe on a rock, then a slam.

His chest crashed against the ground, knocking the wind from his lungs as his body skidded toward the edge. By instinct, he thrust his arms wide and clawed at the dirt and rocks for purchase, fighting the momentum of his overstuffed backpack. He came to a stop, gasping for impossible breath, peering straight over the edge at the roiling surf hundreds of feet below. Jordan lay where he fell, waiting for his diaphragm to unstick, wheezing like a ghost with emphysema.

"Whoa, man. You okay?"

Jordan inched back from the edge and nodded. Up ahead stood a hiker clad in a week's worth of stubble and a hooded, Gatorade-green, long-sleeve hiking shirt. Whether the man rounded the corner in time to see Jordan trip or thought he was literally *crawling* the ledge was unclear. Jordan rose to his knees, relieved to feel his breathing begin to return.

"No hurries, man. Take your time. Not the place to risk a fall."

"Thanks," Jordan eventually said, waiting on all fours for the last of his jitters to dissipate.

"Phew, talk about lucky. Saw you go down. Another foot or so and it woulda been game over." The man punctuated his comment with a lengthy whistle. "No surviving a drop from here."

Jordan braved a look at the tempest below, to where the ocean churned against the rocks like a meat grinder, and knew at once the guy was right. He shuddered, realizing his haste nearly cost him his life. But that acknowledgment, as brief as it was, was immediately piggybacked by the cold truth of Holly's death. Even if she had survived the initial fall—a miracle in its own right—she'd have entered the water shattered and concussed and drowned long before Jordan finished retching.

He snapped his head away from the edge and croaked, "What have I done? So stupid ..."

"Hey, take it easy. You look like you've seen a ghost."

Jordan cinched his eyes closed and shook his head, wishing to disavow the reality washing over him. He killed her. He didn't mean to, but Holly was dead. "I shouldn't have—"

"It's gonna be all right, man. Here, let me help you across the ledge." The hiker gently helped Jordan to his feet. "No shame in being scared. This section freaks a lot of people out."

"I can't ... I shouldn't have ..."

"You're gonna be fine. Just a few more steps." Holding onto Jordan's arm, the man sidled along the ledge, escorting him to where the trail widened around a bend. Once clear of the exposure, Jordan thanked him. His voice sounded distant, unfamiliar, a haunting proximity to the one he used to know. *Before I killed her.*

"Listen, there's some guys living in the valley. They got a boat that comes in every now and then. Ferried some hikers out the other day. I hear it's not cheap, but ..." He gestured back at the ledge, suggesting it beat the alternative.

"In the valley," Jordan repeated, not quite following.

"Yeah, make a left after you cross the stream and go about a mile. You'll hear them. They got quite the setup."

"They live there?"

"Yeah, been back there for years, on and off. Rangers come. They scatter, then regroup. Like cockroaches, ya' know?" The guy laughed. "Hey, what's your handle? I'll tag you when I upload the video."

Jordan shot the guy a puzzled look. *Video?* Only when the man waggled his trekking pole between them did Jordan notice the GoPro mounted on its end. "Oh, no. No. I don't ..." Jordan waved a hand in front of his face as he backed away from the camera's fish-eye lens. He had a fleeting thought to snatch the pole and toss it over the cliff but decided against making a scene. He couldn't risk further attention. Instead, he muttered his gratitude and took off in the direction of Kalalau.

Jordan memorized the man's directions as he hiked. A left at the stream. A mile up valley. They'd been there for years. Jordan didn't need a boat; he needed somewhere to go. A place in the woods to hide. To think up a plan.

"I'm not letting you drag me down." Holly's jeering contempt echoed in his mind, refusing to abate. Now, with his urgency extinguished, he couldn't help reliving their fight. The way she laughed at him. Mocked his profession, his dreams. Her vitriol ricocheted in his mind, boiling his blood, driving him onward with such determination other hikers simply stepped from his path without greeting. With each stride, his balled fists dug their nails deeper into the meat of his palms until the bite was so painful he could no longer ignore the question poisoning his subconscious: Did he mean to push her?

No, it was an accident. He wanted her out of his face. He didn't mean to kill her.

I love her.

True. He did. But Jordan knew if even he were questioning his motive, the police certainly would. He recalled the women who passed who'd heard them arguing. They saw him grab her. Heard Holly's shout. And what about the phone? Only the guilty throw their phone off a cliff.

"I didn't mean to—"

What, Jordan? You didn't mean to kill her? But you did.

"I'm innocent."

Your word against theirs. And the police will say you're a murderer.

Jordan's heart hammered in his chest as he splashed across Kalalau Stream. The beach, his research, none of that mattered any longer. He turned left, as if on autopilot, and marched up the valley with no clear plan. Only a goal: to not spend the rest of his life in prison.

CHAPTER 27
NIGHTSWIMMING

Malia regretted her decision to stand.

Sure, her legs ached with stiffness, but more than that, she needed to prove herself ready to reclaim her freedom. She'd told Park everything she knew, was done with their questions, with captivity. But that was ten minutes ago, before Park and Kahale went into the hallway to talk. Now she stood alone in the interrogation room, waiting. To sit would be to surrender, to admit defeat and accept she had no control over her own life—so she told herself. Instead, she leaned against the corner of the room, feeling as forgotten as an old broom, left to wait until called upon for another mess.

When Park eventually swept into the room, she caught Malia picking dirt from beneath her fingernails. Park's attention roamed from Malia's hands to her sandaled, dirty feet. "Bet you can't wait for a shower," she said, pausing with the doorknob still in hand. The door floated open as Park stepped behind the table.

Malia couldn't tell if Park was suggesting she stank or alluding to her release. Her pulse quickened as she sensed a change in the air, a faint freshness blown in from the hall. She knew not to get her hopes up. If she learned anything that summer, it was that hope only led to disappointment. So Malia stared at the door in silence, afraid a single word would blow it closed for good.

Park clapped her hands and swiped her palms against one another. "You've been a big help today. Thank you. You're free to go."

"Oh, thank God," Malia gasped. She slumped forward, bracing against her wobbly knees, feeling the stress drain away. Then, as that long-awaited verdict set in, Malia huffed a bone-weary sigh of relief and took a hesitant step to Park, searching for the physical reassurance that would mark her ordeal as truly over.

Park raised her hand, palm out, with the robotic detachment of someone halting traffic. "Booking should have any possessions not needed as evidence. Check with them on your way out."

She stared at Park, replaying the woman's drip-fed concern, the motherly advice, the female understanding. Was it all an act? After everything Malia told her about her parents, her love life, and what she'd been through, Park's sudden indifference didn't just feel off, it felt insulting. "Just like that?" Malia didn't know what to expect, but it wasn't this. "For real?"

"Unless you've omitted any details, I see no reason to detain you any longer."

She didn't know why Park's icy demeanor bothered her so much, but she was powerless to melt it. It was time to get out of there. But how? She lost her wallet, had no money; she was effectively stranded on an island where the only people she knew were either under arrest, missing, or the police.

"Did you ... call my dad?"

"We gave him a courtesy call earlier since he filed the MP, but it went to voicemail." Park shrugged her shoulders and offered a win-some-lose-some smile. "We'll let him know you were released if he calls."

Malia bulged her eyes. All this time, she'd imagined her father waiting by the phone, ready to jump at the first sign of her return. But no. And then there was Park. Malia's father filed a Missing Person's Report nearly two months ago, his daughter was questioned all morning regarding a murder, and all Park had to say was that she'd pass along a message if he called? No better than a put-upon roommate.

"So, you gonna see if your friend with the boat will take you back to O'ahu?"

"What—" *Kimo!* Of course.

Malia glimpsed Park's notepad, recalling how long ago she'd written his name, and wondered how she could have remembered. She felt Park watching her, wearing her hands on her hips with a smug look. As if to say, *"What did you expect, Malia? I am a detective."* But Park said nothing.

"Is Waimea close?" Malia asked, remembering Kimo's instructions.

"Not far. About twenty-five miles."

"Oh," Malia said, frowning, hating to acknowledge her desperation. "Is there ... any chance you could—"

"Lend you bus money?" Park asked, again seeming to read her mind. She appeared to be enjoying this. "Yeah. Not a problem."

"I lost my wallet," Malia explained.

"I know." Park pulled a twenty from her pocket and set it down. As Malia reached for it, Park placed her palm atop Malia's hand, holding it firmly against the table. Malia looked up in surprise and saw compassion swirling amidst the mahogany flecks of Park's eyes. The detective leaned forward, close enough for Malia to smell the coffee on her breath. Park tightened her grip, pumping Malia with concern, and said in a wavering voice too soft to be recorded, "Watch yourself out there."

The door clicked shut behind her and, without pomp or ceremony, Malia was free. Her last gulp of stale jailhouse air raspberried through her lips as if from an unclipped balloon. *Finally.* Malia slumped back against the sunbaked door in relief, listening to the distant thrum of traffic. A sound she hadn't heard in months. She half-expected to see her dad waiting beside a tree. The same half of her that wished she could click her heels and be whisked home. The rest of her knew better than to believe in fairy tales—and that her release didn't guarantee a happily ever after.

Watch yourself.

Malia couldn't tell if it was the rote remark of a mother whose child were headed out to play or of a detective who understood the dangers of the world—and didn't agree with Malia's release.

She stood with that thought for a moment. Her only danger was in losing her scholarship to Berkeley. She had to find Kimo and hope he'd take her back to Oʻahu—or at the very least, return her phone. Following Park's directions, Malia clutched the twenty-dollar bill and went in search of a bus stop. She passed two along the main avenue, both for the downtown shuttle. No good. She continued until spotting a sign for Waimea: 25 miles. Park was right. *Crap.*

Her sandal's thong tore through the sole as Malia jogged across a highway intersection. It was the fifth time it ripped free inside of two miles. *Enough!* She kicked the slippers from her feet in frustration, preferring to go barefoot than deal with further annoyance. She turned left onto Kaumualiʻi Highway, no more than a lane in each direction, and tossed out a thumb. She'd never hitchhiked before, but also never found herself barefoot on the side of a highway, sweat running down her thighs, struggling not to trip in sweatpants sized for a linebacker.

The hitchhikers in Honolulu always walked backwards, desperately seeking eye contact with one driver after another, as if guilt alone would land them a ride. Malia couldn't risk stepping on broken glass, even in the weeds where she walked to avoid burning her feet. And so it was with some surprise that a gray Toyota pickup pulled over after less than ten minutes of thumbing it. The truck, splattered in dried mud, bore a bumper sticker beneath its rusted, mismatched tailgate, urging others to "Keep Country Country." The slogan reminded her of something Inoke might have said, and that connection gave her pause. She hadn't seen the driver, but a truck like that, headed out into the countryside … Was it safe? Malia wasn't about to get in the car with a strange man. Why'd she think hitchhiking would be okay? Because it wasn't the big city? She froze, unsure what to do.

"Hey, you need a ride or not?" A woman scooted across the bench seat and poked her head out the passenger window. She wore purple confetti hospital scrubs and had a bright round face and long, black hair tied in a ponytail.

Malia breathed a prayer of relief and jogged toward the truck. "Yeah, I gotta get to the harbor in Waimea. Kikia-something-or-another."

The woman scooped the air with her chin in a shoveling motion like an enthusiastic toucan. "Climb in. I work at the hospital in Waimea. Can't take you all the way to the harbor, but it's a short walk from town."

"Great, thanks!" Malia told herself to keep her guard up, but felt her tension melt upon spotting a child's booster seat in the back. "I'm Malia."

The woman introduced herself as Jade and accelerated hard onto the road, causing an empty soda can to roll against Malia's toes. Jade glanced from Malia's bare feet to her face, looking like she was about to ask something, but instead turned up the volume on the radio. Malia had never talked so much in her life as she did that day, and was happy to drape her arm out the open window as Jade sang.

"You really gonna make me sing by myself?" Jade asked a minute later.

"Oh. I ... I don't know the song."

"For real?" She tucked her chin, casting doubt down her nose. "KONG's been playing it all summer." Jade faced the road, shaking her head, and Malia could tell she was wondering if her passenger had been living under a rock. Malia grinned at the truth within the phrasing. *A three-thousand-foot-tall rock*, she thought. Jade sang one song after another as the road skirted the fertile flank of the island's ancient volcano. They sped past tourist attractions and tiny towns, remnants of old Kauaʻi from plantation times, cruising the narrow two-lane country highway through a waving tunnel of grass. Every now and then, as the truck crested a hill, Malia would glimpse the mountains out the passenger window. Somewhere up amongst the peaks was Mount Waiʻaleʻale, the rainiest spot on earth. A factoid lodged in her brain from school.

Equally cemented in her memory was the day she encountered Jordan at the base of the cliffs, searching for a way out. From deep in Kalalau Valley, the clifftop appeared impossibly out of reach. But from Jade's Toyota, far away on Highway 50, the ridgeline looked so much smaller. Manageable. Of course, if she'd learned anything that summer, it was that everything seemed easier from afar. She gazed out the passenger window, smiling at the hazy mountain skyline, thinking of the hours spent staring up at that ridge, when a sudden picture of Jordan entered her mind. A vision of him tangled in his homemade rope, broken and bloody amongst the rocks—and her, Malia, standing alongside him, torn between the desire to help and the urge to watch him suffer.

"You okay?" Jade asked, watching Malia out of the corner of her eye. "Look like you've seen your last rainbow."

Malia blinked the vision away. "Just thinking about someone."

"A boy, I bet." Jade swatted the air between them. "Sing with me. It'll take your mind off him." She cranked the volume on a reggae song and started bobbing her head, hamming it up. Jade was a mom through and through, acting as though Malia were just another kid needing to be entertained on a drive, exactly like Malia's own mother used to do. Singing and dancing in the seat, shaking rhythm into her knee. But Malia was too exhausted to play along, and thankful when a bluesy Anuhea tune came on. One she remembered from summers past. When she was younger and life was simpler. Jade, picking up on Malia's muted sing-along, arched her eyebrows. "Right Love, Wrong Time?" she said, posing the song title as a question.

Malia masked her regret with a bashful smile. She'd been so focused on getting home that she'd largely managed to avoid thinking about Tiki. Until now. She wanted to believe the connection she felt the prior night on the beach was real. And that seeing him in the hallway meant he might have been waiting outside the station.

I'll never see him again. Don't even know his full name.

A wry chuckle bubbled forth as she recalled her mother saying the same about Malia's birth father. The mysterious "Boy from California." But at least her mom got to experience the romance … Malia sighed. At least Tiki proved reliable in one way. He promised she'd get home today and so far, so good. If her luck continued, she'd get her phone back, call her dad, and have him pay Kimo to boat her back to Oʻahu. And maybe, just maybe, she'd catch her flight to California in time.

"Here's your stop. Harbor's a mile up the road on the left."

"You're a lifesaver. Thanks." Malia exited the car and pushed the creaking door shut. Jade leaned across the seat and, with the tone of a wise old auntie, said, "Forget about that boy. Men are more trouble than they're worth."

Malia laughed and stepped onto the sidewalk. She watched Jade make a U-turn, thinking she was probably right, but suspected it easier to forget a love gone sour than the dreams of what might have been. Regardless, it was time to start putting Kalalau and everything about the summer behind her.

No sooner had the Toyota's exhaust dissipated than the aroma of barbecue took its place, reminding Malia she'd eaten nothing but a small pastry all day. She scanned the nearby shops and spotted a chicken and ribs place across from a small park. She couldn't risk blowing the whole twenty on a plate lunch—she'd need a few bucks in case Kimo couldn't be found—and opted for the loco moco. With two heaping scoops of rice, a hamburger patty, and fried egg smothered in gravy, it was unadulterated comfort in gut-bomb packaging.

She wolfed down the food, tossed the takeout container in the trash, and started toward the marina. She hadn't gone two blocks before a red-painted shop across the street caught her eye. Jo Jo's Shave Ice beckoned, and Malia was powerless to ignore its draw. She jogged across the street and went inside, counting on the kid behind the register to ignore her bare feet. The sign touted sixty flavors, but Malia didn't scan the list. A papaya-lychee combo with sweet cream and maca nut topping, the exact order she shared with her mother every June … until last year. It was time.

Outside, twin roosters strutted around the bench seating as if they owned the place. Malia watched them peck at the rainbow of drops spotting the slab floor and flicked a nut past them. They scurried after it, leaving her alone with the first shave ice she'd eaten since her mother's death. The pastel syrups soaked into the shavings as Malia melted into her memories. Of her mom, the accident, and the awful, awful year spent enduring life without her. The dessert was another first in what she now understood would be a lifetime filled with them. But to Malia's surprise, she wasn't sad. It was okay. *She* was okay.

As Malia spooned her way through the treat, she noticed the squat, beige building next door was a library. She thought nothing of it at first, then an idea sparked in her mind: she'd email her dad to let him know she was safe, tell him she'd call home soon. *Yes*, she thought, wondering what else she'd write in the email, what she'd say when she saw him. Maybe it wasn't too late for them to start their own tradition. Not shave ice, that was her mother's thing, but something they could look forward to. Something for them to share. To build upon during her visits home from school.

Home.

"Hello, Malia."

She froze, stunned by the sound of that familiar voice. Her pulse quickened, but she couldn't look. She'd convinced herself she'd never see him again and yet ...

Malia forced herself to face the sidewalk. There, despite the odds, stood Jordan. Black-eyed, bruised, and shirtless with white-scabbed burns oozing from his legs and hair combed through with sand. He stared at her, through her, just as she imagined a ghost would.

Jordan knew the instant he jerked the spear out, there was no going back. Not to Kalalau. Not home to Seattle. Not ever.

He fled the beach at Honopu at full sprint, his every fiber vibrating from the shock of what he'd done—the uncertainty of what came next. Midnight waters swirled around him, concealing his feet, knees, then his entire body as he trudged deeper into the ocean. Jordan filled his lungs and dove beneath an incoming roller, seeking to rinse his mind of that gruesome image: the gaping, gore-soaked hole, the blood splatter on Malia's face. He could still feel it, the deadweight heft of Inoke's body ripping free of the spear, the warmth of the blood spilling down the weapon, coating his hands.

He was smart to hide his pack before going to Honopu. Stuffed everything he salvaged from the fire into it—his sleeping bag, gadgets, and clothes. Win or lose, he knew better than to trust Inoke and his lackeys. No matter how the contest went. He could have beaten them back to camp, grabbed his gear, and fled into the valley. But this was no longer a fight over the camp. He'd killed a man—and the police wouldn't quit until they hunted him down. That was certain. He'd be a sitting duck in Kalalau. And if he hiked out, they'd pick him up in Hanalei. There was nowhere to go—no way to escape the witness reports. No time to get back to camp and slash the pontoons before Ruby and Darren used the boat to get help.

FUCK!

A wave crashed atop him like a toppled cymbal, halting the adrenaline drumline pounding in his head. Above the ocean din, there was commotion. Screaming. Bloody murder screaming, they called it. As apt a description as any, he thought. But they weren't coming for him. Not to the depths. If any had given chase, they must have followed the coastline along the rocks, back the way they'd come. They'd have to swim given the rising tide, but they could make it.

Could he? Kalalau would be impossible to reach within an hour. And then what?

He kicked away from shore, toward the midnight horizon—toward hopelessness—and floated in the recollections of all he'd lost. His job, his wife, his freedom. How did it come to this? A regretful shove. The need to defend himself. Two people dead. The thought of ending it all right there popped into his mind. Of swimming as far as he could out to sea until exhaustion settled in, carried him under. The easiest thing in the world. To sink away, to vanish without a trace …

But he couldn't bring himself to do it. As a lifelong swimmer, he nursed a healthy fear of drowning, an act far more painful than people believed.

Even as he contemplated death, Jordan angled left along the prevailing current. West. Away from Kalalau. But to where? Land, sky, and sea were as black as his thoughts, his crimes. Only pinpricks of starlight and the halcyon glow of the moon below the eastern mountains helped him tell down from up, the shore from abyss.

"Come on, Jordan, think!"

He initiated a lazy stroke down current, recalling his research. He was certain the mountains melted to farmland in the south. Knew it from his island map, had seen it during the flight over from Honolulu. But how far did the cliffs of Nāpali extend beyond Kalalau Valley? A mile? Two? Twenty? He hadn't a clue, never imagined going any direction other than back along the trail.

He'd never heard of anyone swimming out from Kalalau, away from the trailhead to the west, and that realization provided all the motivation he needed. He'd be the first—or die trying. Either way, no one would suspect it.

Jordan took stock of his situation. The water temperature was comfortable, for now, but without the sun's warmth, hypothermia was inevitable. Whatever the distance was to the next beach, he had to cover it. And fast. Ruby and Darren were only a boat ride away from notifying the police. And once the helicopters were airborne, he'd be an easy capture.

He leaned into his stroke, dipping his face to reduce the drag. The salt stung his eyes, his mouth, and legs too. And for a moment it startled him. The fight with Inoke, the fire. Jordan had nearly been beaten to death. It's why he snapped, why he reached for the spear.

But how did he get the chance?

Malia.

She was in the ring.

Why?

He couldn't recall. It was as though his conscience had blotted out the events of the contest, partitioned his memory in two: Before he killed Inoke. And now.

The hows and whys didn't matter. There was only the stroke. Jordan's muscle memory returned as if he'd only stepped from the university pool yesterday. He rose and fell in the night, cutting a path through the rolling swells. With an eye on the cliffs ever-so-vaguely outlined against the sky, he headed west, well enough offshore to avoid being slammed against the rocks, close enough to spot a beach. He forced himself to calm his thoughts, to squirrel the horror aside and swim with efficiency. The open water was no place for adrenaline. But he had to keep moving. Toward land. Warmth. Anonymity. Going too hard, too fast, would invite fatigue. Jordan had the reserves to tread water indefinitely, but to do so would risk hypothermia. And sharks.

He hadn't swum over three miles at once in years. And never at night. Then again, he'd never swam for his life before.

Left, right, left, breathing every third stroke as he was taught by his coach all those years ago. He rolled to breathe and took in a mouthful of surf. The brine burned his throat, his lungs. He coughed and spit, cursing in frustration and fear. He had to focus. Death was only a single misstep away; blind reliance on past habits would prove fatal.

Jordan scissor-kicked forward and arced his arm through the air, slicing into the water, thumb down and leading, carving an S-stroke beneath him, propelling his body through the sea. Molecules of water glossed across his skin like mercury bubbles, christening him, easing his return to sanctuary.

Cliffs rose like skyscrapers from the sea along this untraveled stretch of Nāpali, nearly as impressive as—

Holly, he thought, recalling the cliffs back in the direction of Crawler's Ledge.

How did this happen? How did everything spiral out of control? *She's dead.*

It was an accident. "I loved her," he croaked, nearly missing a breath.

All true. But as much as he didn't want to admit her death was a gift, she held him back. Everything did. The game? Fuck the game. He'd dreamed up the scenarios in *Driftwood* because he never had the balls to attempt a real survival situation. Not like this. Not like his time in Kalalau.

This is survival.

His confidence surged as he considered all he'd done, how he rebuilt the camp, sourced his own food, knew how to endure. Better than any of them. Video games? Let's see how many can drop the controller and do it for real. Jordan increased his stroke rate, swimming faster than before, fueled by the rawness of his triumph, the battles waged and victories won in his mind. Yes, he'd proven his mettle in the wilds, but now he needed to harness another set of skills entirely. Those needed to get away with murder.

Kill or be killed.

Better fucking believe it.

Jordan lifted his head from atop a wave and spotted a strip of sand glistening faintly against the dark. He'd been swimming an hour, give or take, and gliding on the current with each stroke. He'd probably gone three miles from Honopu. Maybe more. He needed to rest. Find some fresh water or fruit and warm up.

He soon dragged himself onto the sand. Goose bumps coated his skin, but with no fire or dry clothes, he had to keep moving. He staggered up the beach and nearly crashed headfirst into a sign. Shapes stood out as silhouettes, but not much else. Reading was out of the question, but the presence of paths suggested a secluded boater's park or historical site.

Jordan stumbled blindly in the dim light to what appeared to be a grove of fruit trees ringed by a stone wall, likely an ancient terrace. There, he plucked a strange, bumpy fruit from a low branch. He'd read enough Krakauer to know better than to eat anything he couldn't guarantee wasn't poisonous, but had also never heard of anyone cultivating an orchard of toxic fruit. He smashed the orb on a rock and nearly gagged from its stench of festering blue cheese. Still, he needed sugar. Calories. He tore a piece off and bit.

Vomit fondue.

He spit the pulp from his mouth and scratched at his tongue as he sought water to rinse away the godawful taste. He heard rushing water high atop the cliffs. No time for that. He had to keep moving. The beach was a trap. The entire island, for that matter. Too small. He had to get to O'ahu, disappear amidst its inland jungles.

But how to get there? He had an ID, a credit card he couldn't risk using, and two hundred dollars cash in a waterproof wallet. But if the police weren't searching for him over Holly, they'd be looking soon enough because of Inoke. As soon as Darren and the others took the boat—

"A boat," he said, recalling Malia had a friend she hoped would take her home. If he could find the guy in Waimea—and mention Malia— he just might pay his way to O'ahu. And if he couldn't? Jordan would cross that bridge when he reached it.

He strode back to the water, hungry and shivering, but invigorated by his newfound plan.

The ocean felt warm compared to the night air, but his muscles hollered in protest of the renewed effort. Still, he pushed on, counting strokes to keep alert. Breathing every second stroke, always facing the shore to avoid another mouthful of seawater. On every twentieth stroke, he sighted his bearing, aiming to keep closer to shore. And every hundred strokes he paused to rest. He jogged his legs in place, tread-ing water with a light paddle, catching his breath, working the lactic acid from his arms. An hour passed. Then another.

Like a great white rising slowly but surely to devour him, exhaus-tion closed in. His eyes stung from the salt and his muscles screamed in agony, but the cliffs offered no place to come ashore. He had to press on. Death or freedom.

Floating through a lazy backstroke, he spotted a purpling of the sky to the east. It would be at least an hour before sunrise, maybe longer, but the tar black of night had yielded. He'd swam through the dark-ness. Nine, ten miles. At least.

Jordan rolled to his stomach and headed toward shore, hoping to find another place to rest. He heard it first, a change in the ocean's song. A distant shift from bass to treble. A beach. And not a stroke too soon.

He could barely raise his arm from the water, lacked the power to flutter or kick. His feet dragged, as helpless as a dingy as he clawed his way toward safety. His earlier thoughts of cheeseburgers and milk-shakes evaporated from his mind. There was only the swim. Him and the water. Left, right, breathe, sink. Left, right, breathe, and sink.

The westward current tugged like a lifeline, its constant night-long pull the only reason he hadn't drowned hours earlier.

Jordan was on fumes, gasping with every breath, flopping his arms, crying tears of desperation, but going. Still going! And after so many miles, with the faintest navy glow of daybreak rising behind him, he saw it. A flashing red light atop a low bluff. Then another. He angled ashore to a sprawling beach as flat and wide as any he'd seen. He flailed in the waves, a pathetic blind attempt to bodysurf, then collapsed to his knees, not even fully out of the water. He buried himself in the sand, scratching for warmth he couldn't find, and slept the sleep of the dead.

The sound of helicopters flying low and fast woke him in a panic before sunrise. He ducked his head out of instinct, knowing he'd have to be more careful going forward. They flew up the coast toward Kalalau, and Jordan knew they were too big to have been for sightseeing. He soon hit a dirt road and a sign marking the entrance to Polihale State Park. The name rang a bell. The park at the end of the road. The southwest end. He'd done it. He escaped Kalalau by sea.

And unless his memory failed in the night, Waimea couldn't be more than fifteen miles away.

CHAPTER 28
DRAWING DEAD

An aching chill pierced Malia's chest, then snowballed through her body, rolling up the long-awaited relief her dessert had only just delivered. Her shock was so absolute she no longer felt in control of her body. Or even *in* her body. But rather, that she'd become a witness from above, a hidden camera tucked amongst the cobwebs and grime of the overhead tarpaulin watching an unknown girl in lost-and-found wrinkles, lifeless complexion, hand hung frozen in time, suspended above her icy treat as syrup-slicked shavings dripped from her spoon.

Jordan approached, his eyes flicking from her to the street, to the shadows and back. *He* was back. And all Malia could do was chew the air, shaping it, as myriad questions coalesced atop her tongue.

Jordan straddled the small bench facing her, his back to the street. Without a word, he lifted the bowl from Malia's grasp and shoveled several quick spoonfuls into his mouth. He winced and tossed the shave ice into the hibiscus hedge behind her. "Fucking brain freeze."

Malia opened her mouth in protest, but the residual shock of his reappearance kept her silent. Through the fog of her disbelief, a familiar outline took form. He glowered at her, looking every bit as trail weary as he did the day he first stumbled into camp, but the helplessness he exhibited that day was nowhere to be found. This Jordan, the one inexplicably sitting before her in Waimea, bore the cruel glint of a well-used machete, a honed tool possessing a solitary purpose. But whether it was merely a temporary veneer or the hardened truth of a man slipped free of society's sheath, Malia didn't know.

"Well, look who it is. Just the person who can help."

"How ... I thought you ..."

"I swam out."

Malia was confused for a moment, then considered the direction he'd come from. West. From the unknown. "But that must have been—"

"Far, I know. Took me all night. Came ashore some place called Polihale."

Malia recalled flying over a lengthy beach that morning in the helicopter. Was that it? Was Jordan down there, coming ashore in plain sight as they went past? It would have taken most of the day to walk to town. Especially after such a swim. She had so many questions. And Jordan's narrowed, bloodshot eyes suggested he had even more.

"So, you finally caught your ride out with Ruby and Darren?"

Reluctance scratched Malia's throat like glass shrapnel. She swallowed twice to flush free the words, unsure how much to admit, if anything. She needed time to consider her answer, but the slant of his looming presence spurred her lips into a gallop. "The police raided the camp at first light. They arrested all of us."

Alarm flashed in his eyes. "So, someone took the boat to Hanalei and called the police. To let them know I …"

"Killed Inoke?" She couldn't let it go unsaid.

He rotated his wrists, palms faceup in surrender. No point in denying it.

Malia shook her head. "We were gonna go in the morning. The police got there first."

"How? If nobody told them—"

"No idea. Honestly, I thought you must have signaled them with your locator beacon, but—"

"Call the cops on myself? Why would I—"

"I don't know. It's the only explanation I could think of."

"And the police were looking for me? Not just checking permits?"

Malia nodded and dragged her fingernail along the grain of the wooden bench, etching a groove in the drab, rubbery paint as Jordan stared into space. Much didn't make sense, and part of her was relieved to see she wasn't alone in her confusion.

After several moments, Jordan snapped back to her. "But they must have cleared you, else you wouldn't be here, right? Then what? They drive you out here to meet your friend with the boat? Or just take you for ice cream?"

"I hitchhiked. From Līhu'e."

"That so?"

"Yeah, the detective gave me some money, but—"

Alarm bloomed on Jordan's brow like a mushroom cloud, annihilating any pretense of friendliness. The heat of his scrutiny cautioned her to be careful. She was playing with fire, and every misspoken word had the potential to be explosive. Yet rather than be fearful, Malia sensed she might possess the power to affect his course of action. And she just wanted him gone, as removed from her life as he was five minutes earlier.

"The police were looking for you. They know your name. Know you and I"—she lowered her voice—"were friends." Of course there was more than that. Once. She waited for a reaction, eager for him to travel back to that memory, to not see her as a threat. Malia breathed a sigh of relief upon seeing him nod.

"And?"

"They questioned me all day. Wanted to know everything I'd done in Kalalau. All two months. How I got there. Who was in the camp. Why I stayed." Her thoughts drifted briefly to Tiki, but Jordan didn't allow time for reminiscing. Unlike Park's methodical toppling of every stone, Jordan's questioning bore the frantic tempo of an assault rifle.

"What else? Did they ask about me? What did you say?"

"They thought I knew where you went. That I was planning to meet up with you."

His neck vibrated with anxiety bordering on paranoia. "And what'd you tell them? Don't lie to me."

"The truth! That I had no idea." Malia's lip trembled as she struggled not to provoke his anger. She wound the drawstring around her finger and tugged. The pain kept her sharp. "I thought you were hiding. Your bag was gone—"

"I hid it before we left for Honopu."

"The police found it. Part of me thought you might have drowned swimming back to Kalalau."

Jordan smirked at her.

"Yeah. Silly, I know," she said, picturing him swimming all those miles through the night. She wanted to believe she could gain his trust, ease herself away from him, but knew the only type of person who could survive an ordeal like that, especially after taking such a beating, was either fearless or desperate. Jordan appeared both.

"What else?"

"I told them about the storm. The contest—"

"You ratted me out?" His nostrils flared and his complexion turned scarlet.

"No," she said, pulling harder, relishing the cord's bite against her skin. "I told you. They already knew everything. Where you lived, that you were on vacation with—" The drawstring snapped. The blood cinched tight in her purpled fingertip receded, draining Malia's momentum before she uttered Holly's name.

Jordan no doubt read her nervousness in the broken string. "Is that why you're here? Are they listening?" He reached for the hem of her shirt and lifted, as though searching for a wire, but she slapped his hand away as an older woman and two young children exited the shop carrying bowls of shave ice. The children made to sit down near Malia, but the woman whisked them down the sidewalk.

Malia lowered her voice to a whisper. "They found your wife's body." Jordan's downcast eyes avoided her. "A witness said they saw you two arguing." Malia glanced at his left hand, to where the tan line Tiki mentioned was long gone. A pale stripe faded into memory. They all wore the marks of the summer, she thought, and most wouldn't fade come autumn.

"Did you push her?" She didn't want to believe it, couldn't imagine him capable of something so awful.

He shook his head, grimacing.

"They think you did."

"It was an accident," he yelled. "I ... I loved her ..." His stammer faded into echoes, but just when Malia thought he might sob, he slammed his fist on the bench beside her. "It's her fault. Everything! If she hadn't laughed, hadn't provoked me—"

Malia recoiled from the outburst. She gripped her knee to keep it from bouncing. "I don't understand. She—"

"I said it was an accident." A rage boiled in his eyes as he stared at her, head thrust forward, his jaw set. Malia looked away, unable to withstand his glare. She heard him breathe deeply, hoping he might calm himself. Then, in an instant, Jordan stood and grabbed her elbow. "Get up. We're going." His grip was firm, but not painful, yet the shock of his sudden action startled her. In rising, she caught a look at her dessert melting beneath the hibiscus; a brief taste, then discarded without a care.

"Where?" she asked, trying to sound less scared than she was.

"To find your friend with the boat."

Malia stiffened. If she ever told Jordan about Kimo, it was weeks ago. And no more than once by the cliffs when he mentioned climbing out. "How could you remember—"

"I remember everything," he said, and tugged for her to get moving.

"Let go." Malia wrenched her wrist free of Jordan's grip as they rounded the front of Jo Jo's.

Whether because he knew he couldn't drag her all the way to the harbor or because he feared how it might look to passing motorists, he didn't fight her. "If you screw me ..." No need to finish the threat. She'd seen what he was capable of.

Malia bit her lip and burrowed within herself as she led the way past empty souvenir shops and a row of quaint, but seemingly abandoned, bungalows. It wasn't long before the Waimea sidewalk tapered to the shoulder and they were back amongst the waving grass and sprawling countryside. The traffic was sparse and the few drivers zooming by seemed intent on avoiding eye contact with Malia. And who could blame them? She and Jordan were two barefoot wanderers, clearly at the end of their luck. She in oversized sweatpants and a faded tee with a stretched collar. He, battered and shirtless, clad only in hiking shorts that looked as if they'd been through a tornado.

We look homeless, Malia thought. *No, I look like an accomplice.*

Behind her, Jordan discussed Oʻahu to himself in the manner of someone hatching an elaborate plan. He had to get off Kauaʻi. That was his only chance, he said. Malia knew she should turn him in—she cursed herself for not yelling for help earlier, when she'd had the chance—and kept her eyes peeled for a passing cop. That was the deal she made to herself. She wouldn't get anyone else involved, that she'd go along with Jordan's plan, unless she saw a cop.

What about Kimo?

It couldn't be helped. But he was big. Strong. And she could warn him when they neared the boat. Have him call the police. Still, she hated the thought of involving him in this. But what choice did she have? It wasn't like she could overpower Jordan herself. She glanced back and saw him wearing that same forced, rancorous grin he made earlier. The one that said they could be friends so long as she didn't cross him.

She turned back to the road, continuing to chew her lip, gnawing on it as her immediate fear yielded to frustration. She wanted to lash out. Where was her father? What type of man doesn't call the police back when there's a message saying his daughter has been arrested? *If only Park had pretended to be his patient.* Malia clenched her fists, knowing he always dropped everything when the clinic called.

His effrontery propelled her, insulating her against the scorching pavement beneath her feet. She quickened her pace, and not fifteen minutes after leaving, with sweat dripping down her back, they reached the turn for the harbor and paused.

"Was beginning to wonder if you knew where you were going."

Malia ignored the conniving glint in his eyes. A narrow, potholed road led the way to the harbor, hemmed in on both sides by weed-choked trees. She could see the water in the distance. Oʻahu—her home—lay unseen over the horizon. She'd come so far, suffered so much, and the day had taken its toll. From the fight at Honopu, to the arrest, to the hours spent being interrogated. She just wanted it over. All of it. To go home, to be safe, and sleep for days.

How?

Jordan stood nearby, growing impatient. What more did he want from her? She'd saved him from Inoke's assault. Spent hours under Park's accusatory glare. A chill ran along her scalp as a dread thought emerged: he intended to use her for as long as convenient. Then he'd rid himself of her too. Toss her overboard, just as he'd done his other problems.

No. She couldn't allow herself to believe it.

Malia recalled the day he arrived in camp, the look in his eyes. It wasn't that of someone who killed their wife. It was the panicked confusion of a man who made a horrible mistake. And when those fight or flight instincts kicked in, he ran. Straight into the jungle. Out of fear. Fear of nobody believing his side of the story.

Then he learned how to fight.

The harassment, the fire, the knife. Jordan was desperate, cornered like a rabid dog.

"*It's dying in this valley that I'm afraid of,*" he once told her.

So he became the killer instead. But only because Inoke left him no choice.

Malia shuddered as she again pictured the spear erupting through Inoke's chest, felt his vigor spatter on her face. Inoke's death was a kill-or-be-killed moment. But Holly? He loved her, he said, and had no reason to lie. Not about that, not about her death. Malia could accept that what happened to Holly may have been an accident. But two deaths in the span of a single month? The question reminded Malia of a phrase she'd heard Jenna's brothers use during their poker games. "Pot committed," they called it. When you've already risked so much, a few more chips won't make a difference. Anything to not go broke. Or, in Jordan's case, to not get caught.

"Enough standing around. Let's go." Jordan clamped his hand on Malia's shoulder and shoved her toward the harbor.

She gave the desolate ribbon of highway a final look, ready to jump and scream and wave down anyone that passed. No luck. She screwed up. Misplayed her hand. Left alone to survive whatever came next—and she was all in.

CHAPTER 29
ANCHORED

Any remaining hope of finding help at the harbor vanished upon first sight. The dirt parking lot was cratered beyond repair; the doorless bathroom stood graffitied in shambles. No families sat picnicking beneath the small shelter, no fishermen perched upon the rocks. Kikiaola Small Boat Harbor appeared abandoned save for a single boat moored thirty yards from the crescent beach, nuzzled in behind the breakwater.

The *Ka Pua ʻO Annana*. Kimo's boat.

Malia's breath hitched upon sight of it as a sudden wave of emotion washed over her. It had been nearly two months since she hugged Jenna goodbye and walked to the harbor in Haleʻiwa, where she met Kimo. *"You can pay me back proper when you get to Oʻahu,"* he'd said.

Was this how she planned to return the favor? By guiding a desperate murderer to his boat?

Malia needed to think of something. Seeing the boat made it real. Kimo didn't just offer her a boat ride, he said he'd hold onto her phone. Maybe even take her back. He didn't have to do that, didn't even know her, but sought to protect her as a big brother nonetheless.

Like 'ohana.

She had to warn him. For her sake. For Kimo's.

"That the boat?"

"I ... I'm not sure. It was dark ... the night he—"

"Don't lie to me," Jordan said, spinning her by the elbow. "It's his boat, isn't it?"

They were shoulder to shoulder near the water, Jordan pitched forward, scrutinizing her. Malia averted her eyes, wanting to scream for help, but to whom? To Kimo? The boat appeared as empty as the parking lot. No, she was on her own, and it was her damn fault. She should have run into the street back in Waimea. Or told the woman with the kids to call the police. Anything. But like an idiot, she froze, believing everything would work itself out. And now she stood alone in a secluded park with a murderer.

"Go see if he's aboard. Play it cool. Tell him your friend has a favor to ask."

With her heart pounding, Malia hiked her sweatpants up over her knees and waded into the water, unsure if Kimo was aboard, sleeping, or if he'd gone into town. She swam the last short distance, after the water proved too deep to wade, and climbed the ladder onto the swim platform. She held her breath, hoping to see Kimo right where she found him that night, asleep on the bench seating, there to carry her away from her nightmare, just as he once ferried her into a dream. But no. She knocked on the door leading to the berth and called his name, her voice cracking in desperation.

Nothing.

Her loneliness struck like a thunderbolt but vanished in a flash, leaving only a staticky sense of relief. Without Kimo they couldn't leave—and maybe Jordan wouldn't need her anymore. "He's not here," Malia hollered. She approached the rail, eager to leap overboard, only to see Jordan wade out into the water. "Even better," he called, then swam toward her. He flattened his hands atop the swim platform and propelled himself from the water as though launched by a cannon. Seawater sluiced over his chest and arms, down his legs. He wiped the runoff from his face, revealing the sort of malevolent gaze she'd expect in someone taking aim on the family dog with a slingshot.

Malia bumped into the gunwale, backing away as he leapt over the transom. Though he'd only been aboard a scant few seconds, he bore an unsettling air of ownership.

"What do you mean, 'even better'?"

"Exactly that," Jordan said, approaching the controls. "No witnesses. We just take it."

Malia's heart lodged itself in her throat. "You can't steal Kimo's boat."

Jordan shot her a patronizing smirk, then set about trying the handles on the overhead compartments, the side storage cabinets, the dashboard box. All of them locked. He moved in steady strides with the stiffness of a drum major, orchestrating his search with precise movements. He ran his hands along the underside of the seats, checked the cuphold-ers, even peered into the stainless rod holders mounted to the canopy's frame. He shoved away from the metal tubing and crossed his arms defiantly, scanning the boat with a perturbed scowl.

"I'm sure he took the keys," Malia said.

Jordan brushed past her toward the door leading belowdecks. He tugged the upper cover and grunted his relief when it flipped open. He folded back the waist-high door, his lip curled upward in satisfaction. "Looks like he wasn't as careful as you thought. Now, sit where I can see you," he said, pointing at the chair nearest the berth.

With Jordan belowdecks, Malia surveyed the bewildering display of electronics mounted above the steering wheel. Darkened, powerless screens covered every inch of the dashboard. Stick-on labels identified navigational instruments, a fish finder, weather monitor, radar, and all manner of engine and stability controls. So many dials and switches, buttons and toggles. She didn't know how Jordan could steal something so complicated. It was too big to row—over thirty feet by her estimate—but could it be hot-wired? Malia didn't think so. After all, growing up surrounded by water, she'd have heard about it if boats were that easy to steal.

Still doubting him?

She swallowed her rebuttal, knowing better than to underestimate Jordan. If he believed he could steal the boat, then he must know how. Looking out upon the ocean, where she'd be completely at his mercy, Malia asked herself the question she could no longer ignore: How far would she go to save herself?

Malia dug her fingernails into the quilted seat cushion as she absorbed the clatter of Jordan rummaging through Kimo's belongings.

"Bingo!" Jordan hollered, emerging above deck carrying a small toolbox. He placed it on the bench in front of the motor and opened it, revealing a flea market's assortment of weather-beaten tackle and hand-me-down tools. He leaned out over the motor, feeling beneath the cover. "Just got to find the release …" He strained audibly as he stretched so far Malia thought he might fall in, then relaxed as the catch of a lever gave way with a metallic clack. "One or two more," he said, and stuck his tongue out the side of his mouth. Malia imagined shoving him into the water, but what would it gain her? She couldn't outswim him, couldn't outrun him. He'd be back aboard in under a minute. Then what?

No, if she were to fight her way off the boat, she had to put him down for good.

Jordan grunted with success as he lifted the massive cover off the Yamaha 175, revealing a second, inner wall of black plastic armor covering the motor itself. He inspected the bolts and screws holding the cladding in place, then turned to the toolbox. He worked with a fluid confidence that suggested he'd done this before. Not steal a boat necessarily, but knew how to feel his way out of every situation.

"What are you doing?" she asked, surprised he wasn't beneath the dashboard, hacking the ignition.

"Disconnecting the main wire harness. So I can pull-start it."

"Like a lawn mower?" Malia could barely contain her disbelief. The motor was bigger than her and probably twice as heavy. She didn't know much about boats, but had seen enough men struggle with engines a third its size.

"Just need the emergency starter rope," he said, backing out a screw from the coverings. "Should be one around here somewhere."

Malia pondered the words: emergency starter rope. A bitter image came to mind of them heading out to sea without battery power or GPS. No idea how much fuel was in the tanks. If something happened … She shivered at the thought of the engine dying, them never getting it restarted. "But why? Where are you going?" She knew the answer, but still hoped he'd say Kalalau. Or maybe to Ni'ihau, the private island whose grayish outline floated above the horizon like an apparition.

"O'ahu. Can't stay here."

O'ahu? Malia spun toward Jordan in a panic. "But that's over eighty miles away. What if there's a storm? Or we run out of gas? Can you even get there without instruments?"

"Oʻahu's to the southeast, ain't it?" He tapped his watch. "I've got a compass. We'll be fine."

Malia couldn't believe what she was hearing. It had taken all night to cross the channel between Oʻahu and Kauaʻi with Kimo, and unlike the larger islands, Oʻahu didn't have towering volcanoes to spot from afar. She'd seen enough disaster shows to know visibility at sea was only a few miles at best. It'd be so easy out on the open water to blindly cruise past their destination, off into the eternal emptiness of the Pacific— to their demise. She recalled her science teacher once saying that in space, even the tiniest error in trajectory could have caused the astronauts to miss the moon. A boat at sea was no different.

I need a weapon, she thought, then startled when Jordan faced her, as though she'd said it out loud.

Dread shackled Malia in place as she met his stare. With his head cocked to the side, the bloody corner of his mouth hooked in a sarcastic grin, Jordan seemed to relish her finally catching on. Malia tried swallowing, but couldn't, her throat so scratchy dry. He regarded her difficulty with an arched eyebrow, then said, "Find the rope."

Malia's hand beat a nervous drumroll against her thigh. "No." Her voice cracked. "This is wrong."

Jordan rose from where he squatted and pointed the screwdriver at her. "I'm not asking," he said, his tone as thick as tar.

"Screw you. Take the boat. I'm out of here."

He closed on her in a flash, propelled as if from a bow, with the fury of his torment flaring in his eyes. "Don't you get it? You're the only who knows I'm alive. And if I can't trust you …"

Malia squeezed her eyes shut. She shook her head, but it couldn't stop him.

"Once we get to Oʻahu, you're gonna get me money—"

"Money? I have some. Here, take it." She retrieved the sopping wet change from the pocket of her pants and thrust it at him. "Just let me go."

Jordan swatted the crinkled bills and coins from her hand. "Real money. From your dad."

Sparks of hope rose like plankton from the depths of Malia's fear. If Jordan wanted money and needed her to get it, then she needn't worry about being tossed overboard. But then what? Her eyes went wide amid the realization that it was never going to end. The boat ride, the money. Jordan said it himself. She was the only one who knew he was alive. The only one who would know he'd fled to O'ahu. And now he wanted to get her father involved. "You're a monster!"

He bulged his eyes and made like he might slap her—or worse. But he stayed his hand and merely glowered instead. "Awful is watching a woman you love laugh at your dream. Awful is watching her fall to her death and having no time to mourn because deep down you know no one would ever believe it was an accident—"

"But if it was, why would they ..."

Jordan rolled his eyes. "It was over for me the second I ran."

Malia peeked out the corner of her eyes toward the beach, believing that if she could only keep him talking about Holly, she might buy enough time for Kimo to return. "Then why did you run if you were innocent?"

Jordan looked toward the motor, so raw without its sleek plastic cowling. When he turned back, his expression appeared every bit as twisted as the wires and tubes protruding from the engine. He opened his mouth, but the words never came. And for a moment Malia felt as though he might come to his senses, that he'd finally seen the hole he dug for himself and was ready to accept a ladder.

"It's important to talk—"

"Just find the rope," he said flatly, staring at the waves sloshing against the breakwater.

"It's okay. You can tell me—"

Jordan's fury flared as though the sound of her voice was gas to his fire. He whirled on Malia, grabbed her by the throat and squeezed, towering over her in a rage. She thought this was it, that he'd kill her there and then. "Get the fucking rope!"

He shoved her toward the cockpit. Malia slammed into the seat back, which spun as she hit it, spiraling her to the floor. She rubbed her neck out of instinct, so numb with terror she couldn't feel the hurt. Just like last night, only now it was *her* life on the line. She stared belowdecks to where she'd slept so peacefully two months earlier, floating on dreams of anticipation and promise. Now her only wish was to survive. She had to get off that boat. He killed once, twice before. Another victim wouldn't matter. Not now.

Malia took a hesitant step toward the berth, purely for show, then turned and lunged for the rail. Her foot landed squarely atop the gunwale. She bent to spring from the boat, to dive as far as she could and swim to safety.

Too slow.

Jordan snagged her by the waist of her baggy sweatpants and yanked her backward, slamming her onto the floor of the boat. Her head struck first, causing an explosion of stars to swirl before her eyes as pain rippled through her. In a blink, she was on her stomach with her arms wrenched behind her back. She could scarcely breathe beneath the weight of his frenzied effort to pin her down, twist her in knots. The pain was excruciating, disorienting, but she couldn't look away. Jordan dragged her toward the tackle box and, with his free hand, withdrew a fillet knife. He unsnapped the sheath and held it in front of her. "You want me to use this? That what you want?" He leaned into her, his heft rising and falling with the sound of his panting. He rotated the lengthy knife near her face, so close the horror in her eyes reflected in its polished steel.

Fillet.

Flay.

To carve.

"No, please, no! Don't hurt me. You can trust me." Her breathing quickened, accelerating with desperate gulps of air. "After all we've been through—"

Jordan coiled her hair tightly around his fist and tugged her head back, exposing her neck. He raised the knife and leaned in close, so close she could feel the scruff of his unshaven face against her ear. "If you think because we fucked I'm gonna let you go, you're out of your goddamned mind."

Malia had no time to consider the terror boiling within her. Escape was her only option. No matter what it demanded of her, she'd do it. Anything to avoid becoming his hostage.

Jordan grabbed her below the armpit and, with one hand still clutching the knife, hoisted Malia to her feet, her back awkwardly to him. She went limp, dead weight in his arms, unwilling to help the cause and reeling from the knock to the head. He reached across her ribs, binding her arms as he cursed her to stand. Malia looked everywhere but at the blade, searching the boat for something, anything, she could use to pry herself loose.

"Get moving," he hissed, dragging her toward the cabin door. With hands extended, she reached for the canopy's metal supports, the captain's chair, anything she could grab, but one after another, they slipped from her fingertips as easily as eels from a barbless hook. Then, in the commotion, she sensed movement in her peripheral vision. Something on land. A car. *Kimo?*

Invigorated, Malia squeezed her eyes shut and rammed her head backwards into Jordan's face as hard as she could. She felt his nose

break with the crunch of a macadamia shell as a shooting pain rever-
berated down her spine.

"You bitch," he yelled, spitting a bloodstained tooth onto the floor.

Malia's arm slipped free of his grip. She waved it in the air, screaming as the car disappeared behind the bathroom. "Help!" She screamed
again. Louder. She glimpsed the blue sedan emerging into view as
Jordan tackled her against the dashboard. She struck the console with
a thud, slumped to the floor. Jordan closed in fast, grabbed her by the
hair, and tossed her like jetsam belowdecks.

She blinked the agony from her watering eyes as her head throbbed
and her stomach churned with nausea. When her vision settled, she
spotted Jordan standing between the cockpit chairs, blood pouring
from his misshapen nose, dripping from his chin. He angled the knife
at her and glared with eyes devoid of humanity. He didn't say it. Didn't
need to. Find the rope. *Or else.*

Malia scurried away, backing into the crook of the V-shaped bunks.
She scanned the area looking for the rope, knowing Jordan wouldn't
leave her alone until she found it.

Kimo kept a tidy boat. Aside from a cooler and duffel bag, there were
only fishing magazines stacked on a shelf and a portable toilet. Shiny
chrome-plated handles hung flush alongside watertight storage lockers
beneath the bunks. The rope had to be in one of those. She hated for
Jordan to start the engine, but the alternative—being sliced by that
knife—was far worse. Best to take her chances with the crossing, she
thought, needing to believe if she could make it back to O'ahu alive, get
on her turf, she could find her dad. Jenna's brothers. They'd sort this out.

Yeah right. Bullshit.

The bulging plug of a long-held sob bubbled up from within her,
stealing her breath, but she couldn't break down now. She had to find
the rope—and hope that car was still out there when she did. She cast
about the small space as she tugged at the handles, looked under the

floor hatch, searching everywhere. Then she saw it. Not the rope, but there amongst the fishing rods hanging from the wall was something else. Something useful.

She glanced over her shoulder to ensure he couldn't see her, then climbed onto the bunk and knelt with her back to the door. Slowly, without a sound, she reached for the long wooden stock of Kimo's speargun.

Solid as an oak. Deadly. The metal spear, with its pinpoint tip and inflexible barb, rested in the slide, tethered by a sturdy line to a bungee-like slingshot. She lowered the weapon across her lap, keeping her back to Jordan. She'd never used a speargun before, never seen one operated, but figured it couldn't be difficult. She rested the handle against her body and tugged hard on the bungee, straining with all her might, and just barely stretched it onto the metal latch mounted above the trigger.

Is that it?

"Don't hear you looking," Jordan said. Judging by his posture, he stood facing the berth, leaning over the hatch, but she couldn't see his face. Good. She considered his angle of view and held the speargun high out of sight as she moved along the bunk. Once in line with the doorway, and as far from Jordan as she could get, she took aim.

Jordan's hands gripped the side of the cabin hatch. He held the knife in one, pressed flat against the accordion door.

"Let me go," she called out. She noticed a trigger lock and toggled it off before sliding her finger over the cold crescent of steel. Fearing recoil, she braced herself against the boat and tightened her grip, squeezing the stock between her arm and knee.

Jordan leaned into the berth and met her gaze. He saw the speargun aimed straight at his chest. *Just like Inoke*, she thought, picturing the destruction it would do, the hole it would leave. In her heart, she desperately wanted to set the speargun down, to never have to squeeze the trigger, to not see the damage it could bring. But it was too late for that. It was either him or her.

Jordan backpedaled with the suddenness of someone who'd seen a bear. He pivoted toward shore, his attention drawn to something. But what? From within the boat, Malia could only hear the silent swish of water, the gentle tug of the anchor chain's links bumping over the lip of the hull as the boat shifted on the tide.

Then she heard something else. A voice. Someone talking. No. Shouting.

"Help! I'm down here!" She hollered louder than ever, straining to force her voice through the narrow opening. "He's got a knife!"

Jordan turned toward her, his teeth gnashed in fury. He brought the blade up and rushed forward, his rage reignited in the coals of his eyes.

Malia curled her finger around the trigger, held her breath, and squeezed. A thundering crack rang out. Not at all like the *thwoop* she expected. Then another and another. Too many to count. Jordan spun like a dervish, toppling over the seat, spilling out of view.

He never reached the cabin.

The spear tugged briefly against Malia's grip before harmlessly burying itself six inches deep in the bulkhead. Her chest heaved with adrenaline as she stared out the door to where Jordan no longer stood.

Is he dead? What happened? Please be dead.

Malia sat dumbstruck, overwhelmed by her willingness to kill, shocked that she was safe despite her errant aim. What the hell happened? What was that noise? And what stopped him if not the spear? She looked at the weapon in her hands as though it might bite; she dropped the speargun and kicked it aside.

She craned her neck to peer out onto the boat deck. From atop the bunk, she could only see the crimson blood splattered against the white vinyl seats, more pooling along the floor. Jordan's bare feet and legs lay motionless. His body stretched out of sight.

A suffocating level of confusion and nausea overwhelmed her. Then, above the terror still echoing in her head, she again heard voices. Friendly ones. Male, female, together. Shouting. Only now, she could tell they were calling her name. Informing her it was safe to come out.

Little by little, she built the strength to stand, to exit her below-decks trap. Urged on by voices so unexpectedly familiar, yet so out of context she couldn't place them, Malia emerged into the sunlight and braved a glance at Jordan. He was alive, maybe, eyes wide in shock, but prone. Feeble. She stepped around him, daring not to come too close, and glimpsed the multiple gunshot wounds in his side. Blood pulsed from his chest, like water glugging from a garden hose recently shut off. She turned away, unable to stomach further gore, and faced the excitement on shore, hoping her ears weren't deceiving her.

They weren't.

For there on the beach stood Detective Park, arms bent, her gun pointed skyward. A flood of disbelief and gratitude washed over Malia, blurring her vision with relief-stricken tears. She rubbed an arm across her face, then hugged herself as she blinked away the wetness, only to be stunned anew by the sight of Tiki, standing off to Park's side. Malia's relief flowered into an effervescent, inexplicable giddiness as she took him in, wondering why. How?

And then at last, she saw him—her father—exiting the car, running toward the water, coming for her once and for all, just as she'd hoped he would.

CHAPTER 30
OLD DOC, NEW TRICKS

"**D**ad!" Malia's voice cracked as she yelled from the boat, scarcely believing her eyes. Her father. On Kaua'i and coming for her. It was impossible—Park said they couldn't reach him not even two hours ago. Yet there he was. Just when she needed him most.

"Malia! Oh, thank God you're okay." He splashed into the cove in his gray dress slacks and black Rockports without a care. The water soaked his pants as he marched toward her, calling out her name over and over until his words dissolved into a whimper. He trudged through the waist-high water, his arms out in front of him, hands wide, beckoning her to leap into his grasp. She knew he'd catch her. Just as he did all those years ago when teaching her to swim.

Malia dove from the boat and sliced through the shallow water, swimming in a frenzy, her emotions overcoming the drag of the bulky sweatpants, as if the relief she heard so clearly in his voice would vanish if she delayed. And when she reached him, he pulled her into an embrace tighter and lengthier than any she could remember. Not even after her mother died had he held her with such fervor.

"Malia." His whole body quivered as he pressed her head to his chest. "Oh, Malia." He repeated it again and again, the syllables falling one by one into sobs as she melted against him. She didn't want the moment to end, sensing in the desperate way in which he clung to her that Park's observation was true. They were all one another had.

"I'm so sorry, Dad. So, so sorry." She moved her hands to his shoulders and looked up, hoping he saw her sincerity.

Tears flooded Charles Naeole's eyes, bobbing between his swollen eyelids. His lips trembled as he tried to speak, but the words escaped him. His emotions tumbled out in clicks and gasps until he pulled Malia back to his chest, where she felt the blend of joy and fear, despair and worry banging away inside his heart. Dimly, she noticed Sergeant Kahale wading toward the boat, his gun drawn. Then she understood. Her father had just seen a knife-wielding killer gunned down mere feet from his only daughter.

Malia had so much she needed to say but didn't know where to begin. Or when. So she stood, shivering from fright and nerves, snuggling into the solace of her father's hold, the comforting smell of home.

Finally, it was he who broke their silence. "You really had me worried."

"I know." She faced him, sniffling back tears. "I should have told you where I was going. Or sent a message. Or called. I don't know what I was thinking."

"It's okay. You're safe. That's all that matters."

"You must hate me for what I've put you—"

"Shh," he said, rubbing soothing circles along her back. "I could never hate you. We'll talk later. For now, I only care that you're coming home safe and sound."

Malia nodded her head against his chest, thinking of course he wouldn't want to air their dirty laundry in front of the police. No, she corrected herself upon feeling him tremble. He was upset. She could feel it in his bones, hear the candor in his voice.

Still, Malia's guilt wouldn't allow her off the hook that easily. "All day, at the police station, I kept thinking of you. Sitting alone in the kitchen all this time. Waiting for me. Wondering where I went."

"None of that matters now."

"But night after night? I was gone for weeks." She sobbed, unable to restrain her emotions any longer. Her voice shook with distress. "Why would you ever forgive me?"

"Malia, it's okay." He let out a sigh. Then, with hesitation, added, "I knew where you were."

Malia recoiled, backing away from him, and for a fleeting moment her sadness and guilt were forgotten. "What? How?"

The strained expression of her father's agony eased. "Jenna told me."

"Jenna?" Malia stiffened as she processed the implications. "So, all this time you knew? What about the Missing Person's Report? Or the storm?" Malia smiled in disbelief. "I'm surprised you didn't send a rescue party to drag me out of there."

"Believe me, I wanted to. I worried constantly. Oh, how I worried." He looked up to the sky as if settling a bargain he'd made for her safe return. "Jenna didn't say anything until after I reported you missing. When I called over to Kaua'i, the police got back to me a day later to say you were fine. That Detective Bynum was in the area and prom- ised to keep an eye on you."

"The police were watching—"

"I had a lengthy conversation with Detective Park," he continued, ignoring her interruption. "And it got me thinking. A lot. One night, I took your mother's photo down from the wall—God, you look so much like her when she was young—and I sat and talked, crying with it in my hands. Kalalau was so important to your mom. And I know you miss her like crazy. It all made sense. I realized why you'd gone." He wiped a tear from Malia's face, then briefly closed his eyes, as if drawing strength. "And why you didn't tell me. So I let you stay, knowing if I didn't it would only make things worse between us. You're nineteen. As much as it hurt, I had to let you go—and hope one day you'd find your way back to me."

"Oh, Dad ..."

"You've always had your mother's wild streak in you. And I trusted her. About time I trust you too." He stroked Malia's face with the back of his hand. "I know it was only two months, but these creases. This chin. You look so mature."

Malia felt her heart tear from a thousand pangs of sympathy and pride, of love and loss. The only thing keeping her from bursting into tears again was the overwhelming relief she saw in his face. Charles turned toward the beach, and with one arm around his daughter, began guiding them both from the water. Up ahead, Detective Park stood alongside the unmarked car, gesturing animatedly into a radio as Tiki, still dressed in shorts and tank, listened nearby.

"Why is—" Malia cut herself off, straining to understand what Tiki was doing there—and what it was hanging from a chain around his neck. Puzzled, she turned back to her father. "I still don't understand how you're here. Park said they tried to get a hold of you, but you didn't answer."

"I caught a flight as soon as I heard the message—"

"But this doesn't make any sense. How did they know to come to the harbor? Or that Jordan would try to—"

Her father pushed the air between them, pulsing it with his hands, as if pumping the brakes on her questions. "Whoa, whoa. One at a time. Better yet, we ought to let Detective Park explain."

Malia turned back to the beach, not wanting to show her disappointment. She replayed the past hours in her mind as she took the first of several hesitant steps toward the detective. She recalled Jordan's accusation of her wearing a wire; Park's seemingly heartfelt warning as she left the station; their sudden arrival at the harbor. By the time she'd exited the water, Malia's curiosity had hardened into suspicion.

CHAPTER 31
UNCOVERED

Malia stalked forth, tugged by a need for answers. She'd have been killed if not for the police arriving just in time. But how did they know where to find her, or that she was in trouble? Not two hours ago Park said they hadn't heard from her father, yet there he was. She said they didn't know where Jordan went, yet knew where to gun him down. Nothing made sense ... *Unless they set me up.*

Detective Park stood beside the unmarked car, hands on her hips. Whether staring at the boat or Malia, it was impossible to tell. Her face bore a nervous intensity that, at any other time, would have caused Malia to wait until called over. But not today. Not after what she'd been through. If Malia's instincts were right and Park knowingly used her as bait without consent, then Park owed her one hell of an apology.

Malia limped across the narrow beach, her hip throbbing with each step from being slammed to the boat deck. Another bruise for her collection. Malia was five steps away when she thrust a finger at the detective, ready to tear into her.

"You better have a good explanation for this," Park said, cutting Malia off.

"What? I—"

"You think I'm going to believe you just happened to run into him. That it was all a coincidence?"

Malia's knees buckled as Park yanked the indignation out from under her, leaving her dizzied by the sudden upheaval. Her demands for an apology escaped in a gasp, replaced by the cold rush of fear. It wasn't a setup—and Park believed Malia intended to meet up with Jordan. She didn't know what to say, but had to act fast. "He forced me to go with him. I thought I could … He just … How did you …" she asked, stammering through her desperation. "How did you even know we were—"

"Got a call. Middle-aged guy with black and blues harassing a teenage girl in Waimea." Park rolled her eyes. "Mind explaining how he supposedly forced you to go with him?"

Malia allowed the question to hang unanswered between them. She knew she screwed up. Park's explanation made the consequences all too real; if not for a concerned bystander, she'd probably be dead. Malia had considered waving down a passing car, or yelling for help, but … Too scared. Too gullible. Too confident.

It wasn't only tourists who sometimes acted invincible.

"Wait." Malia's voice hardened as she regained her footing. "So, you knew Jordan might make it to Waimea? And you didn't warn me?"

"Me? No." Park uttered a self-effacing snort, as though dreading an I-told-you-so coming due. "Kahale and I thought Detective Bynum was crazy to suggest he might attempt the swim."

Malia glanced toward Tiki, wondering, but Park's trembling hands distracted her. The detective crossed her arms, burying her nerves in her armpits upon attracting Malia's attention, but she couldn't hide the ghostly pallor beneath her tan. Whether to herself or for Malia's benefit, Park spoke under her breath. "Shoulda let him take the shot."

Malia's gaze followed Park's to the boat—toward Jordan—then, unsure how to put it delicately, asked, "Was that your … first time shooting someone?" She'd been so focused on having been saved that it hadn't occurred to her that Park might also be struggling to process what happened.

"It's Kaua'i. What do you think?"

Malia recalled the sight of Jordan slumped in the pooling blood, the gunshot wounds too visible to ignore. She dreaded squeezing the speargun's trigger, of inflicting on Jordan the level of carnage he dealt to Inoke. But Jordan gave her no choice. She took the shot. In the space between her firing the speargun and realizing that Jordan had been downed, there was only the terror of seeing the spear impale itself on the ceiling. Malia didn't dare imagine what would have happened next, if not for Park. "I had a speargun. But … I missed."

"For the better. You don't want that memory."

Malia considered Park's words. "Thank you," she whispered.

"Yeah, well … You didn't leave me much choice." Park glanced at the road, drawn by the sound of approaching sirens. "You're just lucky we knew you planned to get your phone back. And that Bynum figured Jordan might utilize your connection with Kimo as a way off the island."

"But if you thought Jordan might head for the harbor, then why not have someone here to arrest him?"

Park sighed with the abject frustration of someone about to spend long nights second-guessing themselves. "We had cops stationed at the north end of the trail, a checkpoint along the road to Hanalei, and others searching the valley. Even had one up at the overlook in case he found the trail up the cliffs." Park paused, looking exasperated. "And how were we to know you'd get here so fast?"

"So fast? I even stopped for shave ice!"

Park chewed on that for a moment, then arched her eyebrows. "So, I guess I'm not getting my twenty back."

Malia pressed her lips in a hard grimace, shocked by Park's levity, but unable to resist a burst of nervous laughter. "Jokes? I could have been killed," she said, chuckling despite herself.

Park dipped her head, the color returning to her face in waves. "Sorry. Sarcasm comes with the job."

"Everything okay, Malia?" her father called from the edge of the sand. A respectful distance, but close enough to lend support, which she appreciated. She waved her okay, then turned back to Park as an ambulance rounded the corner. The women watched it drive across the grass toward the water, its lights flashing.

"You were lucky today." Park placed a hand atop her shoulder. "We'll need a statement before you go, but that can wait." Her eyes flicked toward the boat, then she excused herself and went to join the paramedics and Kahale.

Malia chewed her lip, struggling to understand how she was supposed to feel lucky in a time like this, after witnessing two men die in the span of a day. Two men she'd spent the summer with, even considered friends in her own unique way. The paramedics waded toward the boat carrying a blaze-orange backboard. Malia turned away, having seen enough blood. And as if by instinct, her gaze locked on Tiki, standing in the shade, watching her, waiting—with a detective's badge strung around his neck, reflecting in the sun.

The twenty yards of crabgrass stretching between Malia and Tiki may as well have been a tightrope across the Grand Canyon. The first step was brutal. To commit to going to him, to risk his rejection all over again required a resolve she could barely muster. Any other day, for any other guy, she'd have said to hell with it. But with one hesitant step after another, Malia drew closer. To him, to the end of her summer, unsure if her heart could survive another fall.

She rubbed her forehead as much to shield herself from the sun's glare as his. Her sweating hand came away slick. She wiped her palm on her pants and smoothed her wrinkled shirt, swept her hair behind her ears. And chuckled at how self-conscious she'd suddenly felt. It was just Tiki. A guy she'd seen every day for nearly two months. A guy who'd seen her topless more often than not, a guy she'd kissed. Once. And, she thought with a sigh, the one she'd spent the summer crushing over. There he was, standing before her, just like that first night in camp when he alone rose to greet her.

Only the man waiting for her wasn't really Tiki. Sure, he had the same earnest brown eyes, the same brown complexion and lean, surfer-fit physique. But he was also a stranger. She wanted a guy who was genuine, selfless, and able to make her laugh as much with his wit as with his silliness. The Tiki she'd known was those things and more. But this one—this Detective Bynum—was an enigma. And, apparently, a liar.

Without a word, Malia reached a tentative hand for his badge and lifted it from where it hung by a chain around his neck. It was heavier than she expected. Shinier too, and cool to the touch. Her thumb bumped along the embossed seal of Kaua'i, the county colors, the word "Detective," as if searching for an answer written in Braille.

"You okay?"

Malia shrugged. "Head hurts, and my hip's pretty sore, but—"

"I meant, are *you* okay?" He lowered his head, his wayworn concern unavoidable. "Did Park fill you in?"

"Not really. I mean, I have my suspicions. She mentioned a Detective Bynum, but ..." She sighed, exasperated. Torn between frustration and relief. "I don't even know your real name."

"Tyler."

Malia played with the name, rolling the syllables around in her mind. *Tyler Bynum*. It had a pleasant ring to it. "Nice to finally meet you, Tyler." The bitter edge of her tone sliced the air between them like a scalpel. "What brought you to Kalalau?" She bulged her eyes for emphasis. This was it, she thought, one chance to set the record straight. One shot to prove what she felt that day by the swing was real, that he wasn't just babysitting her out there.

"Would you like a seat?"

"No. I'm happy standing."

Tyler nodded, ready to come clean. No more bullshit. He licked his lips, then began. "I'm a detective working undercover on a narcotics investigation. I hiked into Kalalau about a week before you arrived, pretending to be a grad school washout needing to get away. The truth is, we had reason to believe Inoke Duarte was connected to an increased presence of meth and heroin on the island."

"He never mentioned anything like that."

"I know. He was careful. I was working to gain his confidence, hoping to meet the guys supplying him, waiting for him to slip up. Anyway, about a week after you arrived, after your dad knew where you were, Park asked if I'd keep an eye on you. Nothing official since your dad revoked the Missing Person's Report and I had a case to focus on, but—" Having sensed Malia's confusion, he stopped to clarify. "I had a satellite phone. Checked in every twenty-four hours or so. Also had backup rotating in and out on the beach."

"Your bag," she said, recalling how rarely she saw him without it. "That explains all those long walks—"

"And how I called in the raid for this morning," he explained, interrupting her gently.

"And your promise," she whispered, noticing the pride he seemed to take in her remembering.

"Was going to schedule an evac for you this morning. I knew I couldn't get you to O'ahu, but I wanted to at least get you to the airport."

A soothing warmth swirled around Malia, bathing her in a whirlpool of gratitude and affection. She had so many questions, but before she could arrange them in the correct order, he continued.

"Needless to say, I'm not really a grad student. Just a guy with an interest in local history."

"And you're not from New Zealand, are you?"

"Did you ever really buy that accent?"

Malia laughed, appreciating that he didn't take himself too seriously. Especially after spending the day with no-nonsense Park. "But Inoke grew pot. He never mentioned hard drugs. Were you really undercover all summer just for some weed? I mean, I know Kaua'i is sleepy, but ..." Malia opened her hands as if to say she wasn't buying it.

"Nothing gets past you, does it?" He smiled in an aw-shucks manner. "I was only supposed to be out there for two to three weeks, tops. Long enough to learn his connections."

"So, what happened?"

"*You* happened, Malia. I was supposed to hike out around the time Skye left. But you were staying. So I floated the idea to Park of me sticking around. Figured I could get some more surveillance on Inoke—and have more time with you." He cupped her hands in his. "So, I stayed."

Malia's heart raced as she stared down at his hands, unable to stay afloat in the current of his story. So many questions remained, not the least of which concerned his rejection of her. "But I don't get it. If you stayed to be with me, why were you so angry when the storm hit?"

"What can I say? Inoke had offered me a chance to meet his crew. I finally had a break in the case."

"So why didn't you go?"

He leaned into a smile. "There'll always be drugs."

"I don't understand—"

"Malia, I've lived on Kaua'i my whole life and never met anyone like you before. Nobody with your confidence, your spirit, your sense of fairness. I think about those days you spent rebuilding the camp, and how through it all, you never let anyone boss you around. And you've probably got plans that go far beyond a cop from Līhu'e. But ..." Any further reservations he had trailed off as he stepped closer to her. He raised a hand to Malia's chin, rubbed his thumb across her bruised lip. His tender voice adopted a wistful yet apologetic tone. "I'm not undercover anymore, so I might as well say it: I didn't want to start a relationship off with a lie."

Malia's chest heaved, rising and falling with her roller-coaster emotions. What she wanted all summer was finally within reach. But she was going home, heading to college. She braced for a difficult farewell and said, "We could have had a lot of fun this summer."

And as Malia stood there, feeling her heart tumble in the wake of his timing, by his careless use of the word *relationship*, he trailed his free hand up her arm, joining the other in caressing her face, and said "Good thing summer never ends in Hawai'i."

With his words still buzzing in her ears, he lowered his lips to hers and delivered the release she'd been yearning for all summer. He kissed her with such intensity, such hunger, she could taste his months-long battle of want and restraint, feel the tremors of her own desires finally being sated. And as she groped at his back, rising on her tiptoes to better savor his desire, the world fell away piece by piece. The ambulance, the boat, and everything they'd been through. Erased like footprints beneath a rising tide.

She and Tyler, together, with Malia eager to create some fresh tracks by his side.

CHAPTER 32
HER MOTHER'S DAUGHTER

The goats picked their way across the cobbles, bleating as they scavenged for fallen passionfruit. Malia lay on her side watching them through the mosquito mesh, the kids barely knee-high in height. They moved as one, the feral adults flanking their noisy offspring in their chestnut coats, corralling them, protecting them from the unseen dangers of paradise. Not unlike the snarling woman who had swept her children away from Malia last summer.

She wasn't surprised by the recollection—they'd pitched their tent right where that family had been camping—but not even that sour memory could curdle her current mood. The scent of fresh coffee wafting on the ocean breeze was all the reminder she needed to know she wasn't alone. That she too had someone watching out for her.

Malia sighed contentedly and sank into the cocoon of her bedding. Overhead, her camping permit scratched a rectangular silhouette where she'd twist-tied it in place. Four measly nights. She could lie there forever, snug in her sleeping bag, listening to the goats, the breeze-blown palms, the rhythm of the surf, but the coffee was hard to resist.

"Look who finally decided to start the day."

"Morning," Malia said, taking the mug offered her. She raised a hand to cover a yawn.

"You know, it wasn't so long ago when you refused to sleep anywhere but your own bed. Really made visiting your auntie on the Big Island tough." Her father floated away in the memory as Malia watched him over the rim of her mug. "I remember we'd finally get you tucked in, and not five minutes later, you'd come running down the hall, screaming about monsters, begging your mother and me to take you home. Guess you grew out of it," he eventually said.

Malia chuckled. "After six months in a dorm, I could sleep through an earthquake."

"I bet," Charles said, his tone nostalgic. "Well, your bed's always waiting—"

"Daaaad," she said, making it clear the topic was a nonstarter. She'd told him a thousand times that dorm life suited her, that there was no way she'd consider moving back home. Not now. Hopefully, not ever.

"I know, I know. Just have to say it. Job requirement."

"Thank you," she said, happy he seemed willing, for once, to let the subject drop. Today was special, after all. For both of them.

Malia tore into an oversized breakfast cookie—perfect backpacker food—and sank into the tranquility of her surroundings. Her father was never the talkative type, preferring to read or watch television over chatting. It used to irritate her, that constant feeling as though her very presence was an interruption, but now she understood. And appreciated it. Him. Being there, at Kalalau. They didn't need to talk to be together.

Twin pelicans glided past, skimming the ocean as she chewed another bite of snickerdoodle. Elsewhere along the beach, a smattering of campers spread out, plenty of space for privacy. After the trail was restored following the storm, and word spread about Jordan and Inoke, the state decided to institute changes in how the park was managed. There would always be hermits, but the majority of the squatters had been chased out. Restrictions on camping permits and trailhead parking reduced the number of visitors, making it all the more rewarding for those lucky enough to experience it. Malia smiled at the memory of the prior day's hike, when she had to coax her father across Crawler's Ledge. The others were right. It wasn't nearly as scary as the internet made it sound. Forty yards and nearly sidewalk wide. Easy-peasy, so long as you didn't look down. She grinned, recalling how scared of it she was last summer. She'd come so far, so fast.

"What are you thinking about?" her father asked, a polite hesitation in his voice. As though aware what a trigger returning to Kalalau could be for her, after all she'd been through.

"Nothing."

"I knew you'd say that." He flicked a passionfruit husk at her teasingly.

"And I knew you'd say *that*," Malia replied, bumping his knee with her own. The truth was that it was hard for her to be back. But she hoped, after today, it might come easier. She scarfed the last of the cookie and drained her coffee. "I can be ready in a few minutes if you want to ..."

"Yeah, that would be good," he said somewhat melancholy. "The sooner we—"

"Before it gets too hot," she said, providing the excuse they both needed.

Ten minutes later, with her teeth brushed, she was ready to go.

"No sneakers?" her father asked, staring dubiously at her bare feet.

"If you only knew," she said, thankful her more risqué escapades had remained out of any public reports.

Malia and Charles Naeole each shouldered a small daypack and headed out. Malia led the way along the campground trail and turned right at the stream to continue up-valley, a route she'd taken a hundred times before. They hiked in mutual silence, respecting the moment. Malia didn't point out the red crumbling slope where she'd seen the goats head-butting one another; didn't mention the path to the rope swing; didn't highlight the entrance to their old camp. She resisted even a glance in its direction. They trudged uphill through the foggy breath of the forest, slipping in the spring mud, sweating through their shirts. They wended across streams, past bamboo thickets and fallen palms, brushing past an infinite palette of greenery. Plants Malia would soon learn to identify, once the introductory classes were behind her. At Community Garden, Malia stepped over the java plum fence, crossing the threshold into the memory of her first attempt at gathering firewood. She paused to embrace the sweet scent of the ripening fruit, then led her father into the valley oasis.

She watched with pride as he spun in place, taking in the banana trees and taro ponds, the mangoes and cherry tomatoes, the breadfruit and papaya. "Garden's been here since Mom visited. Maybe longer," Malia said. Charles nodded respectfully, strolling about with a sense of wonder, craning his neck like a tourist experiencing their first grand European cathedral. Malia could feel him picturing Christina there all those years ago. Perhaps planting a chili pepper, weeding the tomato bed, or channeling water to the taro.

"This is a nice spot," he eventually said, pointing at a patch of sunlit ground. "Pretty view of the ridge across the valley."

"Can see the sunset from here too." Tears pricked the back of her eyes as the permanence of their discussion took root. She told herself she wouldn't cry. Her mother had been gone nearly two years, and Malia now understood that a loss like hers meant facing a lifetime of firsts without her mom.

Together, they knelt in the dirt and unloaded their packs. Malia removed a small trowel and a seedling she'd grown on the windowsill of her dorm room. She dug the hole with reverence, multiple times deeper and wider than needed, piling the soil between them. She dipped her head, signaling she was ready.

Slowly, as if it were a holy artifact, Charles withdrew her mother's urn from his knapsack and unscrewed the lid. He swallowed deeply, then cleared his throat. He raised his face to the sky, steeling himself against the gravity of the moment, but no levee could restrain his torrent of emotions. Malia's innards flipped upon the sound of his cry. Two years of loss and sleepless nights welled in his eyes as he passed her the urn.

Malia's heart raced as she set it down, lest it slip from her trembling hands. "Hi, Mom. It's me, Malia." Her voice cracked beneath the pressure of a pent-up sob. She squeezed her eyes shut, wishing for a do-over. Or, better yet, a never-do. This was her idea, but why? Why would she torture herself this way? Hadn't the memorial service been hard enough?

"Just talk to her," her father said, rubbing circles against her back.

Malia sniffled back another sob and pictured her mother sitting across from her, eager to answer any question Malia had. And little by little, the vision gave her strength. "Hi, Mom. It's me. I want you to know I miss you so, so much. I think about you all the time. So much has happened since you went away. So much I wish you were there for. I'm in college now. Like you always wanted. Studying biology. I hope, if you're watching from above, that I'm making you proud. We brought you to Kalalau. Your happy place. Dad's with me. And he picked out a really nice spot here in the garden. I think you're gonna love it." She wiped at her tears, muttering an embarrassed apology to no one in particular. Malia didn't know what else to say, especially with Charles right there, but dreaded the finality of what came next. She thought it would be different. Something beautiful to observe, like in the movies, but now, kneeling before the dirt hole, she knew the truth. There was an intimacy to this act, to this forever goodbye that was so much more peculiar—and logistical—than she ever imagined.

Tears spilled forth as she tipped the urn, pouring most of its contents into the hole. Malia shuddered as the gray grit cremains slid from the container, not wanting to believe her vibrant mother could be reduced to such dust. She wiped the bulb of snot welling on the tip of her nose, then layered in a heaping pile of soil to protect the plant from the alkaline ashes.

"I'll visit every chance I get. I promise," she said, and placed the seedling in the center of the hole, nestled in amongst the soil.

"I think your mom's already tired of hearing from me," Charles said in an attempt to lighten the mood as he accepted the urn. He sprinkled the remaining ashes gently around the plant as Malia held it upright. He measured this act perfectly, completing a slow, ceremonial loop around the plant just as the last of the cremains slipped from the urn. Malia mounded the remaining soil over the hole, tamping it down with care, and drained her water bottle atop it. She then positioned three large rocks in a triangle around the plant, gravestones to protect it from being stepped upon.

When she finished, Charles motioned her over and wrapped a comforting arm around his daughter.

"You sure you don't want to say anything, Dad?"

After some reluctance, he squeezed Malia's shoulder and surrendered. "Oh, Christina. Where do I begin? The fifteen years of marriage you gave me were the happiest of my life. I wish they could have gone on forever. Sometimes the pain of you not being here is almost unbearable, and I wish I could trade everything I have, everything I achieved, for one more day with you." Malia hugged him toward her. "But for as much as I hurt, I thank you. Though you were taken far too soon, you left behind Malia, the daughter I could only have wished for. And I promise to love and care for her as long as I'm able." He faced Malia, awash in pride, and took a steadying breath. "Though something tells me she'll be just fine no matter what. Your spirit certainly lives on in her."

Malia hadn't realized until then just how much she yearned to hear those words.

She gazed upon the tiny plant, rising mere inches above the soil, and wanted to stay in that moment forever. To be there, the three of them. Malia knew it was time to go but couldn't bear to turn away. She brushed her fingers over the seedling's whisker-like thorns, wondering how it could possibly survive the chilly nights, the inevitable storms. Could she really abandon her mother likes this? Leave her to fend on her own? And just walk away?

It's not fair! It's not fair!

Malia struggled to choke back her rising grief, suddenly wishing she had something to leave behind. To keep her mother company. Maybe a photo? A copy of the one that comforted Malia all those lonely nights last summer. *Why? Why didn't I think of that sooner?*

Charles pulled his daughter close and soothed her against his side. "She's going to be fine. You gave her more than she could have ever asked," he said, as though reading her mind.

They each took a moment alone with Christina's plant, then, while exiting the garden, Malia gave her mother one final look—and understood she'd be okay. That she'd visited Kalalau once before, long ago, and came away rejuvenated. She'd thrive again. Her mother's spirit would live on as strong and vibrant as Malia remembered her.

And as ruggedly beautiful as the dragon fruit planted in her name.

Malia settled into the sand beside her dad, each with a closed book atop their lap, as if any story could have distracted them from the thoughts swirling in their minds. It struck Malia as painfully ironic that it took her mother dying to finally convince her father to visit Kalalau. Of course, she kept *that* observation to herself. But something she couldn't ignore, a part of his response to her garden suggestion, spoke to a truth she hadn't ever considered: Charles knew how special Kalalau was to Malia's mother. And he knew it was where Malia was conceived.

To accompany his wife here, when they had every reason to believe a lengthy life lay ahead of her, meant risking the chance she'd realize she may have made a mistake in marrying him. At home, in Honolulu, he showed no such insecurities. The city was where he thrived. But here? Amongst nature? Malia glanced over. On the surface, he appeared at peace, but she saw the tension in his jaw, the strain with which he propped himself up, the ceaseless wandering of his eyes. It was the look of someone pretending to enjoy themselves while searching for a reason why. No wonder he didn't ever want to come, she thought, seeing how little he fit in.

That her father would have the same doubts and worries as a teenager proved as comforting as it was scary.

Malia would turn twenty in three months, a teenager no more. But what did that mean? *Half plus seven.* She snorted to herself, recalling that silly rule. She turned to the east, eying the grass-covered cliffs in the distance where he'd refused her. *Two more years,* she thought with a smirk, then he'd be thirty and she twenty-two. And the math would pencil out.

"Looks like Tyler had good luck," Charles said, drawing her attention. Tyler approached from afar, carrying a rod in one hand, a fish in the other, and that same ever-present ease that so endeared him to her. She considered the name her father used: *Tyler*. It was the first time she'd heard it spoken at Kalalau. It was his name, of course, and though she struggled to keep from calling him Tiki when they'd begun dating, she was never happier to have something else to call him than now, back at Kalalau, surrounded by those memories.

Malia rose from the sand and jogged to meet him. Tyler dropped the fishing rod and greeted her with a one-armed hug, taking care to not touch her with his catch. "Missed you this morning," she said and kissed him on the cheek.

"Me too. Your dad said you were out like a light."

She narrowed her gaze to sultry slits. "That's not what I meant. Rather be sharing that tent with you."

"Makes two of us," he said, lowering his hand to her rear and giving her a playful squeeze. "So, everything go okay?"

Malia nodded, thinking back to the garden, wondering how to describe it. A ceremony? A burial? "It was nice. Emotional. Harder than I expected."

"Based on what you told me, I think she'd be delighted."

"I just wish she were closer. I thought it was such a great idea, you know, planting her out here, but how often can I really visit her on Kaua'i?"

"I imagine it'll be hard having family so far away. I've been thinking about that a lot lately." Tyler looked skyward, as if to set the hook on what he'd said and reel it back in, but it was too late. Malia could see the regret weighing on him. He'd introduced a story he hadn't committed to telling, and now had no choice.

"What's that supposed to mean? You visit your parents every month."

"No, not them."

"Then ... what?"

"You. Us. It's hard only seeing you every other weekend. And the flights to Honolulu are adding up. Being a cop on Kauaʻi doesn't exactly lend itself to the jet set."

Malia didn't pass on Berkeley because of Tyler. She stayed to be near her father—her *real* one. Charles. But it was hard enough letting go of the ghost whose blood flowed through her veins, she couldn't bear to have Tyler vanish too.

Is he breaking up with me? Today of all days?

Malia backed away, needing space to breathe. "I told you, I can help pay. We can alternate weekends. I can come to Kauaʻi sometimes."

"No, Malia, you have your studies—"

"The semester ends in May."

"Malia—"

"I'll spend the summer in Līhuʻe." Her pulse quickened. "We'll make it work."

"Malia, you're not letting me finish."

"'Cause I don't want you to," she said, bracing for the inevitable.

"I was gonna tell you later, over dinner, but ..." He reached into the pocket of his cargo shorts and handed Malia a leather wallet. "Here."

She opened it, glimpsed the police badge, and shrugged. "It's your badge. So?"

"Look," Tiki urged.

She sighed and looked again. Only then did she notice the difference. "But ... this is a Honolulu badge ..."

"I know. I've taken a position at the Kalihi Department."

Malia gasped. Her hand jumped to her face. "That's right near my old high school."

Tyler's lips curled into a teasing smile as his face flushed. "It's not by coincidence."

"Wow. I ... I ..." The thought of Tiki moving to Oʻahu left her speechless. She balanced the badge in her hand, weighing her desires against the sacrifice it represented. "But you love Kauaʻi."

"I love you more."

Malia rocked on her heels, jolted by his unexpected sentiment. She threw her arms around Tyler's neck and rose to her tiptoes, pulling him to her, meeting his lips with an energy unlike any time they'd kissed before. New, uncharted waters stretched out before them. Boundless. But as thrilled as she was to hear he'd be moving—and even more so to hear him say he loved her—she cautioned herself not to get too excited. They led very different lives. She slumped against him, dropped her hands to her side.

"What's wrong?"

"I want to have you close, but I'm scared. My double major doesn't allow a lot of free time, and Honolulu's dangerous," she said, unable to ignore her father's tone in her own.

Tyler dipped his head. He lifted her chin and spoke. "Purely detective work. Park put a good word in for me. Pulled some strings."

"She did?"

"Yeah, after six months of putting up with 'oh, Tiki' this and 'oh, Tiki' that," he said, raising his voice into the falsetto of a damsel in distress. "Trust me, it was the least she could do. For both of us."

Tyler's dimples returned with his laid-back laugh. And soon Malia was chuckling too, not at Park or him, but with joy. For if he were willing to forfeit the security and comfort of his life on Kauaʻi, the least she could do was let him. Tyler flicked his chin down the beach, drawing Malia's attention to her father's approach. Charles pointed inland as he drew near. Malia couldn't figure out why at first; the silver sheen of cloud-glow produced a hell of a glare.

"Do you see it, Malia? Look," Charles said. "Way in the back."

"Oh, wow. It's beautiful." Tyler leaned over Malia and extended his arm out past her shoulder, guiding her gaze over the forest canopy, to a distant rainbow arching between the ridgetop and valley. "It's like it's—"

"Her spirit thanking us ..." Malia's breath caught in her throat as the rainbow's appearance ushered in a sense of certainty and comfort she'd only dreamed of. For two years, Malia wandered through the gloom, enduring heartache and turmoil, searching for the light that had been taken from her, only to wind up back at the beginning. Her beginning. Kalalau.

Through saying goodbye, she was made whole. And now, graced by that shimmering bouquet of color and flanked by Tyler and her father, Malia basked in the warmest of feelings. A feeling that could only come from sharing paradise with the ones you love.

CONTINUE THE JOURNEY

Learn more about *Shadows of Kalalau* and Doug Walsh's upcoming books at www.dougwalsh.com. Newsletter subscribers receive special offers, along with a free annotated guide to the bestselling time travel romance, *Tailwinds Past Florence,* inspired by the author's around-the-world bicycle tour.

Reviews are critical to an author's success and improvement. Please consider leaving an honest review on your preferred retailer website and sharing your thoughts on social media.

ACKNOWLEDGMENTS

I first hiked the Kalalau Trail in May 2005, following a friend's wedding on Maui. After nine grueling hours spent slipping in mud, wading through waist-deep streams, and feeling as if we might get blown from a cliff, my wife and I arrived at our beach-front campsite shell-shocked, blistered, and filled with dread. It was late afternoon and our schedule allowed only a single night's rest before we had to hike back out. Talk about a rookie mistake. We rinsed beneath the waterfall, trudged back to our tent, and ate our dinner in bone-weary silence on the beach as a woman practiced *tai chi* in the nude before the setting sun. Her companions squatted beneath a low-slung tarp, trading joints and laughter, looking every bit as permanent as the forest. Whispers of a boat for hire drifted through camp on the breeze and come morning, I swallowed my pride and inquired about the rumored Zodiac. Wait behind the bushes, the guy said, and be ready with $150 in ninety minutes. My relief was short-lived. Stubbornness, ego, hubris. Call it what you want, but by the time I returned to our tent, I had sworn off taking the boat. My wife agreed, knowing we would regret taking the easy way out. The hike back was faster, less dramatic. And it was while crossing Crawler's Ledge on that second day where I first conjured the idea of the story that, over the ensuing fifteen years, would grow into *Shadows of Kalalau*. I've returned to Kaua'i multiple times since then (and now, even in my mid-forties, breeze through the hike in under five hours), but I owe this story first and foremost to my longtime friend Luis Perez who invited us to his Hawai'i wedding.

That initial story idea didn't involve detectives, a lengthy interrogation sequence, or undercover narcotics officers. I'll be the first to admit that my inclusion of these elements pale when compared to those of a crime drama or police procedural, but I aimed to get them as accurate as possible. Helping me achieve that goal was Jaycin Diaz, Lieutenant in the Seattle Police Department, with over twenty-eight years' experience. Should my portrayal of police practice fall short of expectations, or ring too loudly of artistic license run amok, I can assure the reader that the fault is entirely my own.

Writing is a solitary endeavor, but revision is a group effort. I'm blessed to have a stable of devoted writers in my corner, encouraging me, nudging me, and offering me the tough love I sometimes need. To the Puget Sound Scribes past and present, who've seen this story from its infancy onward, thank you. David Anderson, Chenelle Bremont, Natalie French, Staci Roberts, and Jeff Weaver; your support and critique is something I will forever be grateful for.

To Sandra Rosner, who graciously and bravely agreed—again!—to be my alpha reader. Your meticulous eye, candid suggestions, encouragement, and friendship has not only helped improve this book by leaps and bounds, but has made me a better, happier writer. Thank you! To Z.D. Gladstone, Wendy Kendall, and Mia Vo, you gifted me your time and your honest, thoughtful, and robust feedback—along with your trust that I would accept it with grace. I can only hope I kept up my end of the bargain, and that I can repay the favor one day soon. Your feedback challenged me, inspired me, and directly led to a clearer, cleaner story for Malia.

To Edward Bittner, Joseph Epstein, and Jessica Walsh, who once again accepted my request to read an early version of the story and who each helped guide and encourage the final sprinkles added before sending the book to the copyeditor.

A love of Kaua'i is not the same as being a Native Hawaiian. I, a middle-aged white guy from the mainland, ventured well outside my comfort zone in telling the story of Malia, a girl whose background, upbringing, and surroundings are so unlike my own. I believe any story is fair game for any author, provided the subject is treated with the utmost care and respect. To that point, I'd like to thank the sensitivity/expert readers at Salt & Sage Books for the guidance, professional insight, and technical expertise that helped mold this book into one, I hope, anybody can enjoy.

Lastly, to Kristin, my forever partner, my inspiration, and my staunchest supporter. I couldn't, wouldn't, do this without you.